The Moscow Enigma

A Novel By

Christian Hirsch

Published in 2012 by New Generation Publishing

Copyright © Christian Hirsch 2012

First Edition

www.newgeneration-publishing.com

 **New Generation Publishing**

Chapter 1

I

The rain pattered hard against the window and, as Alexandra looked out, she saw life as a mosaic cloud of colour and motion. The windswept barren trees braced themselves against the gusts of chilly wind, and she couldn't help but feel sympathy for the trees. She wondered if they felt cold like human beings or if they had any feelings.

Alexandra had always felt more towards nature and animals then she did for humans. Actually, it was men that she never cared about. She viewed men as too one-dimensional and believed they lacked the sophistication that she needed. Everyone saw Alexandra as an enigma. This was completely fine with her. It afforded her the luxury of living a secretive life which was completely controlled by her. No one could crack Alexandra and, for those who tried, she only pushed them away and ultimately out of her life.

She was a twenty-seven-year-old puzzle to everyone who knew her. In some hidden respects she was an adult-child refusing to grow up, and this explained her childish affections and her childlike fantasies and imagination. It was this imagination that would always consume her when she was alone, in trouble or sad, as she was today. Life today was a blurry watercolour that was being damaged by the falling rain.

The rain was cold and the sky was a concrete colour that reminded Alexandra of the grey play-dough putty that was one of her favourite possessions as a child orphan. She thought of how simple life was then all those years ago and wished it would be that way now. She felt that the loneliness of the landscape and the plight of the rain-soaked trees opened the gates of the

3

past, and all of its sadness overwhelmed her.

She reflected on the orphanage where she had lived in for most of her early childhood and on how little it had offered her in terms of physical possessions. The few volunteers and the Orthodox Sisters had been the surrogate mothers and fathers she had never had. Toys and luxuries in those far away days were a premium, which is why she had loved her putty so much. With her imagination, a can of play-dough had been an opportunity to change and devise new shapes and creations into whatever she wanted. Perhaps this innocent can of clay had afforded her control, or perhaps it had been a means of imaginative escape; but, whatever the reason, play-dough had been so much more than just grey putty.

As the rain pattered against the hotel's window-pane she remembered the painful childhood discovery that there was no permanence to any part of her life. Alexandra reflected upon when she once had modelled the clay into a doll, and her pride at having done so. Only after a full week did Sister Ekaterina finally convince her to lend her putty to another girl, which reinforced the fact that life in the orphanage meant that nothing was really hers. Everything she ever loved seemed temporary.

She loved Sister Maria, her primary caretaker, but knew she really wasn't really her mother; a fact crystallised when she finally arranged for a 'real' family to take Alexandra away. She loved the putty and the pink stuffed kitten she often smuggled into her bed - but both of these were only hers if she managed to steal them away from the smaller children. In the end, nothing she loved was hers unconditionally. Life lessons like these proved to be a tough training ground which would affect Alexandra later in life, and they affected her especially now.

The rain washed down the window-pane, and a tear washed down her right cheek. It was often that Alexandra would lapse into the past and find herself staring intently with a locked gaze - looking, ultimately, at nothing.

"Christ," she whispered to herself.

She blinked twice quickly and shook her head to escape the unpleasantness of her childhood, yet the depressing scene of what lay behind reinforced her melancholy. What lay in the room behind her was an escape; albeit with its own shallowness.

The sound of the toilet flushing broke the silence and she quickly wiped away the tear and breathed in deeply. She adjusted her bra and zipped her short shirt and wiggled twice, as she always did when adjusting a short skirt.

Vladimir appeared from the toilet, an imposing man in stature and the typical Russian client she seemed to always have as her John. He approached her, put one hand on the back of her head and the other against her ass, squeezing it firmly.

"Why did you put that skirt on? You know how I love seeing your ass."

Alexandra smiled like a coy girl as she tossed her head back and replied with a sultry whisper, "Hmm, let's spend another hour here and I will show you more than my popa."

Like a little girl, Alexandra never called her popa an ass. The fact was that she also refused to curse and found it beneath her - consequently, all discreet parts of her body were described in the words that she had learned as a little girl.

"But then I would be thinking you were just wanting another five hundred dollars," he replied crisply.

"How could you think that?" she asked coyly and with a wry telling smile. "You know I really like spending time with you. What's another hour and fifteen thousand rubles donation anyways?"

Alexandra was always careful to mention her fee with a client, even regular ones like Vladimir. When she did agree to terms she preferred to call her fees 'donations'. Somehow it sounded so much classier and seemed to disguise the harsh reality that Alexandra was indeed a prostitute; albeit a very high-end call girl.

"I have to go - my wife is awaiting me already. You know the routine. We're done for the evening."

"I was too busy pleasuring you to notice any discussions about your wife. Stay – I want you to."

She tossed her head sideways and brushed back some of the blonde hair that was dangling in front of her left eye. Again, she smiled innocently and leaned back, wrapping both of her hands around his neck. She played the childish whore perfectly and it was probably one of the strongest reasons her regular Johns liked her so much. She was so cultured and refined out of the bedroom, but, once inside, she seemed so much younger than she actually was – all the while emitting the aura of the sexual vixen that she truly was.

It was a dichotomy of sorts because the sex she offered knew no limits, but somehow she could play the role of being virtuous perfectly. She always let the men believe they were dominant and that they pleased her immensely. She knew that men wanted to feel strong and that her juvenile body reminded them that they were with a young girl, which seemed to be a fetish among so many clients. She was sure that was the reason she was so often chosen by them. That, as well as her stunning beauty and captivating pale blue eyes, which pierced everything that fell before them.

It was, however, all a charade for cash. In fact, she usually hated the men she fucked – although she'd occasionally enjoy the sex, when she allowed herself

6

to. She rarely obtained an orgasm from the experiences, and she couldn't have cared less about any of the men she ever escorted. None of them were really that charming and she wondered what their girlfriends and wives really saw in them. Surely it was the money, because that's what she liked. Nevertheless, Alexandra considered herself above these women who settled. She was still holding out for a Prince Charming to appear in her life, even if it was the faintest of dreams and one that was largely forgotten about.

Vladimir released himself from her embrace and went to put his jacket on. He reached in his wallet and pulled out a blue-green one thousand ruble bank note and laid it on the nearby desk.

"A little something extra for you."

Mr Gorban always tipped her. Usually it was a thousand rubles or even a hundred dollar bill when he carried American dollars, like so many of the business men she entertained.

She smiled and strolled over to put on her own jacket, a mid-length leather jacket with fur on the collar and cuffs. She picked up the money and delicately put it in her small purse, and then kissed him on the cheek. "Considering the orgasm you just gave me, I should pay you a thousand rubles."

Of course her compliment was nothing more than an enticing ruse for a future date, but she spoke with such believability and certainty that Mr Gorban could only grin and feel even more of a man as she whispered this in his ear. She then pulled away from her satisfied client, turned off the light, and followed Vladimir out into the hall and to what would be their different directions in the remaining hours of the night.

II

7

Alexandra undressed while she walked to her kitchen. As clothes came off, she tossed them to the nearest piece of furniture as she simultaneously read her mail. The answering machine blinked but she knew who it was. She didn't feel like hearing her parents complain that she rarely called them ever since moving to Moscow eight years ago. If they called, it was always on the last Saturday of every month. Instead her only motivation was to take her shower, which she always did after having sex with a client. It helped her to emotionally cleanse herself.

Although she loved sex she hated the whole routine of pretending that she enjoyed her customer's company, especially after the sex. Most of the time she liked that the men could not perform after their orgasm which meant that, more often than not, her sessions rarely lasted the full time that was paid for. Most men simply wanted Alexandra as a semen vestibule. Knowing that left her detached, and the lure of easy money was her only motivation to cheapen herself this way.

Living the life as a high-class escort did come with its crosses to bear. None of those were worse than Alexandra's personal disdain for her profession; she considered herself educated and cultured yet simultaneously found herself playing the role of arm-candy, as well as a one-dimensional slut, to men that she considered beneath her. She despised that she had to spread her legs for their money, but, at a minimum of five hundred dollars an hour, she lowered herself to the world of prostitution.

Alexandra stood directly under the hot water of the shower and her head hung as she stared at the shower's drain. The water circled about the small hole and she reflected on her uncertainty. She was tired of the secret life, but being an escort was a black hole that sucked her further and further into its grip; leaving her intoxicated, yet bitter and simultaneously ashamed.

As a young girl she had dreamed of becoming a translator in the Russian government or a classical concert pianist. She had dreamed that one day she would work for an important official and accompany his entourage as they travelled the world or playing her piano at venues like Sydney, London or New York. This had been her escape to a world that she believed had to be better than anything she had ever known. All she knew now was that she was alone, with few real friends, and a life in which she played two distinct roles. The circling water around the drain could have just as well been a literal analogy of her life.

She scrubbed herself first with soap, and cleaned her labia repeatedly. She hated the smell and taste of latex, and the thought of the man's penis in her after sex left her feeling contaminated. The incessant cleaning of her vulva was a way to literally and figuratively transform it into a wholesome and pure part of herself again.

After cleaning herself with the soap she then used her pink shower sponge to gently caress herself with the scented shower gel she craved. As a habit she only used Dove products, which included shampoo and conditioner. She loved smelling like vanilla after her shower and besides, the gel replaced the sterile smell of the soap. She had always loved the smell of vanilla for as long as she could remember, and being encompassed by the scent made her feel wholesome and pure again. She caressed herself slowly and methodically. The lather and foam of the vanilla gel encapsulated her, and only then did she close her eyes and feel normal again.

III

Predictably, the Delta flight from Washington D.C. was late touching down. It was a testament to the reality that defined Sheremetyevo airport, easily the most dated of any modern country. The primary Moscow airport was built in the insular days of communism, and remained unequipped to handle the kind of passenger traffic that defines present day Moscow. The delay of seventy minutes was exactly the kind of backlog that was to be expected. It had been anticipated by the two Americans in arrivals.

They had arrived only five minutes before, wondering what was their boss's fate after weeks of being away in D.C. They stood out amongst the ragtag mob of Russian middle class. Their typically American khaki pants, button-up oxfords, wingtips and heavy coats were enough to peg them, as were the McDonald's sandwiches that they were just finishing. Frank glanced at his watch to see the minute hand flick exactly to eight o'clock, just as Florian nudged his partner as he took the last bite from his McRib. "There," he mumbled half-coherently as his head nodded to the oversized information board. The D.C. flight had now changed from 'Delayed' to 'Landed' and then proceeded to switch back and forth from English to Russian.

"Great, only forty-five minutes to go," Frank muttered sarcastically. Florian swallowed hard as he rubbed away the barbecue sauce from around his mouth. He shook his head knowingly as he half-jokingly said "Immigration's a bitch."

Fifty minutes later the two Americans rose to life as they saw the silhouette of the grizzled elderly man who strode confidently through the sliding glass door. It was Ron Billups, a legend in the CIA and the man behind a recent project assigned by the White House itself. Ron approached and barely stopped as he nodded and barked "Gentlemen," on his way to the airport's exit. Like two ducklings lining up behind their mother in the local pond, the three Americans left the interior of the dour airport for an even more dour and dreary Moscow night.

Chapter 2

I

Alexandra hurried down the two flights of stairs and rushed out of her apartment building to the awaiting taxi. It was exactly eight-thirty on Monday morning and, although she only lived twenty kilometres away, her meeting on the Ulitsa Burdenko would take every bit of forty-five minutes. Such was Moscow traffic on week-day mornings. She rarely had morning appointments but, approximately twice a month, she would have to meet her boss and a handful of colleagues to provide translation services for business clients. These clients were usually Americans but more and more often they were Japanese. She was a full-time translator for Khanty Oil, one of Russia's largest state-owned oil and gas conglomerates. Translating both Japanese and English documents, briefs and texts demanded a full work week, but provided Alexandra with a salary that alone would provide her a comfortable life. Moonlighting as one of Moscow's elite escorts, however, gave her a fuller financial life.

In the last two months alone she netted over ten thousand dollars, and that was with forty percent going to Elena, who owned the escort agency. Having enough money to easily buy Prada handbags, Dior cosmetics and Ralph Lauren perfume was something that thousands of Muscovite women fantasised about. For Alexandra, it was a mere reality.

The glum of the city was highlighted even more by the incessant grey weather. A slight drizzle that seemed so permanent made everything outside even bleaker. The traffic moved slowly in this part of the city and Alexandra felt nervous, even though she would probably be early. Alexandra was always fretting over something. Behind the steely external demure was a young woman who sometimes lacked self-confidence and who worried often.

The taxi was finally on the Bolshoy and crossed over the meandering river below. The meeting was in the Balthug Kempinski, one of Moscow's better hotels. Once she met an Israeli client there in its lobby before going out to dinner at an Italian restaurant which was still her favourite. Interestingly, he hadn't wanted sex from her; rather, he had wanted to rant incessantly about the situation in Gaza. Frankly, she couldn't have cared less about the Middle East and never gave it much consideration. She had forgotten about this client. The taxi pulled up to the Kempinski and she exited the dirty Toyota and handed the taxi driver several bills to cover the fare. Walking like a model, her tight dark black jeans tucked into her patent black stiletto boots, she strode to the door. Alexandra, like most women in Moscow, always wore perilously high heels - even in winter. The trick, she learned, was not to totter gingerly but to stride ahead fast and never look down.

She strolled into the lobby and immediately saw Sergi with her colleague Grigory, reclined comfortably in two leather love-seats that filled a spacious corner of the lobby. Alexandra's heels made their distinctive clacking sound against the bare floor as she approached.

"Ah, there you are, Alex," exclaimed Sergi excitedly. "I've been looking over this memo about the offshore drilling quotas that the guys at Teikoku want, and there's a part here I need you to make sure gets perfectly translated into Japanese. Here, Alex."

Before she could even sit, he raised the document and read out loud, "The arrangement will provide a redundant barrier to leaks of hydrocarbons as well as allowing damaged sections to be replaced. Also, the smaller diametre of the tubing must not produce hydrocarbons exceeding two millilitres per minute at an increased velocity, in order to overcome the hydrostatic effects of heavy fluids."

"And?" she retorted matter-of-factly.

"And, I need to make sure this part about redundant barriers is perfectly understood. You know, Alex, you aren't an engineer like Grigory."

She leaned forward and replied with a soft smile, "Sergi – have I ever let you down?"

"Well, uh..."

"That's what I thought. You tell me you want the workover rigs to be coloured pink with yellow flowers all over them, and I will translate that in the document. Guaranteed."

Grigory chuckled. "I remember last year when you translated the notes that were added to the bottom of the Chevron deal."

"And you know that was a lesson for you, my dear boss." She turned to Sergi and tilted her head sideways and smirked.

Smiling coyly, like she often did with her clients, was a way to offset her directness. Being firm with the men who were her work colleagues was something unusual for Russian women. She was treated surprisingly fairly, although she could often feel the men's gazes and occasional flirting. This, however, was a line she never had crossed and didn't dare to. Nevertheless, she knew that most of the men, even the married ones, had mentally undressed her and fucked her many times over. For her, this was a reality that she was desensitised to.

"If you weren't so damn beautiful and good I would already have fired you for insubordination a hundred times." Sergi tried to hide his emotions, but Alexandra knew his threats were shallow.

"But I am good, and you need me."

"You're impossible, Alex," Sergi answered. "One day your confidence will get the better of you."

Alexandra pulled on her long blonde hair with both hands and asked, "What shall we have to drink, boys? Grigory? Your usual fresh orange juice? I could enjoy that right now, myself."

Grigory peered from over his glasses as he shuffled some documents on the nearby coffee table. "Uh... yeah. That would be great."

"And grumpy boss? An espresso?"

Sergi simply smiled and nodded in quiet amusement.

"Don't worry. I'll be a good little woman and fetch you boys our drink. I wouldn't want you to think I was a feminist."

Alexandra rose, shifted her skirt and wiggled only centimetres from Sergi's face, before striding away. A couple of steps later she turned back, grinned, and winked at her boss, who was still staring at the one woman he never could quite understand.

II

Finally the meeting concluded, and Alexandra glanced at her watch. Alexandra looked over at Grigory, and his quick glance down at his stomach was enough of a code to Alexandra that he too was hungry. Alexandra could not recall the last time one of these negotiations had ever finished on time. The director of the Japanese contingent came to Sergi and bowed after he shook his hand. Mr Saitama was followed by three of his subordinates, who individually shook Sergi's hand and bowed respectfully. Then they followed the same pattern towards Grigory, before finally reaching Alexandra at the rear of the large conference table.

She knew the custom of Japan and Japanese well; she had studied Japanese at university for years, and even spent a semester in Tokyo. Her time there reinforced beliefs that covered a full spectrum of stereotypes. As a woman she was always considered subservient to men, but being a beautiful Russian meant that men who had power would often vie for her attention. It was the latter that caused her to post an internet profile of herself in Japanese as an escort for men of 'exquisite taste'. Her rates started at fifty thousand yen per hour, and a business-class flight to Japan was a non-negotiable. It really never ceased to amaze her how beautiful Caucasian women, and especially Russians, were so prized by rich Japanese men. She theorised that the five times she had flown to Japan to engage in a 'date' was each a life highlight for the men she had fucked.

The men shook her hand softly as all Japanese do, and bowed quickly and graciously. "Hajimemashite, Sayonara," she said to each of the three, as she bowed in unison to them.

The truth be known, Alexandra really did not care much for Japanese men. She only learned Japanese because she was pushed to do so by her foster parents. Being accepted to the language studies programme at Moscow's Maxim Gorky Institute was something that came so easily for an over-achiever like Alexandra. So many other students vied to be one of the few chosen for enrolment at the prestigious institution, but Alexandra was accepted easily. She studied both Japanese and English there and, although Japanese was her major, she excelled in English.

When she first visited Japan in 2001 she was taken aback by the formality of the culture as well as how tiny the people were. She stood only 1.70 metres, but seemed to be so much taller than almost every woman

16

and so many of the men. It was on this trip that she had her first Japanese man as a lover. He was thirty, she was twenty. She had always preferred older men but, after having sex with him twice, she dumped him. His small penis and rough treatment of her in bed left her unimpressed and unfulfilled.

As the last of the men left the room, Sergi clasped his hands together as his toothy smile emerged. "It's done!" he exclaimed.

Alexandra merely smiled and flicked away at the loose hairs that had dropped over her right eye. "I'm getting lunch. See you two tomorrow."

III

Alexandra entered the Galereya, which was her favourite place to get a light bite to eat. She had tried much of the menu, but the salads were by far her most desired choice. She took off her long fur coat and was immediately greeted by Arkady, who was widely known as one of Moscow's premier restaurant magnates.

"Ah, Alexandra!" He kissed her once on each cheek and gently led her away from the entrance. "Darling, I'm afraid that we are unusually busy today."

She looked across the restaurant and saw barely an empty seat. "Arkady, it is three o'clock for God's sake!"

"Yes, yes – it is some expatriate club here having a lunch and get-together. I'm afraid you might have to share a table. I think I have a compromise, which isn't so bad."

"Oh, Arkady!" Alexandra sulked and her lower lip protruded like a toddler who had just been scolded.

"Darling, look over there." He pointed to the far corner, where a gentleman sat alone at a table which sat

17

four. "You can sit at the opposite end of the table. What do you say?"

Alexandra exhaled apathetically and bit her lip before succumbing to Arkady's persistence. "Only because I am so damn hungry." She smiled softly, but held her head high and pretended to look more annoyed than she truly was.

"I knew you would agree, darling." Arkady beamed as he began to lead Alexandra away.

Arkady always called Alexandra his darling. As a gay man she felt Arkady was a pseudo-girlfriend to whom she could chit-chat to about small things like fashion. Both of them loved the same boutiques and he always recognised when she wore new designer boots. He walked her over to the table and then handed her the menu, which she already knew by heart.

The man across and opposite from her was a handsome man around thirty-five or so. His features were chiseled, his hair was greying ever so slightly, and she intuitively knew he was not Russian. Alexandra could predict where a man came from almost without fail. The first clue was his shoes and the second his features. This man was surely French, or perhaps German. His posture was too composed and his style was too formal to be American or Canadian.

His eyes met hers, and she felt embarrassed to have been looking at him .

"And here I thought I would be alone for lunch. Hello. My name is Clint. Clint Thomas."

His posture straightened, and with arms folded he surveyed the enticing sight in front of him. A very shapely bottom encased in the tight confines of a black Donna Karan dress was only centimetres from his face. Its owner was currently standing over him, adjusting her coat over the chair next to his. He immediately recognised her, having seen her before at the restaurant.

His gaze drifted down. Long, slim legs were straightened to their full length - all the way from her delicate ankles right up to her gently flaring hips, which tapered into a perfect waist. He couldn't help but admire her sensual curves, and wondered if he would be lucky enough to keep her interest over the pending lunch.

She had a perfectly-fitting dress, sexy high heels and straight shiny hair, neatly tucked behind her ears with a side parting to the left. It was tied back in a small ponytail but he could well imagine that, if let loose, it would fall ever so neatly into a straight shoulder-length bob, framing her face.

Since coming to Moscow eighteen months ago he had been bombarded with seductive, sensual women. Women who poured their curvaceous bodies into clothes and dresses designed to fire the imagination and ignite the senses; women who weren't afraid to entice and beguile, using all their powerful charms for pleasure. However, none of those women were as sensuous as this stranger was.

She was taken by his American accent, and replied in kind. "Hello, Alexandra Malikova." Her soft Russian accent was confident. She smiled at him and then picked up the menu, as much to conceal her face as to actually see what she already knew.

He asked her if he may have seen her at the restaurant.

"Yes, perhaps. Are you in the business of spying on me? You Americans still spying on us Russians?"

He smiled back and nodded, while reaching for his hot chocolate. "First, how did you know that I was a spy, and secondly, is the accent that obvious?" He sipped from his drink before continuing. "Many people think I am European, but perhaps I am a spy from Canada. Did you ever consider that?"

After only a minute she felt he was witty, intelligent and comfortable with himself – a combination Alexandra adored, but that was so uncommon in the few men she ever dated. Most men were so dry and failed to impress her. This man was somehow different. He brimmed with confidence, which Alexandra always considered a sexy attribute in a man. He looked very contemporary in his blue jeans and fitted black shirt, and she could see a gold bracelet half exposed from his wrist. His eyes were deep and his features reminded her of Sting, one of her favourite non-Russian musical artists.

While Alexandra caught herself thinking of Clint as more than just a casual flirt, he was struck by something entirely more profound; thoughts of Aleeka, his former fiancé, who he had lost three years back to cervical cancer. She was only thirty-two when she had passed and had only learned of her cancer months before. He was thirty, and the three years since her death left him in purgatory and stuck between the memory of the past and the hope of the future. Her death was the first truly impacting personal loss he had ever known. Only months before they were to get married, she had been taken from him. Aleeka had been a joyful woman full of life, humour and love. Six months later it took all her strength to utter her last three words to him. Ten minutes later she died, as he held her withered hand. Letting it go was the hardest thing he had ever done.

That final memory haunted him nearly every hour for over a year, until he finally locked away the pain somewhere in a dark fissure of his memory. Suddenly, her death came roaring back to life, and the same buried emotions were now haunting him in the tiny conference room four thousand miles from where it had happened. Alexandra's spirit and mannerisms were so similar that he felt a sudden sense of guilt for tarnishing Aleeka's memory by flirting with a mirror image of her.

Alexandra chuckled softly, which broke Clint's sudden melancholy. "What if I told you this was my first time here? Perhaps you can recommend something that I might enjoy."

"Well.....," his pause then lasting the time it took for him to exhale slowly, "I'd say get what you like because I know this is not your first time here."

"Why do you say that?" she retorted meekly. "Why would I lie?"

"Who knows, but you are. First I saw you here last Wednesday and I remember you were wearing silver boots, black jeans and a black and silver top. Very nice by the way. Secondly, I know the owner here and, from the way he greeted you at the door, I'm betting you are more than a one-time visitor. Lastly, when you answer a question with a question, then it is the sure sign that you are either avoiding something or lying."

His face contained a certain smug look that left Alexandra defeated, annoyed yet impressed.

"How did I do?"

It was at this moment that he realised that his secret interest in her was not so casual. At that moment, he couldn't think of anything else to say. He then realised that she knew she had made an impression with him. This was confirmed as she gently brushed her hair back with her right hand, and smiled at him knowingly.

"Perhaps I have been here a time or two. I will give you that. I didn't know strangers knew that I like coming here. Is my dirty little secret out for all of Moscow? Do tell, Clint from America." Her eyes twinkled and her wry smile made Clint blush. "Well?" she asked, with one eyebrow raised. "Are you spying on all Russian women, or only me?"

Clint's ploy had been exposed. "Okay, maybe I recall you more clearly than all the other women I have been spying on. It could have been your silver boots that blinded me. Who knows the reason?"

She laughed out loud, which forced her hand to her mouth. "Well, it must be those boots because, in fairness, I don't see too many of those on the streets either."

The full effect of his accent washed over her. It was as if she'd blocked it out when she'd first heard him speak, having instead concentrated on what was going on around her. He was absolutely charming and witty and he was coming on to her. Alexandra was both surprised and not. She knew perfectly well she was not that special. Although she was immensely attractive, she was not alone in her beauty amongst a large crowd of Moscow girls. Alarm bells rang, loudly and persistently.

They looked at each other, smiled, and said nothing. Only when the waiter came over and asked, "Madam, have you decided on a drink yet?" was the silence broken.

"Of course. I will have a glass of the Evian, and the veal with mushrooms please."

"You see, Alexandra, you ordered all that without ever looking at the menu. I guess I was right, huh?"

"Okay, okay," she conceded. "Yes, I come here often, but I can't say I remember seeing you before."
The fact was that Alexandra never really minded the patrons of the restaurant. The Galereya was one of Moscow's trendier restaurants, especially among the in-crowd, who went there as much to get noticed as to people-watch themselves. The restaurant was partly sponsored by GQ and was heavily decorated with pictures from the magazine. Even the coatroom tokens were miniature versions of front covers from the

magazine. In fact, the token Alexandra received from Arkady featured David Beckham. Most often the place was full of people – an odd mix of ugly men, beautiful women and awkward foreign businessmen. Clint could have been there shirtless last week, and Alexandra would not have noticed.

Alexandra lifted the glass and took a slow sip, while she gazed upon the man before her.

"Why is it that you are here in Moscow?" she asked in her sultry accent.

"I work for the US embassy, actually. Do really boring things like approve passports, visas, national documents and such. It's a three year assignment."

"And do you like Moscow?"

"Umm... well, yes. Very different than life in Atlanta, that's for sure."

"So you come from Georgia, yes? I have a girlfriend from Georgia."

"Really!" Clint exclaimed. "What a small world!"

"Actually, what a large world," she rebutted. "She comes from Tbilisi, the capital of Georgia. There is your Georgia, and our Georgia." Her emphasis reinforced the typical tendency for Russians to still claim former republics in what used to be the unified Soviet Union. It was a subconscious trait born out of parental habit.

Clint just smiled with pinched lips, as this basic reminder seemed to reinforce that Americans did indeed reduce the world and its scope to their own borders. "Yes, of course."

"Tell me, Clint. What do you like most about Moscow? The nightlife, the beautiful women...?"
She paused without adding more options. Maybe he liked the diversity of Moscow. Maybe he enjoyed the myriad of significant museums, or even the verve of the street which was far removed the shuffle of Atlanta.

However, she somehow knew that Clint was in awe of the beauty of the women, of whom he frequently told his friends about back home.

"The beautiful women? Why would you think that?" he asked, turning a piercing eye on her.

"Wasn't it you who said that, when you answer a question with a question, the answer must be true?"

Clint chuckled and lowered the fork that he was prepared to bite from. "Got me there!" He looked down sheepishly, seemingly in defeat.

"You Americans don't have women like us in your country. I know what you're thinking."

Clint was taken a bit by Alexandra's forthright nature. She spoke so confidentially, almost arrogantly. In this sense she was quite similar to most Russians he had met. Their sense of candour never failed to impress Clint.

"Which is what?" His face was a picture of puzzlement. "What exactly do you mean by that?"

"Russian women are exotic to you. Our beauty, poise and style. Tell me that is not true."

Clint nodded in approval, because he knew this was absolutely true. The women were amazingly exquisite, and he found them so exotic and interesting; probably as much for their incredible model figures and looks as for their refined manners and grace. These were the women of Playboy, and he imagined all of them wore the same kind of underwear as the Playboy models did in their photo-shoots. Undressing them like this somehow was his first instinct – a crude, but innocent, impulse. Although he looked Alexandra in the eyes, he already guessed correctly she was wearing red lace underneath her black dress.

Whatever allure these women emitted, they were like nothing he had ever experienced before in America. Their features were soft, their skin the colour of porcelain and seemingly pure. So many women had perfect bodies and appeared so glamorous, exactly how Alexandra was before him. But it was more than that with Alexandra. She walked gracefully, carried her purse delicately, and her stare was hypnotic.

For a couple of moments the two ate, but the moments seemed awkward, as both wanted to continue their discussions. A mystical connection or spark was there, something neither had expected to feel. For Clint, the luck of having lunch with a woman he had found interesting since the first time he saw her from afar was exciting. For Alexandra it was the unfamiliar feeling of actually finding a man that had more potential than a mere business associate or John.

Eventually the silence was broken when Clint asked, "Can I ask you what you do for a living?"

"I am an interpreter and translator," she said matter-of-factly. "For an oil company based here in Moscow." Clint's eyebrows raised and his forehead creased from his reaction. "English, I assume?"

"And Japanese."

"Japanese!" he replied surprisingly. "Now that's impressive. How long did it take for you to learn Japanese?"

"About four years in all. It was my major in university, but I didn't study just that. Speaking and writing are totally different aspects to learn. I could speak Japanese okay-ish after two years but learning the kanjis and the katakana took me the full four years." She paused in reflection and then continued. "Actually, learning Chinese is harder than Japanese."

Either way, Clint thought that the two years of French he studied in high school paled in comparison. "Hmm, beautiful and smart. What a combination," he replied in a hushed voice and with a crooked smile.

Alexandra simply smiled at him and then drank the

last of her water, before refilling the glass from the nearby bottle.

"I bet that is your line to all the Russian girls you try to pick up here," she said, in a voice singed by sharp sarcasm.

"I didn't know I was trying to pick you up and no, I've never said that before. Really not." Alexandra only looked at him deliberately. She was not buying his rebuttal.

"I've heard all lines from men before. You, Clint, are not original." Her remark was like a sharp knife that sliced his skin, leaving him stung in apparent defeat; but then she continued. "But I believe you."

Perhaps it was because of her own arrogance and self-confidence that she knew his words to be obviously true, or perhaps it was because he seemed natural and more real than most every man who came on to her. Either way, her confession relieved him.

"Maybe we could learn more about each other another time," he said softly, almost meekly. The sincerity in his voice was something unfamiliar to Alexandra and she was taken by Clint's humanity, which seemed almost boyish to her. He seemed an interesting androgynous mix. Masculine and manly but somehow boyishly charming and... innocent, somehow. Alexandra's ability to read men was a life skill that she had honed with experience, and this man seemed different. At least, on the surface.

Doing something she rarely allowed herself to do, she accepted his bait and allowed herself to be lured in. "Yes, perhaps." This time her voice was not filled with anything other than a peaceful acceptance. "That could be nice."

She took her purse and opened it. She took out her brown leather-covered agenda and removed a piece of paper that she tore in two. She jotted down her mobile number and handed it to him, before speaking again. "Only after six o'clock," she said sternly. Her eyes twinkled when she handed him the slip of paper.

"Thank you," he said. His voice was appreciative in a way that was soothing and sincere. Alexandra was not totally sure what to think. Clint, on the other hand, felt as if he were 20,000 miles over the sea.

Chapter 3

I

In a darkened office underneath the main level of the US embassy, a nineteen-eighties-style telephone rang loudly. A line of coloured lights capped the top of its cream casing. The double ring sounded loudly, annoyingly so, and Director Billups knew exactly who was on the other line. When the red light flashed, it could be only one person.

"Ron Billups," barked the recipient. The director leaned back deep into his large chair that creaked loudly, as it always did. The chair was much like its owner – aged, dated and noticeable. The voice on the other end was from the Pentagon, and the director could only occasionally reply with a grunt that confirmed his approval.

Eventually Ron leaned sharply forward and replied with a confident, "Yes Sir, you will have an answer within thirty-six hours." After a few seconds more of garbled verbiage from the other end, the director replied with a final reply. "You have our full support on this one, Sir. It's what we are here for."

He hung up the phone and immediately pressed another of the phone's button and shouted, "Get me the boys. Now!"

It wasn't that Billups was really an office tyrant, but to an outsider it could appear so. He was quick, decisive, but for some who had worked with Ron for any time he could also be seen as fatherly. However when focused he did come across as crass and could hardly be bothered by sensitivities. In his opinion, if one worked in the field for the CIA then they should be immune from such pleasantries in times of importance. As he would often say, "It's still a man's world out there of evil, hate and violence."

The director was right to feel that, actually. His assignments, originating from the days of communism, had always involved indignities that would make the average person shudder to learn the extent of inhumanity that truly existed. Ron's world had seen him lose agent peers to beheadings and drownings. It eventually saw him lose his own agents to military-styled executions. The reality of his assignments was not the one of diplomacy and handshakes that most of his American brethren back home saw on the news. He always felt a disdain towards American pacifists, and he was as old-school as they came. He mocked liberals, feeling that they knew nothing about the brutality that really existed in the world outside their gated neighbourhoods and lush lifestyles in America.

The world was inherently evil in Ron's eyes, and he made no apologies for being politically incorrect or for saying that it was still a man's world. In his experience there had never once been a woman who could measure up to the kind of brutal thugs that truly defined his world. Women didn't break necks, torture victims with ice picks, gouge eyes out and kill other men in ways that Hollywood depicted to desensitised audiences.

A moment later, three men entered the director's office and stood in front of their boss with hands on their hips. "What is it?" asked one, a handsome man with the slightest of southern drawls.

"We have to mobilise. He is coming."

"When?" asked Florian, who snapped to attention when hearing the breakthrough that they had all been waiting for.

"Soon. He comes tomorrow or Tuesday." Ron removed his bifocals and leaned towards the three men.

"This time, we will get him."

II

Alexandra stretched closer to her bathroom mirror until her nose was only centimetres away. She applied her eyeliner gingerly, like she always did. Once finished, she leaned back and looked at her reflection for several seconds. She flicked at her hair and rocked her head sideways a couple of times. First right, then left and right again.

She completed this ritual every time before meeting a client, but meeting her lover meant that she took extra time to prepare herself. It was always this way with her lovers or boyfriends, although this lover was not anything more special than the others that had preceded him. He was yet another of a long list of short-term flings that satisfied her until she grew bored and tired of the routine. Usually it was their excessive time demands or their desire to become serious that were the precursors to the inevitable end. The fact was that she purely enjoyed having a new lover to learn, use and discard every three to four months.

Mikhail was typical of the other lovers of her past. He was older and married. At forty-three he was theoretically old enough to be her father, considering their sixteen-year age difference. His oldest daughter was fifteen and was turning sixteen in two months.

Alexandra had met him when she opened a separate savings account a year earlier. Mikhail was the Vice President of the bank, and they met innocently enough. Eventually, she succumbed to his advances. He seemed charming enough, and enjoyed the sex.

She believed that married men around forty tried harder sexually then the men her age that she would sometimes pick up at the club for a one-night stand. The older men seemed to appreciate her body and its delicate sensitivities far more than the younger studs, who ravished her like the paid clients she had to endure.

She thought married men would never seek permanence with her, because the one thing Alexandra avoided was commitment. Besides a casual girlfriend here or there, she had no real lasting friendships. In the end it was probably due to the fact that she feared permanence and familiarity and saw it subconsciously as some sort of state of paralysis. Having an older married lover in Russia, however, was almost a way of life - even if it was something that Alexandra tolerated as a temporary solution. One day, she rationalised, she would settle down and find someone more suitable.

Alexandra appreciated Mikhail's money and the gifts he bought for her. In fact, the only lovers she ever had were wealthy men. In a way, every man she had ever spread her legs for was for money. Except for the younger men at the clubs, who she enjoyed for what she saw as an uncomplicated 'quick fix'. These were boys she could enjoy unadulterated raw sex with. With her clients she had to do what they demanded, and with her lovers the sex seemed to fit a predictable routine.

She considered herself the model of a post-feminist woman. Since her experience was like so many other women whose men treated them subserviently, she learned early that she would never be able to change this patriarchal mentality and, rather than fight it, she would simply get what she could from them while she could.

Alexandra finished applying her lipstick – a soft rose colour that glistened in the bright bathroom lights. She took her birth control pill and put the packet back into the cabinet next to her vitamins. She left the bathroom and walked into the living room, and reached for the remote to her entertainment centre. As soon as she pressed play, the sound of Jamiroquai filled the roomy apartment.

The apartment was spacious and rather contemporary. In a sense it was typically Russian, but nonetheless it was still considered an expensive and desired flat. The apartment actually belonged to a scientist named Yaroslav.

Alexandra had been a darling to Yaroslav since they first met. He had been a friend of the family's ever since she had been adopted, and he used to live in Perm as well before he found his current job. He had bought her a used parlour grand piano to have in the apartment. Yaroslav loved classical music and when Alexandra played Beethoven's 'Moonlight' sonata at her thirteenth birthday, he became her biggest fan.

Rarely did Alexandra ever play the piano now. Only when she was alone in desperation did the piano find its way back to Alexandra. Her emergence into the piano would be total, and sometimes a full hour would pass before Alexandra realised the time. Only then did she feel complete again, but more and more her sense of detachment from her past sheltered childhood was growing. She was becoming something she did not want, but the metamorphosis seemed uncontrollable.

The door's buzzer sounded and Alexandra quickly lowered the volume and shuffled the CD player to a disk by Lada Dance, Mikhail's favourite pop singer. The ten year gap in the popularity of her music and his was only one of a myriad of differences between the two lovers. She did not, however, mind his choice of music, which rarely strayed from Russian. She pressed the button to let him in, and opened the door to wait for him to arrive. She could hear his footsteps as he ascended the two flights of stairs, and he paused as he reached the platform just a few stairs from her door.

"Come on, old man," she quipped jokingly, "are you tired already? What does this mean for me?"

Mikhail put his hand on the rail and continued his climb up the final stairs with a confident smirk. When he reached Alexandra he pulled her close and kissed her passionately. "It means that I have enough in me to fuck you madly just as you like."

She enjoyed having her lover talk dirty to her. It somehow aroused her but simultaneously diminished her respect of a man who would speak so crudely to a woman, even if it was considered innocent foreplay. Alexandra's logic and standards were often contradictory like this.

"Well, come in and show me," she said as she pulled herself away from his embrace and strolled away into the living room.

The door closed behind her and she turned around to see Mikhail hanging his coat on the adjacent coat hanger. "Would you like your cognac before or after?" she asked coyly.

Usually Mikhail preferred to have his drink before sex, which allowed him to complain about his work, wife, and clients who annoyed him. Sometimes he would brag about his daughter or how fast Anastasia was growing into a young woman who he felt further and further removed from. But tonight he chose the latter. He felt horny, and needed to make love to Alexandra immediately.

Their routine was familiar to them both. Once inside her apartment she would always take off her top and place it over the bedside chair. She liked it when Mikhail would come from behind and kiss her neck. Feeling his lips and breath along her neck awakened her sexual desires. Sometimes she would take his hands and place them on her breasts, which became aroused. This is what she liked, and this was exactly what was happening tonight.

He nibbled and licked the back of her ear, and she

rolled her head in delight. He slowly unbuttoned her white blouse and then slipped his fingers in between her bra and bare breasts. Her nipples were firm and erect, and as he caressed them she moaned softly.

"I've been waiting for this all week," she gasped.

She sat on the bed's edge, and then unbuttoned Mikhail's pants as he took off his shirt. She pulled down his boxers, revealing the erect penis she so desired.

"It better be clean this time," she demanded in a motherly tone.

Alexandra was nearly obsessive about personal hygiene and she refused to give fellatio to a man if he smelled. Mikhail had failed her a few weeks prior – a lesson he had yet to repeat.

"You know I am clean. Taste it yourself."

Tenderly she placed him into her mouth and slowly but firmly sucked his penis, much to Mikhail's delight. He pushed her back onto the bed and quickly pulled off her skirt and panties, leaving Alexandra's lower body completely naked on the bed. He joined her, but, instead of entering her then, he kissed Alexandra passionately while his right hand caressed her breasts. His hands were typically coarse and the dichotomy of his skin and hers couldn't have been more different.

He ran his hands across her body, which intensified their intimacy. Eventually he started a full body kiss, paying particular attention to her heaving breasts. Mikhail loved Alexandra's breasts and would kiss and lick her perky nipples. Her breasts had a pronounced curvature to them; it seemed that, no matter whether she was upright or on her back, Alexandra's breasts always held their shape.

His mouth and tongue eventually found their way to Alexandra's other lips, which by now had become swollen and moist. He tickled her with his tongue, which caused Alexandra to grasp the sheets with both hands and arch her back. She moaned more loudly and then ran her fingers through his hair. She pushed his face deeper into her crotch and spread her legs as far apart as she could.

He liked to pleasure her this way, using his lips and tongue to explore her deeply. There had been times she would climax through this oral stimulation. Rarely did her clients perform cunnilingus on her, because doing that would cost extra. Her fees were for straight sex and oral, but to reciprocate was another hundred dollars per hour. Perhaps that is why she preferred having lovers on the side to fulfil this basic sexual need. It just did not seem right for her Johns to fuck her in this way.

"Fuck me now!" she gasped, her voice nearly trembling in desperation.

Mikhail continued his oral probing for another minute or so before rising up and towering over her squirming body. His penis now was rock hard and he could see that her eyes were fixed to his manhood, and only that. He found a condom and put it on within a few seconds. She took his manhood with both hands and massaged it, all the while staring at it as if it were the first time she had seen it. He finally inserted himself into Alexandra, much to her delight. She tensed as he slowly went deeper and deeper, and then she shouted in ecstasy as he quickly plunged his manhood into the final inch of her quivering body.

Finally, after ten minutes Mikhail could not take the torment of her pleasure any longer. "I'm coming now!" he yelped. "Oh God... now... come with me!"

Alexandra moaned, and seconds later the two shouted and groaned as he exploded sexually. Alexandra's hands dug deep into Mikhail's rear and her legs wrapped around his body in a final act of intimacy and embrace. She enjoyed the feeling of his full penis in her, but she had never climaxed from having a man on top. Only when she was on top could she come, and even then it was only when she allowed herself the freedom to let go emotionally that she could experience any orgasm. Although she had sex often, rarely was she ultimately pleasured.

They lay there, completely still as their hearts began to beat ever slower, until finally Alexandra's legs unlocked and her body collapsed one final time. Mikhail kissed her again before rolling off her. It was a relationship whose end was almost certain, yet the two played on; living in the moment and too unconcerned to face the realities of the future.

Could he possibly keep her and, if so, for how long? Could Alexandra possibly stay 'the other woman' for so long? Surely, she sometimes wondered, he would find another lover to fix his attentions on. This realisation always was to lead Alexandra to her current mentality, which was to lavish every moment with her lovers until she felt the need to dispose of one old lover for another.

There had been rare occasions when lovers would overlap, but she actually preferred the simplicity of having one at a time. It was difficult enough juggling her clients and boy toys with Mikhail and the others that preceded him. Answering to no-one was a mere way of life for Alexandra. Certainly, sex was no different. She fucked whoever she wanted, whenever she wanted.

Mikhail arose from the bed, his torso still heaving from the exertion of love making. He peeled away his condom from his ever-shrinking penis and turned to Alexandra who lay on the bed slowly squirming. Mikhail may have been satisfied, but Alexandra still had dormant desires waiting to be fulfilled. Tonight, like most every night, they would have to go unheeded.

"You were fantastic," he said matter-of-factly as he shuffled to the bathroom.

She rolled over to see him enter the bathroom. He threw the used condom in her wastebasket and turned on the sink's faucet. "You just are so beautiful, and so..." His sentence stopped and she could see him searching for the words as he raised his head in contemplation.

Mikhail collapsed onto the bed and moved nearer his naked mistress. He slapped Alexandra's butt firmly, but not too hard. She turned back with a scowl. "I really love your ass," he said. He inhaled deeply and slowly. A moment's silence fell upon the room, and Mikhail just stared ahead, seemingly just above Alexandra's curious eyes.

"What?" Alexandra asked softly.

"Everything." His tone seemed indignant. "Anastasia's becoming more like her mother. I feel her slipping away. Growing up."

"You mean growing away from you?" Alexandra rose and braced herself against the back of the bed. "You will always be her special daddy, even if it seems she is distancing herself from you."

Mikhail nodded as if Alexandra's statement was what he already knew deep inside. "And Miroslav..." Again Mikhail paused, and his face puckered in disgust.

"What about him?"

"He has become more and more greedy!" Mikhail motioned with his left hand as if he was a conductor. "He has put us in a dangerous position, and I'm tired of his arrogance."

Alexandra was taken aback by his remarks. Although she had never met Miroslav, she knew that he and Mikhail were more than business partners. They went back twenty years, and she was fairly certain that

37

their friendship was probably stronger than his marriage to Marina. In fact, she knew that he and Marina had an open relationship, and that Miroslav was probably the deepest relationship in his life.

She felt fairly sure that they engaged in illegal activities and that they were connected to the mafia underworld somehow. It was in the things that Mikhail had told her. Like the time when he said he had to skip their date because 'the big man' was coming with his 'boys' to have a meeting. Mikhail himself had a bodyguard, and he sometimes waited outside her apartment in his Mercedes when he would visit her. Why would a banking executive need a bodyguard, she wondered?

Anyway, this was the first she had ever seen her lover upset like this. Usually he was stoic, although with Alexandra he tended to be soft and rather kind.

"What do you mean by his arrogance?"

"He thinks the people we work with are stupid! That he is the only one who is smart!" His voice rose in pitch and his anger mounted. "He does business where he needs to stay away, and it exposes me!"

Mikhail stood up and slipped into his shirt. He walked over to her dresser and checked himself in its mirror. He ran his fingers through his coarse dark hair, and put on and buttoned his shirt.

Alexandra rolled out of the bed and slid back into her short dress. "Let me get you a drink."

"Yes. I will have that cognac now."

III

Ten kilometers outside of Moscow center lies a seedy underbelly that is corrupt as the garbage that litters its streets. It wasn't always this way. Only after the fall of communism in 1991 did the area around Gorkij become a slum and a magnet to the mafia. This is a part of Moscow that no tourists or foreigners dare to venture into. It didn't take much to see that Gorkij still has its dowdy communist inheritance. Muddy and slushy streets with poor drainage systems covered this neighborhood giving it a slippery dirty crust. Here one sees starving pensioners who are waiting and praying for death, organized crime gangs, drugs and prostitution –all exposing the glamour of upmarket Moscow.

Moscow is the place where contract killers are hired to shoot journalists and businessmen; where radical nationalists spread seeds of growing discrimination; where corrupted militia authorities rule the streets; where the laws are on the side of the rich and powerful. Gorkij is just one of a thousand places in Moscow where life is hard and progress is far away. The smell of Gorkij's stench never subsides and only intensifies when the summer heat comes. Hell probably smells similar – the sulfur in the air hangs about like a permanent fog.

Igor's shiny black Mercedes sedan seemed completely out of place in the slum rail yards of Gorkij. It moved slowly and stealthily along an alley; as much to avoid the deep potholes as anything. Its black tinted window concealed the muscular driver with dark sunglasses. Igor is a chameleon blending in to every corner of Moscow. He is a powerful figure in the underworld – an assassin who transitions between the glamorous lights of Moscow's upper society and the dark disreputable corners of its criminal outlying neighborhoods.

Although he earns his living from the Kasyamov, he is an independent contract killer who had worked outside of Russia as well. Just the month before he had slit the throat of a Polish dissident who compromised his client's integrity by revealing a banking scheme to

Russian investment authorities. Before he killed Thomasz, he beat him with brass knuckles that left him nearly toothless.

Igor's manifesto is to stay alive and indulge in his affluent lifestyle. He was a former military officer, but when he saw that his fortunes could skyrocket as an arm of the Mafia he had little interest to serve as a mere soldier in a has-been army. At first he completed hits for whichever mob paid him, but eventually he found loyalty with the Kasyanov gang. He would kill anyone although he was not interested in squeezing out anyone from the rival Solntsevo gang or the Dolgoprudnevos. His forte was in killing bankers, Chechens and corrupt individuals who wronged the Kasyamovs.

The Mercedes pulled into the chain linked confines of a scrap yard where dozens of cars filled the muddy property. Three dilapidated shacks were located at the opposite side and Igor pulled up to the largest of these. A few men milled about and watched as the door opened before Igor carefully exited. The comfort of his new 600 SEL was a sharp contrast to where he was now.

The door opened to the metal shack revealing two bodyguards and a potbellied man with a tar stained moustache. "Igor! It's been too long." His voice was husky from too many cigarettes, and his ragged face wore the tell tale signs of hard drinking.

"Only two weeks ago I got my Italian shoes dirty here," Igor said with a heavy accent that almost sounded Georgian.

Igor hated coming to Gorkij, but it was Oleg's favorite place to meet. The scrap yard was, in fact, a chop shop where stolen cars were altered and their VIN numbers changed. Most of the cars came from Russia; however more and more were coming from European countries in the west.

"You are a pretty boy, Igor. You should wear boots like me." Oleg laughed loudly and two of his bodyguards came forward through the door.

Igor strode forward, past the two large nameless men and into the dingy shanty. A nearby table was already prepared with empty glasses and a full bottle of Rodnik vodka. He sat at one end of the table while the other men collected themselves around him. Oleg opened the bottle and poured each of the four glasses half full. It was always this way with Oleg. He saw doing business over 40 proof vodka as symbolic of masculinity and power. Oleg lit a cigarette and took a deep drag from it before slowly exhaling and sighing: "We have a problem," he said in a tone of concern.

"You always call me when you have a problem. That's why I am here."

"You know Igor, I am trying to be a modern man who can change with the times."

Igor nodded in approval and took the first sip from his drink.

"I still like to do my business the old fashioned way which includes…"

Oleg paused while he searched how to finish his thought.

"Bribery. I don't know how else to say it," he said with a sinister chuckle.

Igor slammed his finished drink on the table and immediately Oleg poured him another full glass.

"I pay a lot of money to certain people in order to keep my business successful."

Igor reflected that Oleg was the most backwards businessman he knew; however he was extremely successful in the world of arms trading.

Oleg continued, "So imagine my surprise when I heard that one of my men is secretly dealing with Krokav. Rumor has it he is in Moscow right now."

"Krokav? The Krokav?" Igor asked with an inflection of awe.

"Yes him. And my Minister, Vladimir Gorban.......that double crossing asshole...The one who I thought represented my best interests is working a deal with Krokav that he thinks I don't know about."

Oleg's anger and loathing now totally consumed him.

"Which is why I am here presumably?"

"Yes. My informants tell me that Gorban is dealing on the side which is against our agreement and that is unacceptable".

Oleg gulped half of his vodka at once -causing his face to become contorted as a result. He smacked his lips and blinked twice quickly before Igor responded coolly.

"You know I don't do hits on gangsters, especially king pins like Krokav. That would be.....foolish."

It was a credo Igor had ever since becoming an assassin. He was always clear that victims were not associated with what he called 'family' and Krokav was exactly that. Although not a mob figure per se, Krokav dealt with nearly every mob figure from the U.S. to Japan although Eastern Europe was his playground.

"So how can I help you?"

"No, no – Krokav may think he is better than me, but I've been in this business when that punk was shitting his diapers. It's Gorban I want to teach a lesson to which is where you come in."

"Okay.....which is?"

"He doesn't know that I know all about this little operation he has with the Americans. He is selling them inventory and using his connections at Sberbank to profit. He is holding out on me on that profit which is why I need you."

"Ahh, okay. The bankers."

"And Minister Gorban? Now that is risky." Igor's eyes quickly lost their sparkle.

"That fucking Vladimir Gorban! He refuses me yet he deals with Krokav and the Americans on the side! And who the fuck does he think I am?" Oleg's voice was filled with disdain and he slammed his glass down at the table then angrily poured another glass.

"With my rival, no less! My father says he is insulted by that fucking bureaucrat who thinks he is more powerful than he really is. He must be taught a lesson!"

Igor sipped slowly his vodka and then asked in a hushed voice, "When? How?"

"I want you to shadow these animals. Watch who they are spending time with after hours and take pictures. I know Vladimir is aligned with the Americans who are all soft on our shit Ukrainian step-brothers. However, my sources say there are others who would work against us. This simple politician thinks he can overcome us? Who the fuck...?"

Igor could see a dangerous wave of anger overcoming Oleg so he firmly pacified it saying "You have control Oleg."

"No! I have less control now Igor. But do these new democratic purists at the Duma think they can take back the country that we control? Krokav must learn that his little plan will disappear in a puff of smoke." Oleg snapped his fingers for dramatic effect and stared squarely at his paid killer.

"This asshole will not undo the ten years of work that my family has achieved." Oleg paused and his face changed from anger to dismay. "The Americans and their delusional notions of democracy are nothing more than modern day imperialists. Who the fuck do they think they are? Do they think we are terrorists?"

Oleg again took a long drag from his homemade cigarette and then looked up towards the darkened ceiling.

"They are the terrorists! Fucking Imperialists! How dare Vladimir come in and work with my only rival when I'm paying him bribes to get these contracts!"

Oleg gulped the last of his vodka loudly before wiping his mouth with the sleeve of his shirt. "Cut the head off the snake and the body dies. Krokav's little adventure ends when I cut off the head of his deal."

"You know this will be expensive, yes?" Igor's concern was less of imperialism and more about monetary incentives.

"We will pay you 15,000 rubles a day. I think nearly five hundred dollars a day is enough. Follow him for a week and I want to know every asshole he talks to, every restaurant he eats at and every mistress he fucks. I want names! The names of who is controlling him is what I want most of all!"

"Easy then. What about any hits?"

"My boys are at your service for whenever you need them. For now no one disappears but I may change that."

"You know I always work alone," Igor stated matter-of-factly.

"And your work is always perfect."

Oleg gulped the last of his vodka and then reached into his jacket pocket. He slid a mobile phone over to Igor before continuing, "Use this when you need anything from Ruslan and Pavel. Just in case. Press the green button and it will go straight to them."

Both Ruslan and Pavel looked at Oleg with stern faces that had seen a fair share of brutality and death. Igor, despite being an assassin, saw Ruslan and Pavel as crude muscle whereas he saw himself as a professional. Nonetheless he took the phone and slipped into the inside pocket of his Hugo Boss suit jacket.

As he stood up he smoked one final drag from his withering cigarette before extinguishing the nub on the corner of the oak table. He pulled out a thick envelope and the other men rose simultaneously and the sounds of their heavy chairs reverberated as Oleg handed Igor his money.

"Inside the envelope is everything you need. Addresses and background information. Oh and my father sends his thanks."

"Tell Viktor I won't let him down."

"Tell him yourself the next time you see him. You are his favorite, you know?"

Igor knew that already. Viktor and Igor had shared a similar background in their previous lives. Viktor had fought in the great Patriotic War when he was only sixteen years old. He boasted that he personally killed four Nazi's in one ambush outside his hometown of Sumatra. He had shot to death the last one in the head as he attempted to crawl away. Eventually he left the Red Army in the 1960's before developing his illegal businesses, under the watchful eye of the Kremlin. It didn't hurt that he was well connected and had friends inside the communistic bureaucracy. He saw much of himself in Igor and had even allowed the soft spoken assassin in his home on more than one occasion. He liked showing Igor his collection of antique guns and rifles. It was a means of bonding between two former soldiers. Igor appreciated the words and so smiled as he uttered:

"I will. And thanks for the vodka. It always focuses me."

IV

Alexandra walked into Sergi's office with a smirk and a confidence that was typical of her. The binder in her hands was thick and she dropped it onto his desk just in front of him, barely missing his coffee which sat by the telephone.

"Yes, I said it was okay for you to come in and, yes, you almost knocked over my coffee!"

"It's always okay for me to come in and I missed your coffee by a metre. Don't exaggerate." The twinkle in her eye was a manifestation of the confidence of what existed in the notebook before him.

"I assume this is – "

"This is twenty-five hours of work. Yes, how did you know?" Her brash interruptions were not unexpected for Sergi, however annoying they were. "Complete translation of the deal with Teikoku complete with signatures. All ready to go, and look – it's only eleven. Guess I will go home now and begin my weekend a few hours early."

Sergi picked up the notebook and flipped through some of the last pages. The translation was separated in halves. The first twenty pages or so was the contract in Russian, and the second half was in Japanese. The Kanji ensured that the Japanese portion was much smaller, but it represented at least three-quarters of the total time needed to finish her translation.

"Good stuff, as always." His praise was the reassurance of what she already knew.

Alexandra's and Sergi's relationship was an eclectic mix of professionalism and something greater. Perhaps paternal, in a way. He was now in his early fifties and his youngest son was a year older than Alexandra. Sergi had two sons, and she represented something like a daughter to him. In their four years of working together, Alexandra had been able to manipulate Sergi like a daughter does her father.

Their interplay ranged in gamut from fighting to deep respect. They laughed often and probably argued more than they should. In the most superficial sense, Sergi was more of a father than her adoptive father Fedor, who she never connected with. Her interaction with Sergi was a spark that Alexandra needed, even if it was subconscious.

"Go on, Alex." He waved his hand to shoo her out of his office. He had other projects and matters that commanded his immediate attention. "Get out, and see you Monday. Remember we have the staff meeting at nine."

"Thank God I have you to remind me," she replied sarcastically. She smiled at him and blew him a kiss as she left. Sergi could only shake his head in disbelief and returned to the document he was reading.

As Alexandra walked back to her office, her private mobile beeped. The volume was always turned down low and where others may not have been able to hear her phone ring or chime for a text message, Alexandra had an uncanny ability to hear its near-silent tone. She pulled it out of her purse and looked at the name on the small screen as she entered her office at the end of the hall. She closed the door behind her and dialled Elena. "Hey, it's me," she said in a rather hushed tone. "You have a client?"

"I need you for tomorrow evening at six-thirty. He is Japanese, and we are hiring Svetlana too to join his associate. You are with Mr Takahashi, Svetlana is for Mr Yoshida."

"For how long?" In her mind Alexandra was hoping to be home by ten, because she hated to miss her favourite Saturday night television programme.

"They have booked for three hours and you are

meeting them at the Ritz Carlton for dinner, which is where they are staying. You are to meet him in the lobby just a minute or two before six-thirty, yeah?"

Alexandra knew instinctively what Elena was thinking – easy money. For Alexandra, a client who could afford to stay at the Ritz was probably a good tipper too. Only once had she had a client at Moscow's finest hotel – an Arab from Dubai. Alexandra, who was not given to be overly impressed by much of anything, was taken back by the luxury of the Ritz. That night proved fun. The Arab was not such an unpleasant lover, and she rather enjoyed his extroverted and playful manner. The thousand dollar tip he left her, however, made the largest impression. She may have forgotten his name, but the stack of hundreds was something she would have no problem remembering.

"Fine. I'll be there."

She ended the call by flipping over the phone's cover and then putting her mobile back into her purse. Alexandra's double life meant carrying two phones. She also had multiple email addresses for the different aspects of her life. In a sense, Alexandra was truly the Gemini that defined her horoscope sign. A twin with two halves, where one part of Alexandra was the intelligent, head strong, and career woman, while the other Alexandra was a woman of carnal sin. Alexandra was a living definition of duplicity.

Many thought they knew Alexandra well. Her neighbours were an older married couple who she socialised with occasionally and one time, while over for dinner, they insisted on setting her up on a blind date. They pitied Alexandra for being so often alone and for taking so many business trips away. They often struggled to understand why no men ever came over. Privately, they wondered if she might be a lesbian. Alexandra would just say she was too busy for a steady relationship. One day, she said, she would settle down.

Her parents worried for their adopted child. They lived in far away Perm where Alexandra had spent the remainder of her childhood. She left Perm for good when she was nineteen, as a scholarship student at Maxin Gorky Institute. The scholarship had provided a literal escape from the boredom she felt in Perm and the restrictive confinement of the parents she never fully accepted.

Moscow had quickly become her true parent. It taught her much in terms of life lessons. She quickly learned to be street-savvy, how to fend for herself and how to get connected. Moscow left its scars, as well. Its cold and unforgiving pace toughened her to the harsh realities of being used, and it was where she learned to manipulate others for her own personal gain. Like any relationship, there was symbiosis.

Alexandra finished her email and at the exact moment she hit the 'send' key, her mobile again rang. The number on the screen read 'Unknown Number'. Curiously, she answered, "Privet?"

"Hi, is this Alexandra? It's Clint, the guy you sort of had lunch with a few days ago."

Her mind raced, and a flicker of surprised happiness filled her. She had thought of him a couple times during the busy week, and here he was on the other line. Her mind raced at what to say.

"Sort of?" she quickly retorted. "You mean the guy who forced his company upon me during my private lunch? Yes, I remember him." Alexandra's typical wit was always at its best when quick thinking was required.

"Ohhh..." Clint chuckled. "Forced is how you saw it? I remember you as the beautiful woman who would not stop talking to me. Funny how differently we see it." Clint's candour and cutting humour made

49

Alexandra smile.

"Well... I was calling to ask if you could join me for dinner. Perhaps tomorrow night?"

"I'm afraid you asked too late. I have other plans. You know that a busy modern woman like me needs more notice."

"Yeah, I know. Really and truly you're right, but it was so hectic this week and I wasn't sure what was what until just today. I thought about asking you for a bite to eat this evening but decided on tomorrow because at least it was something of a notice. Then how about next week?" Clint's voice was conciliatory and sincere, and he realistically knew inside she would never to accept a date on such short notice.

Alexandra paused for a few seconds and then replied, "How about this evening, then?" This kind of impulsiveness was atypical of her usual calculating manner. She wondered where had it come from and as quickly as she had said it, she wished it back; but it was too late.

"Actually, yes. That would be even better. Listen – why don't we meet at the Pushkin Cafe? I was there for the first time last month and quite enjoyed it. Do you know where it is? It's right off Pushkin Square."

"Every Muscovite knows the Pushkin Cafe, because it is where all the foreigners like you go." she said with a sense of light-heartedness.

"Oh well, we don't have to go there then if you would like to meet somewhere else. Really, Alexandra, you decide."

Suddenly she felt a sense of guilt, and sensed his sincerity to please her. "I'm kidding. Of course we in Moscow go there too."

"Ah, now I'm feeling better." Clint's relief was evident.

"I really like their desserts. Don't you worry. Want

to meet then at six-thirty? I'm afraid if we go later without reservation then we won't find a seat."

"Great! So... until then, huh?"

Alexandra smiled and felt amused at his relief and apparent joy. She chuckled softly under her breath as she replied, "See you soon, embassy man."

Chapter 4

I

Only a kilometre further south from where Alexandra had just ended her call was a woman that could have been her sister. Both women shared the same physical beauty and delicate features. Torie Popslavskaya was a stunning woman with a model's body that only her husband could appreciate. Whereas countless men had enjoyed Alexandra's nakedness and ravishing sexuality, only two men had ever been pleasured by Torie. And unlike Alexandra, who wore clothing that accentuated her every curve, Torie kept hers hidden in frumpy styles.

The two women may have shared the same beauty, but the two could not be more polar in their differences. Both had come from foster parents who had ultimately adopted them, but only one escaped puberty with a sense of normality. Alexandra had never attached herself to the dysfunctional and cold parental relationship that she endured for twenty years. However, Torie was a mirror of her parents' conservative family values.

Torie was cautious, inward, and softly spoken. Alexandra flaunted her confidence and used her wit and quick mind to penetrate even the most awkward of moments. Not surprisingly, Torie was a mother, and had always wanted to be a mother since her childhood days. For years little Torie's favourite toy was a baby doll that she mothered as if it were real. Not surprisingly, her eight-year-old son was the centre of her universe. Alexandra, on the other hand, was far too self-absorbed to ever contemplate having a child. She was fiercely protective in using birth control, and was always doubly cautious.

But Torie was altogether a different person. Her life revolved around sacrifice and love. She gave herself completely to her Stefan and had never fallen out of love since their wedding days so many years ago. When she had Alexi, then everything from that moment on centred on their wellbeing. It came to no surprise that Torie let herself go and gave little concern to makeup and flashy clothes. Nonetheless, men would still ogle her when she did her daily chores.

A few years prior, Torie was approached to do modelling from a man who was struck by her natural beauty. He saw through the simple girl's conservative clothes and tried to persuade her to come to an audition that following week, but young Torie felt too shy and overwhelmed to go. Nothing had changed for her, and motherhood made her feel too far removed from such things as style and catching men's attention. Alexandra was all about both.

Torie climbed the three steep stairs that led her into a tiny neighbourhood market that sat perched on a corner only a couple hundred metres from her apartment. Torie had been frequenting this store for over two years on a weekly or bi-weekly basis, largely because the married elderly owners treated her as a special customer. The old pair had owned the store since before the fall of communism and somehow managed to keep it to themselves in the turbulent early years. By 1996 the store had managed to expand in stocking some foreign products, which attracted the business clientele of the neighbourhood. Local residents like Torie weren't interested in such imports but rather the stodgy Russian products which, in terms of price, undercut the large grocery store chains that had saturated the city.

As she entered, the stare of the man she passed followed her. She felt his gawk, which was something she had gotten used to ignore. Men still could see through the casual clothes, but Torie was too naïve to know that they undressed her mentally. It was a combination of her ability to focus on Stefan and Alexi, as well as her overriding value system that had never changed.

A simple nod and warm smile from the old woman at the register acknowledged her as she passed and made her way to the vegetables. Torie stood out amongst the store's older and simple patrons. The aisles were narrow and several customers pressed together to get to the small potato section that Torie was at the centre of. Whereas some would feel annoyed at being crowded in a tiny supermarket, Torie felt completely comfortable in this kind of domestic reality. Ten minutes later she approached the counter and smiled knowingly at the same woman who had rung her up twice a week for the last four years.

"Hello, Miss Torie." The old lady always called her by that name. Actually no-one addressed Torie by anything other than her nickname. It was the only example that the proud mother and wife clung to her childhood. In fact very few really knew that her name was not actually Torie, although Torie was the common shortened version that was typically Russian.

"Good afternoon, Mrs. Volkova. Just needing a few things for my husband's favourite dish."

"Cabbage rolls, I assume?"

"Absolutely. What else?"

"That will be three hundred and twenty rubles," the owner said as Torie opened her wallet. "And how is little Alexi?"

"Enjoying second class," she replied with a beaming smile. "And I think he has a special lady friend. He can't stop talking about a classmate named Nika."

As the old lady handed Torie a few coins in change,

she replied with a knowing chuckle, "Oh my! Your little boy will grow up to be a certain Romeo for sure. Here – give him this red lollipop and tell him it is the colour of love."

Torie smiled back as she took the gift for her son. She took the two plastic bags of groceries from the counter and winked at the old lady, before turning away towards the door. "Until next time," she replied as she headed back out into the chilly afternoon.

II

Alexandra hurried into the restaurant's door and was met by staff who offered to take her light camel-coloured fur. Alexandra had multiple fur coats, although few were actually real. A couple ahead of her was now being led away by a blonde hostess who could have been Alexandra's sister. Coolly, she brushed away a bit of hair that had fallen over her right eye, and clutched her hand-sized purse tightly. Unbeknownst to Alexandra, Clint sat at a nearby table that secured not five minutes before she came in. Although her back was now towards him, Clint knew the shape and figure well. She walked slowly, heading towards the adjacent piano bar. Clint rose from his chair and followed; his stare locked to the woman only yards ahead.

"You looking for someone, Madam?" he said, as he gently touched her elbow.

Alexandra spun around and smiled. Her features appeared exactly as he remembered when they last met. Her pale blue eyes were so striking; Clint had not forgotten how mesmerising her gaze was.

"Yes sir. I'm supposed to meet a boyfriend of mine, but you're so cute I think I'll dump him for you."

Alexandra's confidence and sharp wit was the engine that fuelled Clint's fire. Although he had just met her, she was quicker on her feet than anyone Clint had ever met.

"Why, you little vixen," he retorted as his smile widened. He leaned forward and gave her a customary kiss on her right cheek and then another on the left. "Come on, I have us a table over there." His right hand motioned towards the corner only a few metres away.

"I suppose they put us in the corner because they think we will be bad," she said as she followed Clint. Her thick accent was pure Russian and her pitch was very sultry. Her porcelain skin and piercing gaze somehow complimented her hypnotising eyes.

Once at the table he turned to her and replied, "I am a perfect gentleman. Maybe next time we can order a table closer to the middle."

Her stare pierced him and he felt a tingling in the base of his spine as she looked him intensely. Clearly, she possessed him in a way that he had never experienced. He reached for her chair and pulled it out for her.

"I have a special plan for you," he said in an effort as much to break the moment as it was to reveal their plans. "Dinner for two awaits us here, and then we will do something that only takes a few minutes afterwards."

"Where will you take me? What if I want to escape you out of sheer boredom?" Alexandra's brow furrowed inquisitively.

Clint smiled and chuckled softly. He absolutely loved her humour. "You love seafood, yes?"

Alexandra smiled as Clint sat in his chair. "Then I'm all yours, captain." Her reply was laced with a sense of sexuality, or at least Clint's mind thought so.

"Well, based on what I saw you eating last week, I assumed you might eat seafood and then after you eat seafood..." His lips pursed, and he shifted his head from side to side.

"Then what?" Alexandra asked.

"Uh – you will see. My secret," he replied, with a sense of cunning confidence.

Thirty minutes later Clint poured Alexandra a second glass of wine - a full-bodied Pinot Blanc from 1988. "Here's to you," he toasted, as he raised his glass to meet hers. They each sipped slowly, but their stare at one another never broke. Alexandra couldn't understand what it was about him that had her smitten. For the first time she could remember she actually was enjoying the conversational interplay with a date. He was clever, witty, yet there was an honesty that encapsulated him like an invisible bubble. She tried a few times to burst his sphere of sincerity. Often she would counter him, but his replies were always so real and without pretence. After a while she was only partly convinced he wasn't lying just to impress her.

"Come on, tell me about your family now. Somehow we drifted from the subject a while back." Clint seemed excited to learn these most basic bits of information, but little did he know how uncomfortable this made her feel.

"Listen, Clint. They died when I was a small girl."

When she told people this they would just stumble for words before hiding under the typical 'I'm sorry.' For Alexandra, this was only a partial lie. Her father had died but she had never known him. There was so much more to this chapter which remained closed to Alexandra's heart.

"Have you gotten over it?" Clint asked coolly as he sipped from his wine, his eyes appearing over his glass and looking directly at her.

This was the first time anyone had followed up the offensive volley meant to neutralise her emotional tormentors. She paused, looked at him with a mix of panic, and then cut slowly a piece of her lamb. The silence lingered over their table before she replied softly, "You tell me. Do you ever get over it?"

"Answering a question with a question tells me enough. Listen, we move on to something lighter. Tell me about when you were a model." His sneaky smile seemed to reassure Alexandra.

"Why do all American men think that I am a model? I am just normal here in Russia."

"Hardly!" He shook his head as he picked at his remaining food.

Alexandra sipped from her glass before responding, "I told you my life already, and it did not include anything about being a model."

"Well, first thing, I only got a condensed version of your life, and that took you not even three minutes for you to race through. Come on! I bet you have some amazing stories to tell."

Indeed she did, but his naivety to the nature of those stories would elude him and be replaced by what he wanted to hear. Every man wanted Alexandra to be a virtuous creation of brains and beauty. To be so sexually tarnished would negate any of her positive characteristics. Or so she had always assumed. And perhaps Alexandra was more right than she was wrong. Men wanted their madonna-whores to be a fine balance between sexually experienced and conservative maternal caretakers. She was neither, but that was her secret - and her scared childhood was even a deeper secret.

"What was the craziest thing you ever did?" What if she really told him just a fraction of the things that she herself considered crazy? She smiled at him softly as her mind raced.

What if she told him about when she participated in a foursome with three other guys? Or when she and another girl were slaves for a leather-clad dominatrix? What would he think if she told him that she was dominated, that she gave and received cunnilingus with the other woman while she herself was completely dressed in latex? For a moment she thought about actually telling him, but something deep saw his normality, and she enjoyed playing the paradoxical lady instead of the whore. There was time enough for that later. She concluded she wanted to fuck him tonight.

"What? What are you thinking?" His question interrupted Alexandra's long pause and constant stare.
"I was just thinking if agreeing to meet you for dinner was the craziest thing I ever have done."

Clint's lips pursed and his forehead furrowed, as his surprise could not be contained. "Why would you say that?"

"Tell me then why you wanted to be with me?"

"You seem interesting. Could there be any other reason?"

"And if I was fat and wore clothes like American women? Would you have asked me for dinner?"

Clint considered her words and reflected. Intuitively, he knew he would not have.

"You asked me out because of my appearance and because you want to sleep with me. It is a simple but unapologetic reason. There is no need to feel guilty."

Clint was taken aback, and wondered if he was that shallow. After all, there was something deeply exotic and sexual that pleased him innately about her that he rarely, if at all, saw in American women.

"Yeah," he slowly confided, "Maybe to a large degree you are right."

"Stop looking down. All men think the same." Her words seemed to pierce him like a knowing mother.

"Okay, maybe your looks caught my attention, but

after talking with you I really found you interesting. I really saw something in you I wanted to learn more about." His empathetic voice seemed defensive and was tinged with the slightest of guilt.

"What man asks out an ugly woman who is a stranger? We all are judged by our appearance, Clint." As she said this, he knew that this was indeed life's secret. "The cover of our book determines who reads our life story. The question a woman asks is who she lets into her book." Alexandra's philosophical, poignant, yet shallow reality left Clint impressed.

"Yeah, actually I agree. I guess we all are shitty superficial people." He laughed softly and he raised his glass to meet hers. "I toast that we are only animals wearing designer clothes."

As their glasses touched, Clint replied, "Why then did you accept my superficial and shallow offer for dinner?"

"I don't know. Really."

Her answer wasn't exactly what he had hoped for, and left him a bit puzzled. Surely she had some reason? Nonetheless, her empty expression told him otherwise.

"Really not?" he asked.

"The easier question to answer is what do you expect from me? You want me to sleep with you, don't you?" The twinkle in her eye and matter-of-fact expression stunned Clint.

"Whoa! Can't a guy just ask out the company of an interesting woman without wanting to sleep with her?"

"You see, Clint – you just answered my question with a question. According to your theory, I am correct in my assumptions."

"Damn! The human lie detector never fails, huh? I mean, sure – you are fantastically beautiful. What man doesn't imagine it? Really and truly, though, I asked you out because I was interested in you."

Alexandra smiled with reassurance. "I believe you."
Alexandra's vast experience with men meant that she
knew Clint was telling the truth. Alexandra gazed at
Clint's tousled blonde hair, and felt a sudden urge to
run her fingers through it. The delicate strands
contrasted with his strong biceps, yet his skin was
equally smooth and soft. She couldn't help noticing that
his top two buttons were undone and his lightly tanned
skin underneath invited her to kiss it. He caught her
daydreaming, and looked surprised and gratified.
Alexandra hadn't meant to give so much away.

III

Alexandra enjoyed her occasional morning walks in
early Spring. The temperatures were chilly, but not too
cold. She would walk to the nearby Gorky Park through
its tree-lined paths. In all she would be out for one
hour, and she did this when she felt the need to escape
to the intangible world of nature.

And so it was today that Alexandra broke in the new
morning with a walk in her favourite park. It was
pleasing to her to begin in darkness and then finish in
daylight. Sometimes she would make it a point to
appreciate the moment when the sun would break the
horizon. The sky would be a rainbow of blue and
orange hues; from dark indigo where the moon rested,
to the brightest of oranges at the earth's perimetre.
These were the times that Alexandra could value the
wonder of Earth's spectacles, and contemplate her life.
How was it that she felt so alone in a spectacular life of
plenty? The physical trappings that she possessed were
the creature comforts that few Muscovites enjoyed, but
somehow they still failed to fulfil her completely. At
times like this, when she walked alone in the early
hours of the day without the bustle of humanity to

distract her, she felt truly isolated and lonely. She always believed that the ultimate possession was unwavering love, but of whom? Alexandra desired a man, but had yet to meet anyone that she ever would consider more than a temporary fling. She thought she probably would have a child one day, but that realisation seemed so far away. Alexandra wanted more from life. Much, much more.

She entered the small park that was only a kilometre from her flat, and by now the sun had cracked the distant Russian horizon. The morning light was a crescendo of colour, which included the light green of the budding leaves that were exploding from all the trees. Alexandra's childish mind surfaced as she wondered if the trees themselves felt invigorated by the warming temperatures, or if winter's cold had numbed them hopelessly.

Nature, she believed, contained a soul that transcended human existence. This was, for example, why she never plucked away live leaves from a tree or plucked flowers from the ground. To her, this was murder of the unprotected natural world, and she couldn't fathom the pain they most certainly felt from rash humans searching for a momentary pleasure.

She enjoyed alternating between power walking and yoga. Somehow she found the two rather soothing, albeit in paradoxical ways. With power-walking she could be with one in nature and actually work up a sweat, while yoga was more spiritual. Alone and in a quiet room, Alexandra could escape to emotional solitude and connect to something far deeper.

An hour later and Alexandra was stepping out of the shower, when her telephone rang. It was Clint sounding cheerful and full of morning energy. "Hi sexy! Sleep well?"

"Hmm, maybe. And you?"

"Like a baby. I was dreaming of you actually. So gorgeous, what are you doing?"

"I just finished an hour long walk this morning and had a real late night with you, so I'm a bit tired."

"Which was why I was calling you now! Same place, same time, different nightcap?" Clint's voice was laced with unadulterated glee.

Alexandra chuckled to Clint's candour and wit. She had never known a man to be so different, and she simply shook her head to his forthright request for more sex.

"We will see, but I will call you. I'm really busy for the next few days."

"You do what you need, and when you have time please know I'm waiting. Who knows? If you're up for it we could even get out of Moscow on a weekend day." She smiled. Clint's enthusiasm was an unexpected shock treatment, and somehow felt good.

"Out of town?"

"Yeah. Just you and I. We go to Tver some Saturday morning. What do you say?"

"I say one dinner date was okay, but a day out of town is a bit fast. You Americans really go for it."

"When you stop seeing me as American and start seeing me as Clint, then you will know I am unique. I just want to get to know you better, and driving to Tver and being with you without waiters, telephones and stuff would be super."

Alexandra was caught between wanting to go and letting go of her well-protected guard. She wanted a relationship with someone; nevertheless, here at the earliest cusp of one, she felt nervous and unsure. Actually having something serious was so unfamiliar. "Let me decide in a couple of days, yes?"

"Ok. Fair enough."

"I'll call you later, Clint."

"And Alex!" His hurried words caught her before she hung up.

"Yes?"

"Take care. I'm thinking of you. A lot."

Alexandra smiled and rolled her eyes, but not in disdain. "Bye, Clint," she said softly.

Alexandra would not admit that she too had given him great thought this morning while on her walk. Clint captivated her somehow. She wasn't sure how, and she felt sure that he was a temporary distraction, but for now it felt good. Really good.

Chapter 5

I

Far away from Gorkij in the city centre, Alexandra prepared herself for her Asian client. She knew how Japanese men loved their escorts to wear bold colours, so she picked out a red ruched front strapless evening dress by Nicole Miller. She found that its blend of sexiness and conservative fitted her persona well. The right side of her large closet hung clothes only for her paid sexual trysts. Alexandra considered them work clothes of a different sort. On the left side were the clothes for her regular day job and were noticeably less colourful, although just as expensive.

She slipped into the dress and zipped its back before wiggling twice like she always did. She looked at herself before her large standing mirror, and cocked her head sideways. Her slender blue eyes peered through a blonde lock of hair that had just fallen over her face, and she sighed before brushing her hair back in place. Her figure was accentuated by the dress. She checked herself, put on her red stilettos, and then took her coordinated Orla Kiely handbag before turning out the bedroom light and into the hallway.

Alexandra always made sure her makeup and clothes were perfect. Although she often loathed a night out with some clients, it did not prevent her from always being as perfect as possible. Behind the scenes she was always careful about details that few clients even noticed. She had earlier inserted herself with a diaphragm to compliment the six condoms that she carried in her bag.

Alexandra's taxi left the busy Tverskaya and pulled into the semicircular entrance of The Ritz Carlton. She leaned forward from the back seat, and handed the cab driver a five hundred ruble bill. "Keep the change." she said and then slid over to the door. A middle aged doorman opened her door and Alexandra kicked out her long legs, revealing her red stilettos to a small posse of businessmen standing nearby. They simultaneously stopped talking and stared in quiet awe when she graciously stepped away from the white cab. She acknowledged the group with a knowing look, and then lifted her chin as she brushed away her blonde hair from her face.

She entered the luxurious hotel and admired the sweeping staircase and oversized marble table with its gigantic flower arrangement. Alexandra did not immediately see Svetlana and glanced at her watch. She was a bit early by coming at six-fifteen, so she made her way to the comfortable-looking chairs and sofas nearby.

After only a couple of minutes she saw the familiar slender figure in a blue evening dress. She was tall and had presence in her thick-heeled shoes and short leather skirt. Her blonde hair spilled just past her slender shoulders and her translucent skin glowed from the bright chandelier she was now under. Her thick lips were painted a glossy red that matched her heels and the top that barely contained her lush and perfectly rounded breasts.

Svetlana was rather new to the agency, having only started about eight months ago during a college summer break. She was in her third year at university and wanted a break from her engineering studies, but really did not want to work a normal low-paying job. With her body and personality, who could blame her?

Svetlana was lucky - if a hundred girls approached an escort service, five would be lucky to be accepted. In the economic boom that defined Moscow, the escort industry was yet another business that was thriving and growing. Svetlana was chosen for obvious reasons.

"Privet, Svetlana!" Alexandra exclaimed as she motioned to her friend.

"Ah, Alexandra!" Svetlana quickened her pace, and like two schoolgirls they greeted each other with a hug and kiss before playfully examining each other's dresses.

"I love this style, Alex. Who is it from?" Svetlana was nearly the fashion victim that Alexandra was, although without as deep a pocketbook. Brand names defined Moscow's elite and top escorts, and these two flaunted them.

"It's a Nicole Miller. She has so many gorgeous dresses. With your figure they would be perfect."

"We should go shopping sometime!"

"Absolutely!"

Just then, Svetlana's eyes shifted towards the reception.

"I think we're in business."

The two short and nondescript Japanese men who stood near the large ornamental entrance table were their Johns. They were as expected - stocky, shorter than both the girls, but predictably attired in dark fitted suits. They seemed about forty and their fidgeting suggested this was their first time using escorts.

The two statuesque girls strode confidently towards the men, and the men quickly saw who they were hoping to be their evening dates. Once they reached the two Asians, Alexandra smiled and asked, "Mr Nagano?"

"Yes, yes. You are Sasha?"

"Yes indeed," she answered happily. "We are looking forward to being your dates this evening. Shall we go over to those couches and discuss in private?" Alexandra outstretched hand and a polite matter-of-fact atmosphere was established. The group walked over to a large red couch in a rather secluded corner of the lobby. Once there, Alexandra took the initiative.

"Mr Nagano and Mr Shiga, we are pleased to escort you this evening for a minimum of three and-a-half hours as arranged with the agency. If you decide at any point in the evening that you would like extra time, then a donation of $350 or 12,000 rubles per hour will be accepted. Should you desire sex with us, then straight sex is also accepted. Neither of us does anal or alternative sex like S&M or beating. Gentle slaps or pinches are tolerated and a condom must be worn at all times. You can touch us and kiss us anywhere except on the mouth. Do you have any questions, gentlemen?"

The two men looked at one another rather sheepishly, and the long pause meant that everything was understood. Both men nodded and smiled.

Svetlana arose, and said with a beaming smile, "So, then! Let's have some fun!"

III

Two hours later, the foursome were all finally alone again. The evening had gone as expected. Their two Japanese clients had talked solely to the four other Japanese businessmen who had flown in from Hong Kong to discuss a real estate deal that was all but finalised. Meanwhile Svetlana and Alexandra were left to smile, act interested, and to occasionally engage in Russian asides about how bored they were or how ugly the men were.

Each couple were locked arm in arm, and waited by the large elevator. Mr Nagano and Mr Shiga were all smiles and felt confident after the events of the evening. Now the thought of seeing their dates naked and sucking their cocks left each with a growing bulge in their pants. The doors opened and Mr Nagano pressed floor number two for himself, and the third floor for his partner.

Alexandra and Svetlana kissed each other good night as the door opened to the second floor. "Dobry vyecher," the two said simultaneously as Alexandra stepped out of the elevator. Svetlana blew Alexandra a kiss just as the door closed.

Once inside Mr Nagano's room, Alexandra went directly towards the mini-bar. "Can I get you something to drink, Mr Nagano?" Alexandra had learned long ago that it was important to always address a Japanese businessman by his surname even in the middle of sex. "No, no! I want to remember tonight and not have headache tomorrow morning."

Their room was exactly what Alexandra had expected. The dark oak furniture that filled the spacious room was exquisite. A huge four poster bed on an elevated circular platform dominated the room, while two golden antique chairs flanked the huge bed. Enormous mirrors were on nearly every wall, which only exaggerated the interior. An obvious bathroom with its huge Turkish-styled bath was off on the opposite corner, but Alexandra was most taken by the secluded walk-in closet, which was exactly what she had always dreamt of having.

Alexandra turned to her John, tilted her head, and rested her right hand on her hip. Mr Nagano stared at her wantonly from across the room. "Mr Nagano, would you like to relax now?" Her voice was filled with desire; nonetheless, the whole scene was purely acting. At that moment she thought of Clint and the thought paralysed her for a couple of seconds. It was the first time she had thought of a lover while with a John. She quickly blinked her eyes twice and focused on the unassuming client ahead.

"Yes, yes. Very much so. You make me relax.

Maybe massage would be very nice." Mr Nagano's boyish smile could not be contained.

Alexandra walked confidently to Mr Nagano and put his left hand on her shoulder as she began to loosen his tie. She was at least three inches taller than her date, although much of that was due to her stilettos. The warmth of his shaking hand told Alexandra enough. Either he had never been with an escort, or he had very little sexual experience.

As Alexandra worked to unbutton her client's shirt, Mr Nagano began to pull Alexandra's dress straps away from her shoulder. Eventually her dress fell, only to be caught by her bra. She gently pulled the dress away and within seconds she stood in front of her awe-struck client in nothing more than a black lacy Agent Provocateur bra, panties and garter. Her high heels completed the look of the perfect sexual Barbie doll.

Mr Nagano did not know what to do, except to collapse on the adjacent bed while Alexandra followed him. She straddled him as she pushed him down onto his back, whispering into his ear, "Are you ready for a good time?"

Her breath into his ear, coupled with a gentle lick and bite, created a firmness in his pants that she could noticeably feel. Her heaving breasts hung forward, and he desired to see her nipples. His hands reached for her back and within a couple seconds Alexandra could feel her bra coming undone. She rose again and pulled her black bra off, revealing her topless - much to her Mr Nagano's delight. She moved lower and unbuttoned his pants. At that moment she stopped and asked, "Would you like a massage, Mr Nagano, or would you like sex?"

"Yes, sex. Very good!"

She stretched over to her handbag and pulled out a purple condom wrapper. She then pulled her client's pants off and tossed them over to one of the golden chairs. She glided the condom over his erect penis, that was surprisingly thick.

Alexandra took him into her mouth while Mr Nagano ran his fingers through her long blonde hair. She sucked on him delicately for a couple of minutes before stopping, and then lay beside him. She took his hand and placed it on her moistening crotch as he inserted a finger, sending Alexandra squirming next to him with eyes closed. She moaned and arched her back while he once again sucked her nipples and kissed her breasts. He fingered her gently, and after a few minutes she suddenly took his hand away before mounting him. She rode him and his firm penis, delicately digging her nails into his chest while her head arched backwards. Her half-opened eyes saw the large decorative chandelier that hung over the bed, and before she knew it Mr Nagano shouted as he began to cum. His body shook and his hips thrust into Alexandra to maximise his pleasure.

Within seconds the sexual rhythm stopped, and Alex looked down at her panting John.

"What else would you like, Mr Nagano?"

"Oh, nothing more. Thank you. You make love very good."

Alexandra was relieved that, like so many times in her experience, once the man climaxed the party was over. Alexandra slipped back into her dress and sat on the bed's edge to slip her delicate feet back into her favourite pair of Marc Jacob heels. Alexandra turned to her naked client, who simply stared at her in quiet awe. "Would you care for anything else, Mr Nagano? A drink perhaps?"

"No, no. Thank you very much for asking. I want to go to study some documents before going to bed shortly."

Mr Nagano rolled to his side and grabbed his pants that Alexandra had thrown at the bed's base. He slipped into them and walked towards the nightstand where he had set his wallet. He opened it and pulled out three five-hundred ruble banknotes and handed them to Alexandra as he kissed her on the cheek. He nearly had to stand on his toes to kiss her as she towered above him, in a figurative act of symbolism. Her sexual domination was at this moment greater than his business prowess. The symbiosis the two shared was at sharp contrast to the physicality of their appearance.

"Here's a little gift for you to show you my thanks."

"Mr Nagano, you are such a gentlemen, and it has been a pleasure to serve you tonight." Her smile seemed authentic and the inflection in her Russian accent highlighted the word 'pleasure'. Alexandra played the refined role perfectly. "I hope I see you again sometime soon."

"Yes, maybe. That would be very nice."

Alexandra turned to the door, opened it, and looked back a final time at her client. "Paka!" she said with a smile as she waved with her right index finger. Another ignominious night ended just the way so many others had in Alexandra's life.

Chapter 6

I

"Ladies and gentlemen, let's start the meeting now. Sorry for the short notice, but each of you know why we are here, yes? We got a hit on Krokav that he is now in Moscow. Let me tell each of you that Krokav usually only comes to town to personally collect and finish off deals. He's a creature of habit, and this works in our favour."

The director looked around the room and adjusted his notes as he paused for a moment, before saying "As Director of Operations, my job is to make sure we eliminate any threat to our national security. Let's remember why we are all here. Our President initiated this programme so we can act on these threats, and act we will. Any deal this scumbag makes will not go through!"

Director Billups then pulled out his large black-framed eyeglasses and put them on, before requesting "Bill, can you turn off the lights? Or at least the ones over me here in the front of the room?"

He continued. "Alright folks! Here's the deal. The slides from the overhead are going to show you what we know so far. First photo is of Krokav taken last Wednesday. Last Wednesday, people! We thought he was in Syria - however, on Monday he showed up on the grid in Kiev. Then on Tuesday he arrived here in Moscow. Forget the weekend, people! I want to know where he is, who he sees, who he fucks, everything! He is not going to slide away this time. Understand? Is that clear, people?"

The room was filled with eight men and two women, mostly American. All of them nodded in agreement, and looked around to see if anyone would ask a question.

The director paced about the seated group of international intelligence operatives and looked at them in complete seriousness. "The government suspects his clients have included a rogue's gallery of warlords and dictators, including Liberia's Charles Taylor and Libyan leader Moammar Gaddafi, the late dictator Mobutu Sese Seko of Congo, and both sides of the civil war in Angola. Krokav also has supplied arms to the Taliban and, indirectly, al-Qaeda - so you know what that means, people."

The room began to fill with whispered murmurs, before Billups pointed to an agent sitting in the front row. "Jesse, you have a question?"

"Director Billups, if we take Krokav down now do we have enough information to then go after his Saudi and Egyptian buyers? We're still not quite finished on their intel project."

"Krokav is an opportunistic tick. If we cut off the head of a tick then the arms still are there, as is the head, but at least we do some serious damage. We want this guy alive - that is our directive from upstairs. Also remember, folks, we have the help of a special unit that our Russian counterparts have set up. We will be working with them too."

The seriousness of the moment was the realisation of what every person in the room worked for. To get the Godfather of arms off the street would be the result of years of hard work. Krokav was known as the 'Merchant of Death' to everyone in the business for his penchant of arming warring factions, gangs, terrorists, and political coups. Krokav discriminated against no-one, especially al-Qaeda. Also, because Krokav was an old-school Soviet military man, American insiders inherently did not trust him.

"What we do know is the following: up on the

screen, ladies and gentlemen, is Amat Abdul Sellam photographed in Cairo. He has been going back and forth from Algiers every two weeks or so - and I'm telling you, it ain't for the scuba diving. He met with this man, Aman al-Zawahiri, a Saudi extremist who has links to the Caliphate that is operating underground in Turkey and Sudan. It is known that Aman has direct ties to the Taliban forces that are operating near Pakistan in the mountains of Afghanistan."

A man in the corner of the table opposite Director Billups sipped from his water and peered attentively at some documents in front of him, occasionally observing the photos beamed in front of him. Suddenly he raised his right index finger while staring at the documents in his hand. Director Billups was now directly in front of him and anticipated the impending question. He was always the first to ask a question in a briefing. "Yes, Clint. You have a question?"

"What do we know about Krokav's social interests here in Moscow?"

"What we see is a pattern. He usually eats Mediterranean foods and Asian. He usually visits a Thai restaurant near the Tverskaya, and he often hires escorts. He never is alone and has four bodyguards with him at all times, so getting close to him will be a challenge."

A strange expression suddenly came over the director's face. "If we fail to nab this S.O.B then it may take months before we can ever locate him again, let alone apprehend him. We must get this right," he said with a strained expression, as his fingers clasped the podium nervously.

He looked around the room and his eyes locked on one of the few women in the room; a Baltic field operative by the name of Maja Towarowy. Most in the room knew that Maja was a modern day Mata Hari who on more than one occasion used seduction and sex to obtain valued information. The espionage community was a diverse group, but century-old tactics have only been streamlined and improved upon. In that sense, nothing had changed.

Maja raised her delicate hand. "Director Billups? What chances do we have that I can get inside?" she asked in a smooth Polish accent.

"Meet me after the meeting. I may have an angle for you."

Billups looked around the room for more questions. "Ted?"

"Yeah... and what about the Russians? Do we know if he is linked to Kremlin insiders?"

"We don't quite know. The higher-ups have a self-interest to tackle guys like this; however, it's further down the food chain where the problem is. We're pretty sure he's got inside contacts who make things happen for him. We don't have definitive names, but believe me when I say we are working on that. When we get something I'll let you know since this is your area, yeah?"

"Okay, folks. What else?"

"Sure. Uh, let's see... It sounds like we don't have a tactical plan that can guarantee a capture, Director Billups. I mean, our guys can set up and monitor him, but without inside help we are doing this blind."

"Point taken, but this guy is a ghost and we can't have the perfect plan for a ghost who is on and off the grid so frequently. We take what we can get."

"Okay – anything else? Anything? Alright then, Maja, meet me in ten minutes in my office. Florian, Ted and Darrell, I want to see you guys back in the conference room in thirty minutes. I'll hand over all recon to you then."

Director Billups turned on the light switch as he

walked out of the room, and the gather of spies and intelligence personnel was left to mingle and discuss. Networking and sharing of clandestine information was the key to their brotherhood. The unspoken knowledge was that they never knew whether they would see their colleagues alive at the next meeting. Tomorrow was never a guarantee.

II

The next afternoon was not unlike most midweek days. Sergi was anxious on a new deal that could essentially guarantee the financial success of the first quarter. It was at times like this that he irritated others, incessantly pacing and constantly checking on others. After the third visit to Alexandra's desk in two hours she replied before Sergi could speak.

"By four o'clock!" she snapped. Her quick retort and her scowl told Sergi enough. He had been down this road enough times before to know her limits.

"Yeah, yeah," he replied defensively. He muttered as he turned away, while Alexandra only smiled.

Just then, her mobile vibrated on her glass desk. She flipped open the phone to read the text, and immediately smiled when she saw the sender's name. It was Clint, and he wanted to see her this week.

Dinner Wed. night? 7:30? Call me if u can.

The thought to seeing him lifted her - even if it was only a temporary reprieve from the chaotic day she was having. She held the phone in front of her and looked at it for a minute before replying: 80% sure. Will call 2morrow.

Actually she knew she could meet him with certainty, but leaving the door open was a way to omit a sense of uncertainty and independence. She never let on that a man was at the centre of her life, and she wouldn't start now for the charming American.

Alexandra then looked down at the papers before her. They lay there in a scrambled mess that only she could understand. As translations were an inexact science for Alexandra she would usually work piecemeal, working in bits here and there before ultimately pulling it all together. Starting from the beginning and working to the end was just far too linear and boring for her.

The digital clock clicked eleven, which drew her attention —a whole hour and half until lunch! Her concentration would have to improve if she were to finish the twenty-plus page brief that Sergi was obsessing with.

It was nearly one-forty-five before Grigory popped his head into Alexandra's cubicle. "Want to get something to eat?"

Fifteen minutes later, the two sat in the crowded and tight quarters of the noisy deli. As he finished the last of his sandwich, Grigory looked at his gorgeous colleague across from him and asked, "What's up with you, Alex, woman of mystery?"

"What's that supposed to mean?" Alexandra's face was pinched and deeply inquisitive.

"Well, you know. You are the one person in the firm who is simply a mystery. You never attend any company functions, you never mention anything about your personal life, and you never really reveal anything about yourself."

"And that is how it will stay, my nosy friend." She flicked her hair from her face and looked out the window towards the masses which hurriedly walked by. "Don't take it personally. It's just my way. Work is work and I stay focused, so maybe you take the seriousness I put into my job as aloofness. I promise you that I'm not a fuddy-duddy."

"A fuddy-duddy?"

"You know, a bore, a drag. What you obviously think of me."

"Okay then. So tell me about your boyfriend. I assume you have one, yes?"

"Why is it that every man always asks me this question? Why? You could have asked me if I like theatre or the movies or what my favourite type of food is - but no!"

"Um, okay. Where do you like to eat?"

"Jesus, Grigory. You just don't get it. Maybe that's why I don't engage in idle chatter. Here's enlightenment for you. I like all of you but my time after work is my time; I share that with only the people I care most about. Yeah?"

Grigory knew that revelations into Alexandra's life were not going to happen today. He had skirted around her personal life before, but never with success. His coyly planned lunch had fallen flat on its face.

"I think you are an interesting woman, and perhaps I am drawn to your personal life because it is shrouded in such secrecy. My apologies."

"Apologies accepted. Now, wipe the corner of your mouth. There's a bit of mustard," she said in a motherly tone, smiling.

III

"Mom! Why can't I do my homework later? I promise I'll finish it after just one game of Fast and the Furious!"

"The rules are the rules. First homework, and then Playstation." Torie's voice trailed off as she entered the kitchen to fix Alexi's lunch. "How was school today?"

"Boring. And now boring homework."

Torie's head popped out of the kitchen as she retorted, "Homework is what will make you smart, successful, and have lots of money."

"We don't have lots of money. So you guys can't have done your homework, so why do I always have to?"

"Your father does quite okay for the family, and I can guarantee you that daddy always did his homework. Now get those pens and paper out and quit arguing, little man! I'm making you a ham sandwich and chocolate pudding for lunch so you can eat first, and then we'll work together on whatever assignments you have."

Torie loved being a mother to Alexi and would never have considered switching her role as a stay-at-home mother for a paid career. It was all she ever knew and wanted. Emancipation in the form of having her own job, money and social circle was simply a desire which she somehow lacked.

She found such joy in the everyday, and in things which most mothers or wives would casually overlook. Preparing Alexi for morning school, shopping at the local supermarket, and preparing her husband's meal were moments to feel important and contributive. Torie adored her soft-spoken and gentle husband. Stefan valued his wife's domestic contributions and never made her feel beneath him. She felt privileged to have such a husband.

Being an only child left Torie desiring a 'true' family – having a nuclear family that shared in everything was the motivation for everything she did. This was certainly the reality she had experienced in her own upbringing, and the one she continued to live as an adult. When she met Stefan at eighteen she knew that he was all she wanted. Being his wife and a mother to his child gave her purpose. Ten years on, it still did.

Minutes later, Torie entered the small dining room where Alexi had all his papers. "My little prince is working hard I see." She laid the plate with Alexi's sandwich next to him, along with the small plastic tub of chocolate pudding that he so adored.

A moment later, the little boy asked, "Why doesn't daddy allow me to go visit him at work?"

"Well, you know, daddy does important scientific things and only he and his science co-workers are allowed in. He does great things for his country because he is a wonderful patriot."

Although it had been years since the fall of communism, Torie was like so many Russians who were still mentally locked into old-school Soviet-styled thinking. Calling one a patriot was exactly that.

Stefan worked just outside of Moscow at a facility which produced weapon's technology for a variety of arms. The fact was that, in all these years, Torie had never visited her husband at work. For that she would need a car, but she was okay living her life within the relatively small confines of their apartment.

"I want to be a patriot too, just like daddy!"

Torie patted Alexi's head "You will be. But only if you finish your homework!"

Meanwhile, only a few kilometres away, Alexandra was in bed with one of her regular clients, a minister from the Duma that would meet her at least twice a month. Vladimir Gorban was probably her most regular customers and she had grown to know him well, albeit through sex once every fifteen days or so. She knew things she probably shouldn't, as Vladimir liked to talk about inner going-ons and gossip about other Duma ministers. She found it a bit thrilling to be so close to the Kremlin, even if it was by merely screwing one of its more senior ministers.

Vladimir was fucking her as he always did; first

missionary and then doggy-style. His caressing hands and fingers fondled her perky breasts, and he urged her on with a slowly rising tempo. She stroked him back and forth as though moving to the quickening beat of a drum, before slowing to match the pace of his lustful rhythm. His thrusts deepened, his one hand pulled at her hair, and she felt his firmness thicken before finally his passion exploded inside her mouth moaning "Oh yes... ah... yes!"

Vladimir arched his back and stretched himself in a final act of self-fulfilment, before collapsing on the bed. Sometimes she wondered if an older fat John like Vladimir would die during sex. The way he sweated and huffed while fucking left no doubt in Alexandra's mind that the corpulent client's only exercise was when he had sex.

"Oh, Sasha," he sighed with a warm smile on his face. "That was worth every ruble. You are the best."

"Anything for my country, Mr Minister," she said slyly as she walked naked to the bathroom to dispose of the condom. "Anything for my beloved Russia."

Chapter 7

I

The sound of the alarm clock broke the morning silence with a soft digital tone. Alexandra's mind was now focused on what lay ahead. She had taken the morning off her translation work in order to meet with a client who she had been with twice before. After work she would meet Clint for dinner, which had come at the expense of meeting Mikhail. It was the first time she put a man before Mikhail, but, considering her recent fascination with her American interest, it was only a matter of time before she replaced him entirely.

The routine today was as it almost always was. She would forego her morning walk and instead head to the kitchen to have her must-have coffee – vanilla-flavoured Jura. An accompanying pastry complimented her morning brew, and was all the food she needed for the next several hours. She privately enjoyed this time of the morning and would always sit at her breakfast table and slowly sip from her cup as she let her mind wonder.

As she sipped and stared, seemingly into emptiness, Alexandra found herself back at the orphanage she knew as a child. The memory of Sister Maria filled her mind. She wondered where Sister Maria was and if she still was at the orphanage caring for today's generation of unwanted toddlers. Her surrogate mother was a saint in Alexandra's eyes, and doing the work of a God that she herself did not believe in.

Alexandra had never felt a bond with her adoptive mother. Perhaps it was all down to Natali's steely-cold demeanour and the extreme punishments she enforced on Alexandra as a child. Natali's inflexibility and dysfunctional relationship with Alexandra's adoptive father also drove her away from any emotional bond with her parents. Her family was middle-class, but they pretended they were something greater. The incessant focus on manners, posture and piano lessons was stifling, and influenced by the high social positions her grandparents had had before communism.

When Alexandra's parents argued she had retreated to her bed, where she sat remembering the days of laughter and kindness from Sister Maria, who she always affectionately called 'Masha'. Masha and Alexandra had lived simple lives and, somehow, that seemed more comforting and painless than her adoptive life.

As she sipped the last of her coffee, Alexandra was overcome by an overwhelming need to reunite with Sister Maria. But how? Perm was fifteen hundred kilometres away and it had been well over twenty years since she was adopted. All that she could remember about her first six years was that she lived in Perm and that the orphanage was a white and yellow building that sat in a wooden area on the outskirts of the big city. Alexandra thought that finding it again couldn't be all that difficult. After all, how many children's homes could there be in Perm?

Alexandra's adoptive mother was unable to have children, having miscarried three times before. Not being able to bear children had been considered shameful, and it reduced a woman's worth. Consequently, her adoption left Alexandra feeling like she was more a means to an end than a wanted child. Their love was clinical, and they treated her much more as an adult than a little girl. The piano lessons and forced reading left Alexandra longing for her dolls and friends. Her parents wanted her to be a refined lady, whereas Alexandra only wanted a normal childhood. Alexandra additionally felt deprived by not having any baby photographs of herself. The first photos came from her adopted family's celebration of Labour Day. Little Alexandra wore a white dress and held a small bouquet of white flowers. For the first six years of her life there was no family, no photographs, or any tangible manifestations of a childhood. She had brought nothing with her from the orphanage in the day of her adoption.

Alexandra stared into her empty coffee cup, which she held so close to her mouth. She had finished it a while before, yet falling back into distant memories meant she had been unaware of time and reality. At that moment, her mobile beeped twice. As she reached for the phone her other mobile suddenly rang, which meant that Elena had business for her.

"Privet, Elena."

"Good morning, Alex. I have a client that I am wondering if you have time for today. It's late afternoon, around four-thirty, for an hour."

"Yeah. I don't think that would be a problem. What's the story?"

"He's Russian, a big-deal businessman of some sorts. I'm not exactly sure if he is legitimate; nevertheless, he is looking for a girl only for sex and not to be seen with. He essentially described you as what he wants."

'Legitimate' was a term the girls used for men who did their business legally, but Alexandra didn't care one way or the other. The politicians and a couple of her regulars were surely corrupt; however, she saw their money as the same. These Johns who wanted a quickie were the ones that Alexandra loved – no long drawn-out commitments but pure business, which meant that Alexandra's night could not be ruined.

"In and out for one hour, so why not?" she replied.

"Okay then. I'll make final arrangements and text

you the address and his details. I think it will be at the Radisson SAS. He mentioned that would likely be the hotel."

"Fine, then. Pencil me in for four-thirty in the lobby, and I will wear red. That should help him. Paka!"

For a moment, the thought of fucking so many men in the past month bothered Alexandra. She was not a woman who counted, but suddenly the idea of double digits popped into her mind. Suddenly it occurred to her that she had probably had sex with hundreds of men and, for the first time in her life, she wondered if - or when - she would reach one thousand.

'One thousand men!'

The thought chilled her until she quickly summed up that she only slept with eight men last month, which was a normal number. A further mental calculation assured her that she realistically only fucked a hundred or so men a year. Once the math added up, she exhaled as if a weight of guilt had been lifted. In the end the number was surely a third of a thousand, which somehow Alexandra felt far less shame from.

The momentary diversion nearly distracted Alexandra from her text message, which she now began to read. It was from Clint, and she smiled. Hey sexy. Been thinking of u all day. Cant wait 2 c u 2morrow. Call when u can. XXX

It was the perfect way to begin a Tuesday. She had seen him just days before and somehow he seemed to be so much more than a fun date and good sex. Although Alexandra had slept with over three hundred men, he was the only one who seemed to matter right now.

As she entered her bedroom, Alexandra's mind wavered to Mikhail. She now knew her days with him were nearly over. It was always this way, in fact – replacing one lover with another.

"So then. Looks like this red dress will have to do," she whispered out loud. Alexandra pulled a tasteful yet sexy halter dress with a short skirt from her standing closet. Alexandra's tools of the trade crossed every conceivable scenario, and, in this case, businesswear mixed with evening escort wear.

II

The office was filled with activity as Alexandra made her way to an afternoon coffee break. The nearby kitchenette found Sergi talking with another co-worker, a Ukrainian new hire who Alexandra had only passing contact with.

"Ahh, Alex! Have you met Vasily? He specialises in our contacts in South America."

"Buenas tardes, Vasily," Alexandra said as she extended her hand out.

The tall but unassuming man took it and replied rather startling, "Oh, una lengua nunca es sufficiente. Hablas espanol?"

"Yes, I agree that one language is never enough - however, I really only know a phrase here and there of Spanish. I wouldn't say I speak too much. Your job is safe!"

The three chuckled for a moment, before Vasily sipped the last of his drink and then bid the two farewell. "Until next time then," he said, as he nodded and walked away.

"He's a nice guy, even if he is Ukrainian," Sergi said in a hushed tone. Sergi could only say such a thing to Alexandra, who he trusted completely. Political correctness was only a seven syllable phrase in Russia, where gays, foreigners and fat people were the butt of many an office joke.

Sergi spoke of a truth that existed within the

Russian sub-culture where they saw their former republic with the affection of a knowing older sibling who was smarter, more experienced, and simply better. It was an underlying mix of arrogant nationalism that bordered xenophobia. Russians were never known to be self-deprecating.

Alexandra laughed while taking a mug from the cupboard. "Why couldn't you have hired a hunky Brazilian instead? If you are going to surround me with men, then can't you give me at least one bit of eye candy?"

Sergi looked at Alex with the straightest of faces. "Are you saying that I am not eye candy?"

"You're adorable for a grandpa. I'm sure Ira still finds you every bit as sexy as she did thirty years ago when you first met."

Alexandra cocked her head, patted Sergi's head, and smiled while batting her eyes innocently. The banter, which was exclusively theirs, was always this way.

"Damn it, Alex. And here I was thinking of his expertise when reviewing his CV and not who you would like to take home after work."

"Next time, yes?" Alex protruded her lower lip, and her saddened face begged him for future consideration.

"Listen Alex. I wanted to talk to you about something. He motioned with his head to follow him to his office.

"Hmm, sounds serious, boss. As long as he is under thirty, athletically built and clean, then I say you hire him!"

Sergi just rolled his eyes as he walked away.

Once inside Sergi's spacious office, the two sat at a smallish table adjacent to his large desk. On it was a platter with Sooshkas, Alexandra's favourite type of cookie. She immediately took one as Sergi pulled his chair towards Alexandra.

"Listen, Alex, you're something of a daughter to me so I say this without prying. You do great work here. In fact, you could run this show when I retire, but I know you are disinterested. This bores you, doesn't it?"

Alexandra was taken aback. "No!" she stammered. "This work is something I really enjoy."

"I see you as bored. Come on, Alex, otherwise why wouldn't you work full-time?"

"Thirty hours is nearly full-time," she retorted indignantly. "Did Grigory say something to you about me?"

"Huh?" Sergi's total dumbfounded look told her enough.

"Never mind."

"So you take a lot of time off," he immediately quipped. "Listen, Alex. I'm not complaining. Really not. The fact is that I have decided to retire at the end of the year. I'm going to retire a bit early, and I want to recommend that we make a translation division. I want to make you the head of that."

Alexandra focused on Sergi's face as he spoke. The realisation that Sergi would leave felt sobering. His suggested promotion was an afterthought.

"You're going to leave me?" For the first time Alexandra's frailty showed to the boss she always enjoyed cutting down, albeit playfully.

"Yes. I want to do other things. Spend more time with Ira and see my kids. You know Nikolai is near Ekaterinburg, and I don't get to see the grandkids but once a year." His spoke with a regretful tone. "I want to leave here and know that a few of you are going to be okay."

"I'll be fine. Besides, this isn't going to happen for a long time, is it?"

His reply was stern and frank, "Alex. It's ten months from now."

Alexandra just looked down at her unfinished cookie. Ten months would be here sooner than she wanted to admit. She moved to Moscow five years ago, and it still seemed like only a couple of years had passed.

"I can't guarantee that you can continue like this, Alex. You pretty much work a nice schedule. Essentially part-time and with flexibility to go off when you need to. I never have said anything because you always have gotten me the results but... you know... someone new won't understand this. What do we do? Help me to help you, Alex."

Sergi's hand reached out and clasped the top of hers. Alexandra could only look down, as she thought about how difficult it would be to work full time and still manage her escorting. Being off every day at three o'clock afforded her extra time for clients, and being off almost every Friday was something she had gotten used to.

Work was a therapy for Alex; justification, too, that she was more than a sexual outlet for men. Using her brain and degree gave Alexandra purpose while minimising the glaring fact that she was a slut, even if it was a highly-paid one. All this raced through her mind as Sergi continued.

"I know we started small years ago, and it was fine that you worked twenty five hours, but now there are five of you and I'm needing another translator to help Denis with all the German." Sergi was right. The business had moved on so much from those days when she alone did their English and Japanese translations. "I'm thinking of creating a formal translation department and make you the head of it. It's probably worth thirty, even forty percent, more salary."

Sergi seemed to stress the salary as a figurative carrot; however, Alexandra didn't need the money. She could never compensate her escorting with what Khanty would pay. Suddenly her convenient world was rocked, and facing the day when she would ultimately have to leave her secretive life left her feeling somewhat panicked. This was something that she never felt. Alexandra was always unbothered and in control.

"The money means nothing," she muttered.

"I don't know how you do it, Alex, and I'm not asking. Maybe that is why I feel you are only here with half of yourself. You seem to have more money than any of us. I'm figuring your family benefited from our early democratic days, but I've never asked. That's your business."

"I do okay," she said as she nodded in return. If only Sergi knew that 'okay' was actually about three times his salary, then he would truly understand.

"Think about it, and keep this to yourself. In a month or so I will inform senior management that I will retire, and I want a blueprint of where to take the division going forward. I want you in that."

Alexandra bit her lower lip. "Definitely."

III

Forty-five minutes later Alexandra strode into Mya's, her favourite clothing boutique, where many of the clothes she wore had come from. Immediately, Nina greeted her.

"Alex!" she exclaimed as she hurried towards her. "I was hoping to see you this week!"

Nina was one of four girls who worked for Mya at the small boutique, and perhaps Alexandra's favourite. She had only recently immigrated from far away Vladivostok in Far East Russia. Alexandra liked the few people she had ever met from this region. Nina, like most Far Easterners, had a sense of innocence and purity. These Far Easterners were unlike the hardened Westerners, especially the Muscovites, in that they were far more open and friendly. They seemed to trust, perhaps to a fault. Alexandra had once thought of approaching Nina about working in the business, when Elena had solicited help. Ultimately Alexandra privately concluded that Nina's seemingly naivety would prove her undoing.

Nina hugged her favourite customer and customarily kissed both her left and right cheeks before blurting, "I need your help!"

"With what?"

She grabbed Alexandra's hand and led her to the back where the dressing rooms were. "Okay, green or blue?" she asked as she pulled out two dresses from the back office.

Alexandra stood for a moment reviewing each before replying, "Aren't I supposed to be asking you which dress looks best on me?"

Nina giggled a childish laugh. "Seriously, which one? I met a great guy last week and we're going out for the third time. You know, third date? Nice restaurant date, and then…"

"And then… what?" Alexandra replied, as she revealed a sneaky smirk that told Nina everything.

"You know. Then we go back to his place," she replied sheepishly, as her head nodded left and right.

It was exactly this kind of childish innocence that confirmed Nina would never make it as an escort, even though she possessed a body and looks which Alexandra herself envied. Nina was one of so many casual friendships that she had throughout Moscow. Friendships that she knew by name and that she enjoyed superficially.

"Take the blue."

"Yes!" she exclaimed in both relief and delight.

"That's exactly what I was thinking too. Rita said the green, but I just wasn't so sure. You're the best!"

Nina hugged Alexandra tightly for a quick second before replying, "Now, what can I get for you?"

Alexandra looked about and smiled at Rita, who was now at the front door. Her quick search found the wall display featuring a trendy yet classy biker-inspired collection. The deep red cropped lamb-skin jacket was what Alexandra was after.

"The red leather jacket over there," she replied as she pointed. "That is my must-have!"

Chapter 8

I

Wednesday morning broke with a relief from the rain and drizzle. As Alexandra did her power walk around Gorky, her mind wondered forward several hours. Clint filled her mind again and it made her smile. What was it about this man that more and more filled her thoughts? It wasn't as if they really were in a relationship. A couple of dates and one sexual romp hardly constituted a full-blown relationship. She had been down this road before with lovers, but the witty American seemed so much different. He possessed a depth and genuineness that captivated her.

Although thinking of him pleased her, thoughts of a far different matter now consumed her. Sister Maria was a few hours drive to the west, and Alexandra wondered what she was doing and if she was even alive. Alexandra felt an unfamiliar yearning and the sudden question of who her real parents were crept into her mind. She couldn't ever truly escape her unpleasant past. It always left her feeling empty and unwanted. If only she knew why, though. Perhaps Sister Masha could finally provide some answers.

She now walked with purpose, and suddenly the clarity of a plan hatched from momentary reflection came to light. She knew privately that she needed to cross this dark chasm in order to truly move forward. Being given away to an orphanage leaves its scars on everyone, she thought. How could it not?

Her 'real' parents had ultimately disappeared gracefully into the blur of Perm's urban life. Alexandra wondered if her real parents bore any scars of giving her away, or if they had simply forgotten and moved on with their lives as if nothing had ever happened. Or perhaps they yearned to undo the past and wished that Alexandra would show up at their doorstep someday. She had always struggled to bury the fact that she had been an orphan and, try as she might, the feeling that she was a product of exchange left her to tussle with the ghouls of her past.

She gently brushed her hair away from her face, and closed her eyes momentarily. She inhaled deeply and slowly absorbed the fresh March air with all of its ingredients. It was a concoction of damp chill, grime, distant cigarettes and earth that Alexandra had become so familiar with after five years there. As she opened her eyes, a feeling of certainty and calm filled her. The moment gave her direction and purpose. Next week she would face the one thing she had run away from for so long.

Early March had finally arrived, and Alexandra could feel its warming embrace. This winter had been long and particularly wet; however, all that was nearly behind. The winter, like her life, was a chapter that had been completed; yet still remained as a prelude to a greater story that lay ahead.

II

Alexandra entered Maxim's just a few moments later than the planned seven-thirty. A woman, she figured, should never be too early for a date. In fact, this was a common mentality of Russian women -they had, at least on a date, power over a man.

A concierge dressed in white approached her immediately. "Is Madam alone or meeting someone?"

"A friend of mine is probably here already. A Mr Thomas."

"Ah yes! Of course. Please follow me, Madam."

The two manoeuvred through the intimate

restaurant, before she finally saw Clint alone at a corner table.

Clint arose from his red chair and met Alexandra. He kissed her softly on the right cheek and his right arm pulled her towards him closely. She could smell his pleasant scent – a mix of Chanel Allure, aftershave, and his own personal manliness.

Recognising colognes was a tertiary characteristic of being an escort. Having been on the arm and in bed with so many hundreds of men meant that she had experienced scents that ranged from pungent to exquisite. She liked Chanel Allure and could immediately recognise it from its pleasant crisp and clean aroma. It also told her that Clint did not spend more than sixty-five dollars on cologne. It was no secret that Clint was not like so many of the extremely wealthy men she would accompany. Instead, he was a simple bureaucrat living an apparent modest existence. Not exquisite, but somehow he seemed to be doing okay. He certainly seemed more than simply middle class.

"I've been looking forward to this," he whispered in her ear. Alexandra merely smiled and allowed Clint to kiss her once again on the cheek.

Once seated, the two were offered a menu that was covered in a rich but heavy leather. "May I recommend to you our evening A La Carte specials as well? They are listed on the first page. Would the Lady or Gentleman care for a glass of wine, or something else to drink?"

As soon as the concierge turned away, Clint blurted, "Alone at last! God, I've wanted to see you!" Clint could hardly contain his enthusiasm as he reached across the table to take Alexandra's hand into his.

Alexandra smiled coyly before responding, "Me too."

She spoke the truth. Clint was a date that she genuinely had wanted. He was a man who she truly liked, which was so rare. Maybe only one or two men would actually catch her attention as Clint had somehow done. He was genuine, funny and smart.

"How are those passport approvals coming along?" Alexandra's voice was filled with a sarcastic undertone. Clint chuckled softly. "I've been authorising that all good-looking men be granted departure from Moscow while denying any attractive ones from entering. I'm trying my hardest to eliminate competition with you."

"Maybe I like Russian men."

"Maybe so. Maybe not. Either way, I'm here with you now and I want to keep it that way.

It was nearly nine o'clock when Clint glanced at his watch as their desserts were being placed before them. Clint marvelled at his ladyfinger tarte with rum cream, while he noticed Alexandra smiling at her double chocolate cake –a rare indulgence for her.

"Jesus, Alex! I thought mine was good until I saw yours!" Clint's expression was a mix of jealousness and disdain.

"If you're nice, I'll share a bite with you," she responded childishly. "But only if you give me a taste of yours."

"Ah, there's never something for nothing with you Russians, is there?" Clint said as he smiled coyly.

"What do you mean by you Russians?"

"I guess I'm referring to our governments' positions, and how they negotiate with one another."

"I am not Putin, and do not deal like him. I gladly would take without giving, so consider yourself lucky that I offered you a bit of my precious dessert." Her straight-laced expression was quintessential Alexandra, and Clint could only laugh in defeat. "Now, give me a taste of that yummy-looking cake."

As Alexandra reached over to his dessert with an outstretched fork, Clint asked, "We got distracted a while back when I was asking about your adopted mother. I meant to ask how often you go back to Perm to see her."

"Not often."

"As in not often, or like really not often?"

"I haven't been back since I've been here in Moscow."

Clint paused in quiet contemplation before eventually continuing. "Can I ask why?"

"You nosy little devil," she mumbled before finishing her bite. "You must know that my adopted mother and I are two different people. I have my life now, which really doesn't include her much."

"Uh, okay. That's fine." Clint could only nod.

"I mean, I talk to her every so often, but it is the same conversation every time. You have to understand the Communist mentality. She is only interested in when I am getting married, and she couldn't care less about my job."

"I thought your folks pushed you into all these cultural things so you could have an independent future."

"Yes and no. That is a classical mentality from ages ago, when being a true Russian meant you were trained in the classical arts. They read Tolstoy, listened to Tchaikovsky, and admired Catherine. This was Russia's golden age, that the Communists ultimately destroyed. My parents somehow lived in the 1920s, not the 1980s."

"Ahh, I see. You would be the elegant cultured princess for your traditional husband, yeah?"

"Exactly. A smart baby machine who could sing Chaliapin lullabies to her children after a night of entertaining her distinguished husband's guests at parties with piano and ballroom dancing. I think she is still holding out on this hope. If only she knew."

Alexandra chewed hurriedly on her next bit of dessert while she rolled her eyes and shook her head slightly. The thought of such a parody clearly left her with a smidgen of repugnance to the life she ran away from. But just how far away was a secret that both her mother and Clint could hardly fathom.

"I guess she would really think you had gone to hell if she knew you went out on two dates with an American bureaucrat, huh?"

After a slight pause, Alexandra erupted in laughter more at the extent of her real digressions. Clint also laughed loudly and said "I think I'll bring you home, just to piss her off."

"Oh thanks! That makes me feel great."

"Well, you asked about my mother and I'm telling you the truth," Alexandra continued with a slight giggle, as she finished the last of her chocolate cake.

Thirty minutes later Clint's BMW was pulled in front of the restaurant by a valet, and both rushed through the rain into it. Upon entering his car, Clint looked across at Alexandra, who was fidgeting with her coat. "You never told me where we are going next." His stare was sincere and he waited for her reply earnestly.

"To your place. Where else?" She smiled with obvious assurance.

Clint returned a sheepish grin and replied, "I was hoping you would say that."

Half an hour later, Alexandra stood partly naked in Clint's bedroom. She was bare from the middle of her back to her ankles, her soft red dress bunched ruthlessly at her shoulders and her matching thong a crumpled blur, hanging around her feet. Her pale thighs and buttocks were exposed to the man who stood immediately behind her, and his index finger followed the sensual curve of her lower back down to the soft luscious portion of her revealed ass.

"You're so damn sexy," Clint said from behind her, his fingers drifting from her shoulder to the warm bare skin of her back. She felt the cuff of his silk shirt brush delicately against her, then his hand slid slowly around the curve of her ribs to settle on her breast.

Alexandra closed her eyes and let her mind drift to his tender touch and the arousal of his voice. She felt his tender hands move across her body, and tug her dress off her breasts. Her dress now slid down her body, and she slowly stepped out and away from it and to a nearby wall. Alexandra's hands pressed against the wall, and she stiffened her body in anticipation of the assailant who stood behind her.

The stroke of his fingers along her nipple yanked her immediately out of her fantasy and into the current reality of a sudden seduction. Clint took a perked nipple between his thumb and one finger, fondling it slowly and methodically. Alexandra could hardly believe that she was letting this happen, but it felt good. So, so good to finally be indulged by a man who she wanted sex with rather than acting out with a paid client. She responded to his foreplay purely on instinct. Her hips slowly weaved as the pinching of her nipple transferred itself directly to her moistening pussy and stimulated clitoris.

"I want you so badly," he sighed with a husky whisper directly into her ear.

She felt his warm breath flowing across her neck as his free hand lifted her hair. Clint kissed her softly on her exposed shoulder and at the base of her earlobe, which caused her skin to pucker and shiver in delight. She felt his teeth against her skin and then a single touch of his tongue on her neck. But just when she thought he might nibble a bit more, he let her hair fall back into place and reached around her by placing his hand directly on her shaven crotch. His fingers gently slid on her trembling labia. He stroked her gently, just grazing her wanting clitoris while he kissed her neck.

"Does it arouse you?" he asked rhetorically, gently stroking her while cupping both her breasts firmly with his tender hands.

Alexandra heard herself sigh 'yes' in affirmation, but did not feel the words leave her mouth. At this point she was living on instinct and pure desire.

"Hmm, that's what I wanted to hear," he whispered, and, in an instant, he pressed his erection into the cleft of her soft buttocks.

Alexandra did not want to try to break free, but instead her body swayed backwards to press against him, gripping at his hard penis with the cheeks of her bottom. She moaned as she felt him stroke her pussy with his penis. She was trapped between two powerful and distinctive sensations: his constant caress and fondling of her sensitive breasts and the slower, firmer and more direct stimulation of her crotch. She gasped and put her hand on top of his where he was touching her. At that moment she felt his mouth on her ear, and he exhaled deeply, causing her to shudder yet again.

"Go on, take my fingers into you," he whispered.
She felt aroused beyond belief - every invisible hair on her body rose instantly, and she purred like a content kitten getting its face stroked gently. Instead it was Clint who was stroking her soaked lips with his middle finger. She intuitively guided him into a motion that she was familiar with when she masturbated alone, but this felt so much better.
"Are you ready, Alexandra?" he sighed seductively.

Weak at the knees, she nodded and shoved his finger even deeper inside her.

"Show me," he insisted.

She felt surreal and out of control, like some sort of programmemed robot that was being controlled telepathically, as she raised his fingertips and held them shimmering before her semi-opened mouth.

"Taste yourself," he ordered.

Her flavour was sweet, tangy and with a hint of salt, and she licked his fingers gently, slowly gliding them back and forth across her rounded lips. The image before him aroused him mightily. He imagined his cock sliding back and forth so effortlessly from her moistened lips and could not resist the moment to kiss her and take her own fingers into his mouth.

"Now I want to taste you," she said breathlessly. "I want all of you."

III

Somewhere across the huge city, Torie peered out her apartment's window and gazed across the infinite expanse of shimmering lights. The Moscow television tower beamed in the distance, but, aside from the famous city landmark, there was nothing for miles around other than nondescript apartment and office buildings. Alexi had just been put to bed, albeit nearly an hour later than usual. His head cold had worsened from the morning. She hated it for him, knowing his discomfort would mean a restless night.

"What are you looking at?" Stefan stood behind her and began to rub her slender shoulders.

She turned sharply and found comfort by burying herself into his waiting embrace. "Nothing really. I was just thinking of Alexi."

"He'll be okay, darling."

"I know. But I worry. I can't help it."

"You're the super mom, you know?" Torie sighed

wistfully and then smiled after Stefan added, "And the perfect wife."

Torie looked up at her husband and kissed him softly. "I wish I could give you another child."
Stefan was taken aback. "I thought we were beyond this. Are you still thinking about this?"

"Sometimes."

Stefan stroked away her some of the lines that hung on her forehead before replying, "You two are more than enough. Besides, the doctor says it is too risky. You know that, sweetie."

His voice was emphatic yet soothing. "Let's go to bed, darling. You need your rest after such a long day."
Torie looked longingly at her husband. He was so dark and brooding that when she first saw him eight years ago, quite by accident, it had felt as though someone had just kicked her in the stomach. There was an instant pull of attraction, and something she had never experienced before. Or since. Torie took pleasure from this. He smiled now and said in a rather sleepy voice, "Maybe we can practice on that next child."

His sexual reassurance lifted her feeling of inadequacy. They walked hand in hand to the bedroom – a smallish room made even smaller by the large double bed that lay in its centre.

Stefan closed the door behind him and locked it as he did before they made love. It was a lesson learned a couple years earlier, when Alexi walked in on them as Torie was straddled and thrusting herself upon Stefan. Thankfully he was too young to know what was happening, although for months he would occasionally ask mommy why she was riding poppa like a horse.

They made it to the bed in a tangle of limbs and laughter. Stefan was as long lying down as he was standing, but on the bed Torie could move up to kiss him without too much effort. She found his throat, the jut of his Adam's apple. His skin tasted of a hard day's work, and she stroked his bristly face with her mouth.

Torie's green floral dress had ridden up, helped by Stefan's hands. He pushed the dress higher with one hand while cupping his hand around her waist with the other. The edge of his fingers brushed her panties, and she sighed when he began to stroke her. Love-making like this was only once every week or so, yet every time it felt fresh and new.

She looked up to see him looking down at her with an expression of mingled amusement, and something else she couldn't quite decipher. She took her mouth from his and sat up a little, pushing back but not pulling away.

"What?" she demanded.

His hand on her thigh shifted higher, while his other went to prop his head. Stretched out that way, his body seemed relaxed, although their limbs were intertwined. He looked at her with a wry smile. Stefan seemed aware of something Torie was not, an awareness of himself as much a part of him as the colour of his eyes or his powerful arms and chest.

He shook his head. "Nothing, darling."

"It can't be anything," she said. "You're looking at me in that way."

"That way?" He sat up a little but didn't take his hand away from her leg. He widened his eyes and pursed his lips like a guppy. "Was it like this?"

Torie burst into laugher. "Something like that. Yes!"

"Was I doing that again?" Stefan leaned to catch her mouth in an awaiting kiss. He spoke without stopping his kiss. "That's the look I give when I'm in love."

The two kissed softly and slowly, like two old lovebirds who were more than comfortable with each other. The stirring and mindless sex was a distant memory of when they were late teenagers having sex with other in their early months. He nibbled her ear and licked her exposed nipples, which were now firm in expected attention.

"Stefan," she whispered gruffly, unable to take it any longer.

He paused in kissing her to look directly into her eyes. "You want something, darling?"

"I want you! Now!"

It was only another fifteen minutes later that the two lay snuggled in an unrecognisable heap of tangled limbs and heaving chests. Torie's face lay on Stefan's chest, and her gaze was towards a framed photo from their honeymoon.

"Remember our honeymoon, darling?" she asked inquisitively.

"Of course I do."

"We should go again to the Black Sea. I'd love for Alexi to see it."

"Of course, darling. Why not? Maybe this summer."

Torie rolled over and away from Stefan to turn off the bedside lamp, and replied nostalgically, "Yes. Maybe we will."

Chapter 9

I

"Christ! It can't be," moaned Clint, his outstretched hand slapping at the snooze button as the alarm went off at six-fifteen. Alexandra barely moved next to him, although a faint mumble escaped her slumber.

The morning light was enough to illuminate the spacious bedroom. Clint's white dresser, standing closet and bedroom tables appeared milky-coloured, while the sheer curtains from his poster bed provided further translucency. His bedroom was not like that of most men Alexandra had ever seen. The predominant white, brown, bronze and burgundy exuded a feminine touch, while delicate accessories added to the room's softness. Bundles of wrapped twigs filled empty spaces, and a dominant antique mirror opened up the room even more. Tender touches were thoughtfully added, and Alexandra had privately wondered if a woman had been behind the decoration.

Clint enjoyed candles nearly as much as Alexandra, and had many everywhere throughout the house. A batch of various candles were in the bathroom where he and Alexandra had hours earlier taken a candlelit bubble bath.

Clint peered over at his lover, who barely seemed alive. She was buried deep under his fluffy comforter and pillow. A bit of blonde hair and her face was all that peered from under the bed linens.

"Hey there," he whispered softly into her hair-covered ear. "Wake up, Sleeping Beauty."

Alexandra merely mumbled incoherently, "I'm sleepy."

Clint smiled and stroked her tousled hair. "I'll go now and have my shower. Coffee will be waiting for you in fifteen minutes."

Clint left Alexandra and walked towards the white robe that hung on the side of his closet. Alexandra rolled over just in time to see his shadowed naked body in front of her. His lean body complimented his ass, which was firm and taut. She had enjoyed all of him only hours before in lovemaking that left her deeply satisfied.

When Clint left the room, she thought of what had happened and what it all meant. Enjoying a lover this way meant new complications, but ones that she strangely welcomed. She wanted all along for the date to have ended this way. She was ultimately curious about him as a lover. The verbal banter satisfied her mind, his personality pleased her heart; however, he also needed to satisfy her desire. Luckily for him, he had.

The sound of the shower could be heard in the background, and she looked over at his digital clock. It was twenty-two minutes past six now, and she knew that it would take her a full hour to get ready. Leaving his apartment by seven-thirty would easily assure her arrival at Khanty by eight-thirty, unless she was hit by the full brunt of morning traffic. She had no experience in Clint's neighbourhood, so she would see first hand just how long it would take. Hopefully for future sleepovers. The thought made her smile, both outwardly and inside.

"Ah, there you are, gorgeous," Clint exclaimed through his transparent shower door. The bathroom's warm humidity felt good against her nakedness and the smell of his soap and shampoo filled her every pore. She opened the glass door without invitation, and was immediately drenched in the Turkish downpour.

"You're not fully clean until I say so. Understand?"

Alexandra's certainty left Clint to laugh slightly and

respond, "Yes, ma'am."

Her hand immediately took some of his body's soapy lather and rubbed him on his chest. Her hand slowly dropped to his waist, before continuing to his upper thigh. Her gaze never left his stare, which had fallen to her hand, only centimetres from an ever-aroused penis. It became even firmer when she began to wash it with two hands.

He arched his back and let the water run completely over his face, shielding it from Alexandra, who was now on her knees. One hand tenderly cupped his balls, while the other stroked his member into an erect and ready missile. She took him in his mouth and closed her eyes in delight. He tasted clean and fresh from the shower gel. He filled her mouth completely.

"Hmm," he murmured, head tilted to one side and back pressed to the wall.

Alexandra looked up at her lover, whose body was now twisted and coiled with pleasure. "Show me," she said, as she began to massage his manhood with purpose.

Seconds later he exploded in a final act of pleasure, and she took him in her mouth halfway through. She felt his warmth coupled with the stinging beads of water, combining in a dual assault against her pretty face.

All he could do was moan and mutter a muted 'Thank you,' as a look of utter satisfaction blanketed his face. Alexandra rose before him and reached across him for the bar of Dove soap.

She began to wash his chest, kissing his water-soaked cheeks before finally washing off his tiring penis and groin. He had shrunk in seconds, and not even Alexandra's thorough cleansing could arouse him again.

"That should make you squeaky clean for work,

don't you think?" she asked in a girlish tone.

"Indeed. My turn now?"

"No, you go off and get going on my breakfast. I like my coffee strong."

Clint stepped out of the shower, leaving Alexandra to watch him from inside the semi-blurred glass window. She enjoyed seeing him dry off, as if it was him who was a featured zoo animal being viewed by partitioned visitors. In fact, it could just have well been Clint who eyed his naked guest in the shower's chamber as his caged prize. Instead it was Alexandra who slowly caressed herself with the half-used bar of soap while staring at him with quiet satisfaction.

He moved before her steadily, but not hurriedly. His naked muscularity showed as he bent and twisted to dry himself with his large white towel. For a moment he noticed that Alexandra was watching his every move. He smiled at her and winked, before turning away to wipe off the steamed mirror. His ass was so perfect, Alexandra thought.

She loved a well-built man from this view. Seeing how the lower back curved out to the ass and the perfect crescent that formed each cheek was a particular turn-on. If he came back this very second she would fuck him again, as she felt herself becoming horny yet again. Instead he slipped back into his robe, and left her alone to battle her fantasies of a second tryst.

Ten minutes later Alexandra entered the kitchen, where she saw him sitting at a glass breakfast table with a newspaper in hand. He was sipping from a glass of some yellowish juice while completely absorbed by the newspaper. Without ever seeming to notice her entrance he blurted in emphatic disgust, "The Bulls just aren't the same without Jordan." With a look of disdain he quickly closed the newspaper and continued, "I just gotta have my morning American sports."

"Are all American men obsessed with sports?"

"No. Not all? Has that been your experience?"

"Well, Mr Thomas. If I told you that then you would think that I'm very experienced with American men."

Clint smiled at Alexandra's escape from his trap. After all, she'd told him the night before that she had never dated an American and only had passing experience with them. The fact was that she had slept with several American men and had noticed they seemed particularly obsessed by sport.

Clint replied with "Let me get you some of that coffee you demanded," walking over to the professional coffee machine that lay on the counter. "You know, Alex – you've got options here." He nodded towards the machine as he placed an empty cup under its faucet. "This thing makes lattes, cappuccinos, espressos. Hell, it can even make a macchiato if you want!"

"Just a normal coffee will do''.

"One bean strength? Two bean or three bean?" Clint's options began to wear on her patience.

Alexandra just rolled her eyes and exclaimed, "Jesus! Middle strength, and today please!"

Twenty seconds later she could smell the pleasant aroma she had been waiting for. Like so many adults, Alexandra needed her morning cup of coffee. It was her morning ritual. Without coffee she physically felt helpless to carry on; she would feel grumpy and somehow incomplete. Thank God he has a coffee machine, she had thought when she saw it during a quick tour of his apartment the night before.

Clint watched in concerned anticipation. "And?"

She made him wait for his relief. "Good!" she nodded assuredly. In fact, it was good. It was perhaps the best coffee she had had in months and certainly the finest of any homemade coffee outside a fine restaurant. I could get used to this, she thought with silent satisfaction.

II

Florian and Darrell sat amongst the smoky bustle of the lunch crowd, peering sporadically at their target only three tables away. They sat controlled, yet every muscle was tense and on alert. For no particular reason he looked up from his newspaper and seemingly directly at them. Exactly then the two spoke, chuckled and returned to their own lunch. It was however only an act to avoid detection between two spies who had worked together for years.

Across the room sat the man who was responsible for enough deaths, directly and indirectly, to be considered genocide. That it was Krokav only metres away seemed almost inconceivable; however, there he was, albeit flanked by burly bodyguards. There was no doubt – it was him. They'd seen his face and features in so many still photographs, although he appeared more sinister and powerful in flesh..

He had a jutting chin that accentuated a square jaw. His deep set eyes, like so many Russian men, somehow exuded a primitive air. His face could have been that of a wild man from ten thousand years ago; an opinion reinforced by the jagged scar that ran down the right side of his rugged face. The scar was more obvious in person than they had remembered from the photos, but it was there all right – a visible reminder of a life and death struggle from so many years ago.

A cigarette was in his left hand, while his right hand cupped a mug of some drink that steamed before him. He returned to his paper and took a long drag from his nearly finished cigarette, before mumbling silently to one of the men who flanked him. The man immediately left the table and retreated to the back of the room and out of sight. Darrell glanced knowingly at his partner. From where the agents sat it was hard to tell his height, but age-wise he appeared around fifty. Maybe fifty-five at most. He was stout and strong, probably eighty-five kilos or so. His thick neck led to a solid square body. His complexion was pale and his hair was a curly black with obvious traces of grey streaked randomly throughout it.

He stamped out his cigarette and lit yet another as he glanced across the bustling room. Then, putting out his match, he returned to his drink and paper. The American agents felt their heart pulsate and the blood fill their veins. Each knew that they were as close as any agent had ever been to Krokav. If only it could be like the movies where they could walk over with a silencer and execute their target right then. Unfortunately not. Real life dictates that he be arrested on charges of providing arms to terrorism.

Just then his bodyguard returned, guiding a leggy woman wearing a tight black and white checkered dress and carrying a matching red designer clutch bag. Her beauty was indisputable and her curves suggested she was either an escort or girlfriend to Krokav. Either way the agents stared at her, just as many of the restaurant's patrons did. She walked with purpose, her high heels striking the wooden floor with solid confidence.

Krokav's unknown guard leaned over and whispered into his ears before Krokav extended his hand towards the empty chair across from him. She sat and crossed her legs, but it now meant that their target was obscured by the woman's long blonde hair and arched back.

"Are you getting this?" Florian whispered into the invisible microphone hidden inside his cuff. Outside the restaurant sat a black van with tinted windows and other American agents, who were filming everything with high-powered cameras.

"Yeah," was the reply in his earpiece. "We're getting it all."

Simultaneously another agent was taking still photographs of the meeting, which meant that Krokav's bodyguards and the woman would be later cross checked against a database of other projects to see if they could get a name.

"Seen her before?" Florian whispered again.

"Not that we can remember. Looks like a thousand other girls."

In reality, most of espionage was still a low tech world of photographing, following and listening. There were no national databases for men like Krokav. If his bodyguards would be identified it would be by personal memory from another agent or by a low-ranking official sorting through piles of cross-referenced photographs. Espionage was like police work three generations before, where tips came from street informants, breaks came rarely, and the forensics were unsophisticated. An agents' eyes were the most valuable source of information a government could have.

The group that trailed Krokav was a handful of operatives that worked in anonymity and could not be traced on some bureaucratic State Department organisational chart. They were created in secrecy and worked as silent ghosts that reported to only one man, who himself reported to only one man. None of the men inside the café or the van knew why they had to do what they did. The full extent of the bigger picture was purposely kept from such drones. Nonetheless, their work always proved to be the key to success or failure. The fact that they were in the front line and physically amongst the very criminals who were their targets meant many died – most of them with a bullet hole or two in their skull.

Whenever this had happened, there never was any fanfare, state funerals or even investigations. There was never any mention of their murder in any newspaper. Ironically, it was often their colleagues who had to repress the disappearances or deaths by disowning them or denying any federal link. The unknown bigger picture was simply too important in the grander scheme.

After a brief conversation, the attractive blonde stranger rose from her chair and walked away from the group. Their meeting was a mystery; however, what truly excited the agents was not the woman, but a feeling that Krokav would meet a known terrorist. This would substantiate the mission to firmly link him to illegal arms trade while serving up his client as well. Killing two birds with one figurative bullet was always a bonus, and was the reason why five men were secretly watching every move Krokav was making.

Krokav rose, and was immediately flanked on either side by his well-dressed protection. All three put on dark sunglasses, although the weather outside was overcast and gloomy. They fit the bill of mafia or rich criminals perfectly. One of the men stayed behind and paid the waiter at the bar before making his way through the large glass front door.

"We're on!" Florian quickly whispered into his cuff. Immediately Florian and Darrell followed suit and hurriedly laid two one hundred ruble banknotes with the same waiter. They departed the café and turned left, where their car was about a hundred metres away. They walked swiftly but not quickly enough to draw attention, just in case Krokav's men would notice.

To their right they saw the surveillance van creep

out into the rushing flow of the passing traffic. They were only a few car lengths behind Krokav's shiny black BMW, which was heading towards the city's centre. The 740i stood out amongst the drab and dirty compacts that defined all the other cars around. Moscow cars are notoriously filthy in winter and early spring. Some so much that license plates are impossible to decipher, but not so with Moscow's elite. Anything less than daily perfection is further practice of the socio-economic stratification which characterises the country.

The three agents inside had the difficult task of driving in the chaos that defines Moscow's traffic. "Look at that fuck, doing what he wants," exclaimed Logan, who was behind the wheel. "He's all over the place!"

Indeed, Krokav's driver was weaving dangerously through the traffic in defiant arrogance, which typically characterised how the privileged drove in the city. Traffic rules were not their rules to follow but rather for the commoners only. In the event that they were stopped by the police, a simple bribe settled matters before they continued their treacherous driving.

They found themselves in a traffic jam by the banks of the Moskva River. At this location traffic became a tangled mass of metal, stinky exhaust, and frustration. Forward progress would be better off by foot, but, for the trailing agents, it was a welcomed reprieve of the frenetic pace only moments earlier.

Logan said nothing to his two other colleagues, just stared out the van's window, while Marco leaned forward to photograph the BMW. "Now with a bit of zoom we'll confirm where this baby comes from."

"You're assuming it's not a rental?" Logan said in defiance.

In fact, Bill had been here many times before, a

veteran of numerous operations across Europe over the past years. Marco was only just out of the academy and Moscow was his first assignment – a testament to the agency's confidence. Nonetheless, high academy scores were a flimsy substitute to aged experience.

"Ten to one the car has a fake registration or is a rental. If you're looking for…"

"I know," he interrupted with calm resignation. "I know."

"Shit! We've gotta make this light or we lose him," Logan said in terse anxiety. Krokav was a few car lengths ahead and was going to turn right, but they risked being too far behind to make the light themselves. Such was the case at this intersection where only a handful of cars would make it.

Seconds later green flashed, to once again release the cars. The BMW turned left and miraculously there were no crossing pedestrians to hold up any of the turning cars. Krokav sped away and the agents were just able to pass the stoplight as it turned yellow.

"Fuck yeah!" yelled Marco as he looked back at Peter. Victories in the field often come in the smallest packages, so continuing the trail left all three grinning.

"Turning left onto the Krymskiy," Peter said into his headset. All along he was feeding the chase to Darrell and Florian, who were several hundred metres further back. He sat in the van's hollowed-out back at a crude radio desk with some basic equipment and a microphone that could have been State property during the Cold War.

The brownish Moskva flowed underneath, and a long stretch of elite residential buildings stretched directly ahead on its banks. The black luxury car fit well here in Moscow's premium quarter of government, posh hotels and sumptuous apartments.

"How'd you like to live there?" Marco asked

incredulously as he nodded to the stately-looking building only fifty metres ahead.

"Maybe I could afford one month's rent if I pulled all three of our salaries together," mocked Logan. "Jesus! It's at least ten grand a month there."

They turned right on the river's opposite bank, where the traffic was half that leading to the Kremlin. The majestic capital was in near full view. Its grandiose red walls protected it like some medieval fortress from attackers that never came. Now it was being swarmed from a far different invader. One that did not carry a sword or gun, but rather a philosophy that defied its protective sheath for so long. However, old ways die hard and the Duma was not completely as enlightened, as many outsiders believed. By-products of generational Communism were still there in its hallowed and secretive halls.

"Eagle Eye to Nest. Turning right on Mokhovaya," Peter reported to the small command centre which existed in the basement of the embassy. In this operation there were eight agents –five of whom followed Krokav physically, while three others sat in a small room with the highest of security clearances.

"Roger that," came the reply.

Peter adjusted his GPS to a layout that included landmarks. He sensed that maybe they would leave the city centre and he could provide additional dimensions to their location other than an obscure street address that was spelled like so many others.

The inconspicuous chase led them further down the river and past the Kremlin until they crossed back over the city's river once again. Only seconds later Krokav's car pulled into the front of Hotel Baltschug, one of Moscow's most glamorous five star hotels. The imposing yellow and white hotel sat directly on the bustling street while providing guests with views of the

Kremlin, St. Basil's cathedral and the river it bordered.

"He's pulled into the Baltshug right after you cross the Ordynka," Peter said emphatically into his microphone.

The agents were able to immediately pulled into a parking lot directly across the road from the hotel. All three hurried to the van's rear two windows, and Marco steadied his camera in anticipation.

Both bodyguards pushed through the front doors and the driver immediately opened the back door to reveal the striking figure of his employer. Krokav paused and looked around, as if he sensed the agent's presence. He raised his chin and angled his head like a predatory big cat whiffing the scent of his next kill.

"Look at that fucker," Logan said disgustedly as Marco quickly snapped photo after photo.

A doorman approached the car and was waved off by one of the bodyguards, who stopped him before he could reach Krokav. While Krokav and one of the guards briskly entered the hotel, the other guard quickly jumped into the car and waited in it by the entrance. Just then Darrell and Florian's blue Mazda approached from around the bend.

Peter leaned into the microphone, "See him, guys? The black 740 waiting to pull out?"

"Got it!" The response assured them that the two-pronged mission would continue.

III

"How long has it been now?"

Logan was wrestling and fidgeting in a nervous ball of energy and frustration. They had been waiting now for nearly three hours and were at the point that all spies hate in a stake-out. The reality that their target may not leave the hotel until the morning was a sinking feeling that filled their gut like a stone.

"Shit, I'm hungry!" Marco exclaimed wildly.

Marco was always hungry and potentially could eat every hour. How he stayed so thin and kept his flat stomach was more a matter of genetics than exercise. God knows that working this job meant little time for anything else. Such was the case today, as he had to endure the long bouts of boredom and frustration.

"That little diner over there," he motioned with his finger, "Why don't I get us all something? Besides, I could really take a leak."

Thirty metres further down the bustling street was a cheap-looking restaurant eatery whose name was revealed in large red Cyrillic letters. The sign read 'Borchav', and it was a popular eatery in the neighbourhood that specialised in take-away. Marco muttered "Be back in a flash."

Twenty minutes later nothing had changed –this was as the agents had expected. Marco had earlier sent his photos to Gaby back at the command centre. While they could only sit and wait, the guys back at the embassy could at least process their information. Searching for a name behind the bodyguards and woman could take hours or days, and it was unlikely that they could find anything soon. Gaby, one of the agency's best, had her work cut out for her.

Marco returned. "Delivery Boy!" he shouted, with a grin that stretched across his face.

He began to pull out the first of three Styrofoam boxes as he spoke. "We can mix and match if you want." He handed Peter a box filled with small pelmeni, rice and bread before stating to Bill, "You wanted red." His partner was handed a plastic cup of borscht, which he remembered that Logan liked from a previous function where the team went out to lunch together.

"It will do," Logan replied unenthusiastically.

The smells of their food filled the cramped space; nevertheless, the meal was a welcomed reprise to the boredom that it had replaced. They chomped and slurped like a gathering of hungry wolves munching on the carcass of an elk. They ate quickly, as if they only had minutes and not the hours that surely lay ahead. Such was the nature of a stake-out. Things could and did change instantly, and perhaps it was this subconscious conditioning acting out.

It was now four-thirty and they had seen dozens of cars come and go, guests enter and leave, and even a couple deliveries from DHL and Fed-Ex. The rich clientele all looked the same. The men wore the same long black coats, and the women invariably were in some shade of black, brown or dark blue. Any other hue in Russian winters and early spring was rare.

As the van's digital clock flipped to four-thirty-three, Peter stiffened. "The boys said the Beamer is coming back to the hotel, and is only a kilometre away."

Immediately the mood and scene changed from utter stillness to frantic movement. Sure enough, moments later the same black 740i that they had followed hours earlier slowly rolled into the entrance as Peter hurriedly reported back to the base, "Eagle Eye to base, we have contact. Krokav's car has returned."

Their colleague's familiar Mazda rolled past them and around the corner. Their target stopped and sat for seconds, as no-one appeared from behind its darkened windows. The hotel's valet appeared and strode towards the car just as the driver emerged. It was the same husky bodyguard from earlier. He slowly stepped out of the long black BMW and began to walk around its front as the valet opened the passenger's door, revealing the same woman who Krokav had met in he

120

café.

Marco's camera clicked as Logan gushed, "Look what we have here, boys!"

What they had was really nothing more than an insignificant participant in a larger scheme. Whether the lady in red was his girlfriend or a paid slut mattered little.

"Wanna bet Krokav will be getting lucky soon?" Logan solicited in whimsical reflection.

"She's just with him for the money, one way or the other," Marco replied as he continued to photograph the scene before him. "We all pay for sex when you think about it." He turned to Logan in credulous certainty, "The only difference between him and us is that it comes easier."

"Hey man – not me. My lady back home loves me and she knows my shitty salary." Peter's rebuttal rang of the reality that none of the three earned much, and that their relationships were defined more by regular Skype calls than sex.

The valet moved the car and began to circle around the hotel's private rear entrance which allowed Marco and unadulterated shot at both the stout bodyguard and the elegant blonde in high heels. Her long coat glided gently as she embarked on the thick front steps and her hair seemed shiny even from seventy five metres away. She was led by the bodyguard and they disappeared into the hotel. Thirty seconds later Florian could be seen rounding the corner.

"There's our boy," Logan said with calm confidence.

He appeared to cough into his hand, but instead a familiar voice floated from a speaker hung above Peter's workstation. "Going inside for a visual." Within seconds he was gone from view.

Once inside, Florian paused as he quickly scanned

his environment. He searched for the blonde in red, assured that she would stand out in the sea of dull and colourless formality. Once he spotted her then the bodyguard or Krokav wouldn't be too far away.

Then the flash of red caught the corner of his eye and he casually braced himself against the adjacent marble pillar. There she was. And there he was – the bodyguard directly behind, leading the mystery woman to a cluster of neighbouring leather chairs.

Again, he leaned into his cuff. "Got a visual."

The two approached the low brown leather seats only ten metres away from Florian's fixated eyes, and what he saw next struck the surprised agent. "Wait a second. They... they... I know this guy!" His voice was filled with revelation and a hint of shock. "He could be one of ours!"

Peter's reply was quick and direct. "What do you see exactly? Details!"

Florian looked around nonchalantly to ensure his isolation before continuing, "They're meeting another target, but I swear I know this guy from somewhere. I'm pretty sure it was the academy."

Florian's words were met with incredulous astonishment. Logan looked at Marco, who looked both at his boss and colleague in bewilderment. "What the..."

Before he could finish Florian whispered, "They are talking and it looks like the broad is being introduced. Don't know exactly. Now they are all sitting."

"Describe the American," Peter replied emphatically.

"Black suit, dark short straight hair, glasses, about six foot. Could be one-eighty or so. Not that overweight, more athletic than anything."

"Report when he exits. We need a photograph."

"Understood." Florian walked over to the nearby

gift shop and quickly bought a USA Today. A moment later he was sitting perpendicular to the three targets in his own comfortable seat at the lobby's opposite corner. He appeared to be reading the featured article on the Duke rape case, but instead his gaze was what lay only thirty feet ahead.

He saw the three leaning together in a terse dialogue of something unknown. The bodyguard's features were more obvious now. He appeared ethnic; maybe Armenian, the southern influences were definitely there. His features were rugged, and he reminded the men of a modern Cro-Magnon with his thick brow and relatively recessed eyes.

Just then the American that Florian swore he somehow knew leaned away in giddy laughter. He slapped his hand on his knee and placed his hand firmly on the woman's own delicate knee. She whispered into his ear, and within a second the meeting seemed to be finished. The American stranger left with the lady in red. A quick handshake from the American bid Krokav's man adieu, and they left him sitting there as they climbed the steps locked arm in arm.

"Meeting over. Looks like the female subject could be the American's lady friend. They left the bodyguard and are heading up to one of the restaurants on the second floor."

Inside the van, all three agents simultaneously looked at one another in silent disbelief. Each sought an explanation of the link, and all three entertained wildly different scenarios."

Logan broke the silence by stating matter-of-factly, "We've got to find out who the American is."

Logan paced before saying "We've got to interview Flo, because his memory could be wrong. He graduated eight years ago, for Christ's sake."

Logan's comments were fair actually and were

acknowledged by the approving nod of both Peter's and Marco's head. Anyone from 1998 would have changed physically. Besides, what would the odds be that an American CIA agent would be meeting with a bodyguard of a known arm's dealer? They were the main players in the attempt to get Krokav, and they reasoned that anyone else in the agency would surely be known to them.

IV

Over an hour later, and the scene was the same. Krokav's man was absorbed in his newspaper while Florian waited restlessly for something to change. So often the waiting would play tricks on the mind. Night had now fallen on the beleaguered city. The van hummed as the heating battled the biting cold that leaked inside. Every twenty minutes Logan would run the vehicle for five minutes. By now the men felt hunger tearing at their aching stomachs; however, this was no time to take a food break. The urgency and immediate attention of what was transpiring left each pensive and on edge.

Almost in unison Florian's whisper filled the van just as the on-board digital clocked flashed six. "The girl is coming back down."

Eventually she walked towards the oblivious thug, a picture of contrast. His rugged frame and huge features were at polar extremes to that of the waif and elegant lady who now stood gracefully just beside him. He looked up in surprise, and Florian wondered in arrogant introspection, 'Some bodyguard. Good thing she wasn't a hit-man, or he'd have a bullet in the back of his thick skull right now'.

Florian was right. Krokav could have done better than the hulking mass of muscle and bones. He knew that the best protection comes from professionals with more instincts than a wild leopard. A true bodyguard would have seen her even before Florian.

The woman bent over to speak closer to him. The two chatted just long enough for the bodyguard to hand her something from inside his jacket.

"She's coming your way," he warned the others.

"Marco?" Logan said authoritatively. However, there was no need to supervise, as Marko already had his Nikon pressed against his right eye. He was zooming towards the hotel's door in anticipation. "Just about got it," he replied slowly.

Seconds later the woman was revealed, and thankfully for Marco she stood momentarily under the illuminating front lights to button and tie her coat from the pending cold. He snapped non-stop, using this chance to get his shot before she bolted down the stairs and into an awaiting taxi.

As interesting as the woman was, she only provided a momentary break in the action. Gaby still had hours of work to do, but at least she had a relatively new identity-matching software programme at her disposal. Unlike in the movies, it only worked on a general profile of targets who were photographed directly or nearly straight on. It referenced distance between the eyes and other facial common points to get its match, but ultimately it was the human analysing the matches to definitely confirm who was who in each photo. It was unlikely a name would identify their mystery woman; nonetheless, the American remained as their biggest hope in the break that they needed.

Moments after everything had settled back into a monotonous pattern, things picked up once again when Florian announced, "We've got Florian's target coming down into the lobby. The bodyguard is getting up to meet him."

Once again everyone's muscles tightened in anticipation and all eyes feasted on the view across the street. This time Logan turned the van's key, and the van coughed and eventually rumbled to life.

"He's coming out with him. Everyone get ready for a go!" Florian's excited voice was heightened in anticipation.

"Eagle Eye to base. We're about to roll. Subject is leaving with an unidentified target, and we are prepared to follow."

The response on the other end was immediate. "Birdie One, stay put and watch for Krokav. Eagle Eye to roll with target."

For Darrell and Florian it meant staying at the hotel until twelve-thirty a.m. which was the official end of any stake-out that had no second shift. It was unlikely they would have any further excitement in their long day, but, for the three agents in the van, it meant that their involvement was to take a new turn of events.

The unknown man departed the Baltshug with Krokav's man on his shoulder. They waited by the doorman, who appeared to talk briefly with the bodyguard before the familiar silhouette of the BMW glided in view. The valet exited the car and both subjects entered, before it again slowly waited to depart the hotel's protected premises. Logan was cautious not to turn on his lights until he pulled out into the street. Every detail of how not to be noticed was old hand for the grizzled veteran. Tailing a subject at night was always so much easier than in day. Except perhaps in Moscow and possibly this target who seemed to drive with reckless abandonment.

They followed the speedy subject like a lion on the prowl, but only until they reached the Tverskaya, when things ground to a halt. Moscow's central boulevard was a moving parking lot of thousands of motorists.

Slowly they weaved like an undetectable python in the high grasses of the marsh. Their cover was the other cars and their trickery was distance, space and darkness.

Twenty minutes later the BMW turned into the Marriott Grand Hotel. The black sedan disappeared in a sunken garage that was reserved for staying guests. Now, out of sight, the van had to pull off of the busy Tverskaya momentarily in an effort to regroup.

The chase was finally over. Now clues the suspects left were enticing enough to provide them with a clearer, more transparent, scenario. The agents knew where one of the men was staying, and they had their valuable photographs. The next morning's briefing would come soon enough, but right now the three looked at each other with total satisfaction before Logan inquired with twinkling eyes, "You boys want some food?"

"I thought you'd never ask!" blurted Marco, rolling his shoulders and straightening himself upright in his seat. "I know of a great pizza place about five minutes from here!"

"Why doesn't that surprise me?" Logan replied nonchalantly as he looked back into traffic, ready to pull back out into the energetic pace of the big Russian city.

Chapter 10

I

Torie sat at a decrepit wooden table covered in doodles and words, creaking under the weight of her paperwork. This table had seen much in its ancient history but now found itself serving as Torie's work station at the F.I.M Centre.

F.I.M provided Torie with an outlet to help those needy souls who Russian society had so openly shunned. She had always felt something akin to the quiet societal rejects, not the homeless or runaways, but those that suffered debilitating mental illness. These were the people that F.I.M served, and sought to live up to its acronym of Friendship, Independence and Motivation.

What had started as volunteer work had grown nearly three years later to a part time job of three half days. The centre wanted her more and even promised her a management role, yet she refused to let her own Alexi down. If only she were not such a devoted mother and wife.

On this particular morning she was to provide intake paperwork on the Centre's five new applicants. She was the gatekeeper the process of achieving independence for persons who suffered mild degrees of mental illness. Each interview would last fifteen to twenty minutes depending on the condition of each client. While a minority suffered more severe forms of illnesses most were readily functional, but were considered asocial nonetheless. Torie's warmth and gentle manners seemed a perfect fit for a centre whose purpose was to give those afflicted a chance of independent living.

Her office was a tiny room in a building located in a

distinctively middle class neighbourhood. It did not serve solely as Torie's own office, but was rather a multi-purpose room that housed many member records and human resource employee files. Being partly subsidised on governmental funding meant paperwork was plentiful and the office was crammed full of dusty file cabinets that screeched when opened or closed.

She spread her papers out upon the rickety desk and the first of her interviewees walked through the door, a smiling woman with wildly curly hair and a distinctive smile. Her beatnik look was made complete by her disheveled appearance. Her hair appeared to fight the restricting purple beret that capped her head and her oversized blue turtle-neck sweater dwarfed her petite frame. She walked with a distinctive hobbled gait. Torie adjusted the wire-framed glasses that sat perched upon her beaked nose before extending her hand and saying with a toothy grin, "Privet. I am Io."

Torie already knew much of the young lady originally from St. Petersburg. She was from a fairly wealthy family who had relocated in Moscow when her father set up his business' central offices in Moscow. Perhaps it was the profound change of moving the five hundred kilometres to such an urban environment that had affected the young teenager, or perhaps it was the pressure of expectation that she faced coming from a successful family. Whatever it was, Io's incomplete file showed that she was extremely intelligent and sociable, but often relapsed in prolonged bouts of depression and anxiety.

"My name is Torie," she replied with a soft voice that was both melodic and clear. "I want to congratulate you for coming today, and I hope you become a member so that you can begin to enjoy all of our benefits."

Torie and the centre refrained from calling their

membership such debilitating and negative words as 'patients' or 'clients'. Their centre was a place that members paid a one time fee of one hundred rubles to enjoy a wide ranging of services. For three dollars any one of the nearly two hundred members could engage in continuing education, independent housing services, employment services or simple social integration that helped replace harmful stigmatism.

Io sat in a red metal chair that groaned when it felt the weight of its recipient. Torie had already eliminated the typical boundaries that so many others used. As an alternative, she had Io sit next to her table instead of across from her. That way Io could see all the paperwork and be free from the kind of clinical experiences she often endured at the hospitals that treated her with indifference.

"I want to do an intake so that you can become a member of F.I.M today – hopefully this won't take too long. Afterwards you can clubhouse function to join." Torie smiled continuously, moving her hand gracefully as she spoke. Io seemed affixed to this woman who sat before her – a complete opposite in terms of their physicality, yet somehow she sensed Torie's kindred spirit. In fact, it was true. Both shared more in common that either knew; however, it was Torie who had been lucky enough to avoid being dealt Io's cruel hand when she was born.

Io's genes came from two gifted parents who were both highly intelligent and talented in music. Her father played the trumpet and could write music, while her mother taught piano to small children. Io herself could not escape a world of culture and played three musical instruments besides the piano, which often had proved an emotional outlet when she was in the deepest of her depressions.

Torie had been a single child living with a family of

modest means. She had not ever seen a piano until she was fourteen and had never heard live music until her wedding to Stefan. She was gifted with beauty and talents that never were realised and that were likely to lay dormant inside her for the entirety of her life. The two sat presently as polar extremes, but could have become unwitting Gemini twins had Torie been somehow adopted by Io's parents.

After several minutes of questions, that ranged from general personal questions to listing her current medications, Torie asked what she had wondered when she first saw her file. "Why did your parents name you Io?" She then smiled broadly and rested her chin in her interlocked fingers. Io noticed her long painted fingernails in the kind of pink that was her favourite colour, and marvelled at the perfect shape of each.

"Well..." She paused before lapsing into a gaze above Torie that seemed to last ten seconds. "My parents were both planetary freaks and my father had even tried to become a cosmonaut. Can you imagine how my dad felt when he discovered that my mom and he both loved astronomy?"

Io's voice critically stressed the word 'astronomy' and they both chuckled softly, before Io slinked down into the chair so her legs were now completely stretched. She ran her right hand through the tangled curls that framed a long face with round eyes.

"Anyways, Dad always loved Jupiter because it was the biggest planet, but come on! You can't name your daughter Jupiter!" Io's eyes rolled and her expression emphasised her point with forced disdain. "But then there was Io – Jupiter's own moon named after a Greek priestess who became one of the lovers of Zeus."

Io slid back up from her chair and shrugged, "So there you have it." She exhaled softly and Torie sensed that she had often had to recite this story more times than she had cared to.

"Ahh..." Torie replied with satisfaction. "It's such a unique name and I'm sure you become more memorable because of it."

Io raised her eyebrows in approval.

"Well then, Io, shall I take you now to your chosen service unit? Support services is on the second floor and Allesia will surely be happy to meet you."

Torie rose from her own seat and led Io out of the small room and into a spacious reception, before guiding her to a narrow hallway that contained several rooms. In each Io could see a mix of work activities and leisure. Some members were easily identifiable from their steely stare and slouched posture, while the staff maintained a leadership position by talking and supervising. Nonetheless, other clubhouse members seemed to blend in well. If it weren't for their shabby clothes and often unkempt look, they could have blended in with the staff perfectly.

Eventually they entered a larger room above the reception that served as Io's new functioning unit. Here all of F.I.M's social and internal programmes were coordinated and the room buzzed with activity, mostly from female members and staff. Allesia was the commanding figure who sat at the large table that was directing five others in some sort of poster creation.

"They're preparing for next week's open house," Torie stated.

"Open house?"

"It's where the public can see what we do and hopefully make a financial donation. However, mostly family of our members come and see what work goes on and how their loved ones are succeeding."

Torie's smiling eyes were fixed on the nearby group, and twinkled like a proud mother watching her children in their first school play. Just then Allesia noticed her new guests and shouted loudly, "Ahh! Come!" She waved her hands with excitement before being distracted by a stout woman with red hair who had approached her with a box of supplies. It was obvious something was wrong with the middle-aged woman, but only Torie knew that Tasha suffered from schizophrenia.

Io looked at her new colleague with wide eyes.

"What's her situation?" she asked in a whisper.

"Tasha, you mean?"

"That woman with the box." Io nodded her head in Tasha's direction.

"She's actually quite a success. Two years ago she lived in a mental ward, sent there when her elderly mother passed away years before. Then another member… there… Vincent. He's the one sitting there in the red shirt." Torie pointed emphatically to a chubby man with a gaunt face, short straight hair and pencil moustache who was at the table's end. "He was a member, and eventually coordinated F.I.M to meet with Tasha at Ziona." Everyone knew Ziona was Moscow's largest and most infamous mental institutions.

Torie explained, "Twenty years ago the State packed undesirables within its locked gates and walls. Mental disease was treated like a medieval plague where people were shunned by the general public and treated like a curse. Now there is much broader societal enlightenment. Tasha has been transformed from an institutionalised zombie to having some independent living skills. She lives in a group home, comes here nearly every day, and even works a part-time job sponsored by our supportive employment programme. She still has relapses, however, only when she fails to take her medication. Otherwise she functions really well and isn't treated like a patient, but as a peer."

Io nodded in proud acknowledgement.

"You can work too if you ever want," Torie stated with calm certainty.

"I am going to work. Here."

Torie's broad smile was the realisation that her work had purpose and that she had just seen yet another person take a step towards their own personal fulfilment.

II

Across town another kind of meeting was happening amongst members of a totally different kind of group. This was also State-sponsored; but the federal funding was not for personal development or independent living but rather for the continuation of freedom, and the battle against those that jeopardised it. The group that met now worked underground and was far removed from the government that secretly supported them.

Each knew their existence was a parity of truth and lies. The fact was that governmental officials needed and supported these agents, while simultaneously announcing to their constituents that America operated on a higher moral plane than other countries. Their work was never a result of legal or even ethical methods because they killed without trials, eavesdropped illegally, and engaged in illicit activities when undercover or planted with those they fought to bring to justice. The war on maintaining freedom for Americans was dirty and far from the righteous black and white rules of traditionally known engagement. The same politicians who secretly supported them would cast them aside in the face of public outcry.

Director Billups stood firmly in front of the assembly, his gaze planted on the paper before him. The silence from within the room was absolute, and the momentary stillness was surely the calm before the fiery leader's pending emotion. Billups was a man of passion and conviction. His personality was now too conditioned to ever change. Fighting both the Koreans and Vietnamese left him jaded to death and communism.

The latter was the mother of all ironies that he would be stationed in Moscow, the very capital of the country he so despised for so long. No-One believed the director really trusted the former enemy, yet a posting here in Moscow was likely his penultimate assignment before he retired gracefully to the mountains of Virginia where he was originally from.

"What I read here is…"

Again, silence filled the room after Billups stopped midway through. He looked up from the document and flipped away the thick glasses from his face. A look of disbelief and disgust filled his face.

"It says we have new information that we need to process. First off, we need to confirm our facts. Florian?" He scanned the room and squinted to find the agent who added the element of his current torment.

"Where are… Oh, there you are."

"Yes sir." Florian was seated just in front of him and seemingly hidden in plain sight.

"Gaby, what do we have so far?"

The thin black-haired beauty originally from Brazil stood from the back row where she always sat. "I've got no identification on the woman or driver, but we do know that the enforcer that stayed with Krokav is Marat Mogilevich, his bodyguard now over the past year or so. He's Ukrainian originally. We suspect he has now reached the title of Brigadier in the Mafia because of his increased presence and activities away from Krokav. The man photographed with Krokav coming out of the Baltshug remains unidentified; however, we are going to run his photo against the data base with

135

both the CIA and FBI If he has a badge then we should be able to make a match but with a catch."

The director nodded in anticipation of what the obstacle was.

"The software only gives us likely matches, and considering that there are over ten thousand field agents in the FBI alone plus another ten or fifteen thousand in the CIA, we still will have to sift through hundreds of visuals to make a probable match."

Director Billups was quick with his pointed rebuttal. "Seventy percent are white and about eighty-five percent are males, so the numbers are less. I'm sure you can programme the ranges of age to get that number down. Do it! Frank, you're with Gaby on this."

He pointed to the man in front of Florian who sat with an oversized coffee mug in his hand. "I want an ID on this guy now. Yesterday, in fact!"

"We carry on, people." Billups' voice was firm and desperate. "We've got eleven days now and plenty of work. Thanks to one of our agents we have a new lead, but this means even more work. Flo, Darrell! I think you know where you are today. Gaby, Frank! And Clint - I need you in my office in five." He looked across the room of individuals, who now twitched and fidgeted in their seats.

"Any questions?"

No-one answered, and seconds later the director strode off to the rear door and past the anxious staff who quickly scurried about in rapid commotion.

A moment later the door slammed behind Clint as he entered Billups' office.

"I've worked with you too long, Ron. You know something." Clint stood defiantly with his arms folded. "Actually I don't, but you know, I've got a funny feeling about this." He looked down at a scrambled mess of documents, photos and reports.

"These things here tell me nothing and everything. What I know is we got a S.O.B that sells weapons and my job is to put him out of business."

"You mean arrest him. There's a difference."

Ron Billups knew what Clint meant, and it pained him that all along that getting Krokav was not the ultimate victory.

"Shit, Clint, we are the United States of fucking America. We champion our freedoms but are paralysed by them. You think those assholes behind the red wall across from us care about rules and the rights of the criminals?" His face was flushed from frustration and anger. "If Krokav is working with one of ours then don't you think we would know it? Hell, we're here under a presidential order for Christ sake!"

"You mean executive order,'' Clint corrected. Billups knew the fine details of the mission, and although he suspected that the President himself may have known, it was the Joint Chief of Staff who Ron's boss reported directly to. Or so he was told.

"Yes, we would know, which is why that guy probably isn't one of ours. I'm figuring a European who is working for some rogue African. Can you imagine a spook on the streets of Moscow? Jesus, Clint! He would stand out like a fucking Santa Claus on a nudist's beach."

Clint simply laughed as his fingers braced his forehead. "Spook? God, Ron, it's so not 1955 anymore."

"Fuck those politically correct bastards! Spooks, zips, wetbacks, whatever. I never call an honest minority anything when he is honest and hard-working. He's got my respect for overcoming all the cynical bastards like me."

"And the white criminals?"

"Fuckers, pieces of shit, scumbags. Christ, man,

you've heard it all before."

Actually, Clint had. The grizzled war veteran was a throwback to an era when men in the intelligence community trusted no-one. The threat of communism was something so sinister in his prime that it forever jaded him to humanity. He had too often seen agents exposed as double agents, and the greater fear was the unknown. The Russians were good at posturing and shaking the agency to its core. The fact that the Russians were hardly the threat the West thought was discovered too late for a crotchety old hand like Billups to change.

To Billups, enemies were all around and came from outside America's hallowed boundaries, which is why he inherently distrusted Asians and eastern Europeans. Blacks were a different story. He had grown up in segregation and it had taken him decades to fully embrace their inclusiveness. Anyone, regardless of colour or creed, would be marginalised if they did not fit his image of the patriotic citizen that defined the 1940's and 1950's. Old racist terminology was a language that he never truly forgot.

"This supposed American guy. I want you on this. Keep Gaby on this guy and Frank on the others. I want them on a tight leash, if you know what I mean." He thumbed at his cheap spectacles and tugged at his pants to adjust them over his protruding stomach. "Have them report only to you on this, and they are not to talk. It's a code two, understand?"

Clint nodded approvingly and understood what had to be done. Elevating this particular project to where the information was limited within the team made sense however only if the unthinkable was, in fact, true.

"Yes sir," he replied softly as he took a long deep breath. "We'll get it done."

III

There it was in front of her, and Alexandra just sat at her desk with a blanket look of stupidity. She struggled to find the exact meaning of 'quinquennium' in her Russian dictionary, and somehow it wasn't there.

'Shit! How can that be?' she wondered to her herself. Her dictionary wasn't the ordinary type one buys at the book store for several dollars, but rather was Rosen's Comprehensive English-Russian Dictionary. She had bought it in university for around a hundred dollars, which was a nearly a whole week's money in that time. This book had never let her down. Until now. She carefully typed in each letter into Google, mindful of the strange combination of u's and i's. And then there it was in front of her – 'пятилетие' – a period of five years.

She suddenly realised this was the first new word she had learned this year. She reflected back to September when 'indivisible' sent her searching in disbelief. Moments like this were the occasional points in her work that she enjoyed and looked forward to.

Just then her mobile rang, and she immediately saw who it was. She had been avoiding Mikhail over the past days, positive that his calls were for the sexual rendezvous he had grown accustomed to. After her night with Clint she knew that her shallow feelings for her married lover were over. Although she had broken many men before, it bothered her that Mikhail would be yet another. She realised she was slowly but surely gaining a romantic conscience, which is why she knew she would have to take this call.

"Privet, Mikhail."

"Where have you been, Alex? I've been calling for days now!" His voice was mixed with raw concern and a tinge of anger, yet Alexandra couldn't blame him.

"Yes, I know. I've been so busy and have really been thinking of you." Her inflection on 'you' was filled with such sweetness that Mikhail surely felt her sincerity. "Let's meet for lunch soon if you can."

"Yes, darling, I'd like that. How about today?"

"Today?" Alexandra was thrown for the briefest of seconds before processing the inevitability of the moment. Instantly, she knew what the answer had to be. "That would be great, but I'm only free at one o'clock."

"Fine for me. You know I can always take off, so let's meet at our old spot then." Mikhail's voice rose in delighted anticipation; however, deep inside she knew it would be his last joy in seeing her.

"Great," she replied softly. "See you in three hours," she concluded as she glanced at her wristwatch.

She flipped over the cover of her mobile and looked forward into emptiness. Her life was so muddled and empty, and it was only about to become more desperate. Yet leaving Mikhail was a baby step in rewriting her life. She knew that, but nonetheless wished she could walk away from it all with a blink of her steely blue hypnotic eyes. For a moment Alexandra was caught by the questions of fate, love and life. She wondered whether the pains of love were something she had never really felt. She knew that it presented itself with the most sublime of paradoxes. In fact, Alexandra had never really experienced love with a man. In fact the only love she'd really felt was Sister Masha's.

Alexandra suddenly felt empty. She blinked forcefully to escape the misery, and immediately thought back to her plan to find her surrogate mother in Perm. She had been distracted by her new life's mission, but had simultaneously avoided it when she did have free time. I've got to do it, she thought. Indeed she did, and she would; however, first things first.

Alexandra walked into the familiar confines of Mu-Mu Café where she would meet her lover at least twice a month for lunch. It was a popular place for locals and the unsuspecting tourists who rarely frequented the Arbat neighbourhood. The restaurant was typically dim, and the wood-panelled walls seemed a throw back to the eighties when it first came into existence. She scanned the restaurant for Mikhail, but instead saw two men sitting in a nearby booth, staring at her with lustful eyes.

You can't afford me, Alexandra thought as she smiled at them, causing one of the men to raise a finger in acknowledgment.

She walked coolly by the two as they followed her every step before breaking out in a hushed discussion. Alexandra tossed her black coat on the booth's semicircular seat and squeezed in, facing the front door. She sat alone and could see one of the men speaking to his buddy, who stared at Alexandra as a man always did before approaching her.

Just then the front door opened, revealing the shape of the man she knew from his silhouette alone. The curve of his profile and the shape of his body was indeed Mikhail's' and he strode by the gentleman who was readying himself to approach Alexandra. Mikhail came to the booth and leaned over to kiss her on the cheek, leaving the two men to resume to their half-finished lunch.

"I've missed you," he said as he unbuttoned his long wool coat.

"I know you have. Please sit here," she replied as she tapped the seat to her right.

Mikhail slid into his spot next to Alexandra and looked upon her with fascination. It was a combination of lust, desire and friendship. He loved her with his heart, but not with his head. Leaving Marina was never an option, although they both maintained their own lovers. Alexandra needing him as her own was not the issue and it never was. Something had changed now with Alexandra, as she wanted more than a weekly romp in bed and the occasional dinner and lunch.

"Listen Mikhail, I'm sorry to bring you all the way here, but I really need to talk to you and tell you something."

Instinctively Mikhail knew what would follow. His hand turned clammy and moist from a sudden rush of adrenaline, and his eyes narrowed on the woman who sat so calmly next to him. All their time together quickly rushed before him in a single flash - from the time he met her in the Museum of Mayakovsky to the time he first saw her perky firm breasts, only inches from his lips. He recalled their love-making and the last time he saw her only two weeks prior. He knew it was over, and could say nothing. The paralysis of a lover leaving him had never been felt before.

"I'm going to move on, and I don't want this any longer." She said the words slowly.

This, he thought in silent apprehension. Was their relationship reduced to a single unemotional word? Apparently so, but still his mind was racing, his words locked in some sort of state of animation.

"I grew to care about you but I could never care enough, and this was always a short term play-thing for us both. You know that."

Her words stung Mikhail to respond clumsily, "I thought everything was fine between us."

"I didn't say they weren't. It's just that I need to move on without you. It really is not personal because... well..." Alexandra reached across and put her feminine hand on his while she searched for the right way to express herself. "You are a terrific man."

Her smile was the cruel paradox that instantly angered Mikhail. She had become so much more than a lover to him, and there were times he even thought about what would happen if Marina would somehow die accidentally. Marina and he were a brand, a corporation of sorts, that was unlikely ever to be dissolved; however, it didn't mean that he could not fantasise about having Alexandra as his sole possession. Now all that was gone, and the centre of his fantasies simply sat before him with a telling smirk that he wanted to forcefully wipe away.

She sensed his pending rage, and quickly pulled her hand away. Her smile disappeared as he huffed while seemingly lost to say his next words. She saw Mikhail in a way that she never had before. He had never been angry before, and had never had reason to be. Fucking her and indulging all of his manly desires never made Mikhail feel anything except superficial pleasure and satisfaction.

Like one of Moscow's street dogs that becomes cornered and frightened, all Mikhail could do was lower his head below raised shoulders. "I was good to you, damn it!" he hissed through an exposed snarl. He closed his eyes, feeling his rage and disappointment as it pulsed through his veins.

"You were, and that's not the point, Mikhail. I don't want to be your pet anymore. A thousand other girls would trade places with me in a heartbeat, and they would be lucky. This is not about you."

Mikhail sarcastic chuckle and disbelieving nod confirmed his scepticism. "The whole 'it's not you, it's me' excuse, huh?"

"Well... yeah, actually."

"Funny, isn't it? You kicking me to the curb." Mikhail sat in momentary silence as he struggled to find his next words.

"Look Mikhail, I could have just done this by phone or, worse yet, sent you an text or something. I owe this to you because you are a good man who I have no reason to be unnecessarily spiteful to. You are a good man and you will get a lover who worships you. I'm not that girl."

Alexandra crept along the bench towards her coat, and away from Mikhail.

"Where are you going?" He looked at her like a bewildered child, his anxious eyes flitting in uncertainty.

She paused and looked back at her former lover before replying, "Away, Mikhail. Don't doubt yourself, darling. You were wonderful, kind and giving." Her words were poetic poison and were delivered like a melody. "You still are," she concluded softly as she began to leave. "You take care, and don't ever doubt yourself."

Her final words left him speechless and dazed. He watched her stride away and into the bleary brightness that collected like some transcendental portal at the restaurant's entrance. Her definition blurred into a hazy silhouette in an opaque cloud, leaving him misty eyed and heartbroken. She was indeed gone – gone seemingly into a futuristic dimension that no longer would include him.

Chapter 11

I

Alexandra seemed to walk aimlessly in the little market's aisles. There were only four aisles in Riga's, a family-run grocery store which Alexandra often visited. She loved their fresh fruit - tangerines from Israel and cantaloupes from America - but most of all she liked that they carried a variety of Mexican and Chinese products. Alexandra was addicted to salsa sauce and would find ways to incorporate it in many of her dishes. Yet tonight she seemed lost in introspection as she wondered from shelf to shelf with an empty red plastic basket in hand. She stood in front of a selection of pickles and stared at the sea of green before her. She never bought pickles, disliking all things sour. Nonetheless she stood there like a motionless statue and reflected to what possibly lay ahead.

Her mind raced back to the orphanage at a time when she was rocking on a swing, going back and forth ever so higher each time. She could see herself in front of a milky white sky void of any definition, while she laughed uncontrollably. Her white dress spilled out from the seat and flapped in the wind that she generated with an ever growing pace. No-one else was around her; however, she was swinging wildly as if there was no tomorrow or care in the world.

Alexandra's eyes fell, and the fantastical dream was replaced by yellow labels of the dill pickles that she now saw. An elderly woman stood next to her with a checkered scarf wrapped tightly around her head. With her hunched shoulders, large protruding nose and square build, she resembled a troll from Norse mythology. Her piercing eyes looked up at Alexandra whimsically, as if she knew intuitively that Alexandra was dreaming a mystical fantasy that never truly existed. The old lady stared, peering deeply into Alexandra's own private thoughts, and Alexandra thought of her own beauty that would one day surely fade like the dwindling light of Moscow's dusk that was now settling in.

She turned and walked away from the old lady, who followed every one of her elegant strides until she disappeared into the next aisle. Alexandra continued her shopping while simultaneously pondering the next steps of a plan which seemed to grow daily. What had started out as a passing thought was now taking form into something concrete.

Thirty minutes later Alexandra stood before her apartment with two plastic bags of food and her jumbo–sized Prada handbag, while she nervously fumbled with her door key. "Jesus!" she exclaimed with frustration as her unsteady hand fumbled about while trying to balance her evening's groceries. Finally she inserted the key after a desperate stab, and she pushed the cumbersome oak door open.

Alexandra entered and kicked the door closed with the back of her shoe. She dropped her purse on the sofa and made her way to the kitchen, while simultaneously kicking off her heels. In the corner of her eye she noticed the answering machine blinking with a new message. Alexandra worriedly bit her lip.

'Christ! Don't let it be,' she thought to herself. She had hoped Mikhail would not call and was hoping that he would not pester her into anger. She entered her spacious kitchen and tossed the bags onto the counter, and then quickly unbuttoned her coat. She separated all refrigerated products, fruits and canned goods methodically, before placing everything where they belonged. Life was such for Alexandra. Order and organisation was the one aspect of life that stood before all others. If it wasn't, then she could never possibly be successful in juggling two careers and her two identities.

It had always been that way, actually. Perhaps it came from an instinctive impulse to hoard as a little girl. A friend of the family who worked as a psychologist told her parents that adopted children often save everything given to them, and resist letting go. The notion of choice and surplus is unknown to these children, as it was for Alexandra. So it was that little Alexandra would line up her toys by size. Although she didn't have so many dolls and toys she would line them up from smallest to largest against her bedroom wall every night before falling asleep.

Today her compulsive attention to detail was no different. Her wardrobe was organised by colour and by type of clothes. T-shirts were hung before short dresses that were before longer gowns, and all were arranged by colour. Her shoes were lined like a rainbow from light to dark, and the products in her refrigerator were more organised than in the stores they were brought from.

A couple of moments later she entered her living room, and walked before the flashing answering machine. She stared at the black box on the Venetian-styled writing desk; it flickered back at her with its singular red blinking eye. She strode over to it, but before she pressed the machine's button, Alexandra paused puffed with uneasy nervousness.

"Hi Alexandra, it's your mother. Haven't heard from you for a while and wanted to talk to you."

Alexandra exhaled deeply and closed her eyes with relief. 'Jesus,' she thought, as she cancelled the message before it could finish. Avoiding her mother was typical, but tonight she was simply in no mood for a talk with the woman who she found so little connection with. A chat would just have to wait another day.

II

Alexandra stood in Sergi's office doorway nervously. She waited for him to notice her and, when he did, Sergi lowered his bifocals and replied matter-of-factly, "What?" He looked at her confused and with his mouth slightly open. A second or two passed, as both seemed trapped in a momentary trance. "For God's sake, Alex, what is it? You never ask my permission to come in here!"

He was right. Unless she could see that he was on the telephone, Alexandra would always barge in and demand his immediate attention. Sergi would constantly remind her that he was going to have his office door replaced so she could not see him. This, however, was the hollow threat that he had been repeating in vain for years now.

Alexandra entered cautiously like a nervous hunter entering a darkened cave, fully aware the sleeping bear must be near. She closed the door softly like never before and sauntered over to her boss with a serious stare.

"You ain't quitting, are you? Jesus, Alex – you've got a look that is scaring the shit out of me!"

"No, not at all."

She sat on one of his leather office chairs and landed with a heavy thud as if her delicate frame was twice the weight it actually was. She crossed her legs and leaned forward before continuing, "I need some time."

"Time?"

"Time off to… to… well."

Before she could continue Sergi roared in laughter, exposing his yellowing teeth, and slapped his hand hard against his knee. He leaned fully back in a leather chair that reclined with the force of his stocky frame.

"Time off? You scared the shit out of me for this!" His heavy laugh petered to a gentle chuckle, and he lurched forward towards Alexandra and cracked in a husky tone laced with sarcasm, "I thought it was something important."

Alexandra straightened her posture and raised her chin indigently, "It is something important. Important to me."

"How much time are we talking about?" Sergi's jolliness was replaced by a stern look of concern. He raised his spectacles so he could see Alexandra more clearly.

"I need a full week. Next Monday, I'd like to begin."

"Next Monday!" he replied incredulously. "It's Thursday already!"

"The Malloy case will be easily finished tomorrow, and that only leaves the new Shell revisions, but they aren't due until the end of the month." Alexandra paused while she leaned forward and said with straightforward assurance, "Anyway, that's a piece of cake for me."

Sergi rolled his eyes and shifted his lips from side to side while he digested the possibility. "Yeah. Why not?" he replied with a surreptitious glance, before rocking himself back upright and to the state he was in before Alexandra's uninvited visit. "Now, get out of here!" he retorted as his right hand motioned in an attempt to shoo Alexandra away.

Alexandra immediately rose from her chair and looked at her boss, who pretended to be engrossed in a document that was before him. "You're the best boss!" she replied, like a little girl who had just cunningly won over an unsuspecting father.

"Yeah, yeah. Whatever," he answered, like a defeated loser who knew he had been cunningly outwitted.

Alexandra strode out of his office, and just as the door was about to be closed Sergi sneaked a peek at his favourite nemesis as she walked away. A wry smile escaped his shrewd and carefully manipulated facade.

Alexandra, more than most women, was a master of her body, and she depended on it far more than the average woman. It provided her with most of her income and was the rare temple that so many men coveted. She hated the paradox. She was so much more intelligent than most anyone she knew. However, it was her body – that damned mass of flesh and bone – that defined her existence.

Alexandra fed into the paradox by worshipping it herself. She treated it to expensive creams, health care products, and by frequent massages and manicures. She shaped it from constant workouts, and fed it with a steady supply of healthy food and vitamin supplements that she took religiously. She wasn't even sure why she cared so much for her appearance; however, deep down she felt she knew where it came from.

Next week might change everything, she had thought often during the day. But she had to go and confront the whispering voice that so often haunted her thoughts at times like this. She lay on her bed for a moment more, her perfect naked body outstretched. She wondered not about the man she was surely going to fuck in a matter of hours, but about the woman she had fantasised about just as much as her new lover.

Alexandra wondered how her familiar smiling face had changed over the many years. A tiny tear began to spill out from a well that had begun to form from within her introspective eyes. The tear was a tangible reminder that Alexandra was still the lost little girl she was over twenty years ago, on the day she left Sister Masha to enter a world that she battled to find her rightful spot in. She wiped it away and closed her eyes as she breathed deeply and with purpose.

Alexandra sat up, and saw herself in the oversized mirror that hung over her dresser. The person who stared back sat with a glazed stare. The familiar curves and features were there, but the soul and the pain it harboured was exposed like never before. She closed her eyes once again and angled her head back, which allowed her hair to fall freely from off her shoulders. She instantly thought of so much. Flashes of her life passed before her and immediately to the present, where she once again opened her eyes to see her figurative twin staring back at her.

The naked woman looked so much like her physically, but she wondered how different she had become. The stranger in the mirror seemed so pathetic and lost, which was not what the confident woman on the bed that others saw her as. The sad image in the mirror was one in the same, and Alexandra felt hatred towards her own duplicity. She had indeed become something she barely recognised.

The little girl who played so innocently as a child and who dreamed of having a perfect husband and three babies had long ago been replaced by a jaded fighter, sceptical of people and of ever finding true love. How had it happened? she wondered. What had happened to becoming the veterinarian or the archeologist she wanted to be when she was an early teenager? The poltergeist staring back at her was an empty spirit trapped in a shell that despised her unfulfilled fantasies. She was rich, yet had fallen prey to selling her dignity to achieve her affluence.

She tightly shut her eyes as if the reality of her life could somehow disappear behind the darkness of her eyelids. No, she thought. I'm better than them.

Convincing herself that her life held some sort of influence was the battle Alexandra often fought. Her fine social charms and lady-like graces were proof that she was a socialite on the basis of her intelligence. Indeed, Alexandra could mingle with Moscow's upper echelon, and could succeed in becoming a chameleon that blended in perfectly. A classical education served her well, as did her worldly experiences, even if most of them were a result of paid trips by lovers on extended 'dates'.

She opened her eyes once again and rubbed her face and eyes as if the eradicate her temporary worthlessness. Alexandra needed to catch her taxi that she had arranged in twenty minutes, and she still needed to dress and apply her makeup. She disappeared into her bathroom and grabbed her makeup bag, which was huge. No woman should need such a wide array of liner, blusher and lipstick but, without such a plethora of choice, Alexandra felt incomplete.

Exactly twenty minutes later her mobile rang, and she peeked out her living room window and towards the street four stories below. A car waited in an illegal pedestrian zone with a soft stream of white smoke bellowing from its tailpipe. "Privet," she replied while striding towards her coat rack that stood directly by her front door. "Your taxi is here," replied a deep husky voice on the other end. "My number is URH 29."

Moments later, Alexandra watched Moscow pass from inside the dirty windows of her taxi. The small Hyundai crept along in the massive traffic like a spider crab fighting the tidal forces it crawled against. Eventually it would make it to shore, but only after a constant battle of nature and a head-first clash of the strong oceanic tide.

The city was alive in the chilly March evening.

People were walking everywhere like an unorganised army of ants, zipping all around their taxi when it was stuck in a jam or at a red light.

How the city was changing, she had often thought. Moscow was a fusion of West and East, Russian and everything else. Stalinist-styled buildings, once its only architectural style, sat shoulder to shoulder with modern structures that had sprung up wherever there was a free lot. The old hard-liners who once ruled the country with an iron fist had surely fled the fickle city by now. How could traditional communists bear to see their empire's capital resemble that of the once-hated West? Everywhere the city bore the new scars of capitalism like gaudy makeup on a circus clown. A huge neon hand grasping a twenty metre long Nokia mobile flashed atop an office building next to her, while the golden arches of McDonald's loomed directly ahead. She passed a KFC, Starbucks and a Zara before they turned again to yet another crowded street full of Western-branded retailers.

The driver said nothing, and Alexandra gently leaned against the window. His radio had played throughout the journey something unrecognisable and she thought it could be Georgian folk music.

Total crap, she thought. Alexandra had always hated the folk music that was still so popular with Russians. She was of a new generation whose early exposure to music had been influenced by the trance and house music that flooded Russia in 1991. David Guetta and even Depeche Mode were the sounds that she would lose herself to.

Eventually the taxi pulled off the busy street and forced itself into a tiny space between two parked cars in front of her restaurant. She handed him three hundred rubles as she said, "Keep the change." As she slammed the filthy door closed, she adjusted her short plaid skirt and tugged at her stockings. She instantly resumed the posture and grace that had temporarily eluded her, before striding confidently to the restaurant only twenty metres away. She opened the heavy oak-panelled doors which revealed a smoky, cavernous, but well-lit interior full of gold, red and silver.

The doorman relieved her of the door and motioned with his outstretched hand to a smiling woman with jet-black hair. She stood behind a padded podium and seemed anxious to greet her new guest – almost as if it were her first day on the job, where the thrill of novelty hadn't yet worn off to resignation.

"Dobry vecher, Ma'am. Welcome to Casanova's," she said with girlish enthusiasm.

Ma'am? Alexandra thought to herself as she felt the weight of her eyelids, longing to fall. It was Alexandra's unusual and instinctive reaction to when she felt old. Christ, I may be only two years older than her.'

"Are you dining alone or meeting someone?" she asked in the juvenile pitch of a twelve-year-old girl.

Before answering, she saw Clint weaving between two tables and smiling at her with a boyish grin as wide as the Povarskaya Street directly outside. "Alexandra, Alexandra!" he shouted, as if she hadn't already noticed him. She noticed the patrons around him suddenly stop eating and look up at the childish commotion he had caused with his enthusiasm. A second later, Clint stood before Alexandra at the table. He kissed her emphatically on her cheek before turning to the somewhat startled hostess and replying, "She's with me."

"You think she couldn't figure that out?" Alexandra quipped with a telling smile.

"Damn, you are gorgeous tonight," he said as his

eyes ran over her entire body.

"If you are going to check out my ass, then be careful you don't run into one of these fine patrons."

"I wasn't checking out your ass," he replied with hushed indignation. "I was checking out your sexy legs," he whispered into her ear.

Clint pulled out the large red leather chair covered in golden rivets. Alexandra marvelled at the gigantic seat, which looked borrowed from some eighteenth century Baroque palace. She let the chair embrace her, feeling its warmth immediately as Clint walked around the table.

"Hmm, I like this place!" she exclaimed in girlish satisfaction.

Clint plopped into his own chair and replied with a satisfied smile, "I knew you would. Isn't it cool?"

The two sat across from each other, and their eyes locked into a comfortable gaze for a few seconds. Neither spoke, but both smiled like two teenagers on a first date alone.

"God, I've been looking forward to seeing you," Clint said.

"You say that every time I see you." Alexandra's quip was pointed and sharp, but her smile eradicated any ill-meaning.

"It's because I do," he said as he leaned back into the chair. When he did, the cracking of the leather resonated as a dull backdrop to his reply. "You know Alex, I've got all this work going on and...and..."

"And there's so much going on, yet I keep finding myself thinking of you." He paused momentarily and gazed at her wantonly. "A lot," he concluded.

Alexandra felt the sting of his overpowering honesty like a needle's prick, drawing not a drop of blood, but rather jabbing at her uneasy consciousness. Somehow she believed him; however, it was easier to make herself believe he was lying. He simply sat there, smiling at her innocently like a pre-schooler at Christmas who was overwhelmed with the pomp and pageantry. How gorgeous and perfect he must see her at this moment.

Perfect? she thought. If only he knew. She forced a wry smile and then looked up to the waiter, who was approaching their table.

"Would the madam and gentleman care for a beverage before dinner this evening?" The waiter stood before them in perfect posture, and with a bent arm that carried a draped white handkerchief. Alexandra thought the scene couldn't be more quintessentially perfect. Then the thought occurred to her that she was actually dating Clint.

The thought sent a rush of blood through her body so rapidly that she clutched at her cloth napkin with one hand, and at the edge of the tablecloth that hung near her lap. She grabbed at each with instinctive panic while Clint calmly reviewed the wine list, unaware of his date's sudden panic attack. She could feel a lump in her throat, and her body's heat flash left her desiring a cold drink. "I really need a glass of Rosinka," she blurted.

The waiter nodded while Clint peered over the menu with a surprised look. "Rosinka?"

"Water," she replied in a hushed tone.

"Ahh. Would you care for wine, or is water enough?" he asked softly.

She regained her composure quickly to coolly respond, "You pick."

Clint smiled, and she did likewise. However her forced smile only concealed her embarrassment, and the sudden reality that she was truly becoming involved with a man in a way she had steadfastly refused... or rather, not known.

How? she wondered as she looked at Clint inquisitively.

The better question was why? Why was it that Alexandra felt these raw emotions that suddenly raged throughout her? Why did fear, anxiousness and uncontrolled hysteria seep from every pore? If Alexandra could only shed away the many layers of protective emotional armour that clung onto her like a compression-fit shell, then the answer would be painfully obvious. She had never given herself to a man beyond her sexuality. Looking at this gentle man standing there reminded her that she wanted more than sex and simple companionship.

"Alex?" Clint asked. His words filled her ears, but it took a couple seconds for Alexandra to register their meaning. "Alex? You there?" he asked again.

She blinked her eyes twice, smiled widely, and then replied matter-of-factly, "Of course. Have you decided?"

"I asked you if you would like the house Cabernet." His tone underscored that she had been caught while lost in her emotions.

"That sounds wonderful," she responded emphatically as she looked directly to the waiter. He nodded slightly in agreement and replied, "Two glasses of the house Cabernet and one glass of Rosinka. I'll bring the Madam her water immediately."

Alexandra looked at Clint again and smiled knowingly. Maybe this is worth a shot, she contemplated.

"What? You've got something going on in that head, Alex!" Clint's tone was of nervous anxiety. She would hardly come clean with her private thoughts. Not for now, at least.

"I was merely thinking that you've got to learn the brands of bottled water if you're ever going to survive in this city."

She giggled softly and reached her hands across the table, cupping his own. She felt his tender skin and the warmth that it exuded before she continued, "I've wanted to see you too; I just now realised it more than before."

III

Hours later, Alexandra was again in the bedroom she remembered so well. Clint was there before her and moving ever closer. She could smell his cologne, and the wolfish tang of perspiration. Their combined scent grew stronger as he embraced her and began kissing her mouth with a savage softness. She could feel her knees weaken, and as he moved towards her neck she breathed in a deep breath of the surrounding humidity. His hands were now under her perfectly starched shirt, and he stared at her hidden breasts, which heaved up and down from inside it. The outline of her aroused nipples poked from inside her lacy bra and he began to swell in excitement.

"So," he murmured. His head was slanted to one side, but his cool collected composure defied his desire. Most men would have attacked her flesh like a hungry lion on a weakened zebra, but not Clint. He casually stood before her and looked straight at her with a telling smile.

She held up her skirt with one hand, leaving the other by her side as he began to reach down between her legs, and she let herself be overtaken by his caressing. First her breasts were teased, and now he began to manipulate her ever so gently by stroking her – everywhere, that is, except directly on her other lips, which moistened in anticipation.

Her clitoris swelled and begged to be stimulated, or at least all the nerve-endings told her this – the same ones that had been aching for this since before she even arrived at his apartment. Alexandra gasped as a single finger grazed the front of her vagina, and she began to wiggle her hips instinctively to the sexual rhythm playing inside her body.

"Hmm," he murmured in approval from beneath his breath.

Alexandra bit her lips and nearly closed her eyes under the heavy eyelids which seemed like miniature hanging weights. Her body ached to lie on his nearby bed, as purely standing was becoming increasingly difficult. One of his hands now stimulated her perky tits, while the other stroked her swollen pussy. Clint kissed her ear and slipped his tongue into it as he began to finger her.

"I think I might fall over," she moaned in a gravely low-pitched voice that ached for more.

"Well, brace yourself against the wall, because I've only just begun," he chided while he increased his rhythm, like some sort of sadistic punishment. He continued to stroke her insides like a guitarist playing a slow ballad.

At first he stroked in a sort of melodic rhythm that left her floating in a hypnotic state, but then his movements became more aggressive, more rapid. His ballad became a full-on rock concert that left Alexandra's body convulsing and quivering, shaking to the sound of the measured and constant beat. What started so slowly was now a violent storm of sexual passion where the puppet master's fingers controlled his wanting puppet from within. Alexandra floated outside of her physical body like some sort of departed spirit rising to heaven.

And then she came. Alexandra exploded right then in massive wrenching waves, while Clint's free hand embraced her weakened body, cradling and supporting her as she double backed the crashing waves of pleasure that continued to wash over her.

"Oh, God," she whispered as the orgasm began to die. He held her for a little while longer while she struggled to raise herself upright and regain the feeling of her legs, which had seemingly deserted her. At that moment she could feel his own organ on her exposed thigh, through the cloth of his trousers.

Finally her desire to lie on his inviting bed was realised, as he lifted her quickly onto it. He lowered her on top of his firm mattress and she was relieved to finally be off her feet. However, her reprieve was short lived as he turned Alexandra over so her face was nearly buried in the softness of his large pillow. She felt his hands graze her again, wanting – she was still turned on though, and welcomed the attack.

She felt her skirt come off and she knew her ass was nearly fully exposed to the stare he surely was enjoying. She could not see her lover, but she knew what was happening at that very second. The familiar sound of his zip whooshing down left her tensing in anticipation. His hand pressed on her back, flattening her even further, while his other hand slipped aside her thong. Then there was the sound of the condom package being torn and the slight delay that it took him to put the rubber on.

Before she could think of what would most certainly happen next, she gasped at the sudden feeling of being filled by his swollen member. His cock simultaneously rushed in and he began to thrust hard, while occasionally stopping to push even deeper inside her, leaving Alexandra to gasp in appreciation.

She turned her head to one side and gasped to every thrust, feeling him swell even further. She could barely see her lover and she knew that he was nearing the end. His ever thickening cock assured her of it. She closed her eyes and waited for Clint's explosion, as she could again feel her own orgasm coming. A second, a third and a final deep thrust sent them both into a synchronised climax that seemed to last a full thirty seconds. In fact, it was surely far shorter; however, time and space stood still while they both came.

The two lay on top of the bed as a singular heap of heated flesh, pumping blood and lost thoughts; their bodies intertwined like twisted vines across a trestle. The afterglow of their passion dimmed into a softer tender moment of reflection, where each drifted to the thoughts of their own fantasy.

Alexandra's eyes remained closed, as if to stay trapped in the moment and to squeeze every final tingling sensation that her body still produced. Clint's breath began to slow and he indulged in his dominating position over her. He felt like he was a protective human blanket which covered her nearly completely.

"You feel so... so... perfect," he whispered in her ear, which was only a centimetre or two from his mouth.

His words broke the sensation that she was floating alone in some sort of gravity-free blanket where the physical real world seemed so far removed. Clint's bedroom had become a portal to a fourth or fifth dimension where reality relented to a surreal world of fantasy and pleasure, far away from the vulgar city that lay outside. Alexandra's eyes remained closed as she indulged in feeling, enjoying every last bit of the moment he had given her.

It then occurred to her how long it had been since she had had sex that left her feeling so satisfied...and so out of control. She wondered how she allowed him to ravage her like he had. How was it that she relented without thinking? She had always been the predator who carefully manipulated every single moment in every single sexual escapade, but not tonight. Not the time before with him, either.

"I want to stay," she demanded with authority.

He looked at her with puzzled confusion before answering, "I never wanted you to leave."

She leaned forward and met him with a slow passionate kiss, feeling his tenderness and sincerity in the hand that touched her cheek softly. The polarity left her feeling woozy and wanting to crawl deep underneath the inviting sheets that Clint exposed as he pulled off the thick burgundy and cream comforter.

He motioned for her to be first to enter the inviting bed with an outstretched hand. A moment later they were again intertwined as a singular mass of humanity – embraced as a cuddled pair in a spooning position that left each contented. She felt completely protected and secure. It felt good, yet strange. She buried herself as deep as she could into his embrace, and absorbed every bit of his enveloping warmth.

I like this, she thought. "This feels so damn good." Nonetheless, it was a thought she was somehow afraid to say out loud.

As if her lover was reading her mind, the silence was broken at that very second by the faint whisper of his words. "What are you thinking?"

She imagined that her thoughts had escaped and hung over her, like words trapped in a bubble from a cartoon character. Her eyes darted back and forth as her mind raced for a reply.

"Nothing," she blurted. She closed her eyes and winced in embarrassment at the silly and unbelievable answer.

"Yeah, sure." Clint's answer back proved he had read right through her transparency. "Come on, sweetie. Open up." His reply was so soft and gentle that she closed her eyes to appreciate its tone more, and then she digested the words:

Open up.

The two words stabbed her like an impaling sword through her gut. In that second Alexandra wanted to tell him everything, to pour out every bit of darkness and truth in a tsunami of honesty. For the first time in her life she wanted to flee her figurative second skin, and reveal the inner person she had repressed for so long. She couldn't. Not right now.

A minute passed where all that could be heard was the distant traffic of the city around them. They laid together, breathing slowly and calmly as each absorbed one another and the moment.

"What is your biggest dream?" Alexandra asked softly. "One that you know that you never can fulfil?"

"To be a writer." His answer was quick, and guaranteed that it was genuine.

"What's stopping you?"

"Besides reality? That's what usually gets in the way of dreams, isn't it?"

His reply left her suddenly feeling its truth. Reality was the cold emotionless entity that forced its malevolent will on everyone. It certainly had for her.

"I'm leaving for a trip," she said.

Clint raised himself partly from her and propped up on one elbow. "When?"

"In a couple of days. I'm going away to Perm for a few days."

"I didn't know," he replied with melancholy. After another moment of long silence Clint continued,

"What's in Perm?"

"Family." Alexandra's reply lacked any emotion, which left Clint wondering.

"I thought you said your parents were dead?"

Alexandra's eyes rolled in the irony. "Yeah, I did, but family can be more than parents alone."

The truth was that Alexandra had three mothers in Perm to whom she felt a full range of emotional attachment. Her adoptive mother she knew well but cared very little about, while Sister Masha she barely knew and wanted to care more for. Then there was also her birth mother, who she never knew but who tugged at her thoughts.

There was so much for him to learn about her. Then again, there was still much for Alexandra to discover about herself. If only he knew then he surely would leave. That was the thought she couldn't eradicate from her mind. If only he knew, she pondered in quiet introspection.

She thought of how to change the subject, and then a sense of melancholy overcame her. "Where would you go if the whole world were about to end? Where would you want to spend your last days?" she asked softly.

Her question seemed to come from nowhere; however, pillow talk was often such between them. Clint smiled at her from behind and chuckled lightly.

"I know exactly, but you first," he replied.

She felt him press against her, and his chin which resting neatly on top of her head like a bird comfortably perched atop its swing. She thought for a moment and let her mind naturally drift to the one place which always remained in the back of her mind.

"There's a place..." She stopped while she suddenly remembered the first time she was there, and could see it through her naïve childish eyes from so long ago.

"Yeah. And?" he asked.

"There's this lake outside of Perm called the Gayva. When I was a little girl my family would visit it every summer and rent a cottage along its shore. I'd watch the sun set and try to catch the sun rise every morning. It was always so quiet and peaceful there. Sometimes I wish I could hear the sounds of the water slapping the beach, and the elk in the distance. I miss that."

Alexandra's voice was filled with nostalgia for a time long since forgotten. Clint wondered privately what the scene she described could have looked like. He imagined snow-capped mountains in the background and spindly pine trees lining the lake, while large eagles soared above.

"Describe it to me," he demanded. "What does it look like?"

"The lake wasn't that big. It would take forty-five minutes to circle, and it was heavily wooded all around." She paused and closed her eyes to recapture the essential elements. "The wooden cottages were small and dark green." She chuckled when she recalled that they had no air-conditioning and only a basic small electric heater in each room. "The mornings were always so fresh!" she reminisced in laughter.

"You mean fucking cold, right?" he replied in soft laughter.

"Okay, they were cold!"

Alexandra paused and thought back to the many times she was there, and then recollected, "The deer, really big ones with huge horns, would walk around in the distance. You could hear them so loudly and clearly. I used to think they were calling just for me."

The two lay together, and were enveloped as one. He squeezed her tightly as the story faded into a still but reassuring silence. She smiled when she thought about her childhood favourite place. "That's where I'd go to if the world would end." Her words were certain, yet the tone was hopeful. Dying there seemed to be a happy experience for Alexandra, and Clint's hidden smile meant he understood.

"There's a little hotel that sits on its shore that I would buy, you know?"

Clint nodded and mumbled approvingly.

"I've always wanted to buy that hotel. They rent these cute little pedal boats as well as small electric ones. Poppa would always take me in one."

Her voice was filled with such happiness, and Clint hugged her a bit tighter. He thought about telling her where his fantastical escape was, but just when he was about to speak, the gentle signs of his lover's peaceful slumber replaced the moment. She lay in his arms asleep completely encapsulated within his protective embrace, and she breathed with gentle deliberation, lost in her own serene dream. Clint buried his forehead into the back of her hair and inhaled her flowery scent of perfume, shampoo and soaps. He wondered if she was now dreaming – if so, he hoped she was again at the shores of Gayva. He wished she was sitting on its gravelly shore and watching the sunset from behind the distant horizon as her wild deer called for her to join them inside the nearby forest.

If only he knew.

IV

Alexandra knew that she had always chased the men who were unavailable in some sense. Either they were married, emotionally unavailable, or sometimes too cowardly or broken from previous experiences to ever become really emotionally involved. More often than not they were too self-absorbed or shallow to really be capable of caring for her deeply. These were the ones she chased.

She wondered why she did this and realised that her sense of freedom was vitally important to her and, in her experience, only the men that ran away or weren't really involved didn't threaten it. Her other lovers had been demanding, controlling and possessive. Alexandra needed to be free to follow her impulses and not to plan. She had no desire to be stuck at home with children and a man who, she felt, would soon stop appreciating her once he knew he had her secured. She'd never been with a man who gave her complete freedom while also being there for her one hundred percent. The permissive freedom she needed was not so much one to be with other men, but to be as social, unsocial or impulsive as she liked. However much she liked a man, she disliked the feeling that came with a relationship –the pressure she needed to see someone a certain amount to avoid offending them. Sometimes she felt like being untraceable for a week or so at a time, for no particular reason than that she liked her space.

With Clint things were different – his stability was actually what attracted her, and it was this that made her think that perhaps this relationship would last longer than her others. At the same time she was aware of the fact that perhaps she was attracted to this quality now as it was so new and because she was tired of ultimately being alone, even when with a lover.

She also knew the novelty would wear off and that he would probably soon start to become more controlling, which would eventually leave her feeling restless, caged and in need of freedom. Stability, and someone's loyalty, came with a certain demand upon her conscience, and she was not used to having to listen to her conscience or anyone's demands. She cherished her freedom, although it made her lonely, and, while she could surrender it for a year or so, she knew it would take a very special person to manage the balance.

She was not sure she could commit to any one man forever. Then again, she hadn't seen herself falling this much before she met Clint. Perhaps, in time, she would fall more and might, one day, actually be able to commit whole-heartedly. It was something she slightly wanted and yet feared. She reasoned that to give your whole heart to a man was surely going to end in tears, and they would be her tears.

Alexandra liked Clint's naivety. It was something she had lost – something she could never get back and, while she felt herself superior in some ways for being so much worldlier, at the same time she felt more sullied for it. Clint offered her an open heart – something she was not brave enough to do. She also found him very attractive. Not only physically and intellectually, but he also had the irresistible combination of being both strong and vulnerable. When he smiled or looked at her it was sometimes with a certain shyness that she found appealing, and which made her feel safe.

She had been in love once before and it had taken her over two and a half years to really get over it. She doubted it would take so long with Clint, but she was unsure how much it would hurt. Alexandra had never anticipated that losing her first love –Denis - would hurt so badly. In fact she had never intended to fall in love with Denis at all. He had been a married man and a wealthy one, and she had initially been attracted to the restaurants he took her to and gifts he bought her as much as she was to him. She enjoyed the way he would spoil her, and his romantic gestures. Such as when they went to a hotel suite in Sochi and he had arranged for rose petals to be sprinkled over the floor, the bed, the warm waiting bubble bath - or when he arranged for a horse and carriage to take them to dinner.

She had thought he adored her and always would but, when she eventually fell for him, his attitude had changed entirely. No longer attracted by the chase, he suddenly found that in the place of the elusive, sexual and independent woman he had been dating, there was a vulnerable girl who showed the beginnings of jealousy and possessiveness. The more Alexandra had cared for him, the less attractive she became to him. He had no intention of leaving the wife he loved –or the children he loved even more. Alexandra had become an annoyance. The way he had ended the relationship was not graceful. He simply failed to turn up to the restaurant they had arranged to meet at. Later the next day – after several missed calls and texts from Alexandra – he simply texted back saying that it was not working and that he no longer had romantic feelings. He only answered one of her calls after that. Denis informed her that she was becoming a nuisance and that his wife was there, which was very inconvenient. Alexandra gave up calling after he answered the phone twice, pretending that he could not hear who was on the end of the line.

His behaviour had left Alexandra totally disorientated and broken. She had difficulty in forgetting him, which actually took several months. Immediately afterwards she dated and slept with numerous men and clients but she was never with someone who she didn't, at least at some point, think of him. Eventually she forced herself to stop thinking about Denis, and she forced herself to write out and focus on only his negative qualities or comments. Even today she sometimes wondered what she would do or say if he called her. Ultimately though she would always remember the callous way that he abandoned her, and know that she would never see him again.

After him, Alexandra had never given her heart to anyone so completely. Deeply she knew she wanted to, but was terribly afraid. For now it was better to give men the chase that they desired, or give them the aloofness that drove them so crazy. No, she knew now that Clint would morph into quite a different person if she loved him without reserve, and she knew she had to resist the urge to let him into her heart completely.

Chapter 12

I

Clint stood behind Gaby who was pounding at her keyboard with an index finger from each hand. It wasn't a simple keyboard from any ordinary computer. The contraption in front of her towered above and had multiple screens, gauges and coloured buttons. Gaby's right hand then grabbed a pencil and began scribbling on a mousepad. The face before her on the primary central screen was of a man who could have been anyone. Superimposed on it were dotted lines that seemed like the marks plastic surgeons use for reference as they carve up their patients.

"So what do you have so far?" Clint asked with his arms folded.

"We've got this upgrade software that unfortunately requires a lot of manual manipulation before we can let it do its thing."

"Its thing?" he asked.

Clint's forte was processes, not the details in how technology worked. To him Frank and Gaby just fed the machine, and somehow it gave them what he needed. He knew it was more than that, but really had no idea just how skilled the agent before him was.

"Well before we were using the popular recognition algorithms from a software programme called Eigenface."

"Okay.... and?"

"Well, the problem is that the technology is changing so rapidly that it makes Eigenface old-school."

"So what you are telling me is we can't find our guy because the software is obsolete?"

Gaby let out a laugh – well really it was more a

171

nasal snort than a laugh.

"No, no – not at all," she replied with emphatic firmness. "Now we have this three-dimensional face recognition that uses the visual details of the skin and turns the subject's unique lines, patterns and the spots apparent in a person's skin into a mathematical space."

"So a facial fingerprint, then?"

"Exactly! The chance of recognising subjects is shown to increase by up to twenty-five percent."

"So what's up with the manual stuff you said you are doing?"

"Well, I ran the bodyguard through the old programme, but came up with nothing. I'm flattening photos using it.''

Clint leaned forward and could see how Gaby was able to manipulate the face manually – it looked as if it was turning ever so slightly before him. "And then?"

"Then it won't take too long. If he's ever been photographed by one of our own then I'm pretty sure we can identify him." Gaby paused and, by the sound of her exhale, Clint knew he was about to hear the word 'but'.

"But that is going to take a lot of time to do this. I've got a few hundred to do still."

"How much time?"

"Probably another five days, maybe six."

Clint's head fell in disgust. He ran his fingers through his hair in frustration. He wasn't angry at Gaby, but rather cursed the greatest enemy to the espionage community – time. He looked over at the work station next to Gaby, and Frank merely nodded his head without provocation. Clint moved in behind Frank, while peering over his shoulder at the figure in one of the screens.

"How close do you think you are?" Clint asked, as if he already had resigned to the certain explanation that surely would follow.

"I don't have anything, sir. Both the woman and our mystery man are ghosts. It's going to be tough at best. Look," he said as he pointed to his computer screen. In it was the woman who Marco had photographed; however, her features were unclear.

"Even after I blow it up, the face is just too darkened and blurred for a definitive match. She's also wearing a hat, which adds this shadow right here. The nose is really important, and this is the best shot, so I'm working on it, sir. Just don't hold your breath."

Clint peered at the woman, and he skewed his head while simultaneously squinting. She resembled his new lover, and he thought how similar they were. However, beautiful blonde and slender woman all looked alike from far away photographs. This one stared out from under a hat and huddled in a coat which hid her unquestionable sexy curves.

"This is often the case, sir. These guys get a different woman in every city. She's probably a call girl or something."

Clint just rubbed his nose and bit his lower lip before replying, "And the guy? He's the important one."

Frank just looked at him apathetically and with a pouting frown that told him everything.

"Work on him. He's the priority." Clint left the two through a slender metal door that creaked as it opened and closed. At the end of the hall was Ron Billup's office, which he strode confidently towards.

He stood before the grey door – it was without any distinction or pomp. Only a small rectangular plastic plate with the title 'Director Billups'. He tapped twice on the door with his knuckles, and the reverberation echoed loudly through the hall.

"Yeah!" came the quick reply.

Clint half-opened the door and stuck his head through before speaking. "Nothing on Gaby and Frank's two bogeys. It doesn't look good."

Ron peered over his out-dated glasses, and shrugged his shoulders. Clint then cautiously entered his office and gently pushed the door closed. The look on Clint's face implied he had an idea, and he stood fidgeting with his hair.

"What?" Director Billups simply stared back with a look of total bewilderment sketched across his face.

"You've got a way apart from normal channels to access additional identity files, yeah?"

Ron just looked at him, confused, with his mouth slightly open. He squinted sharply while throwing himself back into his chair. He stuck one of the legs from his spectacles into the corner of his mouth. "What are you thinking?" he asked in a tone laced with both curiosity and a hint of anger.

"Sir, I'm thinking we may be looking at this the wrong way. What if the two subjects are somehow on the inside and beyond our internal data bank? If we could access every governmental agency and contractors sponsored by us, then maybe...."

"Wait a minute!" Ron snapped forward like a cobra striking at its prey, and he tossed his glasses atop some papers that were predictably scattered over his cluttered desk. "You want me to divert this into an internal investigation before we emphatically conclude that those two aren't some yo-yos from the outside?"

"I've got a hunch..."

"A hunch? A fucking hunch! Great!" He shook his head disbelieving as a sarcastic chuckle escaped his disbelieving smirk. "You expect me to go to my boss and say, hey – my guys think it might be one of your guys because we have a hunch?"

"Uh, no sir."

"So what, then? What's the God damn point?"

"Let me put it this way." Clint strode over to the empty chair in front of Billups' desk and flung himself into it as he continued, "Say we don't get a hit. We discover this in... let's say five days, because that's the timeline we have to assume. And I'm here again in this very chair telling you we got zip. Absolutely dick shit nothing. Then what?"

"We continue with the mission. Did you forget Krokav is who we are after? The biggest weapon's dealer in the whole fucking world. That guy?"

"Yes, of course, and we don't deviate from that. Something tells me Florian's memory is right."

Again Ron tossed himself into the back of his chair, and the sound of its aged leather creaked and groaned as he squirmed uncomfortably and searched for a reply.

"We can still run a parallel investigation, but just expand our search," Clint added empathically.

"Who are you thinking?" Ron's reply suggested he just may be open to the idea, and Clint quickly pounced on his opening.

"Contractors. And Blackwater too. Blackwater scares the shit out of me."

Ron leaned slightly forward and exhaled softly, as if he was defeated to compromise. "I'm not going to Director Whitaker with hunches and speculation."

The two sat staring at each other in desperation - each was trapped in distinctively different thoughts. Clint was acting on his instinct, which had rarely let him down, while Ron pondered the formality of protocol that had served him well throughout his career. He hadn't become a director by following the play-book and its rigid rules. The seconds passed and as they sat with blank.

Finally Ron pushed a file away, and slid his arm into its place. "I can do this. I've got an old buddy in the Pentagon who heads up all the federal records on our contractors. He handles only defence and technology and not civilian contracts, but that's the best I can do."

Ron's face instantly transformed into despair and regret as he continued, "God damn it all if I ever live to regret this. I'm going to retire soon!"

"I'll take it, sir. Let me know when we can get the additional files, yeah?" Like a spring releasing itself from its coil, Clint popped up from his chair and headed to the door. As he opened it he then stopped and looked over his shoulder. "Thank you, sir. I hope I don't let you down."

"If you don't then it means we have a far bigger issue than containing Krokav."

Clint paused at the door and sighed deeply. "I know, Sir. I know exactly."

II

Perm was the kind of city that its refugees want to forget. It was a centre of manufacturing during the reign of the Communists, but now it was like so many Russian cities that were dying a slow death of mass migration. It didn't always used to be that way. In former times Perm was a vibrant mix of commerce, industry and nightlife, which bordered a figurative desert of nothingness. Moscow was six-hundred miles southwest and Ekaterinburg was its closest metropolis neighbour; albeit an additional two-hundred miles southeast.

Like so many of Russia's larger cities, Perm was a patchwork of neighbourhoods, mostly poor slums or middle-class sections that comprised a city of just over one million inhabitants. Alexandra's orphanage was one of four that the city created in the 1970's when pregnancy amongst teenagers and unmarried women was widespread. It was Russia's dirty secret that people never discussed and that the Party leaders tried to sweep under the rug. That was until the rampant number of abandoned babies finally forced their hand. Alexandra's orphanage catered to the young and shamed women in Perm's south-eastern quarter called Yuznoye. She never knew exactly how she ended up there or the events that followed. She was born in a Perm hospital, yet which one exactly remained a mystery. Her birth certificate was in the city's archives, but was something that Alexandra had no access to. The Communists had decided long before that orphan's records would remain sealed. Male orphans would grow to become soldiers, factory workers or simple farm help. Females were often trained in service sector jobs like waitressing, room maids, or cleaning ladies in governmental buildings. Their education was simple. Humanities and higher mathematics were the kind of courses that simply were not considered.

Whether it was days, weeks or months after Alexandra's birth, all she knew was that Sister Maria somehow had become her surrogate mother. Of course, Alexandra always knew she wasn't really her mother. After all, she was one of over a hundred children in the orphanage.

Alexandra escaped her dreary destiny on a Spring day in 1985. The Malikovs came quietly to the orphanage administrators in private shame and desperation. Natalie had miscarried for the third time the previous November. The doctor's news that she was unable to bear children was the lead weight that crushed her and Fedor's world. They had both wanted a child so badly, and unlike most couples in that time it was a daughter that they preferred. The thought of funnelling their artistic and classically-educated backgrounds into a piano-playing ballerina was their ultimate fantasy. Somehow a boy just didn't compliment the dream like Alexandra would.

Their hearts melted the moment they saw Alexandra playing alone with her pink stuffed cat. Although so many other children packed the playroom that day and scurried around the strange guests, it was quiet Alexandra who they decided on immediately. Nonetheless, they would have to wait for another six weeks before Alexandra could leave the unassuming orphanage. The wheels of Russian bureaucracy moved slowly on a low priority such as adoption.

Alexandra remembered the day she was taken away. She didn't understand what was really happening. She thought she was just going away for a short time or for some sort of holiday. However, for her to comprehend that she would never return to the only home she ever knew was beyond her childish mind. Eventually the reality crystallised, and the frantic-paced world she left was replaced by quiet structure.

At first there was the unfamiliarity of space and ownership. Dolls belonged only to her. Games were always accessible. Her bed was so large that she could spread her legs and arms and still not reach the sides. Yet the comfort of aimless living was substituted with formal arrangements. Soon her parents demanded contributions to the household chores, and, within one month, she began piano and dance lessons.

She hated such formalities. At the orphanage she lived in a fairytale world complete with imaginary creatures and friends. Alexandra could replace her boredom with imagined games of hide and seek, and she often pretended to be a Czar princess while the other children were her humble court. Sometimes Alexandra would take a simple twig and use it as a regal wand and tap other smaller children on their heads as if to anoint them into her royal court.

Now her new mother demanded so much, and she would crack her hands or rear with a wooden spoon when Alexandra stepped out of line. That didn't happen often as Alexandra truly feared her strict mother, realising she would often give way to rants and tantrums. Natalie would sometimes break down and cry after moments of hysterical volatility and abuse. Alexandra merely receded back into her imaginary world where no-one shouted or disturbed her.

"Why do you make me do this to you?" Natalia would sob to Alexandra.

Alexandra would never answer. Instead she would just stand in quiet stillness and hope for the return of normalcy. Eventually it would come; however, it led Alexandra to escape more and more in a world of make-believe. The same world where she lived as a princess who longed to return to her palace and the only friends she had ever known.

The orphanage was an ironic refuge and point of normality for little Alexandra as she grew up. Now she was older, she daydreamed along a desolate highway. She felt that the pull of her past was a magnet and her car was the steel that slowly was being drawn by some sort of undeniable force.

She thought of Sister Masha's kindness and attention and wondered again what it would be like to meet her. The fact was that the Sisters really did not have much time for individual care; however, somehow Alexandra imagined that she was more special than the other children. She remembered fondly the three or four times in a day when Sister Masha would sit with her and compliment whatever she was doing. Praise was the emotional candy that fuelled little Alexandra's existence, whereas Natalia's praise was only given after a personal sacrifice from her. The thought that Sister Masha may be dead caused Alexandra to blink and shake her head. I need her, she thought to herself.

It was almost five o'clock when Alexandra finally reached Perm. No place in Russia smelled quite like Perm. Somehow all the factories made the city smell overripe, like fruit left too long in the sun. It smelled pungent, like a drunk's breath after a drinking binge.

And it smelled of sweat. Alexandra had never entirely forgotten the industrial unique stench of the city, which reminded her of a smelly locker room. She was sure that the people of Perm didn't notice it, but she did. As a teenager she had fantasised about a place smelling of exotic flowers and expensive perfumes, of beautiful cities full of grand buildings and populated by smiling people wearing bright colours.

She had thought that place existed in Moscow; she'd seen it in the magazines she coveted throughout her whole childhood. Although her parents were not poor, they certainly were not rich. The piano, dance and fine manners seemed an empty and clumsy façade to the harsh realities that they lived in a grimy industrial void. None of that mattered. Alexandra had promised herself that someday, somehow, she would live in Moscow - and she did. For now, though, she was back at Perm to confront what she always suppressed.

She had left at eight and only stopped twice for less than ten minutes. The little compact she rented coped well; nevertheless, it left her legs aching as she stepped out to get gasoline on Perm's perimetre. She went inside to buy a map and asked for directions.

The man looked up to her with his sunken eyes; the sight of her beauty ignited them into a sparkle. He smiled and motioned with a crooked index finger over his shoulder. "Down the road until the red light where the flower ladies are. Then you turn right and eventually you are there." He smiled and swayed a bit to his left and then right in a wobbling motion, like a defective matryoshka doll.

"Thank you," she replied with a soft smile and a nod of her head.

Alexandra drove away from the stares of the old man and the twenty-something attendant. In her mirror she could see the old man peering from within the window while the gangly attendant stood in apparent awe. Alexandra could only chuckle from under her breath, and looked over her left shoulder to a road that was now void of any traffic.

She had followed the old man's directions and was now in a busy neighbourhood that could have been any of Moscow's poorer areas. Large apartment blocks looked as if they were ready to collapse, and a myriad of shanty kiosks served as points to buy flowers, snacks and magazines. People hurried about, most carrying plastic bags of products recently bought. There were surprisingly few cars to battle but, then again, she was in Perm. Moscow's traffic dwarfed every other city, which gave the perspective that there was little here in Perm.

Alexandra pulled into a parking space in front of a stretch of stores, hoping for directions. The scene was far removed from the sights that Alexandra usually was familiar with. What lay before her was gravel, dirt and dilapidation. Impoverished souls scurried about the deteriorated store fronts. Most were elderly women and small children who skipped about obliviously.

She entered a flower shop and immediately the three women inside turned to her, freezing in a gaze that was either fear or awe. In fact it was neither, but rather the deep curiosity towards a stranger so out of place that it required a stare to register. Alexandra was definitely not from this neighbourhood, but therein laid the paradox. She was indeed from this neighbourhood and it struck her immediately that she could herself been one of the two women who stood behind the counter in inquisitive silence. As much as she battled with the emotional scars of being adopted, it had saved her the fate of forever living in poverty.

"Privet," she muttered awkwardly.

The singular customer returned to foraging through some colourful begonias that filled the opposite corner, while the older of the two elderly women turned and walked away. A stout woman in her early fifties stood holding a cluster of pink roses that matched Alexandra's Chanel blouse. Her formless checkered and soiled dress resembled a cheap tablecloth, and was a far contrast to Alexandra's fine silk top. The woman did not speak; nonetheless, an uncomfortable smile and a nod of her head signalled her embarrassment but willingness to assist.

"Do you know of the children's home that is here in the neighbourhood?" Alexandra was careful to lower her tone and speak softly so the other women could not hear. It was uncomfortable for her to be there, and she imagined what the woman thought. "I'm afraid I left the address and directions at the restaurant."

The fact was that there were never any directions. Alexandra was here on pure memory and instincts, as if she was a salmon returning to the familiarity of her birth home. Except salmons intuitively knew their birth home because of some sort of mysteriously programmed DNA that humans lacked. Alexandra only ever remembered the orphanage in vague clips and fuzzy general details.

The ageing woman lowered the flowers onto the counter and privately thought how much of a shame it was that Alexandra had most likely tried in vain to become pregnant but had failed – leading her to the orphanage she now sought. She wondered how handsome the husband must be that surely awaited outside in their expensive car. A sympathetic smile escaped her withered lips and she leaned forward and whispered softly, "You mean Orphanage Number One?"

And so it was that Alexandra was reminded that older children's homes often lacked the dignity of having a name. The Communist assigned them numbers; in this case they must have been 'Number One', 'Number Two', the only other orphanage she knew of, which had opened up just at the time she was adopted. Alexandra only knew of this orphanage because a few of her friends left for it in the weeks before her own departure.

"Yes," she replied nervously.

"It's not far. It's near the forest on the Morozova."
Alexandra tilted her head and raised her right eyebrow for the information she truly needed. "And where is that?"

"You go back out here and immediately take the first right and then keep driving until the gasoline station. You take that left and then keep going. I think it could be another kilometre. I don't know because I don't drive. My nephew lives down there and the bus takes me. Maybe it's further." She smiled fully for the first time, revealing darkened and crooked teeth.

Alexandra leaned forward and bowed her head. "Spasibo," she replied.

She walked away and noticed in the corner of her eye as she opened the door that both the other women looked at her again. She knew the woman at the counter would tell them why she was there and the false assumptions that she had made, but she didn't care. Her journey was finally nearing an end, and the anticipation of nervous energy was rising.

Moments later, Alexandra drove slowly and leaned over the steering wheel, while looking out of the front window with concentrated intensity. She searched for the physical landmark of trees in a sea of concrete, asphalt and dirt, but she couldn't see 'Morozova'.

"Shit," she murmured in frustration.

Just as she thought she would have to ask for directions yet again, she noticed a street where trees gathered at its end. She made the right onto the street that curiously had no street sign, and drove approximately four hundred metres. Buildings on the left side disappeared as a forest emerged instead. Gradually the street became more residential, and softer in appearance.

Alexandra looked over to the right and followed the houses until finally she saw what seemed unbelievable. She braked immediately and felt herself lurch forward and then back again, as the car suddenly stopped. There it was. A medium-sized building with a waist-high gate around its parameters. She saw the Cyrillic letters spell 'Number One', as if the small children running about the grassy front yard was not evidence enough.

She sat in quiet awe, and at that very moment a flood of emotions overcame her like a giant wave. The children ran about and laughed innocently, unaware of their sorry plight or bleak future. She noticed two girls about six years old holding hands at a swing, and imagined that could have well been her and her friend Inna twenty years earlier.

The building itself was better than most in the area. It was three storeys and painted an awful yellow and green, with a large red door that invited her to come inside. She vaguely remembered that this was the area where classes and activities took place while the longer base was the sleeping chambers and administrative rooms. In her memory the building was part-hospital and part-school. Yet the clinical nature of each was replaced instead by a warmth that it exuded – a warmness barely remembered until now, when she could feel its tug once again.

No-one noticed the blue car and woman. The few children frolicked about, oblivious. They were children being children, and exempt from such crude demons like self-actualisation or introspection. That was left instead for adults, one of whom that now sat staring at the playful childish world of innocent naivety.

Alexandra smiled, and her eyes became misty in nostalgic reflection. It was exactly what she had expected, and yet was different. The joy of discovery jerked at her soul, which stirred like it never had before. At least, not that she could remember.

She wanted to cry and laugh simultaneously. Home lay before her, only metres away inside the picket-type fence and playing children in hand-me-down clothes. It was her point of origin, and there was no denying it. She felt a moment of pride as a tear slowly trickled down her flushed cheek. A nervous laugh escaped her as she quickly wiped away the tear and looked down.

The orphanage was the antithesis of Alexandra in all its form, and she cried for what she had become. There it was before her, and it emitted a radiant cloud like some sort of mystical fog. Its values and existence were insular concepts that saturated those who came close to it physically, and Alexandra had just fallen prey to its magical lure. Anyone could easily feel its purity, its blameless innocence and its greater purpose. Alexandra certainly did.

Who would have thought she would become everything the orphanage was not? She was rich while the children's home could barely clothe its extensive brood with ragged leftover shirts and pants. Alexandra operated in a seedy world of sex, whereas the Godly orphanage was partly run by Orthodox nuns. Whereas Alexandra had lost hope and the trust in others, the children and nuns only lived on hope – optimistic hope of tomorrow and that the young lives might grow to fulfil their potential.

Alexandra shook her head in a clumsy physical attempt to erase the guilt and pain that she was left feeling. She looked across once again and saw a little girl in a knee high plaid skirt who had wandered up to the fence and stood facing her, only metres away. She stood, emotionless; one hand resting atop the metal fence gazing at Alexandra who sat looking back. Seconds passed as each thought the other to be the most beautiful thing they had ever seen.

Alexandra's beauty radiated even from within the car, and the nameless child dreamed of becoming such a princess on the outside world. In turn, Alexandra imagined her to be the perfect daughter that deserved a better life. Her features struck Alexandra as so tender and pure. Just then the little girl waved to her, her tiny fingers curling softly. A smile replaced her stoic and saddened expression which left Alexandra to smile instinctively back as she waved herself.

The sudden thought of whether she would ever have such a child of her own was simply too much to bear. The panic it caused, the sheer emotion it stirred overcame Alexandra right then and there. She put the car in drive and pulled away quickly, leaving the orphan to watch the imagined princess disappear down the street just as she had seen so many others do.

III

The grey sky hung low over Moscow, and the air was filled with a damp mist A husky banker who rushed to his car parked in a nearby car park only a few hundred metres away from his office. He huddled as much as he could against the headwind, and he raised his briefcase in a feeble attempt to shelter himself against the annoying elements.

Moments later he climbed the stairs to the garage's fourth floor, which was reserved for employees of the nearby offices. He opened the door and walked slowly while he shook at his coat to clear some of the rain which had accumulated. His car was at the opposite corner and was not unlike most of the other luxury cars that were parked about. Nearly all were black, and were mostly German. Having an Audi, BMW or Mercedes was a physical Russian expression of success, as was the case for Miroslav, who fumbled for the remote-control door opener tucked away inside his coat's breast pocket.

He pressed the button and the darkened Mercedes nearby flashed its rear lights twice. The sounds of traffic filled the garage, as did the high-pitched siren from an ambulance that raced below. He popped his trunk and tossed in his leather briefcase, before taking off and shaking his coat clumsily.

Miroslav entered his car and before he started it up he suddenly felt the cold sting of a something sharp at his throat. The icy metal was the polar opposite of the hot hand which grasped the side of his head in a lock that left him paralysed, at the mercy of the unknown predator who pinned him from behind.

"You have something I want," he heard.

The voice was sinister in its hoarseness and depth. Miroslav felt the warm breath across the back of his neck, and he could smell the sweetness from his assailant's breath. It was a mix of mints and alcohol that combined in an aroma that left his naked hairs standing on end and pimpled in fear.

Panic settled in as he was caught in a vice grip that left his torso completely immobilised. His arms were free, but were powerless to alter the situation. His mind raced and his fear led him to an obedient compliance.

"What, what do you want?" he replied frantically.

"I want the codes and the account number."

"Which one? I run a bank with thousands of accounts, for God's sake!"

At that moment Miroslav felt the pinch of the large blade as the man adjusted its tip to his Adam's apple. "Don't fuck around, Mr Asimov. You know the one."

Miroslav's eyes flitted nervously and he raised both hands slowly in front of him, careful not to alarm his attacker. "I really don't. Tell me which ones and can give them to you," he whimpered softly.

"The one you are using for the weapons' transactions."

"The American one? Condor?"

"Call it what you want. The account that American used when he came to see you after lunch. I think you can remember."

"I don't have access to the full code," Miroslav retorted as he struggled to speak clearly – his voice raspy from the strain of the assailant's tight grip "My partner gets half of the authorisation code just before he comes in. Really! I only give him a password!"

"What is the password?" The voice lowered to a growl and again the knife and hand that locked him tightened like a python, slowly squeezing its helpless victim.

"It... it changes every time. I only get a phone call from my contact that someone will come and then a moment later the password comes from an text. I don't know what the account is being used for. I swear!"

The desperation in Miroslav's voice was legitimate; however, he was not telling the truth. Miroslav was dealing in something he knew was illegal, and was being paid a thousand dollars every time the unknown American came to him. The details of the account and the fact that he was involved in weapons surprised him, which sent his mind racing.

"Who sends the text?"

"I don't know!"

"Don't fuck around!"

Miroslav whimpered as he felt the sharp prick of the knife as it slightly pierced the tender skin at the base of his neck. He felt the warmth of the tiny trail of blood that now ran down his neck and gathered at his white shirt collar.

"Okay, okay! Jesus fucking Christ! It's Gorban. I'm sure you've heard of him! What are you going to do? Threaten a minister in the Duma?"

"Probably - but first, the American. When's he coming again?"

"I don't know, really. He comes... I don't know... maybe twice a month."

"What was the last password?"

The assailant's questions seemed to become more and more filled with frustration, and Miroslav could sense his irritation by how tightly he locked him against the seat.

"It's in my phone still. I can't remember," he snivelled apathetically.

At that moment Miroslav thought of his wife and two sons, had wondered how he had gotten himself into this situation. How was it that his life was at the hands of an unknown who could end everything with a slice of the ominous knife that could – it seemed - decapitate him with a single slice?

Just then Miroslav felt the grasp loosen ever so slightly, and he heard the voice from behind. "I want you to put your hands on the steering wheel and only then will I let you go. You will not move them and will stay this way for five minutes. Do you understand?"

Miroslav felt the welcoming relief of life shower him, and he felt a joy so profound that he wanted to cry. He shook his head rapidly and struggled to speak. "Yes, yes!" It was all he could say as his body completely weakened, like gelatine.

His arms felt like twin steel girders, but he lifted them slowly and clasped at the wheel only inches away.

"Yes, yes," he muttered again while a subconscious smile escaped him as he began to weep in quiet desperation. At last he was free from the terrible grip.

Miroslav heard nothing except the rustle of some clothes from behind. His eyes widened to catch the sound of anything, and his imagination ran amok. He wanted to hear the rear door open and the assailant's footsteps disappear in the distance; however, he instead heard nothing more than the crunching of the stranger's jacket or coat.

Just as he wondered if he should speak, he felt the cold of metal against his temple. Just as the chilling reality occurred to him, the silence was broken by a soft whoosh and the unmistakable splat of brain matter and tiny skull fragments striking at the driver's side window. Miroslav's lifeless body hunched over immediately and fell like a raggedy doll against the steering column. The side of his face exposed the panicked face of a man whose last thought was fear and terror. A large black and red exit wound was over his left opened eye.

A hand slowly came over Miroslav's chest and into the inside pocket of his suit's jacket. It found his mobile phone and slid back out like an elusive snake slithering stealthily away from any danger. The door eventually opened, then closed once more. Finally the footsteps of the invisible killer could be heard, but only by the living – of which there were none around. They disappeared into the stairwell and the slam of the door was the last sound emitted from within the parking deck. Only the traffic and the incessant horns filled the ears of the dead man hunched over in a heap.

Chapter 13

I

Torie tugged at little Alexi's arm as if it were a leash attached to an unruly dog. Alexi continually wanted to stop and look into the shop windows that were full of colour and tall mannequins while Torie pressed ahead, already running behind her strict schedule. His eyes widened when he saw featureless faces and their stiff poses.

"How can they see, Mommy?" she asked in childish bewilderment.

"They aren't real people, darling. I've told you before that those people in the windows are all plastic and wood."

"But the one lady was moving and bending. I saw her," he retorted in absolute certainty.

Torie rolled her eyes a bit before calmly replying, "She was the lady who works in the store and dresses those dummies."

They came to an intersection where Alexi could finally be released from his mother's suffocating clutch, even if it was only for a moment. The traffic was so thick that the cars seemed to swallow the city, as if the roads were merely a moving parking lot to the buildings and shops that surrounded them. Torie looked down at her little boy, who stood with his head staring up and eyes rounded with inquisitiveness. He loved walking about the giant city. Being around so much excitement, moving cars and scurrying people fascinated him and existed as a polar reality to the calm subdued life that his parents enjoyed when they were all together in the tiny apartment.

"After we go to the store, Mommy will make you your favourite sandwich when we get home."

"Will you make it with strawberry jam?"

"Strawberry?"

"I want strawberry instead of grape."

Torie's face soured in confusion, as she had never remembered Alexi ever having strawberry jam other than when he first tried it two years ago and spat it out. Nonetheless she had learned that her son had a habit of flip-flopping his interest spontaneously and relented without question, "Okay little man, strawberry it will be."

She entered the door to the sound of a jingle. Torie nodded to the old lady behind the counter, who nodded back. Rarely had the owners ever spoken, yet their crotchety personalities somehow endeared them to her because they reminded her of Stefan's parents. They too were quiet and hard-faced, seemingly dour and stern; however, underneath the rigid unfriendly exterior was a warmth and generosity that was truly charming. It just took a while to eventually experience it.

Torie smiled and made her way to the rear of the third aisle where jellies, jams and baking products were neatly stacked. "Do you see one that you like?" she asked as she folded her arms.

Alexi looked at the several choices and focused on each of the labels as he scanned his multiple choices. His mother's finger outlined the five or six choices, and she warned him that the other red jams were in fact different flavours. "These over here are cherry and this here is raspberry," she stated with motherly assurance.

"I know Mommy. I can spell now," he replied. His wide grin could not contain his pride at being able to read some words, although Torie doubted he had learned the difference between 'raspberry' and 'strawberry'.

"Good boy. Now, which one do you want?"

Torie's hunch proved prophetic when his tiny hand reached for the glass jar with the bright green label. Green had always been his favourite colour, and she somehow knew that he would instinctively choose the one jar that was twenty rubles more than the others.

"You picked the best one," she replied with a smile and a gentle pat on his head. "This one is with the best berries in the whole world."

"Really?" he asked with wide-eyed curiosity.

"Of course, darling!" she replied without hesitation.

"Now let Mommy get these other things we need, and then we can go home and begin your homework."

Alexi grumbled incoherently and the protrusion of his lower lip, slow shuffle and hung head showed his obvious discontent.

"Come on, little soldier! You do want your sandwich, right?"

Alexi followed while he pouted and Torie's small hand-held basket quickly filled with goods. After all, it would be another week before she would come again. Like clockwork she only ever did her shopping here on Monday, after picking up Alexi from the kindergarten school that was located just around the corner and across the street.

They made their way to old lady at the single check-out, who nodded when Torie stood at her side with her wallet in hand. She reached under the counter and revealed a red lollipop the size of a ruble coin and handed it to Alexi, who stood with a huge grin and rounded eyes.

"What do you say to the nice lady?" she said with a mother's strictness.

"Thank you," Alexi replied coyly.

"And thank you," Torie whispered to the owner as Alexi ripped away the plastic covering.

"I meant to give you that when you were here a couple days ago," she replied as she swiped each article across the flat laser.

"You mean last Monday when I was here with my son?"

The old lady instantly seemed confused and her pace slowed as she reflected back in time. "I thought it was Thursday." She finished swiping the eggs and some bananas that were the last of Torie's groceries before concluding, "Who knows? My memory is so bad. I bet it was Monday. 320 rubles, please."

Torie handed her three one-hundred bills and some coins which paid her exactly, before stuffing her sack methodically. "Thank you again," she said with an appreciative smile before grabbing Alexi's free hand and heading out the door. Alexi looked back and licked the sucker as the bell jingled over them and the city revealed itself once again. They disappeared immediately from the watchful eyes of the shopkeeper, as the two blended in with the outside sea of humanity which zipped about in a million different directions.

II

The small diner could have been any of thousands in the city. It was dilapidated from neglect and years of disregard. The facade needed painting and the front window was cracked a crack. Only the red stickers that spelled its name stopped the fracture from making its way completely across the dirty window. Inside wasn't much different. A few metal tables were arranged with accompanying yellow plastic chairs as three prints of the Eiffel Tower, Big Ben and New York's skyline hung on the empty walls. The posters somehow justified the clumsily coined slogan of 'Moscow's only international snacks', although Slovij's didn't serve anything French or English. Perhaps the greasy French fries and crude hamburgers supported such a motto, but certainly not the ninety percent of typical Russian snacks that it sold.

The diner was a front for Viktor and his syndicate to wash dirty money and for his men to eat for free. This little restaurant was the heart of Viktor's territory – the seedy southern part of Moscow where law enforcement is largely corrupt and businesses get their monthly shake down from the Godfather everyone knows but who is never spoken about. Some things just exist as they are and are better left unsaid.

The sleek Mercedes parked out front stood in contrast to the many junkers parked about. An occasional late model Toyota or Ford could be seen; however, everyone who saw Igor's set of wheels knew he was a man not to press. Inside Igor was waiting – nursing a cold beer imported from Bavaria. Igor was marvelling at its frothy head and sipping slowly, enjoying its earthy flavour, unlike the crappy beers from his homeland that he occasionally drank.

Just then the doors were opened by Russian and Pavel, allowing Oleg to walk through like some coroneted king making his grand entrance to an awaiting court. Igor couldn't have cared less about such formalities and ceremony. In his eyes Oleg was just another sponsor that bankrolled his comfortable life, and this meeting was nothing more than a necessary formality he had to endure to get paid.

"Igor!" Oleg exclaimed as he stopped, his arms reaching out for their customary hug. It was always this way, actually. Meeting in a home of the mafia or a business they owned was something akin to a family reunion where guests were greeted as if they themselves were part of an extended family.

Igor rose and brushed at his suit, before smiling and kissing his sponsor once on each of his cheeks. "I have good news for you, Oleg".

"I was hoping you would. Viktor is becoming impatient, but is hopeful with the... um... news he wants to hear."

Both men nodded knowingly –they knew exactly what the 'news' was, as each knew exactly without having to articulate it.

"Anyway, forget such vulgarities for now. What interests me is enjoying a drink with you to celebrate our progress." He turned to the waiter who stood patiently by the bar, and motioned with his raised finger. It was the immediate sign that sent him scurrying to the table like an obedient and well-trained dog.

"Yes sir. Your wish, please."

"Two vodkas for now," he replied without ever looking at the man.

A moment later the two men faced one another with raised half-filled glasses of forty percent proof vodka.

"To the project," Oleg said with a beam across his hardened face. Igor nodded in approval and both men downed their drink in a single manly gulp. Each sent the empty glass crashing down on the cheap table, and the subsequent 'clang' echoed through the empty interior.

The two bodyguards stood nearby at the entrance with their backs turned to their boss, waiting to turn away any patrons who were unlucky enough to want to come inside. The waiter and elderly bartender were anointed insiders trusted by the mob family. They existed solely on the crumbs and protection of their employers. Secrets heard stayed with them, as each knew that any leak would mean a certain and painful death at the hands of a hulking understudy looking to make a promotion or pass an initiation.

"So tell me, Oleg. The plan."

'The plan.'

Those were the two words that meant everything right now for each of them but for completely different reasons. They had come to discuss why they were there in the dingy restaurant; each so far removed from the riches that normally defined their existence.

Without the constant flow of weapons the Viktor's family business would be severely reduced because they had not expanded in such crude industries like drugs or prostitution. The family had found its way as career military men who had all-important access to unused weapons after the fall of Communism. The subsequent accountability had allowed them to siphon off hundreds of small arms and everything in between.

For Igor, the success of 'the plan' meant a certain paycheque from his favoured employer. He couldn't care less about the instability their work brought to many African governments or guerrillas that fought injustices in countries that were defined by civil skirmishes and conflict. The only cause he supported was his own, and if that meant killing Russian bankers or politicians, then so be it.

"It seems the Americans need weapons for some sort of secretive mission. They are using the bank to apparently make payments into an account called Condor."

"To who?"

"It is Krokav – that is for sure. And the information I got from the banker was that Gorban is behind this. You were right."

Igor gulped the last swig of his alcohol and raised his glass to Igor for another refill. Doing business meant talking with the sweet smell of whiskey, cognac or vodka on his breath, and he thirsted for more. This particular vodka that Oleg had brought was special.

As Oleg poured into his empty glass, Igor continued, "We both know that the Duma controls the Sberbank and, if we have the despicable Krokav and Americans both involved, then it really does mean that you are being double-crossed."

Oleg slammed his glass hard on the table and ran his empty hand through his thick hair as his face tensed. His eyes filled with imagination and his mind raced with even greater fantasies. Fantasies of revenge, deceit, double-crossing and panic. "I want revenge on Gorban! That's for starters! I pay that bastard for nothing?"

"Calm down, Oleg. Calm yourself." Igor spoke with cool composure – like a man who already had crossed the chasm of despair that Oleg now teetered on. "First off, I did what you ordered and terminated the banker before he could harm you further." Igor sipped again from his glass and smacked his lips in delight before chuckling with a laugh that was as sinister as it was joyous.

Oleg nodded approvingly and clamped his teeth while he seethed some more. He gulped at his vodka before again filling his own glass nearly completely.

"Listen, Oleg, killing Asimov only makes things messy. Suspicions will be raised and it could force our hand."

Oleg took a deep breath and then inhaled so strongly that he seemed to suck all of the heavy air from within the room. He sunk into the back in his chair as if the weight of his breath had filled him like some sort of sandbag. Igor was right. Killing Miroslav was necessary, but did threaten to expose the full extent of the double crossing.

Oleg's mind raced at how this was happening. He thought he was the government's favourite source of illegal arms trade, and that his connection to a couple of key ministers inside the Duma was a lock. If they were now using Krokav instead of him, then everything would seem lost.

Oleg could not comprehend why his family had been pushed to the outside, and he felt he needed his father Viktor to provide the answer. Perhaps his father would save them, just as he had done a couple times before when things had turned for the worse.

The last of Oleg's drink was gulped crudely. "Okay then, my friend. Follow your instincts and lead me to the fuckers behind this treason."

Igor nodded as his hunch was confirmed. Oleg was as predictable as they come, and his orders were already known before he entered the seedy restaurant twenty minutes before.

Oleg's hand removed the same tan envelope as always from inside his jacket. His paycheque was slid across the table. "As always, send my regards to Viktor and tell him that I look forward to ending this."

Oleg seemed to snap instantly out of his funk and retorted quickly, "Don't kill Gorban yet." He paused and seemed to contemplate what to say next, and then after a few seconds of calculated consideration he added, "Until I tell you to waste him."

Igor smiled like a child being given a toy. Killing was his forte, and the thought of being a mere private investigator tortured him deeply. At least he knew that he would be able to use his Kruger soon enough, and that pleased him immensely. It made him feel powerful. God-like. Unique and tough. The dog-eat-dog nature of the area in which he had grown up, and his disinterested, tough parents, had let Igor to value feeling powerful above all else. He associated feeling and being humane with experiencing pain and saw no point in indulging any better impulses he may have felt growing up. Igor liked his one-dimensional, simple approach to life, and he was richly rewarded financially for his lack of conscience.

Chapter 14

I

Alexandra turned right onto the street that she knew would lead her to the one place that could stir her very soul. How was it that mere mortar, bricks and concrete could raise this much emotion? Fear collided with hope and clarity superseded doubt. The building a few hundred metres away was both her tortured prison as well as her centre for redemption.

She thought of the little old lady who must now be every bit of sixty, if not older, and what she would say to her surrogate mother. The fact that she could hold the key to finding her birth parents was the paradoxical irony that tugged at Alexandra's emotions. Privately she still tussled at whether she really wanted to know the identity of her 'real' parents. She was sure they were no longer together.

She had been told by her adoptive parents that her mother was quite young when she gave Alexandra away. That was all she knew of her mother; however, her father remained an even bigger mystery. The only known fact about him was that he was an older married man with his own family. What happened after the pregnancy with Alexandra did not leave much to deduction or imagination.

Alexandra sat in her car, which was aimed towards its final destination like some sort of cocked arrow waiting to be delivered to the red bulls-eye. Except, in this case, the hunter's fingers quivered like fluttering autumn leaves in a forceful wind – her hand a bundle of anxious nerves gripping the steering wheel. Alexandra's right hand slowly lowered to the gearbox, and with cautious reservation she slid the lever from 'Park' to 'Drive'.

She parked across the street next to a cluster of some old pine trees that she had probably seen often as a child. Alexandra's mind reverted to the childish state that it often had over the years when considering nature or the world around her. She wondered just how many generations of children the trees had seen, and the thought of her standing at the gate's limits over twenty years ago, looking out across to this very spot left her feeling nostalgic.

Alexandra stood next to her car, facing the building, where she could see her imagined childish self staring back; except it wasn't Alexandra. The ghost was a six-year-old idolised phantom who stared with hopeful eyes and long straight blonde hair. She smiled wistfully when she recognised herself in the future, and was now thankful she had returned. The little girl stood motionless while the real-life children bustled about in the background; one kicking a blue rubber ball to three others, while four children played skip-rope with an aged and thick brown cord.

Alexandra felt her eyelids close, and when she reopened them the poltergeist had vanished. Little Alexandra had disappeared in an instant, and the only thing in front of her now was the invisible barrier of doubt that she had to take her final steps to overcome.
The gate had a box with a simple white button that rested underneath a speaker. She pressed the button that somehow creaked when pushed, and she then heard the crackling of the speaker in response.

"How can I help you?" The voice on the other end was void of emotion and the response seemed terse and passionless.

"Uh... privet. My name is Alexandra, and... well... and..."

"We accept no solicitations," the voice barked before Alexandra could finish. "We only allow entry if you are a potential foster parent or mother in need. Only if you have an appointment."

Alexandra took a half step back and cleared her throat, which allowed her the one second she needed to gather her thoughts. She leaned back into the nondescript box and her mind raced. Everything was suddenly so clear. As if her brain had just been doused with a drug where all of life was revealed. She sighed deeply and smiled – her first in days.

Alexandra had her answer, and she knew what to do. She felt that she would probably never again stand on this spot, which is why she attempted to experience every sensation that surrounded her. The air smelled clean and the gentle wind grazed her delicate face. Eventually she pushed the button at the fence and softly replied, "Thank you. Thank you anyways."

II

Mikhail arrived at his apartment building and stopped at the front door – the overhead lamp providing just enough light for him to find the correct key. As he fumbled with the large number of keys, a man approached from behind. Mikhail had not given notice to the nearby parked car and the sound of its door slamming shut.

Just as the front door key slid into the lock, a firm hand on Mikhail's shoulder caused him to shudder in surprise. "Mr Markov, we need to talk," the tall man stated matter-of-factly as he pushed Mikhail through the now half-open door.

"Who are you?" Mikhail demanded in a mix of panic and insistence.

The hand was firmly clasped onto Mikhail and did not allow him to fully face his mysterious visitor. "Consider me a friend –you need help regarding a potential problem linked to some unscrupulous associates."

Mikhail could not see who had pushed him towards the nearby elevator; nevertheless, he could make out that the man was dressed in a dark suit and wore a long coat. Both hands were now firmly on his shoulders and were guiding him to the elevator.

The doors of the elevator soon opened, and the two men entered. Mikhail was finally free from the stranger's clasp and he turned to confront his tormenter.

"What do you want from me?"

The man before him was a powerful figure much larger and sturdier than the ageing businessman who stood defiantly across from him.

"My employer would like some answers."

"What answers? What is this all about?" Mikhail's voice raised in anxiety, already thinking of what weapon he might be able to use within his apartment if the stranger were to suddenly attack him.

The reply came in a calm and hushed tone. "We'll have a glass of vodka and talk through things inside your apartment."

Just then the elevator stopped, and the doors opened to reveal a hallway lined in typical Communist red wallpaper. Mikhail opened his apartment door and flipped the light switch, revealing a luxurious interior. The stranger looked around the tidy and spacious flat – a testament to Mikhail's meticulous attitude.

"Now tell me, why did you force yourself on me. Is this some sort of robbery?"

"Mr Markov, does it look like I need money?"

"Well…"

"Speaking of money, I want to know a bit more about your banking friends, but only after we have a drink. Please." His hand motioned to the nearby standing globe, which served as a bar. It was if he had been to the apartment before and knew immediately where the alcohol was kept.

Mikhail opened the globe to reveal a wide selection of drinks from which he pulled out a half-filled bottle of premium vodka. He poured two glasses and handed one to his uninvited guest, who was now seated in a nearby leather chair.

"What exactly do you want to know?" His question was slow and drawn-out.

"Tell me, Mr Markov, about Condor."

"Condor? I don't know what you're talking about," he muttered back.

The stranger leaned forward: "We both know that you are familiar with everything about Condor. I want you to think about your future. I want you to think about why I would be here."

He reached into his coat pocket and casually pulled out a black Kruger and began to tighten the silencer that was attached to its muzzle.

"Whoa, whoa, whoa!" Mikhail stammered as he raised his hands defensively. "There's no need…"

Before he could finish the brute interrupted, "I think you will tell me everything now. Or you will force me into consequences." The muscular hit-man placed his empty glass on the adjacent table and nonchalantly laid the metallic pistol on his lap. However, it was aimed directly at his host.

"Okay, okay! You obviously have found out that the account exists. I'll tell you what I can, but believe me, I still don't know everything. My boss was the main contact, but he is now dead. All I know is that it went to the highest levels in the Kremlin. I really don't know much more than that."

"Start talking and we both are saved from a… shall we say, stressful evening?"

"Condor is an account where a foreign sponsor

deposits money as payment for small arms."

"The foreign sponsor is the Americans?"

"Yes."

"And?" The stranger twitched his gun at Mikhail. "Why Condor in the first place?"

"The Americans are... shall we say, concerned. The deal is where a Russian arms dealer ships small arms and other weapons to Kurdish tribal moderates located in the Kunar Province of Afghanistan. Then the Americans reimburse him into Condor."

The intruder motioned with his left hand for Mikhail to continue after a slight pause.

"American administration officials don't want their public to know that they are giving one set of terrorists weapons to fight another. So they approached the Kremlin."

"Why involve Moscow?"

"The logic would be to use a Swiss or offshore account, but the Americans have come to us for two reasons. One was that we had experience with Afghanistan, and apparently some of their military people are working with ex-Russian soldiers who were in Afghanistan before. Our Russian guys made alliances that the Americans now can use."

"And the second reason?"

"The second reason is that Russians are good at keeping secrets, and we have contacts with the dealer who is actually providing the arms."

"Who is your contact man? Who makes the payments?"

Mikhail leaned forward to reply. "Do you really think that they would be that transparent? I don't own the bank, the Kremlin does."

"A name, Mr Markov. You are dancing and I don't dance." He waved his Kruger upwards as he replied.

"The deal isn't that way. I can see the transactions.

Money comes in and goes out. The accounts are accessed remotely with PIN numbers that I don't have access to. If you want the money then I can assure you that I can't help you."

"I'm not after the money. My client wants names first."

"Then I'm afraid that is the only thing I cannot tell you." His reply was defiant and certain.

"Mr Markov, I'm not leaving without a name. Or two." He emphasised his point by an additional turn of his silencer.

"I... I really don't know." His answer seemed genuine and laced with pensive fear; however, the unwanted guest only pursed his lips in disbelief.

"That's unfortunate," he retorted indignantly.

"Look. On two occasions some American CIA guy came in and made a download from the account on a disk. I got a call from my boss to tell me that he would come in, identify himself as Condor, and I was to allow him into the account. That's it, I swear!"

"He went by the name of Condor?"

Mikhail nodded quickly and stammered, "That's the only contact I've had. Really!"

"What did he look like?"

"All Americans look the same. A bit overweight and dressed in a cheap suit."

"Details, Mr Markov. You can do better."

"Maybe the guy was forty-five, even fifty. His hair was turning white over his ears. And, oh yeah! He had a cleft chin. You know, a dent in his chin."

"Much better, Mr Markov. Much better indeed." He rose from his chair and stepped towards Mikhail, who just looked up at the imposing figure that now loomed over him.

"We will be in touch. You can count on it, Mr Markov. This gives you some time to find out who the

American is. Understand?"

Mikhail could only sit in his chair, shaking inside, but he knew that he was now centrally involved in something he had only ever been a minor part of. At least he was alive – more than his boss and friend.

III

Clint's office phone rang to the sound of the double low-pitched beep which indicated an inter-office call. He quickly focused on the digital extension that appeared before him. and then immediately picked up the receiver. "Yeah, what do you have?"

"Sir, I think you should see this." Frank's voice was filled with urgent concern. Then, in a hushed tone, added: "But perhaps we should meet in the conference room."

Clint knew instantly that whatever Frank had found was sensitive enough to protect from his adjacent colleagues. "I'm leaving now," he replied without hesitation.

A moment later he entered the small room and closed the door behind him softly, as if to avoid detection from the bustling activity only yards away.

"What do you have?" His question was direct and demanding.

Frank's face was flushed with anxiety as he sat at the table with a single folder. Clint knew that whatever was inside the folder was big.

"Sir, you were right. However, right now it really doesn't make any sense."

"It? What is 'it'? Start from the beginning, Frank."

"When you told me to cross-check the files from the CIA, I got this hit." He took out a file with a photo of a man and slid it over to Clint. "But I think you will see that it doesn't make sense."

Clint quickly scanned the photo and saw that it was a man named Simon Wolf, who was more than a simple field agent. He was a Deputy Director who had worked under the Committee of Armed Services, but had been reassigned to an undisclosed role which involved reporting in the Pentagon.

Clint squinted at the report and tossed it down in disgust. "Shit! He's undercover."

"What do you mean, Sir?"

Clint needed a second to collect all the thoughts that flooded him before he continued. "It doesn't list his current role, and only gives an address at the Pentagon. That's what the agency does when they want one of their men to be invisible. They give him some bullshit title and a phantom office at the Pentagon. And presto – he's working undercover!"

"But he's working for us, yes?" Frank's question was naïve.

"Of course, but it's not that simple."

"How so?"

Clint sat still, his neurones firing wildly. His mind raced and he struggled to comprehend the implications. He looked at his colleague and thought of what had to be done first and foremost. In the academy he had learned to 'contain the situation', and his years of experience confirmed this to be true. Frank's information had to be contained.

"I assume you told no-one of this?"

"Absolutely not, Sir. I called you immediately."

"Good. It has to stay this way. Only you, and Director Billups will know about this." He leaned forward and sprang from his chair as he grabbed the folder tightly.

"What do I do next, Sir?"

Clint stopped and paused at the door while he scanned his mind for an answer. "Work on the girl,

210

then. She's probably a nobody. Google Moscow escort services and see if you get a hit. Have you tried that?"

"Uh…"

"That's what I thought."

Clint turned and opened the door quickly. However, just as he took his first step out the door, he swiftly turned to his dazed associate. "Good work on the real target."

He made his way down the hall and eventually back to the familiar door that always remained closed. He tapped emphatically on it and heard the approval he needed to enter its sacred space. He opened the door to reveal Ron Billups fumbling through a handful of papers, just as he always seemed to be doing.

"What?" he snapped angrily.

He checked that the door was completely closed before he continued. "I have something."

"Well, it better be something damn important to interrupt me. You know I have that conference call with the Joint Chief of Staff."

"Yes, Sir. It's vital."

Clint simply stood with a confident smirk and poise that defied his boss' grumpiness.

"So what the hell is it? You gonna just stand there?"

"We are both validated. I've got a name on our mystery man from the Baltshug, and it isn't Slavic or European."

"CIA?" he asked with his typical snarl.

"Yep!" Clint tossed the folder down onto the desk before him. Ron slowly took the file and opened it half-heartedly as he sighed with resignation. "A Simon Wolf who is now off the grid, but I'm guessing you'll be interested in where he spent the last six years."

Ron looked over the file with eyes that quickly scanned the entire page. "Jesus!" he blurted as he suddenly realised the implications. He snapped the folder close in a subconscious reflex to prevent its secret from escaping; nonetheless, Pandora's Box had already been opened. The twisted scenario spread out from the folder and permeated the heavy air that both men reluctantly breathed.

"Who knows about this?" he demanded as he ripped off his eyeglasses.

"Only Frank; however, I've already contained him."

"Listen, we just... we..." Ron slumped in his chair, searching for the words to complete the thought of what exactly had to be done. Actually he knew, but the clarity of his linear plan was bombarded by the million other scenarios that intruded his brain. His head felt like a field filled with exploding landmines and the force of the surprise onslaught suddenly attacked him.

The conference call abruptly faded into oblivion.

"We just what?" Clint asked patiently.

"You leave it to me. I need to take this to the Director." He paused again, and the anguish on his face resembled a wooden war mask that prepared him for battle. "We can't assume anything yet. Got that?" he barked.

"Yes, sir. I'm just following protocol."

Ron just looked at Clint standing in front of him. He paused momentarily before continuing, "Just keep doing that. In the meantime, the focus is still Krokav."

"Yes sir." Clint deliberately turned the cold metal handle of the door. Before completely departing the office, he turned back to Ron, who sat with a stunned stare and said, "We'll get them. We'll get them all."

Chapter 15

I

Alexandra peered out of her hotel room and saw the bustle of people below making their way to work. The day was dreary and the different shades of grey in the sky added to her melancholy and disgust. She glanced back to the yellow-framed plastic clock that hung above the entrance door, before collapsing into bed exhausted. The thought of moving forward and the long drive back to Moscow left her tired and depressed.

She glanced over at her mobile, which she had kept turned off for the past three days. It lay on her bedside table and had remained there since the evening before when she had been tempted to call Clint. She knew that her spirit was too vulnerable to speak to him after such an eventful day. Alexandra feared exposing her toxic past and present, while desperately wanting to let it all out and feel his emotional acceptance envelope her from afar.

She rolled over and clutched at the phone, before throwing herself back onto the bed and into an exhausted heap. She held the phone up with both hands, pushed the central button, and waited impatiently for a connection. Deep down, Alexandra knew she was going to receive messages. She figured that joining the real world would help her to break her from the paralysis that she had been feeling since yesterday.

The phone beeped twice – a quick scan showed that she had three missed calls and two messages. She responded by rolling over and facing the emptiness of the sparsely furnished room. She felt tired, even though it was only 8:45.

Alexandra hadn't slept that well. The night was an unkind enemy that had tormented her with strange

213

images of the past and future. In her dreams she had been followed by a dark wispy figure. The figure was shadowy and appeared as a hazy blur. Then she recalled that she had also dreamed of herself trapped in a hotel with a faceless man dressed in a tuxedo who carried a red bag of some sorts. None of it made sense, and she shook her head to clear the images one last time.

She looked at her mobile and dreaded pressing the button that her thumb already rested on. She sensed she knew who had called and, after a quick push, her certainty was confirmed. Mikhail had called twice.

"Shit!" she muttered.

Alexandra knew he would eventually call. He had only needed some time to calm down and think things through. She was sure that he would attempt to win her back, but right now she was completely uninterested in facing him.

In fact, she wasn't quite sure if romance of any kind was important, although she felt a pang towards Clint. Her head was swimming with emotions and uncertainty. Predictably sex and men were the last thing she felt she wanted - a stark contrast to the woman who had arrived only days before. The last two days had been an emotional feast that had filled her completely. She had gorged herself with emotional stimuli. Ultimately, it had left her feeling weak and unsteady.

It was a strange sensation to feel so drained. She had always been totally in control, and emotions were usually reserved for the bedroom. Doubt, confusion and fear were so alien to Alexandra. Guilt had been non-existent; however it was the present overriding feeling that swallowed Alexandra. It was why she feared Mikhail and why the thought of a stranger fucking her was such a turn-off – even if the money was good.

However, leaving sex behind would be a battle for another day. Prostitution had long been a part of Alexandra; however, she had always known there would be a day when she could would walk away. Despite this, it always seemed to be far removed. The money was intoxicating, the sex sometimes consuming, and the easiness of it all was so captivating. For some reason it all now reversed itself, and Alexandra knew that there must be more to life than making easy money and disposable lovers.

She thought she should get it over with and pressed the green button of her mobile, and waited for the answer on the other end.

"Da," spoke the familiar voice. Mikhail always answered the phone with a simple 'yes'.

"You called."

"Alex – we need to talk. I…"

"Listen, Mikhail," she interrupted, "I'm really going through a lot right now and I don't have time to argue with you."

"I don't want to argue. I need you, Alex. A lot is going on. For God's sake, Miroslav is dead and I'm under so much stress. I really need to see you."

"Miroslav is dead?" she replied with astonishment.

"Just several days ago – killed in the park garage right here at the bank!"

"That's terrible. I'm sorry, Mikhail. I know you two were close."

"I need you, baby!"

"I'm sorry, but I can't meet with you anymore."

"We can work this out!"

"Can't you just please leave me alone and find another girl?"

"But I want you!" His answer was resolute and sure. The pause between them was a vacuum that sucked life out of each. Alexandra eventually continued, "Mikhail, you have to respect that I want more for myself now. And it's nothing against you. You were... you are wonderful."

The compliment was exactly the fuel that Mikhail's lifeless spirit needed to hear. Immediately he chimed in, "So, then, let's work this out together." His plea was more of a beg than a statement, and Alexandra could sense his despair.

"Look, I'm not in Moscow right now because I need to get away from it all. And that includes you. Can you please just let me go and leave me to remember you nicely? Can you do that for me?"

The silence after her question told her that Mikhail was nearing defeat. She bit her lower lip, closed her eyes and slowly exhaled.

"You fucking ungrateful bitch! I gave you everything!"

Alexandra was taken aback by his outburst, and she held the phone away as he yelled, "You think you can just throw away people like some fucking piece of trash? You treat people like shit, and..."

"Hold it right there!" she retorted.

"No, bitch! You are going to learn!"

Alexandra had heard enough and felt too drained to battle Mikhail's petty anger. This was exactly what she wanted to have avoided, but there she was hearing Mikhail's venomous tirade when she only wanted a mature and pleasant end to what had been an enjoyable relationship. She had hoped for closure, but he instead opened fresh wounds.

"Good bye, Mikhail." She spoke with finality, and her tone was soothing and calm.

"I'm not finished with you!" he yelled back angrily.

"But I am. I wish you well. I really do."

She closed her phone, leaving her to recline back on her bed in a lump of frustration, sadness and further guilt.

It was all coming back to the singular emotion she had never felt. It was so alien and new to her. Guilt. A distinct sentiment that consumed her and felt so heavy and wrong.

How can this be? she wondered.

Perhaps it was some sort of delayed rite of passage into adolescence that she was facing. Maybe it was because she was away from Moscow and alone in an environment that was so different. Perhaps she was just feeling sentimental because of seeing the orphanage again. Deep inside, Alexandra knew it was a combination of all of these.

Her whole adult life had been defined by hedonism and answering to no-one. Leaving her adoptive parents was the escape into a life where she could literally flee the responsibility and structure of an artificial world that she never had liked. The piano and the dance were Natalie's desires, not hers. The forced conservative values left Alexandra numb, and the appeal to Moscow's liberalism was the allure that began to seed itself into Alexandra by the time she was eighteen.

Somehow it all made sense now. Perhaps not because she had had a moment of self-realisation, but rather because she only now truly was facing her life. She blinked her eyes quickly and shook her head slightly as if to clear the unpleasantness of it all; however, the ugliness of who she was remained. The shame of her shallowness just couldn't quietly be ignored. There it was still, and it refused to let go of its paralysing grip – guilt. That sudden, dirty and new emotion that Alexandra couldn't run from.

She turned back to her phone, as much as a means to eliminate the sudden strange feeling that had overcome her as it was to see her other message. She pressed the green button to her voicemail number and listened to Elena's message. Elena had tried her work number, but eventually turned in desperation to Alexandra's personal number that she had been given for 'emergencies'.

She listened to Elena outline a triple-priced tryst with Mr Nagano, who she had met only a couple of weeks prior. Mr Nagano was back in town and wanted her to fuck him and an associate in a threesome. Normally this rate was double, and Elena had indicated to him that 'Sasha' no longer did threesomes, yet at triple the price it was worth asking. She needed an answer by nine o'clock and it was now 8:50.

She dialled back to Elena, who answered in a huff. "Where have you been?"

Alexandra wasn't in the mood to explain and frankly never felt the need to with Elena. She was one of her top girls and didn't remotely feel guilty for failing to tell her that she had left town.

"When is it for?" Her cool and collected reply immediately cleared Elena's initial bad mood.

"In exactly one week. At 5:00. You would meet Mr Nagano and his associate for dinner at his hotel and then have the threesome. Are you…"

"I'll do it," she interrupted.

"Well… ok. I'll…"

"Just give me the details."

Alexandra's voice was dead and her flimsy patience indicated that she had already tuned herself back into the only life she truly knew.

"Alright then. Alex, are you okay? You sound…"

Again, Elena was cut short when Alexandra replied abruptly, "Yeah, yeah. Just finishing some long overdue errands. You know how it is, yeah? Never seems to be enough time."

"Yeah, I guess so." Elena's own half-hearted response showed she wasn't convinced. She had never been one to pry in her girls' private matters, especially the breadwinners like Alexandra.

"I'll call Mr Nagano right away. We'll talk soon."

"Yeah. Until then."

Alexandra tossed the phone on the bed again and rolled over, sliding her head back under the pillow. The immediate darkness was a pleasant reprieve, and she wished she could fall back asleep. However, her mind raced, and Alexandra knew that her journey back to Moscow had to begin. She threw back the pillow and sighed deeply.

Christ, she thought. Gotta go.

II

Clint quickly strode to the locked metal door that separated his section from the rest of the embassy. His group was sealed away in a remote corner of the embassy's basement that even the janitors didn't have access to. He slipped his personal I.D. badge over the scanner, which flashed green and emitted a high-pitched beep. The door opened, revealing the hub of activity of his associates, but his focus was elsewhere. His pace quickened and he spun around the corner to where the conference room was. He turned the handle and flung open the door to see Frank seated at the large table's corner.

"Sorry, Frank. Got here as quick as I could. Fucking traffic!"

"Yeah, yeah. No problem sir. It's only 10:40."

"Ten minutes is still ten minutes. What do you have?"

As Clint shed his jacket and placed it on the back of his chair, Frank began to speak.

"Okay, Sir. What I found were a couple of things."

He opened his light blue folder and placed two photographs on the table between them. He first pointed to the photo on the left, and continued, "Thanks to the data bank you gave me access to, I found out who this guy is. He's actually a State Department officer who works with the Committee of Oversight. His last assignment was working with a committee headed by Vice President Cheney on small arms."

"Makes sense, actually. Kind of explains why he is here."

"Well… there's more."

"And?" Clint's raised eyebrows caused his forehead to furrow and crease as his curiosity was piqued.

"I dug into this committee and could only find a little bit. Even with my skills I could only get so much, but it actually looks like the purpose, from what I could see, is to buy and sell arms that go under the radar. Some project called 'Condor' keeps popping up, and bank accounts linked to Sberbank."

"Sberbank?"

"Yeah. I found lots of IBAN and BIC electronic codes, all of which funnel into this bank right here in Moscow."

"How much are we talking about?"

"A lot! Like crazy amounts. A few million in all."

Frank pointed to a series of yellow highlighted transactions and the scribbled hand-written sum on the paper's side.

"The D.O.D. never really knows, because they are channelled through the Oversight's Special Task Force which has executive privileges. Besides, they only get notified when the individual amount is over a hundred thousand dollars. Notice how many transactions are just under this. There are hundreds."

"Let me guess," Clint said, looking thoroughly at the document.

"Yes, they don't have to be registered with the Defence Department because they are considered to be 'discretionary' by approval from the President. Under a hundred grand, and no-one knows."

"Mother of..." Clint threw himself back in his chair and refrained from finishing his thought. His mind was already way ahead of his words, and his eyes flitted with possibilities.

"And this guy, Simon Wolf, is shown meeting with Krokav, which probably means...."

"Don't talk to anyone about this," Clint interjected. His body lunged forward and Frank immediately became silent.

"I'll speak to the director immediately, but, until then, this stays under wraps. Got it?"

"Of course, Sir."

"I'll need everything you got, yeah?"

"Yes sir. Of course."

"And what's this? Got something on the broad?"

"Actually... yes. I took your advice and spent some time online looking through tons of escort services, and..."

Frank's paused and looked sheepishly at Clint with a look of guilt.

"What is it?" Clint demanded impatiently.

"Sir, I'm worried if there is an IT audit I could be compromised. I did spend a lot of time on these sites, you know."

"Don't worry. It ain't going to happen, and if it somehow does then I've got your back. Now, what is it?"

Frank exhaled as if relieved before continuing, "I found this girl as a probable match to the woman

Marco photographed. Her name is Sasha, but of course that's got to be fake."

He spun the photo towards his boss, who picked it up and looked at it attentively. Clint was struck and Frank noticed that.

"Do you see something, Sir?"

Clint continued to stare at the internet photo, as the familiarity caused him to reflect.

"No. Not really."

But actually Clint did see something. He saw a woman remarkably like his Alexandra. Her eyes and face seemed so similar, but the hair was definitely different. It was perfectly straight and longer than Alexandra's. However, the figure could have been the same and he felt a peculiar feeling of revelation. Clint had always heard the myth that every person has a twin, and somehow he was staring at Alexandra's twin, coincidentally was an escort living in Moscow.

Amazing, he concluded in silence.

"I doubt that is her name, but I ran this photo through the software and came up with a high degree of probability. Over 95%, sir. The problem though is that Marco's photo is from some distance, and when you blow it up then we lose clarity for a perfect match."

"This is probably her. I'd bet on it," Clint snapped as he flung the photo back on the table. "It says on the header that it's from Moscow Elite. What do you have on that?"

"Only what I could get from the internet. It's all here."

Frank handed Clint a few sheets of papers with everything that he had. Clint rose from his chair and looked down at Frank. "Good job, Frank."

For now, a meeting with Director Billups was paramount. As Clint strode quickly out the door, Frank eased back into his chair for a moment of self-congratulation. Moscow was only his second assignment since the academy, and the intrigue of what he had uncovered was exactly the kind of thrill he wanted when he enlisted. Clint's acknowledgment was the proverbial pat on the back that stroked him and made him feel worthy.

Meanwhile, Clint now stood facing his boss's office door.

"What is it?"

"I've got something. You have a moment?"

"Not really, but..."

"That's what I thought." Clint was already inside the office and closing the door before Billups could finish.

"The identities of the two in the photos. I've got something you may want to know, especially the guy."

Directors Billups' face was a cold stare of expressionless confusion.

"The guy that Florian swears is one of ours?"

"Yeah, him. And he is."

Billups dropped both sets of papers and leaned forward, almost with indigent anger. "Shit! Now I suppose you're going to tell me he is CIA?"

"Not really. A State department guy working on a covert project selling arms. It's being directed by the office of the Vice President."

"What the hell?" Billups eyes squinted.

Clint continued, "Sir, I think we stumbled on something. I was hoping you could elaborate. Is he involved in the operation?"

"You think I'm hiding something, don't you?"

"Sir, I don't think I should interfere unnecessarily. Now is the time for disclosure."

The two sat looking at each other for a moment, and Clint felt sure that his boss would now tell him what he suspected. Director Billups replied, "I wish I could, but

I don't know anything about this guy. Simon something or the other, right?"

"Wolf. Simon Wolf, sir."

"You sure about this?" The furrows on his forehead confirmed the truth as much as did his words.

"Here's what we have."

Clint handed him the folder with the State Department employee profile, plus his work history and synopsis of assignments.

"You think this guy is working with Krokav?"

"Yes, sir. But the part that bothers me is that all the transactions, which are probably linked to arms, are exempt from the Defence Department review. You know what that means – we could be arming God-knows-who!"

Billups exhaled slowly and muttered disbelievingly, "And working against our very own project. Jesus Christ!"

"So why have us? If this is true, then surely they would have known we would discover this. Shit, Sir! This is like another Iran-Contra!"

"We could be wrong, Sir. The evidence is…"

"Circumstantial, but compelling. Shit, Clint. God damn fuckers working right under our noses while we are out in the dark fumbling around like idiots."

Director Billups' fury could be tangibly felt. Their whole project could be a misguided puppet operation.

"Sir, what do you want me to do?"

"Keep your guys on Krokav and this State Department fucker and see what shakes out. We only have a few days before Krokav leaves again. Shit! And here I thought we were chasing bad guys from Syria and Saudi Arabia."

"Of course."

"And what's up with this bimbo? You going to tell me she's also an operative?"

"No, sir. Just a five-hundred-dollar-an-hour escort. We think Krokav is using her, so we're keeping an eye on her too. Nothing too important."

III

Mikhail opened the front door and flipped the light switch on. He tossed the stack of mail onto the adjacent marble top desk and he threw his hat onto the nearby bronze coat rack. Suddenly he felt a sharp pain in his neck and a tightening pressure that caused him to jerk in response.

"That wouldn't be a good idea, Mr Markov." The husky voice was only centimetres from his ear; he was in a vice-tight grip.

"You again. Now what do you want?"

"Just to talk. I'm assuming you have gotten what I asked for."

Just then Mikhail's right arm was released from the painful arm-lock, and he shook it in a feeble attempt to shake out the dull pain that he now felt.

"How did you get in here?" Mikhail said then, seeing the gun, mumbled fearfully. "There's no need for guns."

"Just in case, Mr Markov. Please sit down over there."

The man in black pants and matching turtleneck pointed to the sofa at the room's opposite corner with his free hand.

Mikhail sat slowly - all the while eyeing the intruder with the shiny black gun. He raised his hands and leaned back defensively.

"Put your hands down, Mr Markov. In fact, pour yourself a drink."

The killer motioned with his gun to the two bottles that sat on the side table next to the sofa. "But slowly."

"What do you want?"

Igor shook his head and pinched his lips tightly.

"Why is it that a man always says those four little words when staring down the barrel of a pistol?"

"Mr Markov – I have a bit of a... well... a new proposition. I'm not as interested in the American as I am in Condor and Gorban."

"I know it was you who killed Miroslav!" Mikhail hissed, which interrupted his intruder. His raised voice was filled with anger and he wanted to cross the gap and kill the man across from him, but he was powerless to do anything more than scowl.

"Relax, Mr Markov, or you will meet him. Maybe I did, maybe I didn't. It was quite the news on television a few days ago."

"What do you want?" Mikhail clutched the arms of his chair firmly and stared back at the casual killer who now sat with his legs crossed.

"Well, you should know that Mr Asimov was involved in some very interesting financial transactions that affect my client." Igor uncrossed his legs and leaned forward. "And you are going to fix that." Igor paused and slowly took in a breath before continuing, "By the way, how are your wife and daughter doing on holiday?"

"Huh?" Mikhail slowly receded to the depths of the leather chair.

The stranger casually waved his gun towards their pictures, which sat on the mantel only a metre from Mikhail.

"They are so beautiful and... pure. Can you imagine what one would be like without the other?"

"Are you threatening..."

"Of course I am! You'll do what is necessary if you ever want to see one of them alive. Right now I'm thinking the little girl would be the greater tragedy. Anastasia is her name, yes?"

"You wouldn't kill a little girl," Mikhail gasped. "She's only ten, for God's sake."

"It's in your hands, Mr Markov. You see – I know you've been a bad man at work too. Fucking that young brunette that works with you. Kristina is her name, yes? What would your colleagues and HR say when the photos I have of you two coming and going from the hotel you go to twice a week? You seem so..."

Igor paused and smiled as he searched for the right word. Mikhail simply gritted his teeth and seethed.

"Ah, I know! You two seem so cuddly. I bet Mrs. Markov would like those photos as well."

"Just tell me what you want."

"So I have your attention?"

"Just go on."

"You see, Mr Markov, you are going to do a little money transfer. Those Condor payments are going into the account of my client."

"Jesus! I told you I don't know what Miroslav was doing. How can I find the accounts?"

"With a phone call, for starters. You and I will make a phone call to the man who is making the deposits."

Mikhail nodded slowly and wiped the sweat that had formed on his forehead.

"Then you will transfer the payments into a special account my client has open in Geneva. He is waiting impatiently for this, Mr Markov."

"When?"

Igor reached into his jacket and pulled out a mobile phone, tossing it to Mikhail. Mikhail caught it and held it tentatively as if it was toxic and somehow dangerous.

"I will call you on this phone, which also has software installed in it that lets me know where you are.

Like when you are at the Holiday Inn fucking Kristina, for example."

Igor chuckled and his wide smile relished his power and the embarrassment of Mikhail. The smile immediately turned before he continued, "One false move and the girl meets her grandmother up there." He waved his gun heavenwards and his nonchalant expression told of his seriousness.

"I will kill her, Mr Markov. No doubt about it; and if you fuck up, I will kill you too."

"I understand."

"I'll be watching you. You do know that, yes?"

Mikhail's nervous nod that followed meant that he did.

Igor straightened himself in his chair and crossed his legs as he scratched his chin. "Enough with all these threats. We are businessmen and this is merely a business deal. That's how you should see this, don't you think?"

Mikhail slowly nodded, but didn't speak. His eyes never left the man who sat, smirking, across from him.

"So I guess we are done then," Igor said, rising from his chair. He fidgeted with his jacket and took a step back as he motioned for Mikhail to get up.

"After you," he said with authority.

Mikhail got out of his chair and cautiously passed him, while never leaving him with his fearful eyes. He walked to the door and opened it slowly, hoping that the whole experience was some sort of dream or joke. Igor left and disappeared into the darkness.

Chapter 16

I

It was 7:35 and Alexandra was the first employee in the office. She stood in the kitchenette and turned on the coffee machine while she reflected in the absolute stillness.

It felt good to be back to work. She marvelled at the quiet that she had never appreciated before. During the afternoon the office was always so chaotic and noisy, but now it was completely empty and barren. She pressed the maroon button that caused the machine to groan and churn. Seconds later her coffee began to pour, and Alexandra breathed in its fresh aroma.

For days Alexandra had been without her morning stimulus, and now she grasped the warm mug with both hands. She raised her drink to her nose, closed her eyes, and breathed in the smell of the rich beans. She blew softly on the liquid's surface, steam warming her cheeks.

Just then the sound of the door opening broke the silence. Alexandra spun around and recognised immediately the smile and the curve of the face.

"Well, I've seen it all," said the man who stopped in his tracks. "What in the world are you doing here?"

"I missed you, boss."

"For some reason, I don't buy that."

Sergi walked forward, embraced Alexandra in a hug and a kiss on her forehead. "It's good to see you back."

"It's good to be back," Alexandra whispered.

"Why early? I thought you had taken off the whole week?"

"Well... I finished what I needed and... well... here I am."

"Okay then! Shall we have some cookies? I got a fresh batch on Tuesday."

"Deal!"

"Actually, I want to talk to you about something. I've made a decision."

Sergi paused as his knowing gaze fell upon his favourite employee.

"Yes, really," she replied with a telling smile.

They took a plate of cookies and walked into the office. Alexandra sat and leaned deeply back into the brown leather that creaked when she adjusted herself. "I've thought about it and have come to a decision."

There was a long pause, and Sergi's eyes never blinked as he waited with pensive anticipation. "Well?"

"I think I will do it. I'll go full time. It's best for me."

Sergi clapped his hands together in a sound that pierced the quiet. "Fantastic!" His voice boomed and he leaned forward suddenly. "This will be great! When did you decide?"

Alexandra didn't actually know. It was somewhere between Perm and Moscow late the previous evening. She only slept a few short hours and was restless the whole night; hence why she was here so early.

"Recently. Not long ago, in fact."

"I'm going to work on the details soon enough, but trust me on this, Alex, you'll be happy!"

Sergi was so giddy and Alexandra smiled with him; however, her acceptance came with a price that sank her soul. She was happy, but not like Sergi. Accepting this offer meant letting go of her present. The future would be simpler, and although she knew this day would come, it felt strange to let it go. She knew she needed to let Elena know soon.

"Come on! Let's have a toast!"

Sergi rolled himself to the cabinet behind his desk and opened it to reveal a stash of fine alcohol. He reached for a clear bottle with a fancy black label as Alexandra exclaimed, "Oh no you're not! At this hour?"

"A bit of scotch in the morning is exactly what this calls for, my dear."

He grabbed an empty glass from the table and poured the honey-coloured drink slowly.

"A toast," he said as he raised his glass.

Alexandra raised her coffee mug and leaned it across to meet Sergi's glass.

"To your future!" Sergi said with seriousness.

"To yours," she replied.

"Mine is winding down, Alex. Yours is just beginning."

Sergi was right and Alexandra felt the truth of these words. She was about to embark on a new life path – a simpler, more dignified path that she wondered if she could accept, but one that she now embraced nonetheless.

The two sipped from their glasses and Sergi looked across at his protégé. "Listen, Alex. I don't know what your personal situation is, but I want the best for you. You're something like a daughter to me, you know?"

Alexandra nodded and took a deep breath, before Sergi continued, "The funny thing about life is that it slips away so quickly. Finding out what makes it worthwhile is the key to happiness. I think this will help create a path for you Alex. One that can lead to you to find your own happiness. I know you aren't that happy, are you?"

Alexandra was taken aback. She felt his words and his insight like a sudden dagger that pierced her protective bubble. Was it that obvious? she wondered. Indeed it wasn't, but Sergi was intuitive.

"Well... I wouldn't say that," she replied.

However, her answer was a thinly veiled rebuttal that lacked authenticity. Last night alone confirmed her desire to change. Alexandra was feeling somewhat empty, and this bottomless void had been nagging at her for weeks now. Now she felt bare and naked.

"You're fine, Alex. I'm not suggesting you aren't, but I know you could be happier."

The conversation felt heavy and the mood had changed. Sergi smiled like a paternal father who knew better, and she sensed warmth in his face, not smugness or conceit.

"Well, maybe," she resigned.

Alexandra clutched at her mug and sipped slowly from it, as if to hide her face. Her eyes peered over the rim.

"I've worked with you enough to read you like a book."

"Anyways, let's not get too serious. Here's to happy futures," he said as he raised his glass to Alexandra.

They toasted and Alexandra replied, "And to yours."

II

"I have a new idea about how to proceed."

Oleg leaned back and exhaled. Smoke drifted around his face, and he squinted at the man across from him.

"I'm listening." Igor sipped from his drink and bent slightly forward.

"We have the unique situation for... how do they call it? I think it's called a win-win. From what you just have told me, I think we can limit our exposure and ultimately increase my satisfaction."

"How so?"

"A simple hit on the Minister could only raise more eyebrows," he answered coolly. Oleg chuckled slightly as he continued, "Of course, killing that bastard Vladimir would give me great pleasure. No doubt about it." He shook his head and his wide smile confirmed the delight of the thought of his new nemesis dead.

"Killing a Parliament Minster is risky," Igor stated with calm certainty. "I can do that, but it would be better if you were suggesting something else."

"I am."

Meanwhile, a few kilometres away, Alexandra peered out at the dreary end of yet another damp and chilly March day. The taxi inched its way through the congested intersection and Alexandra's mind drifted to the future.

She hated meeting Oleg, and concluded this would be her last meeting with him. In fact, Alexandra wondered when she would tell Elena that she would leave the business for good. She felt a bit for Elena, who was, strangely, a surrogate mother to her. Alexandra seemingly had many superficial mothers and mentors. It was Elena who believed in her and was the reason Alexandra lived a financially lucrative life. She knew that Elena would feel disappointed; however, Alexandra suddenly realised just how quickly another beautiful girl would replace her.

It was this feeling of nothingness and superficiality that made her realise that she needed more in life. Fucking brutes like Oleg was truly beneath her and left her feeling more and more like she was selling out. Nevertheless, her agenda was full and two other clients within the week were already planned. Next week was her period and her week off. 'I'll tell her then,' she concluded with absolute conviction. In a matter of minutes she would meet her long-term client who she met once a month since last summer.

Oleg had used many of the agency's girls for years and mostly used Tatiana, a busty Czech who was truly a nymphomaniac. She was the only girl who could frequently work multiple clients in one day but for some reason Oleg's new pet became Alexandra when they met in July. Ever since then she would meet him on every third Friday in the mediocre Holiday Inn that bordered the Gorkij neighbourhood. Fucking expensive escorts in a cheap hotel was some sort of weird fetish for Oleg. For Alexandra, his thousand dollars was the same whether it was here or at a five star hotel.

Alexandra knew Oleg was one of the few clients who was part of some underworld that she cared little about. He had bodyguards and he always carried a gun – a huge silver one that he liked to show her. He bragged about his importance and always carried three mobile phones. She really didn't care, but pretended to. Sexually he was rough, and his thick penis felt uncomfortable. The fact that he fucked her roughly and talked dirty to her made her feel not only sore, but cheap as well. Luckily he tipped well, but more and more she began to regret her monthly commitment.

Alexandra pulled her tiny mirror from the small red handbag that matched both her dress and shoes. She powdered her face while her eyes never left the mirror. Looking her best was a habit that she would likely not likely break soon – even if she was no longer an escort. The taxi stopped suddenly and she hurriedly shoved her mirror and powder back into the bag, paid, and left the car in a hurried dash. As she began to walk towards the bar, the hulking shape she knew so well came from around the corner.

It was Pavel, one of Oleg's own bodyguards. He smiled at her and his giant frame glided effortlessly across the lobby. Privately she had sometimes wondered about what it would be like to be with Pavel, and certainly concluded that sex with him would be better. She had never been with such a muscular man and, although they had barely spoken, she suspected his accent and features could be influenced by some sort of Armenian background. Even though he was a bodyguard that had seen and done God-knows-what, she sensed gentleness in him, and he was always respectful in his handling of her.

"Madam," he said in a soft voice that was both deep and melodic. "Mr Kasyanov awaits you in the restaurant." He extended his hand and bowed his head slightly. Alexandra took his lead and followed him into the well-lit restaurant and past the buffet that two staff members were filling.

The restaurant was essentially empty except for Oleg and a man in black. They were huddled together and spoke quietly, but ate nothing. In fact, it looked strange to Alexandra that two men sat together in a restaurant with no food and only one drink at the table. Oleg had just handed the man an envelope; the same kind he had gave her as a tip after sex. She knew that money must be inside and that some sort of deal was being made, although it really didn't interest her.

Just then Oleg saw her and Pavel approaching. "Ah, Sasha!" Oleg's face lit when he saw his date arrive, and he immediately rose to his feet.

"Privet!" she responded, leaning forward into Oleg's embrace.

She noticed the stranger looking her up and down while Oleg kissed each of her cheeks. His features were distinct, and he struck her as a boxer or as another bodyguard. But boxers and hired muscle didn't wear such expensive suits, and she noticed the subtle red strip in his suit, which meant he was wearing Prada. His shoes were too refined to be any simpleton and he reeked of Italian design. As she pulled away from Oleg, she knew exactly what kind of businessman this stranger was.

"My business associate and I were just finishing," Oleg stated matter-of-factly.

As if on cue, the goliath stood, dwarfing Alexandra with his mass. The man in black nodded without any sign of expression. Somehow he seemed more of a machine than a man. A fucking Terminator she thought to herself, as he muttered something undetectable.

Pavel stepped aside, and the two giants who now stood next to one another resembled well-dressed professional wrestlers.

"Have a good evening, Oleg. We stay in touch." He nodded his head and then acknowledged Alexandra. "Ma'am," he said softly, before turning and walking away.

"A great guy, Igor is," Oleg exclaimed as his arm reached around her back. "I guess we are done here. Let the fun begin."

Oleg seemed particularly giddy and his mile-wide smile was something she was not accustomed to seeing. Usually he was serious and hurried. She assumed his love-making was a mere reflection of his lifestyle, which always seemed stressed and rushed.

A moment later the three were in the elevator, with Pavel standing in front as he always did. Alexandra noted that he never looked at her when they were together. It was if Oleg had instructed him to avoid this when he was in their presence. To him, she was invisible.

As the elevator ascended, she felt Oleg's finger run down the base of her spine and towards the crack of her ass. This was a particular erotic sensation for her, and she couldn't prevent her nipples from hardening and her skin from puckering instinctively. She tossed her head back, causing her chin to protrude upwards, as if to deny the intense affect of his touch.

"When are you going to tell me your real name... Sasha?" he whispered into her ear.

His breath tickled her inner ear and she leaned back into his ear with the faintest of replies. "Never."

Immediately he grabbed an ass cheek with power and squeezed hard. His sinister smile revealed that his rough play had just begun, leaving Alexandra confident that she would be sore tomorrow morning.

The elevator finally opened, freeing her from his violent grip. A moment later she stood behind Oleg while he slid his card key in to open the door. They entered, while Pavel stayed outside. A knowing look from Oleg assured his bodyguard that the next hour or so was his to be free.

The room was the same as always. Small, forgettable, and lacking any ambiance. The firm bed was large, and the only highlight in an otherwise average interior.

"You want anything different this time, Mr Kasyanov?"

His angry reply was immediate. "When are you going to start calling me by my first name? After one year of fucking?"

"I respect you as a client, Mr Kasyanov, not as my lover."

Her answer was indignant and drew the line that he may be able to have her physically, but not emotionally. Alexandra was not one to become familiar with her clients, even though some regular Johns seemed interested in taking their relationship beyond pure sex.

"Which is why I like us just the way we are. Besides, your tips are always so generous."

Oleg replied with laughter as he took off his blazer and loosened his tie. "I think that is why I like you so much! It's like fucking a sexy businesswoman who just left a board meeting. Since I met you, I now know what it is like to fuck me!"

"Except I don't call you bitch," she retorted sarcastically.

Oleg stepped closer to her and grabbed her chin. "Don't take it personally. You just bring the animal out in me."

"Oh I don't, Mr Kasyanov. I really don't."

She doubted that he truly understood exactly what her response meant, as she began to unbutton his shirt and undo his tie.

"The envelope with your extra money is in my jacket. You want it now, or after I fuck the shit out of you?"

"Later's okay."

"That's what I thought," he replied, as his hands clutched her face.

He stared at her with a vicious gaze for a second, before diving into her neck like a wild lion lunging into its hapless prey. The fury with which he kissed her left her feeling more assaulted than caressed; however, this was nothing different to previous meetings. Nonetheless, Alexandra moaned as if his wet mouth and sloppiness actually turned her on. Instead she closed her eyes and imagined Clint and his naked body. Oleg's mouth and hands quickly found their way to her breasts, and he clumsily fumbled at her back zipper, which he eventually undid. The red dress fell to her ankles. Her nipples were completely frozen and his tongue flicked at them, before finally his mouth enveloped up them completely.

Alexandra kept her eyes closed, which continued the fantasy. Now her mind drifted to Clint's expression, tellingly appreciating her bosom. Although it was Oleg who assaulted her breasts, she imagined Clint's mouth tenderly sucking.

"On the bed, bitch!" Oleg shouted.

He pointed emphatically, and her fantasy dissipated at that instant. Still, she managed a wry smile, and obediently obliged by slowly stepping to the bed. She slithered on it and looked back at Oleg, who was fixated on her raised ass. From this angle, she was perfect. Her breasts seemed a full cup size larger and both halves of her tight ass were perfectly smooth. Alexandra's blonde hair fell across her face and, from Oleg's wild expression, she knew his attack was imminent.

"Fucking beautiful," he howled as he unbuttoned his pants and clumsily stepped out of them.

His penis was like a tree stump and surely as thick as it was long. His balls were dark and his pubic hair was a wild mess that she would have trimmed if he were her lover. Oleg stepped forward as Alexandra pulled out a condom from her purse. With Oleg she bought the extra-large ones and always a strip of three.

"Put it on, bitch! Hurry up!"

Oleg was desperate to fuck her and he held his cock with one hand, which was now only an inch or two from her face. She delicately unfolded the rubber with her fingers before sliding it over him with her mouth.

"Yes! That's it! Suck it good!"

She followed the instructions and began at first by sucking him slowly. One hand barely wrapped itself around his base, while her mouth completely surrounded the top of his penis. She sucked in one rhythmic oral dance. Her right hand stroked him as did her mouth. Meanwhile she titillated his head with her tongue, and took him ever deeper inside her.

"God damn it, baby, you're good!" he yelled approvingly. "Come on! I want that pussy now!" Oleg stepped away and pulled himself from her mouth.

"How do you want it?" she asked childishly and with a sheepish grin.

"I'm gonna fuck you like a dog."

She turned around and dropped on all fours. She widened her stance to open herself completely. Again, she closed her eyes and imagined Clint sliding into her. Alexandra's body tensed as his cock poked nearby in a desperate search. She bent down and reached back for it. A second later she eased his shaft into her opening, and closed her eyes again with baited expectancy.

"Oh yeah. Now that's one tight pussy."

Oleg began slowly, but a few thrusts later he was already fucking her harder and harder. Within a minute his penis was a figurative jack-hammer pounding back and forth with such force that he had already pushed her forward a full metre on the bed. He clutched at her hair and pulled it back like the reins of a horse. She reached at the bed's headboard and braced herself to the primal battering which Oleg gave as he gritted his teeth in a sadomasochistic grimace. Alexandra felt no pleasure, only suffering and discomfort.

Oleg was screwing her just as he said he would. His hips were moving with the speed of a machine-gun, and exactly like those of a dog humping a bitch. The only thing missing from this full-on assault was his tongue hanging out, and the silly look of content that a dog displays when mating.

Eventually Oleg slowed and came to a stop. She heard his panting, and she opened her eyes once again.

"Suck it again."

He withdrew himself from her and she felt free from the imprisoning vice connection that had paralysed her. She spun and took him once again in his mouth. The taste that had previously been lubricated latex now tasted sweet, but slightly salty. Tasting herself was a far better alternative, because she had never gotten used to the medicated flavour of an unused condom.

Alexandra hoped he would come, yet knew from experience that Oleg took a while to climax. She also knew that he liked to fuck her in all the normal positions – from behind, on top, and then with her on top. The reality was that this sexual attack had only begun.

A moment later Alexandra found herself riding him, which was easily the only position that gave her pleasure. She moved her hips slowly and in a smooth rhythm that maximised her inner sensations. Oleg clumsily played with her breast and his fingers pinched her nipples.

"Yeah, bitch, ride it good," he told her. "Show me those tits."

Alexandra had long ago tuned Oleg out, so his comments were hardly anything more than guttural outbursts that interfered with her fantasy of being fucked by her own lover. She smiled and purred because Oleg's thickness pleased her – at least in this position. She controlled everything at this point and couldn't even hear her John mumble the profanities that continued from him.

In her private thoughts she saw her lover's profile and chiselled chin. His smile and tender eyes exuded the romantic warmth that assured her that her sexuality was a gift, not a commodity. Alexandra leaned forward, still with eyes fully closed, and let her hair fall on Oleg's face. Clint would have gently brushed away her tresses at this point, but now she was feeling the sudden tug of her hair.

"Now I'm going to finish this," he insisted angrily.

Oleg pushed her off and almost body-slammed her. He ripped open her legs and crawled forward, aiming his thick cock at her vagina, which remained open in an inviting gape. A second later he was once again inside her and his hands held her ankles to form a 'V'. He panted as he fucked, and the angry scowl that formed during their sex never left his face.

He pumped as hard as he could, and Alexandra whimpered in a combination of painful pleasure. His forehead was full of perspiration and his body began to smell of sweat instead of his musky cologne that didn't smell much better. As if he was a runner sprinting to the finish line, his fury climaxed to a humping which could not possibly be any faster. Alexandra kept her eyes closed, but his attack made it impossible for her to fantasise. Instead she clutched the bed sheets as tight as she could in an attempt of sheer survival – her own face as contorted and convoluted as his.

"Yeah bitch! Oh yeah! Oh yeah! That's it baby! OH YEAH!" he shouted in a tone so loud that anyone in the outside hallway would have surely heard.

He exploded inside her like some sort of massive volcano, and she knew that he would fill his condom just like always. His eruption seemed to stretch her even further; she moaned, and eventually collapsed in pure exhaustion from the beating that she had just received.

Oleg's thrusting had mercifully ended, and he gave a final gentle prod in a last ditch effort to maximise his orgasm. He seemed woozy and he huffed and puffed like the out-of-shape man he was. His breathing was rapid, yet it eventually slowed as he stood above her. He dropped her ankles, which sent her legs crashing down on the bed and, for a second, she just laid there in a shocked state of paralysis.

Thank God it's over, she thought, before finally composing herself and reaching down to raise herself up against the backboard.

"Yeah," Oleg panted, "You're the best whore there is."

It was a bittersweet and ironic compliment that Oleg had been saying immediately after sex for months now. Alexandra wondered how she could be a good fuck when she only lay down defensively and tried to survive his sexual mugging. Nevertheless, this time it stung even more than usual when he called her a whore. Her body tensed and it was all she could do to say nothing in return. The fury was there, boiling inside her, but she calmly closed her eyes to collect herself and hide her rage.

This is the last time. I can manage, she concluded to herself. I'm done with this fucking asshole.

Alexandra opened her eyes and smiled coyly. "No, you're the best fuck I get. Wanna go around again?"

She knew he was done, and she also knew stroking his ego would land her a big tip. It was all about the money with Oleg. Alexandra would suck as much out of him and the industry as she could, just as he extracted as much sexual humiliation and self-pleasure from her. It was a cruel reminder of the stark reality of being in the sex industry. Self preservation and humility had its price. For Alexandra, that price had finally neared its end.

III

Alexandra tapped her fingers on the table while she waited. The Galereya was busy as usual, and Arkady came over for a second time.

"Darling?" he asked sheepishly as he shrugged his shoulders.

"She's coming. Just a couple more minutes. Until then, I'll have another one."

She pointed at her nearly empty margarita. Arkady only smiled and replied, "Take your time, love. I'll have a new one brought over to you immediately."

It had been a while since Alexandra had seen Arkady, and she paused at the comfort his familiarity brought to her. He usually recognised her designer labels and anything new that she had recently bought. She wondered how life would change without so much money, and if her limited circle of influential friends would soon figure out that she could not afford to engage in their affluent lifestyle.

Alexandra kept her eyes at the entrance and saw people come and go. She remembered the first time she came here and the first time she met Arkady. It was two years ago and the day was much like today – chilly, sunny, and a bit windy. She had made an immediate impression on Arkady when she came in, wearing a Prada chiffon dress and matching Jimmy Choo pumps. From then on he was smitten, like so many others were instinctively when Alexandra was near.

A slim waiter with a model's face came over with a fresh new drink. "Ma'am," he said formally as he placed it before her.

She smiled back, and then began to reflect as he left. She felt as everything she had grown to know would soon be gone and for the first time in her adult life she felt fear. Somehow everything had changed and she wasn't sure why it had. It began a few short weeks ago, and had seemed to grow every day. Now she was a ball of nervousness waiting to tell Elena that her life could no longer accommodate being in the business.

Finally, Alexandra saw the graceful figure of her friend and boss. Elena brushed by people at the front of the restaurant and walked confidently ahead. She slowed and explored the surroundings in search of her lunch date, yet failed to see Alexandra alone at a table only a few metres away.

Alexandra quickly raised her hand and waved it in an effort to catch Elena's attention, until she finally saw her. Elena rolled her eyes, sighed, and threw out her arms as if embarrassed at the obviousness to where Alexandra was.

She hurried over and huffed, "For God's sake, there you are! Right in front of me!"

Elena quickly took off her jacket and plopped down across from Alexandra and began to complain, "Would you believe the traffic? And I was meeting this prospective new girl who was late."

"Don't worry," Alexandra replied with calming reassurance. "You're only twenty minutes late. Besides, I don't have a boss who checks up on me."

"Make that two bosses who doesn't check up on you!"

Alexandra chuckled softly and looked down in simple acknowledgement. "Yeah, that's for sure."

Elena smiled like an approving mother, and placed her hand on top of Alexandra's.

"So about this girl. What do you think, Alex? She's a dark-haired Ukrainian. Gorgeous girl, only twenty-two though."

"It's really your decision." Alexandra had never been one to advise Elena on her stable of girls and felt ill at ease to give her opinion.

"Well, you know, dark hair is becoming more in vogue now, as are small-breasted girls. The thing that has me wondering is that she is barely an A, and I've never hired less than a B."

Alexandra couldn't avoid getting sucked into Elena's conversation, and she thought how to answer while slowly sipping from her drink.

"It is a trend, for sure. I definitely think a lot of men want as young a girl as possible. Small tits compliment the fantasy. Sick bastards, when you really think about it."

Elena huffed in agreement. "Everything goes in cycles. Just a few years ago it was all about getting bigger and bigger. I couldn't have had enough blondes," she sighed. "Now the trend is shorter hair and flat-chested girls just out of school."

Elena bit her lip as she took the menu and began to thumb through it, before eventually concluding, "I guess I'll bring her aboard."

A moment later, Elena slammed shut the menu and looked at Alexandra, who was patiently waiting.

"Now, what brings me here?"

Before Alexandra could answer she was saved by the waiter, who came forward to take their order.

"Chicken salad with prawns for me," Elena declared.

"And I'll have the veal cutlet with asparagus."

The waiter smiled approvingly, nodded and asked, "What can I get the ladies to drink?"

Alexandra looked at Elena and answered with a question, "Two glasses of the house red?"

"Works for me," she replied.

"I'll bring the drinks out immediately," the handsome server countered before spinning away and out of sight.

"So, where were we?" Elena huffed.

"Why I want to talk to you. Remember?"

"Oh yeah. I'm simply a mess this morning. Can't slow down."

Elena flicked at her hair and pursed her thin lips. At forty-eight, Elena was still very attractive. She had kept her figure and was herself a part-time escort fifteen years ago just after the fall of communism. Even in her mid-thirties, Elena was able to book as many appointments as she wanted. It was a couple of years later, when foreign investment and a wave of expatriates began to define the Moscow scene, that she got her idea for Moscow Elite. What started as a small niche service catering to foreign businessmen soon grew into the giant company that Alex was part of.

"Oh, before I forget... I've got a couple of dates that I'm giving you priority on. When we are done here, remind me to see if I can pencil you in." She leaned forward and tilted her head as she whispered sarcastically, "Asians. Little dicks, big money!"

Alexandra could only smile and chuckle ever so slightly.

"In fact, this is exactly what I want to talk to you about."

"What? That you only want Asian clients from now on?" she retorted, snapping back up in her chair.

"No Elena. It's the business altogether. I've really been doing some thinking," she stressed with an urgency.

"Ohhh... I see." Elena sat back completely in her chair, and her expression turned sombre. "You're thinking of quitting, huh? My girls always say the same thing before they bail."

"Actually..." Alexandra swallowed hard before she could continue, "Yes."

"Shit. I didn't see this coming."

Elena looked away, out into the restaurant that bustled with activity. Somehow she didn't hear the clang of the plates and the chatter that filled the room. The waiter then appeared and placed their drinks between them in a scene of solemn stillness.

Barely looking, Elena reached for her drink and downed half the glass in one large gulp. Her disappointment was obvious, but Alexandra could barely know the full extent to why.

"Is it the percentage, or did something bad happen?" she muttered as she faced Alexandra once again.

"Because if it is, then…"

"No. No. None of that. Really not."

Then it hit Elena. Alexandra could see the realisation wash over her completely as she leaned forward with absolute certainty.

"It's a man. You've met someone, haven't you?"

Alexandra could only tighten her lips while her shoulders slumped tellingly. "Well, yes… but…"

"Don't let a man do this to you," Elena interrupted with emphatic authority. "Don't you go out on someone else's terms!"

The authority in her voice came from both her experience and the simple fact that Elena cared so deeply for Alexandra. The disappointment she felt came purely from the fact that she saw some of her girls as surrogate daughters. Perhaps it had something to do with losing her only daughter when she was thirty, or the simple fact that Elena had no other family she could truly call her own.

She leaned forward, nearly blanketing the table with her torso, and whispered with absolute authority, "You've got at least five more solid years, probably more. For God's sake, if you took this seriously you could easily be the top in the business."

"He doesn't even know about my escorting, and this really isn't about him Elena. It's about me." She stressed her final word in a futile attempt to convince Elena otherwise. Elena merely huffed like a mother who knew better.

"Besides, I can commit myself to my work now. My boss has offered me a full-time position and a promotion."

"That job is a simple hobby, Alexandra. For God's sake – do you hear yourself? You'll be lucky to afford one nice handbag a year on that measly salary. You can do such more with yourself."

Elena could barely look at her favourite and most-cherished employee. Her maternal tone was exactly that of a mother trying to argue a point to her stubborn teenaged daughter. It was if Alexandra was a teenager who wanted her mother's permission to get a huge tattoo, or for her to understand why she wanted to quit college to join a rock band that had yet to achieve anything.

However, here were two adults, and the older adult was too jaded and entrenched in her business to truly understand Alexandra's motivations. Alexandra had been guided by deeply personal convictions as she struggled to find self-actualisation and her rightful life's path. The industry would always limit this, and, until she moved from it, Alexandra knew that her life would remain a shallow and temporary lie. She wasn't even sure that Clint had been that catalyst, but she was absolutely sure that she couldn't go on like this.

"That's exactly what I intend to do – to do more with myself. Elena... I'm still young."

Elena sighed loudly and shook her head with disappointment. The waiter reappeared with their meals, and again the two were served in an uncomfortable and awkward scene.

A few seconds passed and the sobering friction seemed to tug at them, but for different reasons. Elena truly didn't understand, and was still stuck on the mention of a man. For Alexandra, her discomfort was letting down a woman who she owed so much to, as well as feeling a need for Elena to understand her.

They flicked at their food and seemed to have lost their appetite. Each wanted to speak, yet both felt they wouldn't be listened to. Eventually, Alexandra broke the uncomfortable silence with a simple plea.

"I owe so much to you, Elena. I don't want you to think that I am abandoning you, but I just don't want this anymore."

Alexandra took a bite from her plate and then a sip from her glass. She looked across to see Elena looking down, fumbling to stab a prawn with her fork.

"Listen, I'm not going to quit right away. You have me for a few more weeks. At least through June. That should give you more than enough time to find someone. Believe me, Elena – if it was anyone other than you I'd walk away today. I owe you that."

Elena knew Alexandra spoke the truth. She reached across the table and clasped Alexandra's arm and replied, "Just be happy, dear. Make sure he's worth it."

"It's really not about him. Really." She stressed 'really' in a persuasive attempt, although Elena just sat there with a resigned look.

"Listen, I'll stay in, but let me decide who I do and not. Also just so you know, I'm done with that pig Kasyanov."

"Did he...?"

Alexandra answered before Elena could finish. "It's nothing other than him fucking and treating me like a two-dollar whore. Warn whoever else becomes his favourite that he will leave them aching for at least a whole day afterwards."

"That bad, huh?" Elena furrowed forehead; her squinted eyes and clenched mouth showed she understood Alexandra's pain.

"Let's just say that I need today off for sure. I really don't know how Tatiana managed."

"We all have had our experience with those kinds of guys. Reminds me of this Polish guy I use to have when I first started. Honey, the myth is that size matters, but only up to a point. I know what you mean."

Alexandra chuckled and whispered, "Actually, just give me a normal cock and I'll come every time."

"Me too, honey. My vibrator is only sixteen centimetres." Their chuckle and confessions seem to lift the air and reunite the pseudo-mother to her daughter. "You're off from Kasyanov. I assume then the Asians are still on?"

"Of course," Alexandra replied with a twinkle in her eye and a soft smirk on her face.

"So now tell me, darling. What about this guy that you've met?"

Alexandra then leaned sheepishly back into her chair and began to smile widely.

Chapter 17

I

"Mr Markov, you have a gentleman who insists on seeing you right now."

Mikhail responded to his secretary with predictable annoyance. "He's not on my calendar, so tell him to make an appointment with you. Tell him I'm in a meeting."

Olga knew otherwise, but replied, "Yes Sir."
A moment later, Mikhail's speaker phone crackled again.

"Mr Fokin says he is a friend of yours and that he has to return the document you gave him the other night when he was at your house."

Mikhail's pulse suddenly leapt, and his eyes darted back and forth in panic. Shit! he thought to himself while he jumped from his chair and ran his hand over his face.

"Mr Markov?" Olga's voice begged for an answer that Mikhail was too stricken to give.

"Yeah... okay then... yeah... send him in."

A few seconds later the tall figure of the man who had threatened him came through the door. Again he wore all black, and his expression was just as cold and menacing as before.

"So, Mr Fokin. It's good to finally have a name behind the man."

"I just made it up. Do you think I'm that stupid?"
Actually Mikhail hadn't thought it to be an alias. He was too panicked to think clearly and he simply stood there like a planted robot – too stiff and without the free will to act normally.

"My client and I have decided you can help us get what we want in a more... impacting manner."

His telling smile assured Mikhail right then that he was powerless to disagree. Instead Mikhail collapsed down into his chair like the dead weight that he was. Defeated and discouraged by his current predicament, Mikhail quietly uttered, "What do you want me to do?"

"You are going to have a little discussion with someone and I'm going to help you with what to say."

Mikhail's mind raced as to where this was leading, but he knew it wasn't good. He wondered what dark path he was about to walk, and suddenly felt contempt towards his old friend Miroslav for unwittingly putting him in this situation.

"Okay. Then will you leave me and my family alone?"

Igor sat down in the black leather chair across from his desk, and looked at the beleaguered face of his victim.

"Actually, yes."

The two simple words immediately raised Mikhail's spirits, but somehow it seemed so unbelievable. It can't be this easy, he thought. What dark motive was his tormentor really up to, where a simple conversation would free him of this unwanted grip? Also, what about the money transfer? All these topics and thoughts flooded his head in a whirl of confusion.

"You will meet with a man named Vladimir Gorban and have a chat about this Condor project."

"I told you that I really don't know much about it. Miroslav was involved, not me!"

Mikhail's raised voice indicated the passion of his innocence, which Igor somehow believed; however, the fact that he wasn't involved previously did not exempt him from this present calling. He couldn't escape Condor and its dark secrets any longer. He would soon assume Miroslav's role, and Mikhail doubted that he would be able to walk away as if nothing had ever happened. Miroslav lost his life over Condor, and Mikhail felt confident that his would soon be over too.

"Miroslav is now dead! You expect me to believe that I can have one conversation to ensure me and my family's safety?"

"Mr Markov, you can believe what you want. You really don't have a choice. In my line of work I rarely have the opportunity to not kill someone. The easy solution is to put a bullet in your head right now! Your value to my client is far better when you remain alive and have a simple discussion with Mr Gorban. If I were you, I'd consider myself extremely fortunate."

Mikhail sensed what the killer said was somehow authentic.

"Of course," he replied in absolute obedience. "Tell me what to do."

Igor smiled as he leaned towards Mikhail, who looked back with a blank expression of servitude.

"Mr Markov, do you know who Vladimir Gorban is?"

Mikhail shook his head, although the name was vaguely familiar. Maybe it was a client from the bank or someone he could have met.

"He's a minister in the Duma."

A minister, he thought. This can't be good.

"You'll also be wired and tapped."

Mikhail exhaled and, oddly, felt more relief than fear. "You want me to extort a minister on tape?" Fuck! he thought in silent disbelief.

"I wouldn't call it that, Mr Markov. Think of it purely as a conversation, and everything will be fine. You say what we tell you, and then your problem is over."

It all sounded too easy, too contrived, and too straightforward to be this simple. Mikhail still felt resignation, but his thoughts were for the safety of his daughter and his wife. He may have been fucking women on the side, but he truly loved his wife. Alexandra and the others were just sexual playthings.

"Alright," he agreed quietly as he let out a deep breath. "How do I do this?"

Igor pulled from his jacket a thin envelope, and tossed it atop Mikhail's desk.

"Here. Everything you need to say is here. Consider this the homework assignment of your life, Mr Markov."

Mikhail dragged it methodically across his desk, as if there was a bomb were inside that would explode if moved too suddenly.

"You will also wear a tiny earpiece so I will be... listening. I hope you don't plan anything stupid, Mr Markov. You'll be outfitted with a mic, a camera, and I'll be listening to every word you two say." Igor smiled. "I've always wanted to be a Hollywood director."

"So when, then?"

"Next Tuesday, actually. A day before your precious family return from their little holiday. That gives you a few days to study your lines very carefully."

"And all this wiring and shit?"

"We meet here in your office at nine o'clock first, and then you will ride with me."

Mikhail immediately thought that his life would end on the drive back, and he suddenly felt scared and fragile. He imagined the hulking thug tormenting him, before finally shooting him in the head. But what could he do? Mikhail felt powerless and used. Meeting Gorban didn't worry him as much as the dreaded ride back from the Kremlin.

Mikhail could only hang his heavy head into his sweaty palms. "Yeah, sure. Whatever."

Igor cocked his head and stood up before him. "This isn't whatever. This is everything for your Anastasia and your measly corrupt life. Soon you'll be hugging the women of your life again, and all this will be over."

Mikhail couldn't imagine him ever seeing either his wife or daughter again. It occurred to him just then that he would write a letter to Marina and mail it to their home. He would explain everything – the blackmail, their own jeopardy, and how he really loved her. If he somehow lived then he could intercept the note but, if not, then it was there for her to understand how desperate he had been.

Suddenly it occurred to him that he couldn't possibly be able to intercept his mail, and his mind raced to an alternative. Frantically his mind raced to who he could possibly trust with such a letter and then it hit him – Olga!

"Mr Markov?" Igor's voice broke the mental planning.

"Yeah, yes. I got it. Tuesday. Nine o'clock."

"You'll want to pencil me in this time. The name is what, Mr Markov?"

"Fokin, I think."

"Very good. I'm glad you remember. It means you'll do fine next week when it really counts."

Mikhail slumped back in his chair in a fit of overwhelming frustration and fear. The world around him seemed to spin out of control and his mind raced so fast that he could only hide his eyes behind the palms of his hands.

The letter remained on his desk and on his mind; however, for now, Mikhail simply hid in the forgiving darkness that his hands provided.

II

Torie rose from her chair and was readying herself to leave work when Boris came by. Torie smiled at the twenty-something member who had only joined the centre a couple weeks prior. He was rather severely afflicted mentally as well as being bi-polar, but was nevertheless functional. His IQ was reportedly seventy-six, which meant he didn't have to live in a state-run institution. He was lucky to have been spared such a fate. Being in prison would have been a better destiny.

Before joining the centre, Torie had no idea just how repressed the mentally ill community was. Suffering from any physical or mental ailment was something she knew was a great national stigma.

Almost any Russian would see Boris and feel terribly uncomfortable and demand his exodus to an institution; however, Torie saw tenderness and empathy. Boris, Io and the countless members she worked with amongst every day were her extended family to care for, and she strived for their improved life quality.

She bent over slightly so that she could look directly into his hypnotic gaze. "Boris, I want you to come back tomorrow so you can help me cut out name tags for the new members that come on Friday. Are you going to do that for me?"

Getting the members to work in her supported service unit was one of her leading tasks, and she found that she was able to have the highest attendance rates of any other unit by fostering fun, team spirit and delegation. Her members liked her and she kept them involved. The alternative would have been either sitting around the number of couches and chairs or, worse yet, having never discovered the centre in the first place.

"What's your son's name?" Boris asked shyly.

"Alexander, but everyone just calls him Alexi."

The long pause and stare from Boris meant he was processing what Torie had told him as if her statement was a complex algebra equation.

"He's pretty."

Boris' face barely changed expressions, yet she managed to see the faintest of smiles when he spoke. His innocence was perhaps all he truly had, and Torie fed off of this energy that her members omitted. Moscow was so cold and the people seemed so hardened. Most of her neighbours and environment were defined by aloofness and sterility. The weather was so frequently bleak and the Muscovites somehow had become living manifestations of their grim and dour environment.

However, Torie was unlike most in the big cold-hearted city. Her heart was larger than life and she saw sunshine everywhere where others only saw grey. Sunshine was everything from the birds chirping in the midst of noisy traffic to the colourful fruit stands in front of dilapidated buildings. Her work was a secondary passion to her family, and fit perfectly into a consistent, holistic life credo and belief system. She believed in the goodness of everything and somehow prospered in a city and populace that saw her as naïve and peculiar.

Torie was the quintessential optimist, and she derived great pleasure by helping those in need. F.I.M recognised this instantly and valued her contribution. Although Torie had relatively few friends, most of those that she did spend personal time with were from the centre. Oksana, Irina and Polina were more than other unit leaders from work, but rather her three closest friends.

"Yes he is, but he takes after his father," Torie bemused in typical modesty.

"You're beautiful."

Boris' eyes lost their glaze and seemed to twinkle as they met her own eyes for the first time. All Torie could do was smile. She always smiled when people pointed out her beauty. The fact was that Torie was a beam of sunlight as a person; however, it was her internal beauty that radiated.

Torie smiled brightly, reached down and placed her hand softly on Boris' cheek before replying, "Thank you, Boris. And you are a handsome young man too. I'll see you tomorrow, right?"

After a few seconds Boris' reply assured her of his attendance. "Yes ma'am," he replied softly.

Torie glanced at her watch and saw that it was just after one-thirty. She knew that she had a full forty-five minutes before needing to be at the day-care centre.

She bid goodbye to Boris and Polina, who had popped into the room momentarily to put on her long overcoat. A few minutes later she was descending into the city's underbelly to catch her train.

She found a nearby free seat and then peacefully closed her eyes. She thought about what she would do later in the afternoon and evening and how she could please the two men of her life. It was often that Torie would use the quarter hour ride to contemplate life and her family. It was her own form of meditation.

The noisiness of the tracks and train had been replaced by the calm serenity of images of her family at the Black Sea. She marvelled in the beauty of her simple life and the happiness she derived from it. The love she felt for Stefan and Alexi showered her spirit, and she smiled brightly. She decided then that she would fix Alexi his favourite sandwich – chocolate paste spread - and give him an extra Choco Pie when putting him to bed for being such a good little boy. Choco Pies were his favourite sweet food and he probably could eat a whole box of the little cakes that were nearly exactly like American Moon Pies.

She also knew that she would make love to her husband that night and would change into her sexiest underwear before he came home. It never failed to arouse Stefan when he saw her in a thong and half-cupped bra, exposing most of her delicate nipples. They hadn't made love in five days, and she knew that a tender massage and love-making would ease some of the recent stress he was getting from work.

She let her mind wonder even further and nearly fell asleep. Her stop was the fifth along the route and, like some sort of internal alarm clock, her eyes reopened just as the train began to brake for her final destination. The door reopened and a slew of people gathered around the entrance, allowing her and four others to exit into the brightly-lit underground cavern.

It wasn't long before Torie was bounding along the sidewalk, weaving amongst the throngs of people on the busy thoroughfare of shops and mini-markets that defined her neighbourhood. She always enjoyed window-shopping along the packed Yamskaya and didn't seem to mind that she rarely bought anything for herself. Stefan would often have to insist that it was all right to indulge herself with a new outfit or pair of shoes, but somehow she thought that to be frivolous. Instead, she liked spending her money on Stefan, and especially Alexi.

III

Across town, Alexandra lay naked as her client rose from on top of her. His ejaculation had filled the purple condom that he now pulled off as he looked down at her and asked, "You okay?"

Vladimir had probably fucked her twenty times before, but this was the first that she seemed so detached and uninvolved. She barely moaned, and she lacked the animation or passion of before. He felt as if she was one of those artificial dolls one could buy from a sex shop.

"Yeah. Sure. Why? What's up?"

Alexandra hadn't even noticed that the last two minutes of their sex was little more than the minister pummelling her on top while she lie there like a dead woman, looking at the blank hotel wall.

"You seem... distracted. You weren't there," he added, almost apologetically.

"Really?" she replied, with near-shock.

Of course her one-word answer was purely rhetorical, because she hadn't been 'there' at all. Instead she was thinking of Clint, who she was to meet in two hours. She was wondering why she was still fucking clients, and every one now seemed harder and harder to engage. Somehow, perhaps out of some basic human conditioning, she still would instantly get moist and ready for their physical assault; however, her mind was no longer there. Her mind had been her secret weapon, even over her stunning body. Now, however, it was the very thing that was undoing her.

"You know," she said as her mind raced for an explanation, "I have a bit of a headache and a sore stomach."

It was the best she could do at the moment. A headache seemed such a cliché, but it was all she could think of. How could she tell the powerful figure who loved to fuck her regularly that she couldn't stand him, his touch, or his boring fucking? How could she reveal that she was finally – maybe - in love? How could she let him know that his touch made her skin jump and, that when he filled her inside, she felt guilty and vile? Instead she could only smile and act.

"You were fantastic, as always. I really needed you today and am so happy I could be with you. This was relaxing and exactly what I needed," she replied with the softest of smiles, and touched his cheek.

Alexandra was back in full role-play. Clint had begun to consume her and take over her mind. He had already taken over her body, as her sexuality would explode the moment he kissed her. She would fall victim to him and give herself completely like no other man before. Such was his power and her loss of control.

"Good, then. I sure needed you, Sasha," he confessed as he exhaled in relief. "I really was looking forward to this the whole day."

If only Alexandra could say the same. Instead she was regretting their meeting, and kept thinking back to her promise to Elena. She was fucking for Elena, and wondered if she could honestly make it through the summer as she had promised.

"Listen, I know I've asked you this before, but if you ever decide to want a threesome then let Elena know because I'd love to hook up with you and one of the other girls. I'd tip you well," he said with a twinkle in his eye and a lift in his tone.

"Hmm... I know you would, and I'll think about it. You know, I'm really a one-on-one kind of girl, but if I ever would do this then it will definitely be with you."

Of course this was a lie, and Alexandra had no desires to be with another woman. A few years ago it really interested her and she had her chances, but somehow it had never materialised. Now she was beyond the fantasy, and especially now since she was with Clint.

"So, then. Will I meet you soon?" he asked, yet the question from his perspective was purely a statement of fact. For Alexandra, it was a question to which she knew the answer. Alexandra would never see the fat man naked again, not even for the five hundred dollars that he paid Elena, plus the one hundred dollar tip that was all hers. In all, she made four hundred dollars from him, and before she always thought of it as easy money. Vladimir was straightforward and uncomplicated – the best kind of client - who also tipped twenty percent. However now she would rather work a full day for the same money!

"Absolutely," she mumbled hesitantly. "As always."

She wouldn't, though. This time when she was handed his hundred dollar tip she didn't have to smile at him again. Another thing was now clear. The threesome with Mr Nagano was off. She couldn't keep doing this, especially with multiple clients. Now she would have to let down Elena, which she dreaded more than the fuck she just had to endure.

Chapter 18

I

Mikhail's buzzer went off and, just as Olga spoke, Mikhail interrupted. "Let him in."

"Uh… yes, sir. Right away," she replied in surprised resignation.

Mikhail's large office door opened seconds later, and Igor entered confidently. He was carrying a black leather briefcase that matched his typical black clothing. If ever there was a cliché of a hitman, then Igor was it.

"Good morning, Mr Markov!"

The unwanted tormentor sounded cheery and his broad smile revealed an expression that couldn't be more of a polar opposite to his. Mikhail sat dour and depressed. He was pensive, preoccupied and fearful. He truly thought that his life would be over by noon.

"I hope you studied your notes well," he said as he placed the briefcase on top of the edge of Mikhail's desk.

"Yes."

A one-word half-hearted answer was all he could muster. His eyes still focused straight ahead and he barely noticed that Igor had just opened the briefcase, exposing a host of electronics. He slowly turned his gaze to the attaché case that also revealed papers, folders and a gun that was firmly held into place by a built-in clip.

"Will I need that?" he asked, pointing towards the gun.

Igor looked towards his pointed finger and then chuckled as he continued, "No, Mr Markov. Hardly. I hope I don't either."

"So then," Igor continued as he pulled out a set of tiny thin wires that were nearly a metre in length, "I'll set you up now with the microphone."

He approached Mikhail, who sat in a mix of trembling fear and resigned peace to his seemingly pre-planned fate. Mikhail marvelled at the brute's huge hands and how subtly they manipulated the delicate wire.

"Open your shirt," he barked authoritatively.

Mikhail undid his tie and unbuttoned the first three buttons. Igor quickly placed two patches on his chest and slid the wire through his shirt button. The scene was like a mother fixing their toddler's bib in preparation for a feeding. Mikhail sat slumped, and did nothing while Mikhail worked feverishly. Clearly he had done this before.

Igor reached in his kit and pulled out small scissors and then turned Mikhail's jacket inside out just enough to expose the brand's label. He snipped at the inside material and then cut away the button where the breast pocket was.

Mikhail was amazed how the end of the long attached filament could so quickly be outfitted with a button, which actually wasn't a button at all. Instead it was a camera lens. A bit of tape then secured its place on the inside of the jacket, leaving the operation finished and Igor looking smug.

"Now fix your shirt and your tie."

A few seconds later, Mikhail was finished. He could feel the discomfort of the tape that was just above his right nipple. The smallish black device was a miniature television that Igor adjusted. Mikhail could see his office through the lens of his jacket, which appeared as black and white on the monitor.

"I'll expect you to sit as still as possible when you are there. Don't move too unnecessarily."

Mikhail nodded knowingly.

Abruptly the killer placed the device back into the briefcase and then pulled out a small box, which he opened before Mikhail's inquisitive eyes. The tiny flimsy-looking instrument sandwiched between the enormous crude fingers seemed like it would surely be crushed if barely squeezed.

It was Mikhail's earpiece that wasn't any bigger than a large fingernail clipping. Mikhail had seen hearing aids, but this was altogether different. It was so small that he wondered how it would ever come back out after being firmly placed inside his ear.

Mikhail then felt his large fingers fill his ear, but, surprisingly, he could barely feel the hearing unit. Mikhail himself touched at his ear where the apparatus felt to be a piece of ear wax – a bit annoying, yet quite manageable.

"Now we do a little test."

Igor sat down across from him in the same chair he had sat in the week before, and pulled out a black slender stalk. He flipped a small switch at its tip and spoke into it softly.

"How does this sound?"

Mikhail perked straight up when he heard Igor's voice. Amazingly, Mikhail could hear the stranger's voice as if it were some sort of inner voice resonating from inside his head.

"Jesus! Yes! That is clear."

Instinctively he reached for his ear, but, as he prodded at the entrance of it, Igor reprimanded him. "Whatever you do, you will not touch your ear when you are there. Understand?"

"Yeah, yeah. Sure."

"Lastly, Mr Markov, you are getting a new watch."

"A new watch?" Mikhail was again paralysed in a state of absolute confusion.

"Take off your watch and wear this. Make sure it is on the right wrist."

He handed Mikhail a watch which seemed unusually light, and felt cheap.

"This is your microphone, and I want you to try to sit like this."

The black-dressed thug sat in front of him with his right hand extended on the edge of his own desk. By doing so, it revealed the watch slightly as his cuff receded.

"This way the sound quality is even better," he advised.

Mikhail slipped on the watch, careful to put it on his right wrist as told. He had no idea why it mattered which side it was on, but, at this point, the less he questioned the better he felt. Mikhail knew what lay ahead. He had read over and over the typed letter that Igor had given him – now it was clear what the expectation was. He would incriminate a corrupt Duma official, yet he wondered how he could ever return to the normalcy that the hit-man had promised.

Mikhail was hoping that everything was just a secretive bribe; however, the information provided in the letter was too descriptive to live with. It seemed certain that such secrets would cost him his life. He wished he could have avoided this moment and this day. He had longed that Marina and Anastasia would have appeared in Moscow early, and that they all could simply run away. Of course they hadn't, and he now sat in his office chair like a sorry zombie.

"Okay then. We're ready."

Igor motioned to the door, and he closed his briefcase with a slam. Mikhail rose slowly and cautiously, his eyes never leaving the man standing before him. Again he felt like a dead man walking – wired up like some sort of science-fiction spy. He felt weird realising that everything he saw, heard or said would be controlled.

Damn Miroslav! he thought to himself again. Perhaps this was the fiftieth time he had cursed his former friend. Damn this all!

II

The lunch crowd at Galereya bustled just as it always did at this hour, and was no different from one month ago when Clint and Alexandra first met. Both had decided to celebrate their two month anniversary together by revisiting the same restaurant.

Arkady came over to pour their champagne.

"I always get warm and fuzzy over a love story," he said as he poured the first of the two glasses of champagne. "I think you two are absolutely adorable together."

"I figured I better take him before you do," Alexandra quipped instantly.

Both Clint and Arkady laughed, while Alexandra's straight face hid her own giggles that desperately wanted to escape.

"You know it, girlfriend," Arkady quipped. "Now I'll leave you two lovebirds alone while I pair up other potential couples."

Alexandra said nothing, but her eyes said it all. With him they always did her talking, and they always could transform him in an instant.

Clint could do nothing, just as always. He was always a prisoner to her humour and eyes – the deadly combination which he assumed had held other men hostage.

Alexandra slowly sipped from her drink, before leaning forward and finally placing it back on the table. "Okay. 'A', I was thinking I love you. 'B', I was thinking just how damn hot you are or 'C', I was thinking that these past months have been one of my best months because I met you."

The pause between them was long, and both smiled warmly at each other as their eyes were locked together. Finally, Clint spoke.

"And 'D', all the above? Where is that option?"

Alexandra chuckled and threw herself back into her chair. She was disappointed that he had usurped her on an option she should have thought of.

"No 'D' this time. Come on now, which is it? 'A', 'B' or 'C'?"

"It's all the above, Alex. That's my answer and I'm sticking to it," he replied, with a slight chuckle that wouldn't stop.

"Okay, you stubborn American. It was 'C'. Happy now?"

"Yes, Alex, I am."

His tone and face suddenly had turned serious and sober. Clint was happy about his relationship with Alexandra. They were spending more and more time together, although it was still limited. Each lived a secret life from the other, yet somehow both had made one another a priority in their limited free time.

"Meeting you has been really good for me. In ways you don't know; so yes, I am happy."

Alexandra's face was a mix of satisfaction and puzzlement, as she had no idea what depths he hinted at; however, it was enough for her to delicately raise her glass and reply, "A toast to more happiness."

Clint's glass met hers and, as they clinked, he thought how their budding relationship was proving to be the exact remedy for the guilt and pain of losing Aleeka. At one time he swore off any other relationship, although he knew deeply that he would love again. And now it was Alexandra who made him feel alive and happy once more.

"I can't believe this has happened so fast," she said with surprise and astonishment. "In one way it seems like yesterday, and another it seems like a long time. It's like I've known you for months and months."

"I know what you mean," he replied matter-of-factly. "I never expected this when I first saw you, that's for sure."

"What did you expect?" she countered.

Clint could only pause in momentary reflection as he thought how to answer. The question was simple; however, his feelings and emotions were too complex. Condensing everything down to a simple answer gripped him in a trapped quiet. He could have never have expected to be feeling what now overcame him a mere two months later.

Finally he answered, "I didn't know what to expect, honestly. I was just hoping I could see you again, but I never really thought much beyond that."

His confession made him instinctively reach for his drink, as if he could somehow hide his nervousness behind the glass sphere that would partially conceal his face. Nonetheless, Alexandra read his emotions as if they were written on the forehead that he couldn't fully veil.

She had years of experience with interpreting men's emotions, actually. For years now, Alexandra shape-shifted herself from an educated woman of culture to an impassioned slut when in the presence of her clients. Being so close physically to so many men had given her a metaphysical bond to the other sex, so Clint's nervousness was easy to read.

Alexandra believed him. Still, she assumed he was like every other man she had ever met, who initially saw her as a potential plaything. How could she assume anything differently? She only knew men as sexual, and most of her contact with them somehow involved the pursuit of sex, even if it was her own. Only later did she discover something different with Clint. He seemed to genuinely care for her, and he talked about the mundane and ordinary as well as their future. He wasn't solely fixated on her sexuality, which she readily gave him, but rather on her person.

"I guess I felt the same," she countered. "But I wouldn't have expected this. I wasn't looking for a relationship, but... you know... in a way I was."

"Like how?"

"Well, like every girl who has big dreams and still holds out for a Prince Charming to come along. I'm really jaded towards men for the most part."

The source of her confession struck both for the same reason; only Alexandra hadn't a clue that her lunch date knew exactly why she felt this way.

She continued, "Then I met you and you had so many more dimensions. We just connected in a way that I haven't felt. Ever."

"Wow!" Clint gasped with sudden surprise. "Ever?"

Alexandra paused and her face reflected her seriousness. "Yeah. I guess so."

Clint was smitten right then and there. This was exactly the women he believed in. At moments like these, she was his beautiful blonde angelic Madonna.

"So, then. Let's make a toast!"

He raised his glass and met hers, as both smiled as they always did. The expensive glasses pinged, omitting the quality pitch that only expensive crystal can.

"Here's to us," she said in return.

III

Mikhail watched in absolute silence as he looked out of the window. The city raced by and the buildings were partly illuminated by the bright sun, which peered out through the darkened thick clouds. The heavens were an ominous mix of emerging sun and threatening black. What he stared at above could just as well symbolise his life at this moment. He wondered if he would live to see another sunny day or if he would die today, Monday, March 28th, when everyone else was purely thinking about the challenges of a new work week.

The two men didn't speak at all until Igor muttered, "Think of your family."

Mikhail turned and looked at him in disgust. "Why else would I help you?"

Igor just gave a half-hearted smile and replied, "Who knows, Mr Markov? Who knows?"

Mikhail searched around for any clues he might be able to use if given the slim chance to talk to the police. He had memorised the licence plate, but when he saw the Hertz sticker on the glovebox his hopes were initially dashed. Still, he thought that the car could be traced back to the man who looked straight ahead in serious contemplation. Bastard surely didn't use his real name, he thought. Indeed Igor hadn't; yet Mikhail could only hope.

The facade of the Ministry of Defence suddenly came into view. The great building seemed to grow in size and rise above them like some sort of mythical living entity. A few minutes later Igor pulled into a narrow road that bordered the great complex, and he drove directly by the huge Stalinist styled building until finally an unassuming entrance appeared. Two rifled guards stood waiting, and Igor pushed a button that slowly rolled down his window.

A straight-faced uniformed man who couldn't have been over twenty leaned down and peered inside the car; however, he said nothing. Igor also didn't speak, but revealed a badge attached to a red lanyard. The guard simply motioned with his head to proceed, and mumbled, "Okay."

"Governmental entrance," Igor said to Mikhail, who sat quietly, absorbing the whole experience.

Mikhail was partly consumed with his pending meeting and partly in awe of what he was experiencing. Every Muscovite wonders what it is truly like inside one of the hallowed ministry buildings like this. Now Mikhail was where so very few ever were.

The slender driveway quickly led to a grey, unassuming building. They parked in a small lot nearly filled with a predictable fleet of black BMWs and Mercedes'. "Come on!" Igor ordered.

Mikhail complied and followed his giant host to the door that was only metres away. Again Igor revealed his badge, and the right door cracked open immediately. Inside was a long hallway only partially illuminated by a few exposed light bulbs hanging clumsily overhead. Their steps resonated like those coming from inside a metal chamber, and the acoustics inside meant that anyone at the end could surely hear them. Where they were going still remained a mystery to Mikhail, and he was surprised that after such a long walk they still hadn't come across a single person.

After trudging up twenty or so steps Mikhail could finally see some evidence of life after all. The last stair led to a glass door where he could see a handful of people walking about, as well as a large counter with an attractive blonde sitting behind. Mikhail opened the door and after a few steps Igor surged ahead and approached the pretty blonde, who casually looked up and asked, "Your appointment is with who, Sir?"

"Mr Gorban is expecting us. Mr Markov is here to see him."

"Very well, then. Please sign in here."

Mikhail saw the signature of his chaperone, and began to wonder if Fokin could actually be his real name. Igor had consistently used this name since they met, and Mikhail made a mental note to check that with the car rental company should he have the chance. For some reason Mikhail now seemed consumed in finding out the true identity of the man he was hostage to.

Little did he know that Igor was actually too trained and too experienced to be discovered by such an espionage virgin. Mikhail would never be able to track down this professional hit-man. Igor had lived this long because he had learned to be stealthy. A few times Igor had turned his hunters into prey, killing them when he found out he was being looked for.

The long-haired secretary advised, "Third floor. Room 303. You can take the elevator right here."

She pointed casually to the elevator doors directly adjacent to her counter, and the two nodded in thanks as they moved away. As the doors closed behind them, Igor spoke without looking at Mikhail. "You'll be on your own now, but remember – I'll be watching you. Don't fuck this up!"

Mikhail knew his time with the stranger was nearly finished. His mind turned to the pending meeting, and he began to feel nervous and unsure. Being a vice president in Sberbank meant meeting influential people, but not like this. He certainly never had to be confrontational. Mr Gorban was a Duma minister and surely was too well connected to let a mere banker influence him. Mikhail nodded and mumbled back, "I won't."

"Good, then. I won't be joining you, but I'll meet you when you are done."

"How will I find you?" Mikhail wondered.

Igor chuckled and released a cocky sneer. "Mr Markov, I will find you. I always do."

The elevator settled to the third floor and the doors opened slowly.

"Go on," Igor said, as he nudged Mikhail in the back.

Mikhail stepped out clumsily and looked back just as the doors slowly shut, leaving the man in black behind.

"Stand just in front of his door until I tell you it's okay to enter."

Igor's voice filled his head so clearly. He wanted to touch his ear, yet immediately remembered not to. The instinct, he knew, would be hard to eliminate. The sign read 303 with Vladimir Gorban underneath.

"Now I'm ready. Proceed," the voice in the earphone demanded. Mikhail tapped on the door firmly with his bare knuckles.

A second passed, and then a couple more. Mikhail's mind raced at the possibilities and, just when he was ready to knock again, the door flung open. What stood before him was a middle-aged woman with pursed lips.

"Please come in, Mr Markov. Mr Gorban is waiting."

"Yes... thank you," he stuttered as he followed obediently.

Mikhail followed the frumpy-looking woman through the spacious room and to the door of Minister Gorban himself. The secretary then opened her boss's door to expose an ageing pot-bellied minister with a thin moustache. He was about the same age as Mikhail but with far less hair.

"Come in, Mr Markov."

The minister walked to meet his guest. Mikhail approached and extended his hand, but the minister only gave it a loose perfunctory shake before rushing back to the protective confines of his desk. A super-sized black leather chair awaited him, and he seemed to launch himself into it. Gorban then casually pointed towards the frail and well-used chair in front of his gigantic mahogany desk. The door closed and it finally came down to just the two of them – or three, when Mikhail thought about the silent ghost who was listening from afar.

For some reason Mikhail had imagined the office to be somehow bigger, more prestigious, or even more impressive. Instead his confines were no more different to that of his bank's middle managers. Mikhail sat, and he was quick to remember what his trainer had instructed him to do – sit upright, still, as motionless as possible.

"So, Mr Markov," the minister began. "We have a situation here and, before I received your email, I had no idea you were involved. Imagine my surprise."

Of course Mikhail hadn't sent any email and, in fact, he only knew a bit of what he was jumping into. His puppet-master was controlling everything, and he truly felt the manipulation that was now upon him. Mikhail replied coolly and deliberately, just as the text he studied suggested. "We need to talk about how to carry on with Condor."

"Yes, Condor – that pesky project from the Americans. What can I say? Miroslav had that running so well, and then he ends up dead for God knows what reason."

Hearing that his boss and friend was dead still affected Mikhail. He tensed upon hearing of it again. "Now I am in charge," he said calmly, as he tried to stay focused. "As I told you in the email, I discovered this account from my own audit, and approached Miroslav, who was also my friend. He didn't tell me much on purpose except that it was an account created for you. Everything else I wrote in the email."

"And who made you in charge, Mr Markov? I never knew you to be involved so highly."

Mikhail didn't know what to say, but Igor came to his rescue "Tell him that you were contacted by the American. The one who came every month to Miroslav."

Mikhail instantly answered as if he thought of the answer himself. "The American, who always came to Miroslav?"

He didn't know the name of the American, as it all was loosely scripted in his notes. His capturer wanted the name, and it was one of his tasks to complete. Gorban, however, coolly leaned back in his chair..

"Ahh – Mr Wolf did, huh? It's strange he didn't tell me this, though." The minister seemed suspicious, and Mikhail could only bite the inside of his cheeks nervously.

"Lean just a bit back," Igor instructed.

He did - still Gorban sat quiet and puzzled. Finally he replied, "Well then. It looks like you're our new bank guy. Did Mr Wolf explain to you the terms?"

The ploy had worked – Gorban had fallen for the ruse. "Answer no," Mikhail heard.

"No," he replied obediently.

"Well, you do everything that Mr Wolf instructs and you'll get one thousand dollars per transfer. You'll be provided one code from me and one from Wolf when he is there to see you. Of course, you will use your discretionary right to approve the transfer yourself without oversight."

"When is the last of these payments?"

"The deal is set up through the end of this year. At least. You'll earn a few thousand more dollars, don't you worry."

"Do we continue to pay Mr Pilkin?" he asked in an attempt to goad his subject into confirming the name.

"Of course. Why wouldn't we? He'll provide transport of the arms to the tribal Afghans."

"Just checking. I wasn't sure if you were planning on changing buyers."

"Only our own Mr Markov. However, I suppose a simple banker like you wouldn't know the finer details of Russian life, would you?"

Indeed Mikhail wouldn't have. Only now had he crossed over into the dark underworld of corruption and crime. He knew he would pay for it, too. One doesn't deal with unnamed killers and corrupt Duma ministers and not get away cleanly.

"No sir, I wouldn't." Mikhail nodded in agreement, a look of desperation across his worried face. Again he heard Igor's voice in his ear. "Come on. Get the name."

Mikhail was just readying himself for the next part of the scripted play. He was going to ask the minister this, but now his manipulator demanded it.

"Minister Gorban. I would like to ask you something off the record, just for my information."

"Hmm… you can always ask," he replied, as he leaned forward tentatively.

"The man who I am paying. I think you underestimate me as… what do you call me? A 'simple banker'? What if I tell you that I know it is Krokav?"

Vladimir leaned back now and smiled brightly. His large grin couldn't mask the thoughts going through his head.

"I see you're a smart man, Mr Markov. What's in a name anyway? You just need to assure everyone involved that these transfers stay secret, especially from the Americans who are behind this."

Again Igor whispered into his earpiece. "Find out who the Americans are."

"These Americans that I am helping. Who exactly are they?"

"Why does that matter, Mr Markov?" Gorban asked indignantly.

"If I have to put my life on the line then I want to know the fucking gangster who I am helping." Mikhail leaned forward and whispered softly, "Call it insurance."

"How do you know this anyway, Mr Markov?"

"I'm not an idiot, and I was close to Miroslav. Besides, I'm curious."

"This whole arrangement is from our beloved imperialists in Washington. I don't need to tell you how high this goes – just use your brain. They send me this Simon Wolf babysitter and I play superintendent to this little charade. Naturally, for my own fee."

Mr Gorban leaned forward and scratched his cheek before continuing, "But what's in a name anyways? You and these men who sell arms will never come into contact. You are a different piece of the puzzle altogether. Well, I think we are done here. Thank you for sending me the email last week, but from now on let's meet another way."

He scribbled down something on a small tablet and then tore it away before handing it to Mikhail. A simple glance revealed a phone number which surely was the Minister's.

"You never know when the eye in the sky is checking, if you know what I mean?"

Mikhail just smiled and shoved the paper deep into his pants' pocket. Internally he wished that Kremlin insiders would find this email, although he doubted they would. He thought that maybe a real computer expert would be able to trace the IP address which could exonerate him, but the sudden realisation struck him that he was getting ahead of himself. First he had to survive the day.

"Good day, Mr Markov. I'll be in touch."

Gorban led him to the door and opened, it letting Mikhail to shuffle out, breathing heavily. His secretary barely gave him a passing glance and instead typed feverishly with absolute concentration. He let himself out and said nothing as he heard Gorban's door close behind him.

"Now go into the elevator and I will meet you in the lobby. Wait for me by the front door."

"I did what you want," he whispered strongly, "Now just leave me and my family alone."

"Shut up!"

Mikhail had pushed too far. The reply was firm and laced with abrupt fury.

"I give the orders. Just wait by the front door and don't touch anything on you."

"Okay," Mikhail replied meekly.

A moment later he entered the elevator. Just before the door closed a hand stuck through and caused it to re-open again. A balding fat man entered. Their eyes met briefly, and Mikhail stepped backwards to give him room. He turned his back to Mikhail and allowed the doors to close.

A few seconds later they reopened to reveal the lobby, with much more activity than the seemingly quiet hallways of above. The man bolted out. Mikhail waited and waited some more. The longer he stood by the front door the more uncomfortable he became. His palms became moist.

Finally the huge black figure came towards Mikhail like a gliding Grim Reaper, moving effortlessly but directly towards its imprisoned prey. Just before he reached him he motioned subtly with his head to follow. They left the building walking single file and back out to the parked car.

When in the car, Igor stated "I have what I want, Mr Markov. You did your job."

"So, please just leave me and my family alone?"

Igor casually looked over at the pleading man, whose panic-stricken eyes were the same as when they first met. He smiled and then looked back at the road, which was only half-full, before turning on a side street that was empty except for a couple of parked cars.

"The lovely ladies in your life will live."

Mikhail did not know what to feel first – relief, happiness and mental exhaustion all swept over him like an emotional tsunami. He exhaled and his head unexpectedly fell forward. He wiped both hands across it and over his damp forehead, glistening in the Moscow sunlight.

Mikhail was overcome that he had made it through his tortured capture, and felt silly for trying to remember details which he could relay to the police. For all he knew the driver had his influences with the police as well. If he could so easily get inside the Defence Ministry, then surely his reach extended further down the State-sponsored food chain. Mikhail looked over and, with a thankful and reassured expression, mumbled with sighed relief, "I'm glad this is finally over."

No sooner had he completed his reply than the muffled sound of a gunshot filled the car. Mikhail's head instantly snapped right from the force of the bullet that pierced his skull. Igor slowed to a stop and sat the long barrelled gun on Mikhail's lap as he rolled up the window and took out a handkerchief from his suit's breast pocket. He leaned over his dead victim and wiped at the bit of blood spatter on the dash and on the lower part of the window.

Igor's eyes were actually only centimetres from the frozen stare of Mikhail, and he stopped to look at him for a second. Oddly, he felt a remorseful. The killing of innocents seemed to slowly be chipping away at his impenetrable armour, as the thought of Mikhail's wife and child entered his mind. He blinked quickly to escape the momentary guilt, and rose back completely in his seat. His arm reached back to the rear floorboard where he picked up a baseball cap, and he put it on Mikhail to conceal the gore. Exit wounds, he knew, could be visible to passers-by. The drive to where he would dump Mikhail was still twenty minutes away, and everything had to go according to the assassin's plan.

Chapter 19

I

Igor pinched at the bridge of his nose and sat at the same grimy table as always. Slovij's was one of those diners trapped in time that would never change. It was cheap and low-rent when it opened twenty five years ago, and hadn't changed one bit since then. Only the odd fresh coat of paint was added to renew the grey that eventually replaced the interior wall's original white.

The smallish yellow plastic chair creaked under the weight of the large hit-man. Igor didn't identify with the crude and simple ways of Oleg, but remained loyal to the gang mainly because of Viktor. He wished he could deal more with Viktor instead of his ill-tempered son; nonetheless, this current assignment was easily his most profitable in a long time.

Igor looked across at his host, who sat smiling while the two bodyguards predictably flanked either side of the entrance.

"So, what brings us here today?" Oleg asked with a sudden sternness.

"I thought you should know something that will... well... enlighten you."

Oleg's eyes were firmly planted on Igor. "And?"

"First, Mr Markov has been taken care of. Just as you asked for. The Minister is on his own now, which means everything is on plan."

Oleg smiled brightly as he leaned forward and replied, "That's why I hire you. Now that pig Gorban goes down!" He began to laugh softly.

"I hate to dampen your fun, but you may have a new... well... issue."

Oleg's expression transformed into a stare of concern.

"What kind of issue?" he demanded.

"You may have a problem with your lady friend. Remember when I called you a few days ago to ask where you found your whore? You know – the one I saw you with recently at the Holiday Inn?"

"Yeah," Oleg countered with obvious curiosity.

"She appears to have other clients that I would call... well... a conflict of interests."

"Like?"

"Like Gorban. Just this week I've seen them meet at his hotel. It's not good when you do the math." Igor sipped from his drink and squinted his eyes emphatically before continuing, "It looks like you might have a mole, or an insider."

Oleg could only clench his teeth and begin to seethe. Igor had seen him like this before, and every time was predictable. Oleg was like a volcano that took a while before he ultimately blew. He would boil inside his rage, churning and bubbling from inside, before ultimately shouting and losing his temper.

Now Igor watched in uncomfortable silence as his benefactor brooded and slowly come to realise what the implications of his information meant. Seemingly everyone was conspiring against Oleg, but only one person must be behind it all – Sasha.

"How many times have you seen her with them?" he asked, attempting calm.

"Well... only once but, you know, I've only been on them for a little while now. It's definitely her. I never forget a face and I've got some photos of her with him inside the hotel. I have the pictures here if you want to see, but I have better proof than these photos."

"Bitches and backstabbers. Fuck them all! Let me see the photos!" Oleg exclaimed, crashing his hand on the table with a thud so powerful that Igor's glass shook.

Igor could only sit and watch Oleg's anger mount. No matter how hard he beat and abused the flimsy table, nothing would change the fact that those closest to him could not be trusted. It was bad enough that his business partner was sneaking behind him on a deal he knew nothing of. One could almost expect this from such an insubstantial and feeble alliance between the two cartels; however, his regular paid mistress came as a total surprise.

"Are you sure it's her?" Oleg demanded as he took the photos from him.

Igor was sure, and would have never noticed if he hadn't seen her with Oleg only a couple weeks before. He had paid one of his many underworld contacts to break into the registered address of Moscow Elite, who didn't take long to find the registry of client activities. Grigory gave him what he needed. 'Sasha' was often booked, and on two of those occasions the names Mr Gorban was listed as appointments.

To make absolutely sure, Igor had waited on the day of their appointment to see if she would come to meet Gorban. Just as he expected, Oleg's sexy escort, who had strolled away from him in the hotel a couple weeks back, was the same woman he saw. Igor could hardly forget such a stunner. The photocopied ledger he brought with him was the final bit of tangible proof that he needed to convince Oleg. Mr Gorban had been a paid client for many months.

He handed him the ledger and pictures. Oleg searched through each carefully, and with a look of total disgust. The last photo was laid down neatly on the stack of already viewed pictures, and a response finally came from the crime boss.

"Kill her. She's too risky," Oleg demanded emphatically.

As simple as that, Oleg was finished with his favourite bitch. With a snap of his finger he could terminate her life. Actually it didn't really surprise Igor, and he had expected such a response from his hot-headed employer. Nonetheless, Igor could understand. Maybe it was all coincidental, maybe not. Nevertheless, her usefulness was likely to already have been served. Killing her now would likely prove irrelevant, although he understood that it was a reasonable risk to eliminate. It didn't seem too far fetched to believe that she was possibly working with Vladimir in some plan against Oleg.

Sasha would have no trial or jury. Her jury consisted of one hot-tempered man who was convinced on the flimsiest of circumstantial evidence, but it was enough to seal her fate. A death verdict handed down against her in a matter of less than a minute.

"You know, my fee…"

"I don't give a shit about your fucking fee, Igor. Shit, man! Do you think I can't afford a grand here or there? What do you take me for?"

"Just stating that she is a business deal outside the normal terms. That's all." Igor's calm and reassuring tone was at a stark contrast to the aggravated and annoyed Oleg.

"You can never trust bitches," Oleg lamented. "They fuck you over every time. That's why I fuck them hard, because they have it coming! Sneaky bitches are all just useless leeches that suck your money and use you!"

Oleg grabbed his vodka and gulped from it as if it were an antidote for the poison he now felt. He looked at Igor and shook his head in disbelief before continuing his tirade, "This bitch fucked with the wrong motherfucker!"

"Let's hope you kept your pillow talk to a minimum," Igor wistfully replied.

In fact, Oleg hadn't. He openly bragged about his guns and his business deals. Oleg never gave too many details; however, Alexandra certainly had her fill of stories about how much money he made and how his guns were all over Eastern Europe and even the world. Oleg assumed she had told Gorban everything.

"Call me when it happens. I want to know."

"You know I always do."

"She meets with Vladimir tomorrow according to the registry. I will follow her and if it is right then the hit will happen. If not, I'll need to pick another time."

"Sooner the better, my friend."

"In the meantime stay away from Moscow Elite. Or change agencies," Igor said, smiling a toothy grin.

"I pity the whore I fuck next," Igor replied with a wry smile.

II

Clint buried his head deep into Alexandra's hair, and thought back to when he last saw his lover. Her smell was exactly as he had remembered – that wonderful scent that reminded him of fresh flowers after a spring rain. Alexandra smelled just like that, with the faintest hint of vanilla.

"Hmm… I could just stand here and smell you forever," he whispered wistfully. "You are a living bouquet of flowers, and just as beautiful."

Alexandra spun around and faced Clint with a delicate and knowing smile. "Trying to get into my panties?"

"Maybe."

He tried to smile innocently and do his best imitation of acting coy. Alexandra simply kissed him softly and, as she pulled away, took his lower lip with her.

"Well, maybe I'll let you," she replied coolly and then walked over to the side of his bed. "Just this once," she stated with a smug smirk, as she began to unbutton her silk blouse.

Actually, that day was much like most days when they were together. Once inside Clint's apartment, Alexandra would always take off her sweater or jacket and place it over the bedside chair. She liked it when Clint would come from behind and kiss her neck. Feeling his soft lips and breath along her neck awakened her sexual desires. Sometimes she would take his hands and place them on her breasts, which only heightened her excitement. This is what she liked, and this was exactly what was happening tonight.

Clint was already behind her, and his warm hands were cupping her breasts that were fully aroused and firm to his touch. A purr escaped from her glistening moist lips, which formed a nearly perfect circle. Alexandra's own hands capped his as they began to caress her sensitive torso.

He nibbled and licked the back of her ear while she rolled her head in delight. He finished unbuttoning her white blouse and then slipped his fingers in between her bra and bare tits. Her nipples were firm and erect, and as he caressed them she moaned softly.

"I've been waiting for this all day," she gasped.

Suddenly Alexandra escaped his tender hold and sat on the bed's edge. She unbuttoned his pants while Clint took off his shirt. She pulled down his boxers, revealing the erect penis she so desired and he so wanted to give her. Tenderly she placed it into her mouth and slowly but firmly sucked it, much to his enjoyment.

Clint pushed her back onto the bed and quickly pulled off her pants and panties, leaving Alexandra completely naked. He joined her on the bed, but instead of entering her then, he kissed her passionately. She loved his touch and always marvelled at just how soft his hands were. He didn't ever use creams, but delighted in having hands and feet that were as soft today as they were when he was a young boy. He ran his tender hands across her face, which only intensified their intimacy.

Eventually, he started a full body kiss. Clint's mouth and tongue eventually found their way to Alexandra's other lips. He tickled her pussy with his tongue, causing Alexandra to grasp the sheets with both hands and arch her back. She moaned loudly while running her fingers through his hair. She pushed his face deeper into her crotch and spread her legs as far apart as she could. He licked softly, then harder, and began to suck her swollen clit firmly.

He liked to pleasure her this way, using his lips and tongue to explore her deeply. Eventually he would insert a finger to increase her pleasure, and the combination of finger and tongue heightened her primal desires. An oral orgasm from Clint would so consume her that it would take up to five minutes for her to return fully to her senses.

Alexandra could take no more. "Make love to me now!" she gasped, her voice trembling in desperation.

Clint rose up, towering over her squirming body. His penis now was rock hard. She tensed as he entered, and then she squirmed in ecstasy when he quickly plunged his manhood into the final inch of her. They kissed deeply. At that moment a man and a woman could not possibly be any closer emotionally or physically.

They were poetry in motion, and performing a sexual dance in bed. The principles of lust meant both were synchronised and acting as one. They kissed and embraced each other as if it were to be their last time together. They alternated positions over and over again, whispering how perfect and wonderful they made each other feel. Love-making like this, they would always conclude afterwards, seemed too perfect.

Finally after fifteen minutes Alexandra could not take the torment of his pleasure any longer. "Come now, come now!" she yelped. "Oh God... now... come with me!"

Clint too was ready, and seconds later the two shouted and moaned in one fulfilling sexual explosion. Alexandra's hands dug deep into Clint's rear and wrapped her legs around his body in a final act of intimacy and embrace.

They lay completely still as their hearts began to beat slower. Finally Alexandra's legs unlocked and her body collapsed one final time. Looking deeply into each other's eyes, they realised their relationship was not purely sexual, but instead a deep romantic connection to the other.

"You know that I am falling madly for you, don't you?" asked Clint.

"I know."

She smiled to reassure him, all the while aware why he asked this question. They kissed some more and Alexandra felt his warmth within her, but she relished this most sacred of acts. It was the first time she had let him come inside her without a condom – an act of commitment that very few men had ever before enjoyed. She pressed closer to his body, looked into his gentle eyes, and wished the moment would not end. Deep inside she knew that she had to end her life of paid sex, and being with him now taunted the morality that she didn't know existed.

Clint shifted his naked body and slowly relocated directly aside Alexandra in their favourite spooning position. This was always the time they appreciated the most. After sex the two would always snuggle and whisper fantasies still to be realised, until finally Clint would fall asleep. He would always be the first to doze off.

Clint appealed to the deepest of her desires. To Alexandra, Clint was perfectly androgynous – he was sensitive, deep, empathetic, as well as a good listener. He seemed to truly understand her female self and to genuinely be sympathetic to women in general. He always knew exactly how to articulate what she felt, as if he had experienced many of the topics she would expound on. Yet, simultaneously, he was an all-man's type of man. He loved sports, was into cars and was openly heterosexual in his humour.

When she made love to him, she would melt. Rarely had she experienced such sexual pleasure as she did with Clint. She would do anything for him in her desire to please him. The thought of another lover never crossed her mind when they were together, and this was unique. Often when she had fucked Mikhail, she had thought of another man.

With Clint she had found the connection at every one of her personal and private levels. She loved this new feeling of falling in love with him, although Alexandra thought privately that she was hardly what he deserved. If it just weren't for her circumstances and alternative lifestyle, then the torment wouldn't be there. However it was and, after the sex, she felt guilty and treacherously selfish.

"I want this," she murmured calmly.

Clint's familiar deep rough voice questioned, "This?"

"Us. This. You know... I want this, what we are doing."

"And what do you think we're doing?" he asked rhetorically. She knew he was playing; nonetheless, his resolute reply masked it well.

"Starting something we can't stop."

"I'm not interested in stopping it."

Clint's reply was absolute and exactly what she wanted to hear. His words wrapped her like a warm blanket on a cool night. She smiled softly when he buried his face into the back of her head and sniffed deeply.

"You know, there's something about me I've never told anyone before," she whispered in dead seriousness.

"What is it?" he replied empathetically his body compressed against her more tightly.

"You have asked me before about my parents and I always brush them off, but now I want you to know why that is."

She paused, inhaling deeply just as someone does just before a confession. Clint could only hold his own breath as the two lay snuggled in anticipation.

"Okay then," he replied softly, waiting to hear what she would say.

"I think all my life I've resented the fact that I was an orphan. I never connected to my adopted parents because I was always daydreaming about my birth ones."

Alexandra's admission was so deeply personal that he didn't know what to say or how to feel. Being an orphan was too far removed from his privileged and traditional upbringing for him to comment foolishly. Instead he could only squeeze her more tightly.

"You'll find your way," he said softly as he nuzzled the back of her neck. His continual inhaling of her hair tickled, and she flung back around to face her lover.

"What are you doing?" she giggled.

"Absorbing you."

His boyish smile and puppy eyes met her own, which sparkled in his presence. She could read him like no other man. He said nothing, yet his silence spoke volumes. Alexandra had found the man of her dreams after all. She had always dreamed, but never had earnestly searched. She lay there as his finger glided across her forehead and down her cheek. She suddenly felt that she had no interest in fucking another man ever again; and then it came back.

Guilt. That damned one-syllable word that pierced her soul with a pain that felt like a razor's slice.

Damn him! she thought. Damn him for being able to casually lie there with that silly smirk, and to be able to melt her. For ten years she had been screwing men for the sole purpose of egoistic pleasure or money, and now she had become emotionally soft after sex with Clint. Alexandra didn't know how he did it, but right now she didn't care. She was his psychological slave; nonetheless, at least she retained the dignity of keeping him at bay with this hallowed secret. Letting him know this would be a final act of submission that she simply wasn't prepared to indulge.

"I'm falling in love with you, Alexandra."

The words hung for a moment, as if they were trapped outside of her in a cartoon strip's bubble. They had entered her brain, but somehow seemed to linger between them as she lay frozen from what he had just said.

Did he just...? she thought as she turned to face him. Meanwhile, Clint just gazed at her. She didn't know what to say, but could only sense an overwhelming feeling of completeness like never before. Alexandra was feeling something completely new and fresh, and it left her dazed and overwhelmed.

She felt her eyes water, and blinked slowly to prevent the tear she felt from escaping. Her hand met his. Clint's soft eyes followed her every movement until she leaned forward and kissed him, slowly exploring the depths of his sensuous mouth.

It was the kindest, most genuine thing a man had ever said to her, and she truly didn't know how to respond. Every woman dreamed of these types of authentic romantic moments, but Alexandra was paralysed in a grip of confusion and splendour. Her heart beat like a drum, yet she felt fearful and simultaneously pensive. She wanted to shout out loud, yet cry from the impact of his words.

All Alexandra could do was to explode in a broad smile that beamed the light of a hundred suns.

III

Igor sat outside Alexandra's fitness studio while she worked out. Body and Soul was Moscow's largest and most comprehensive gym – a full four stories that had every conceivable machine or exercise possibility.

Oleg had remembered she worked out there, and Igor had verified it. Inside Igor's target was sweating, in full motion, and lost in thought. Outside was Igor, who sat in perfect repose while his mind wondered in deep contemplation. In a way, the two individuals couldn't have been more diabolically different – she a willowy woman of beauty, Igor a hulking mass of raw features. He sat perfectly still at this moment, while the blonde beauty worked furiously on the Nordic exercise machine in the third floor. Yet their lives would cross soon enough.

Igor thought deeply about what he was going to do. Killing a woman was never pleasant. Surprisingly he had only ever killed one woman before, but that hit was nothing like this. She was a banker, as corrupt and vile as any mob guy. She was also as sinister as any man he had ever killed before or since. Still, it had bothered him, and it was probably one of the only kills he could easily recollect today. Eight years ago he killed Valentina Aparina in her bedroom. It wasn't her bland nakedness or her rhyming name he remembered, but the feeling that somehow whacking a woman was wrong. That same feeling was what he felt right now.

Alexandra had only slept with one man associated to Oleg's business, and Igor wondered if she was truly connected in an effort to harm him. It wasn't Igor's job to question the judgment of his sponsors and, frankly, he could appreciate why Oleg had chosen to terminate her. Nevertheless, the longer he sat waiting, the more uncomfortable he was beginning to feel.

Igor probably didn't know it, but the killing of Afghan women that he had witnessed by fellow troops had impacted him. That war was hell reincarnated; however, as bad as it was in Afghanistan, the conflict with Chechnya was even worse. He was barely twenty when he first went to Afghanistan in April of 1985. By the time he returned to Moscow two years later he had seen his fair share of brutality and death; however it was the sheer vulgarity of war with the Chechens that left him even more emotionally scarred.

It was here, some ten years later, that he saw firsthand how low war could be. He lost count of the times he saw fellow troops brutally beat and rape Chechen women as if they were nothing more than human receptacles and outlets for pent-up sexual energy. Sometimes they were killed, most often not however they were always degraded as much as possible. The men who fucked them never saw them as a mother, a sister or even a grandmother. Their humiliation in front of gloating soldiers was probably the deepest of embarrassments a Muslim woman could face. Igor had never stooped so low.

Igor never thought about why he avoided killing women. Perhaps it was purely because it never came up. He took this hit without reservation, but only now did the realisation of its emotional messiness begin to play on him.

Emotionally messy was how Igor thought of any involvement with women. He kept his distance from any kind of relationships, and had his last serious girlfriend just before heading out to Afghanistan. Then he had been only eighteen. Ellie was only seventeen at the time, and was the first and only girl whose virginity he took. After the war he only engaged older women in their mid-to-late twenties, and none that he cared to have a relationship with. Marriage and commitment were messy inconveniences that didn't fit his work. Now, at forty-one, he usually fucked prostitutes or women he would pick up at nigh clubs. Ones he knew cared less about seeking anything other than sex and free drinks.

He glanced at his watch and knew that Sasha would be finishing her workout soon. She had been in the gym for just over an hour and he had learned from staking her out that she always finished at six o'clock. By 6:20 she would invariably leave the gym.

Only a couple moments later he looked up and noticed his target walking towards him. Somehow Alexandra had managed to leave the gym early and cross the street without him noticing. Igor jumped to attention and focused on his target, only twenty metres away. She soon passed him, completely unaware of the man who was aware of her every movement. He pulled out his black BMW into the flow of traffic and slowly followed her. Igor was careful to have his right hand blinker on so that cars behind him would assume he was merely searching for a parking space. He couldn't follow her like this forever, but preferred his car as a quick getaway as opposed to foot.

Igor reached inside his coat's pocket and felt the base of his gun. The elongated muzzle he so often used lengthened the pistol, yet was absolute necessary if he was going to have to kill her in a crowd. Igor always felt his gun before a hit. It was some sort of conditioned response that he had acquired during the Chechen war when his gun rarely left his hand. That habit had served him well, and now he drove with one hand on the steering wheel and the other barely caressing his weapon.

Sasha walked along the sidewalk, weaving like a slippery serpent around and through other people, all the while totally oblivious to the large black predator that lurked in her wake. Dark tinted windows concealed the killer.

The blonde finally stopped and disappeared into a little grocery store, and Igor slid the car into an empty space. A break in the cars that sped by him allowed the hulk to jog across the busy street and to the sidewalk. Igor entered through its glass doors.

Once inside, the killer scanned the simple interior. His target was along the back wall where the refrigerated goods sat. He casually stopped and pretended to give notice to the pasta that was now directly in front of him. However, his real attention was to the woman who was now at the checkout counter while two of the other patrons also strolled to the cashier. Shit, he thought in frustration.

Five or six more seconds, and he could have made a silent hit in the perfect spot. With no-one around and the near silence of one or two shots, his target would have slumped into his arms without even a casual notice. How long she could have laid on the back floor before the next customer found her was anyone's guess.

Yet one thing was for sure – he could have easily slipped out and been far from watchful eyes.

However, his opportunity had gone, and he followed her as she left the store. There she was, stopped on the sidewalk only a few short strides away. She was fiddling with her pocketbook. Few people were near as she opened her purse and reached for her ringing mobile; his own hand reached for the metal contraption that served as his singular tool.

He quickened his pace and his hand now felt the familiarity of the trigger. The butt of the gun felt warm and like an old friend to his calloused hand. With another couple of strides he would finally be upon her. Finally, he was. Curiously she spun around, just as she flipped her phone's cover to say hello. Instead she turned directly into her killer who loomed over her like a darkened monolith. His silhouette consumed her. Their eyes met once again, except this time she would not walk away.

As if time and space somehow stood still, his gun now pointed directly at her chest, their eyes interlocked and her answer of the mobile with a simple 'privet' all converged together as a singular event. No sooner had she uttered her last word, Igor had pulled the trigger. A muted 'whoosh' filled the air, and her eyes instantly widened as the bullet pierced her torso at blank range.

Death had come instantly for his target, and he caught her as the phone fell to the ground. The elderly couple walking by barely noticed what had just happened, and, if they did, it would have looked to them that the woman had merely walked into a tender hug of her lover or husband.

Igor had his Sasha, just as he had originally planned. He dragged her a single metre in between two parked cars and gently laid her down, leaving the groceries and phone as the only visible evidence of where she last stood. Blood poured out of her chest and began to stream towards the street's gutter, only centimetres away.

A final look into the woman's eyes struck him as he noticed just how angelic she was. She was exactly the kind of woman he desired physically and, perhaps in a different life, they could have been lovers or more. They had never spoken, but Igor confirmed her tenderness from the single word he heard her speak.

Only then did it strike him what he had done. Suddenly he would have to live with a new Valentina Aparina who would haunt him long into the future. Killing men was so easy, but now her ghost would pre-occupy his mind in a final act of revenge. He was instantly sure of that.

Igor rose and saw many people coming from both directions. He quickly stepped out into traffic and towards his own car. Igor dodged one car, then two, and finally a third as he heard a scream that pierced the noisy Moscow air. Somehow the ensuing shouting and shrieks could be heard over the cars and trucks that the killer now jogged through.

As he reached his car he turned and noticed that a group of five, maybe six, people now stood over the dead body. One woman was pointing towards Igor and shouting something, while others began to notice. He quickly got in, turned on the car, and pulled out immediately. He sped away in a matter of seconds and disappeared into oblivion. Another murder in Moscow's broad daylight had just happened, the fifth of the month. Only this time the police would be left with no motive, little evidence, and vague eyewitness details.

Sasha was indeed dead and Igor had killed the last of his required hits. The only thing left to do was to call Oleg. Oleg's pending joy was now Igor's current torment. Where it had come from he didn't know, yet all he could see was her face.

Chapter 20

I

"Sir! I think I have something!"

Frank had the same look as he always did when he found a break. Clint knew it already. It had become an unspoken synergetic relationship, not between boss and employee, but rather lone wolf and his willing partner. Clint had gone beyond the initial scope of the project and had instead begun to focus more and more on a tertiary angle of the case that had become personal. Bad guys and potential terrorists abounded; however, slowly his attention seemed to be on a more sublime tangent of the mission. He knew that involving as few people as possible would be the best way to satisfy his secondary personal investigation; however, he still needed help. A naïve and willing rookie like Frank was exactly the right person.

Clint motioned with his head and walked towards the conference room which served as their secret getaway. It was the mother of all ironies, actually. In the cramped and relatively tight quarters of the agency, operated by a group of spies and intelligence personnel, no-one really knew of Clint's and Frank's investigation. Except for Director Billups, but even he knew nothing of the tangent that Clint was now exploring. If Billups had known that Clint - his best agent and head of the project - was sleeping with a known figure in the mission, then he would be pulled immediately and sent back to Virginia. Clint himself wasn't certain, but he had to find out for sure.

As he led Frank to the conference room, Clint felt that every passing hour was an hour closer to a revelation that he had to have. He had wondered now how the girl in the photo could look exactly like his

Alex, and he undertook his private investigation more for himself than the agency. He was too deep now in both the mission and her to just walk away. If the girl was somehow Alexandra, then the prudent thing would to dump her. The inconvenient truth was something he simply had to know.

Frank walked by him as Clint closed the door softly. Frank perched half sitting on the conference table and had that anticipatory look.

"Go on! What is it?" Clint's patience was long gone.

"Matchmaker," Frank blurted out.

"Match what?"

"Matchmaker – the software I installed to compliment Eigenface. This way we can identify anyone from nearly any angle."

"Yeah, so?"

"Okay, let me explain."

Frank took a deep breath as he always did before he inevitably began a long-winded babble of which Clint usually only understood half to two-thirds. Usually it was always something techie or dealing with how his software worked. Clint was only interested in the bottom line, and 'Matchmaker' was sounding ominously suspicious already.

"I took all the photos we have on all our subjects – from Krokav to the escort – and entered them in this new application called Matchmaker. After that, I tapped into all the local agencies that we have partnered with, from the different embassies to the Moscow police department. Matchmaker then automatically cross-checks its files against anything that our partners pull up, and lets me see what they see. I've been doing this for weeks now. Just in case, if you know what I mean."

The glimmer in his eye indicated his cunning pride.

"Fucking brilliant! Is this legal?" Clint asked sternly.

"Well... yeah... I guess so. I got it approved in Langley."

Clint just shook his head in disbelief and said, "Go on."

"Well, anyways. This just came through on the police wire."

Frank handed him a folded piece of paper and waited like a pensive teenager showing a report-card to their parent. Clint's eyes darted as he read, and then a look of sheer shock froze them. He privately mustered all his strength to avoid displaying any more emotion than he had already shown.

Calm and collected, but a raging fire inside, Clint asked "Who did all this?" then added "The director needs to know."

"Yeah... I mean... I think so, sir. She's just been whacked. The crime scene photos from the police report registered a hit with Matchmaker. Now we have her name, finally. It's all there."

Clint could only look away and try to come to grips between two diabolically opposing feelings. His sworn duty to office somehow seemed so shallow compared to the raw emotion he now felt. This was never supposed to happen.

Damn! Damn, damn, damn! he thought to himself as his mind raced. He couldn't do anything. He just stood there weak in the knees and feeling completely overwhelmed.

"Go on, Frank," he mumbled. "And thank you."

It was obvious that something was not right, and Frank was taken by his boss' unusual reaction. He had thought that this break would result in a different reaction. Instead, his boss seemed so far removed and unsure. He left meekly.

Clint took a seat at the table, looked at the paper once again, and re-read every translated word before eventually burying his head into his hands. All the emotions that he had felt years ago were back. He wanted to cry; however, was too confused and torn to do anything other than sit in darkened silence and try to slow his mind, which raced a million miles per hour. He felt dizzy and light headed, angry and saddened.

Alexandra was dead, shot down in broad daylight along a busy thoroughfare. His nagging fear that the girl in the photo was her now confirmed – it was Sasha after all. Obviously the agency wasn't the only ones who had ultimately linked her to Krokav. Now Clint had to balance his personal feelings with what the next steps meant to an unknown bigger picture. Clearly, this was nothing he could so easily transition to.

What to do, what do I do, damn it? he thought as his face slid out from behind his hands.

"Sir?" Frank asked tentatively. "Are you okay?"

"Yeah, yeah," he replied and snapped back into an artificial sense of alertness. "I was just thinking how... well... what this means for the case. Was just thinking of what to do."

What to do was tell the director and move on. A minor player had been eliminated, but a weapon's dealer at the centre of the mission was only hours away from delivering a huge cache of artillery to Afghan rebels. Clint knew this as a trained professional; however, his insides were wrenched with personal feelings that told him otherwise.

How he had fallen so hard for Alexandra, he didn't know. By the time he learned that she was an escort to God knows how many men, it was too late. He had fallen in love with her and wanted to believe in the person he still believed in. The fact that she slept with figures of the criminal underworld seemed a mere inconvenient obstacle that somehow was pressed to the background.

Of course it never was that easy, and Clint knew it.

II

Clint stood in Yuri's office with a look of despondency and shock. For all the cases they had worked on, Yuri had never seen him like this.

"You okay?" he asked inquisitively.

Of course he wasn't. His lover had just been assassinated in cold blood and right now he couldn't see straight, let alone keep the outside world from knowing his pain. But he had to. No-one inside had known of their relationship, and it had to stay this way. Right now the only person who could help him was standing in front of him with a look of bewilderment on his face.

"Yeah. No. Actually I've got this mother of a headache, and I'm having a hard time concentrating."

"Shit-man, I've never known you to have headaches. Is this new?"

"Guess you have to start at some point. I'll be fine."

Yuri was more than a lieutenant in Moscow's police force. He was the closest thing to a true friend that Clint had in Moscow, and one of the few Russian police agents he could trust. Yuri was so different to every other Russian cop he knew. Born in Siberia, he was not the typical hardened Muscovite, but jovial, simple, earthy. He himself had never gotten accustomed to his eastern Russian brethren, hence his own slight disdain to the typical crude and aloof folk of Moscow. Clint and Yuri had met through a cooperative initiative by the two governments, pitting the agency with local law enforcement to assist on grunt work that could be expedited by the Russian police.

Clint moved to the desk where the case file and crime scene photos were. He picked up the top photo and looked stunned at what he saw.

"So what do you have?" he asked directly.

"Not sure, actually. You really think this woman is somehow linked to your case?" Yuri's expression was puzzled.

"Looks that way. That's why I'm here."

"Alright then. Here's what we have. We've got a victim named Victoria Popslavskaya, age 27, married, mother of one. So she gets whacked point-blank by some guy all dressed in black. Black sweater, cap and sunglasses. Gets away in some luxury import, most likely a BMW."

"You say she is married with a child?"

"Yeah, eight years married. Their kid is six."

Clint was flabbergasted and had to sit down at the only chair in his office. He felt dizzy and instantly nauseated. Alexandra was married? She was a mother too? And her name wasn't even real.

The questions he asked himself were so overwhelming and hard to fathom. She had spent nights with him, professed her emerging love. It was bad enough that he had discovered she was an escort. She was still polished, refined, classy, and not like the cheap hookers that ran the darkened alleys in need of cash for their next fix. Being an escort at Moscow Elite was different, and had convinced him that this discovery was merely an inconvenient obstacle to hurdle sooner than later. Now everything else was a total lie, which left him nearly gasping for air.

"You okay?" Yuri asked his friend again.

Clint blinked out of his state of confusion and shock, and tried his best to hide the emotions that fired inside him like some sort of volcanic inferno. His heart raced and he felt as if he had been kicked in the gut by a bucking bronco; the discovery that his lover was someone so deceitful was just too much to bear.

"Yeah. Just feeling a bit dizzy," he confessed, only partly hinting at how he truly felt.

"I can get you some water and a tablet if you want," Yuri said empathetically with his heavy accent.

Clint waved his hand and shook his head as he grabbed the file. He opened it and read the details intently and searched for every detail. Still the words Yuri spoke seemed stuck in his head.

"So we have a background that suggests she was a saint and just a normal woman."

"Well... yeah. Which is why I don't see a connection to your arms' case. You say your woman was an escort?"

"Right now, it looks that way."

Clint didn't know what to hope for. Perhaps it was all some big mistake – that she wasn't a high-end hooker after all. In fact, their names were completely different. However, if not, that would mean she was still a diabolical liar who lived two lives. The thought that she could be both hadn't occurred to him. He pulled from his briefcase his own files and opened one folder to reveal the photo which Frank had retrieved from the internet.

"This is what we have," he said as he slid the photo to Yuri, who stood at the table's edge.

"Sure looks like the same. Hairstyle is a bit different though, and here she's all sexed up. But damn – that has to be her. The eyes are identical."

Indeed they were. Alexandra's eyes were probably her most striking feature. Any man would be struck by them. Most were.

"So it seems Mrs. Popslavskaya went by 'Sasha', huh?" Yuri deduced.

Clint felt Alexandra's deceit deepen. Sasha was indeed the nickname for Alexandra, his lover's name. Alexandra, Victoria or whoever she was had managed to weave in and out of reality with three identities. She had wore three different faces with ease, and all the while fooled everyone. He couldn't help but feel bitterness sink in, and it occurred to him that one of those three identities had led to her being killed. Clint couldn't tell his colleague that he knew her personally as Alexandra, a supposed translator. Yuri would just have to assume his victim was a simple married mother who might allegedly have been moonlighting as an escort.

"If your dead victim is this woman that we've identified with our software, then indeed she is one and the same." Yuri sighed and looked at Clint's photo once again. "Sure complicates things. But definitely gives us a possible motive. We'll have to question the pimp. You have that name already?"

"No. Totally out of the scope of what we are dealing with. Hell... before she ended up in your lap she was barely in ours."

"So how did she become a subject of interest?"

Clint hesitated and sighed as he answered. "You're not going to believe me if I tell you."

"It would make it a lot easier. Come on, man! I've got a dead body with no leads. Now you come in here and tell me she's some moonlighting escort mom who is associated with whoever you Americans are on. Also, if you are involved then it can't be simple. So what gives?"

"Krokav. She was seen with him and another subject that I can't divulge."

"Krokav? Like the guy whom both our governments keep tabs on twenty-four seven? That Krokav?"

Clint could only nod his head subtly.

"Oh, Christ man! Can you drop a bigger bomb on me? Do you really think that he was involved?"

"I can tell you that I doubt the pimp has anything to do with it. Krokav though? Maybe."

"I don't know," Yuri said with a heavy tone of doubt. "Experience tells me its one of two people, and I have something on my side that is willing to bet you that I am right."

"Like what?"

"Like experience. Experience tells me that escorts don't get whacked. Murder is almost always committed by someone close to the victim. In my world, over seventy percent of murders are committed by someone the victim knew."

"I don't know, Yuri. I think you're wrong."

"You know what I think? I think the husband found out that she was doing this escorting, got pissed, and paid to have her hit."

Clint could only bite his tongue and force himself to hold back what he knew. Yuri was right, actually. His theory was sound, and Clint's mind wondered. Maybe she felt emotionally abandoned in her marriage, which is why she sought his affections. Yet still there was the escorting. The more he learned about Alexandra, the more embattled he became. Clint had thought she was so straightforward. Instead he had started to give his love to a woman he barely knew, and who had deceived him mightily. "You could be right," he conceded.

"Listen Clint. I'll go now and check out this escorting angle. I'll talk to the pimp, see what records she has on her, and get a confirmation if your Sasha was her. First I'm going to have a nice long talk to the husband. What do you say we meet for dinner around eight and we'll compare notes?"

Clint said nothing, his mind was still foggy about everything. He sighed slowly and seemed lost in a stare as he just moved his head. He knew he needed more, and that the answer to her death was probably something more sinister than her husband's hit. Something just didn't add up. He needed more time.

"I'll take that as a yes? Get some tablets for that headache, yeah? I'll keep this picture of yours until then. I think I'll need it for the husband and the pimp."

"Yeah, sure. Take it. I've got her picture already."

Clint had Alexandra's picture all right. What Yuri didn't know was that it was a mental picture of her. He didn't need a glossy photograph to recognise his love, but rather experience and memory would serve him. He knew every inch of her face and body, but memories would be all that he would ever have again. And then it hit him.

"I know what we're going to do first," he exclaimed as he bolted out of his chair.

For five minutes Clint had sat lethargically and looked like a dying man; however, now he was instantly full of vigour. His expression wore the look of a man rediscovered and with a plan.

"Jesus! Now that's an instant turn-around. What are you thinking?"

"You're coming with me to the morgue."

"What the…?"

"Just trust me on this," he interrupted as he scampered by on his way out. "Come on!" he shouted as he slammed through the door. Yuri could only shake his head and follow like an obedient dog chasing their master. "You drive!" he shouted.

Five minutes later, the two were in Clint's car and amongst the vehicular chaos that is Moscow traffic. Moving so slowly allowed Clint's mind to race and to fall back on images that tormented it. Three hours ago Frank broke the news that his own lover was dead – the woman he had thought he'd see tomorrow. He probably had yet to totally grasp what had truly happened; his body and mind partly encapsulated within some sort of self-inflicted and subconscious defence mechanism against such trauma.

Now his icy stare was fixed forward, but, in actuality, to nothing. He drove on autopilot and was too self-absorbed to properly react should he be suddenly called to an evasive manoeuvre or quick reaction. His two hands gripped the steering wheel as if it were the neck of the unknown assassin who had stolen his beloved from him.

It all just made no sense. Then again, maybe it did. Clint struggled to fathom how he could have fallen and begun a relationship with a married woman and a mother. The same woman who somehow could live another existence fucking men and carrying on with him as if her real life was something so shallow that it could be easily left. Alexandra had spent nights with him and told him things that he now shuddered when he thought about them.

How can it be? he asked, in deep contemplation. It just doesn't make sense.

It was the question he couldn't help but ask himself continually over and over since he found out. The only logical explanation was that the wrong woman was photographed. Victoria Popslavskaya was surely not his Alexandra Malikova, and he was going right now to prove it. The software and photos were no substitute for his own eyes.

Clint drove in a passive rage. Going to the morgue in his current state of mind and belief hadn't prepared him for the unexpected reality that he may be wrong. He was a man in denial and going there to prove himself right, despite the near-certainty of what was true.

What was true was the fact that Clint had never been to Alexandra's apartment, and he had always met Alexandra on her time. Clint suddenly realised that he had also never met a friend of hers. He had fallen in love with a Moscow enigma. What he thought was real now looked to be nothing more than a superficial fantasy.

Clint had always been such a good judge of characters, and all this conflicting information simply didn't make sense. The words that she had spoken, especially recently, haunted him. Clint had been around enough liars to know one when he saw one.

Ironically, he had been just as guilty of deceit as she, as Clint had yet to tell her his true work. Only in the past days did he begin to wonder when that day might be. Alexandra's supposed confession of falling in love with him had made him begin thinking of this.

He blinked a few times to escape the confusion and rubbed his right hand across his face, just before turning onto a large road where the traffic was less congested. As he sped along, he began to feel anger towards Alexandra. He had been duped and played. He started to hate her duplicity and how she could shun her motherly obligations for a good fuck. It was this that bothered him more than knowing she was an escort.

Clint still loved Alexandra; however, now he truly struggled to accept just how wrong their relationship had proven to be. In the end he felt played and used, but drove on nonetheless. Still he needed to see his lover for the closure he so desperately needed.

III

The footsteps resonated through the sterile hallway of the antiquated morgue as if they vibrated from inside the barrel of a steel drum. Clint strode forward, taking nearly a half step more per stride than Yuri, who practically jogged in toe.

"Two zero two. Look for it!" Clint barked. Room 202 was where he was headed, and Yuri's task of searching every name plate that was posted along the way only slowed him further.

"What was his name again?" he shouted at his leader who was now five metres further ahead.

"Nimonsky! Doctor Nimonsky performed the autopsy."

"Fine, but there are no room numbers, only names on these plates." Clint once again led; however, this time he walked slower and looked back at his friend who seemed to take a full five seconds per door.

Yuri was clearly not convinced they were in the right area of the large and sprawling morgue. The labyrinth of halls and rooms was astonishing, and, oddly, no-one was around to ask for help. Yuri was the translator and had been here twice before but, from how confused he appeared, it was hard to believe.

"This is correct, for God's sake! Where the fuck is..."

"Here it is!" Yuri interrupted, now pointing to the door that they both stood immediately next to.

Clint responded by slamming through the doors that flung open when he forcefully pushed on them. Yuri simply followed him like an obedient terrier trailing his master.

The room was large, well-lit, and stood as a stark contrast to the desolate gloomy hallway that they had spent the past minutes in. Two men dressed completely in green scrubs stood at a table over the corpse of an unknown victim at the room's opposite corner.

"Who are you?" said one of the two in Russian through an operating mask. The voice was muffled and could have come from either of the two, but Clint hardly cared.

"Victoria Popslavskaya! Where is she?"

Yuri translated to the stunned pathologists who merely stood in frozen bewilderment. Neither Clint nor Yuri had actually noticed that the doctors were in the midst of carving up another sorry soul who had come to this ugly fate – cold reality on an icy metal slab, getting butchered, only to be sewn back together again.

"Where is she?" Clint hollered agitatedly.

Again Yuri shouted the same before the one doctor demanded, "And who are you? What gives you the right to interrupt our work?"

Yuri strode towards the doctor and met him at the side of the table, covered in blood and alongside the remnants of some faceless victim. The stench suddenly struck him like an invisible straight jab that he blindly walked right into.

"Oh Jesus!" he stammered as he simultaneously coughed.

Clint stood further back, not immune to the smell of death that lingered in the room in a sickening haze. Yuri spoke some Russian and flashed his badge before ultimately pointing back at Clint, who stood impatiently, nervously tapping his fingers on an empty table. The three Russians seemed to talk over one another with gesticulative hands before finally one of the pathologists stormed towards Clint.

"Follow him," Yuri shouted to his partner.

The doctor tugged away at his protective mask and Clint could now easily see the human stains on the front of his scrubs that were all smeared with marks of red. He wondered how such a job could exist and what kind of person it took to look completely inside another human.

The leader in green came to a wall with many handles and surveyed the wall with his pointed finger as he incoherently mumbled something in Russian. A few seconds later he grabbed at the handle to the right of their knees and pulled it with an abrupt tug. He barked to the onlookers to give way, sending the three observers scattering around the pull-out table that contained the shrouded figure. All at once, all four were around the fully extended victim, Clint and the one doctor at one side while Yuri and the assistant gaped at them from the other.

"This is the woman you want," said the doctor in a heavy Russian voice.

"So you do speak English after all," Clint mumbled sarcastically. "Pull away the cover," he ordered in anticipation.

Clint tensed as the doctor's hands reached for the top of the white sheet. Only the two extra humps of the chest proved it was a woman under the sheet, but otherwise she was an incoherent mass of humanity that could have been anyone. However, this wasn't just anyone. It was Alexandra – shot and killed earlier today, and the American spies already knew.

The doctor was methodical, nearly sadistic in the way he carefully rolled over the sheet, fully aware that the agents were desperate to see her face. Her forehead, then the eyes and finally her full lips came to light once again, before her face was finally fully exposed.

She lay there in a state that was both serene and tortured. Her eyes still open seemed to still grasp her terror at the gun which surely was her last living memory; nonetheless, she seemed so surreal and angelic. Her skin had lost its glow to death.

Clint blinked at the sight of the woman he had fallen in love with, and his pulse quickened while his body tightened at the morose sight. Her ambient frost could literally be felt; the result of being stored away in the cold chamber at two degrees Celsius. However, Clint felt the fire of his passion and the anger of his rage boil. He stood hiding his secret and fighting with all his strength not to tear into an uncontrolled rage. Beads of sweat, escaping his forehead, were the only evidence of a fire that he masked so coolly and nonchalantly.

"Sir?" the doctor asked cautiously.

Only moments before Clint had been a ball of impatience, but now seemed paralysed and captured in some sort of trance. He stood fully consumed by her death and the finality of it all. At last the spell was broken in the form of the slightest of head tilts, and he reached for the top of the sheet the pathologist held. He took it and pulled it further back, revealing the dead woman's lower neck and cleavage. His eyes fell upon the secretive spot where Alexandra's only flaw existed – near her left breast she had had a tiny birthmark the size of a fingernail. He looked there, and then lowered the sheet further. His eyes were frozen, yet his mind raced wildly. The other men gave uncomfortable glances at each other.

Yuri finally broke the deafening silence when he calmly asked, "See something?"

A second of silence passed, then two and then five or so. Finally he spoke. "No."

His one syllable, one word answer denied any break to the thick tension that filled the room. He lowered the sheet even further, revealing the single gunshot wound that pierced her tender torso exactly where her heart was. It seemed so surreal to see his 'Alexandra' so lifeless, but the body before him was merely the shell of a woman who once captured the imagination of everyone.

"Are you family of the deceased, sir?" the assistant asked empathetically.

Clint took a deep breath and replied as he slowly exhaled.

"No. Not at all."

He finally allowed his gaze to leave her, eventually turning to the doctor and saying unemotionally, "She's just someone who the police and I are interested in. I think we're done here."

The doctor began to delicately roll the white sheet back over Alexandra, and a final look at her was enough for Clint. He turned and started back to the door slowly.

"Come on. Nothing more to see," he barked to Yuri.

Yuri also left the doctors standing alone, and he looked puzzled as he approached Clint. "What was this about anyway?" he asked in a hushed whisper.

Just then the door once again reopened to reveal the anguished face of a stranger dressed in a dark blue suit.

"Doctor Nimonsky?" he asked in near-desperation. "Are you Doctor Nimonsky?"

The doctor threw up his hands in exasperation and replied in Russian, "For God's sake! It's a circus in here!"

"I'm just looking for my wife! Victoria Popslavskaya is her name. At the entrance they said she was here."

Clint was taken aback, and stopped suddenly. Yuri flanked him, and they both saw the man's obvious desperation. His panic and stress was clearly visible. Death and loss will do that to a person, and Clint had seen his share of it over the past years. Being a spy and working with the results of espionage had meant the untimely death of two field agents, one of which was his best friend. This, coupled with the loss of his own fiancé four years earlier, meant he knew a grief-stricken relative when he saw one.

He rung at his hands and fretted as he stood there before continuing, "I am Mr Popslavski, Victoria's husband. I want to see my wife."

The doctor took a step towards the man and motioned with his hand. "She is here, sir. You can see her now," he said with a stretched hand towards his lifeless wife, who was again covered. The desperate husband raced past Clint and Yuri without even the simplest of casual glances. Had he thought twice, he would have surely wondered who they were and why his wife was already out of her chamber. However, he didn't notice. He was too consumed in grief to notice such intricacies.

Again the Doctor slowly rolled down the sheet, and as he did Mr Popslavski could not contain his tears. He completely broke down at the time her face was fully exposed, and sobbed inconsolably. The assistant handed him a crude relief in the form of a nearby towel, which Stefan grabbed and cried in.

"What will I tell my son?" he huffed as he sobbed. "How can he manage without his mother?"

The four men had no answer, and Clint felt this man's pain. Only a few years before he watched his own beloved Aleeka slip away from the physical world, and asked himself nearly the same questions. It took him almost a year and the complete immersion into his work to find a way to manage without her, but eventually he did. One hour ago he had felt virtually the same pain all over again. Hearing that Alexandra was dead brought back deep buried emotions that left him quivering, just as her husband was now.

The doctor touched his sleeve and calmly leaned forward. "Mr Popslavski. I hate to be so formal, but my assistant will need you to sign a couple of forms indicating that this is your wife and that an autopsy will be completed tomorrow morning."

His body instantly snapped back and he replied in a venomous shout, "You aren't going to butcher my wife! I won't let you!"

"I'm terribly sorry to inform you that all murders and suspicious deaths require the city to perform an autopsy. Please understand, Mr Popslavski. Please."

"Some psychopath shot my wife! What else do you need to know? Leave her dignity intact!" His voice was a mix of raw anger and absolute despair. He couldn't keep his eyes off her, and he couldn't stop crying.

Yuri approached the sobbing husband and gently clutched at his arm. Immediately the big man spun and demanded, "Who are you? Why are you here, anyway?"

"I am Yuri Richov, a lieutenant investigator in the police. I am here to begin an investigation into your wife's murder. Perhaps we should go outside and talk."

Yuri's words seemed to calm the man and his obvious panic was replaced by the resigned desperation that he was powerless and completely unprepared to deal with all that just happened. Nonetheless, Yuri couldn't believe his luck.

"Okay... okay," he replied meekly, now walking away, leaving the three others to breathe out collectively.

Clint was left alone in his thoughts. He felt as though he was drowning in the rush of memories of their times together, and the enormity of what he had just seen. It seemed so strange to share the room with a man who loved the same woman as he.

A little over an hour ago the mystery of his lover's life had been cracked by his colleagues as if she was a non-entity who had never laughed, cried or shared real human emotions with anyone. To them she was a manipulative prostitute who selfishly used men only to be executed herself. They saw her as an escort who lived a double life as a housewife and as a secretive slut for cash – that would be her eternal legacy in the file. The damn non-changing file that would tarnish her reputation forever. He wondered how his lover's husband would react. Privately he knew the man that had just stumbled out the door would never accept the 'official' record although the evidence was straight in front of him.

The doctor and his assistant were back at their table and were again behind the face-masks that covered their mouth and nearly all of their face. For a moment Clint felt as if he was a ghost or a traveller who had leapt back in time. The scene was exactly as it had been only moments ago. He turned, breathed in, and walked back out the door. He knew what he had to do.

Chapter 21

I

The conference room was packed. Fitting all the people who worked in the agency in a room that seated seven meant some were left standing. They all knew that the director would burst through the door at any second and fill the empty podium before them. Gaby hurried to complete the order of the slides from the slide projector before the big boss could enter.

Florian leaned into Clint's left ear and whispered, "What do you think this is about?"

"Must be some break," he whispered back with a casual shrug.

In fact, Clint knew far more than he led Florian to believe. Last night he found out from Yuri new information about his lover and had met the director at their favourite restaurant, a dive near where Clint lived. They always went there after hours when there was a big case or they needed time to talk away from the office. Billups had told him that he would call a meeting in the morning, and now he sat waiting just like everyone else.

Only when they came in this morning was the memo circulated that a 9:30 briefing would be mandatory. Krokav was leaving in a week and time was running out. Some were sure that an ass-kicking by the crotchety director was coming. A couple individuals were less certain. One of them was Clint, who now stood perched in the back corner. He had confirmed to Billups the death of Victoria Popslavskaya and knew that the director was fine with the progress of the mission. It wasn't often that his boss was agreeable, but at least a few hours ago he seemed fine.

Clint stood in the half-light and kept thinking of what he wanted to do next. 'Alexandra' had impacted him hard, but seeing Victoria's body on the cold metal table like that truly scared him. Years before he had thanked God that his beloved Aleeka hadn't suffered the indignity of being mutilated by an unsympathetic pathologist. His last sight of Aleeka was seeing her gaunt but vaguely angelic features from within her casket, and he swore he would never revisit death like this.

Then it happened again. The image of Victoria's nude body gripped his mind in a vice. A plan he had concocted the day before continued to race in his head, and the more he thought the more certain it was what he had to do - even at the risk of his own career.

Just as he settled into an assured confirmation of what would follow, the director burst in the room like always. He frantically made his way up to the podium and motioned with a single finger for the lights to be dimmed, before nodding to Gaby. He quickly scanned the room.

"I see we have everyone here."

He then looked back at the screen that showed nothing – just a white blank slide that surely was a mistake.

"Folks, this is what we now have," he said emphatically as he pointed to the void behind him.

"What we do have is these relatively unimportant details, like the following."

A snap of his fingers revealed the next slide – a picture of Alexandra from her website. The image captivated Clint, yet jabbed at his heart cruelly. He hated this aspect of his lover, but was now reminded of it every few minutes.

"This is Sasha, a.k.a. Victoria Popslavskaya. Sasha here has been photographed by our field operatives with this man, and this man."

Each time Billups said 'this man', a photo appeared. First with Krokav, then with Vladimir Gorban. With each slide he identified the men that everyone in the room was already familiar with.

"Now she's dead, a victim of an obvious hit, but, from whom, we can only guess. The police will have their hands full and I want one of our guys all over them. Logan! You become fast friends with Yuri. I think you know his connection to us."

"Yes, sir!" Logan replied emphatically.

"This woman was, apparently, Mother Theresa. Police say that everybody they talk to claims she was the Virgin Mary. I want to know how a woman like this can somehow be doubling up with the likes of those scumbags."

Actually, the director's question was a good one. The police weren't the only ones wondering the same, and Clint had already seen a translated a faxed copy of the police report from Yuri. Her husband swore that this was surely some sort of smear campaign fabricated by the police, and that it was impossible for his wife to have been an escort. Clint knew the truth, and was now driven to get to the bottom of the enigma.

However, the evidence against the dead woman said otherwise. An initial statement by Moscow's Elite's owner said it was Victoria Popslavskaya, although no original documents could prove it yet. The woman Yuri had spoken to already, an Elena Victova, would soon provide photocopies of her identity and employee files. However, Matchmaker proved the facial likeness from the agency's photos with over ninety-seven percent accuracy. There was no fooling the software which had multiple photos of Alexandra, as well as Clint's own confirmation. The woman he saw looked exactly like the woman from the photos. Victoria's husband would soon be presented with the truth.

"And don't forget that ten days ago we had a hit on this man, Miroslav Abramov, a banker who we suspect was working with Krokav. What we don't know is if Sasha here was known to have associated with Mr Abramov."

Everyone in the room was probably thinking the same thing. The connection was loose, and so what? So what if a prostitute was dead?

"Which gets me back to this slide."

Again, Billups snapped to the empty slide before continuing, "Nothing! That's what we think we have, but somewhere there is a connection. Escorts don't get whacked like this for nothing." A startling police photo filled the screen of Victoria dead on the sidewalk, blood covering her torso.

"This, folks, was a professional hit. I think we will have more bloodshed on our hands, so let's all get cracking and squeeze as much information as possible before we lose more subjects like this."

Director Billups surveyed the room and then asked, "Questions?"

Logan raised his hand and spoke. "Could it be possible she was working for a rival gang?"

"Everything and anything is possible. You're going to find out. Anything else?"

No-one really knew what to ask and they just sat uncomfortably in their chairs, before the director slapped his hands sharply twice and barked, "Get cracking!"

The light switch was flipped, illuminating the brooding figure in the back corner. Clint was one of the last to leave and then, right there, he decided to do it.

First he would pop by Billups' office and tell him where he had to go, but right now he had to call Yuri. Clint dialled Yuri's mobile and slipped into a corner of the long hall where Billups' office was. Yuri answered with a simple "Privet," and Clint spoke low and cautiously as he looked around.

"Hey Yuri, it's me. Listen buddy, I need to meet you in thirty minutes on something really important. You free?"

"Well... not really... but... I mean, I guess I could..."

"Super, then. I'll meet you at your office in thirty and then I'll explain."

"Well... okay," replied the less-than-convinced voice on the other end.

Clint moved forward to the ominous door of his boss and rapped it twice, just like always.

"Yeah!" shouted the hoarse voice from the other side.

Clint peeked in and saw his boss still standing at the edge of his desk and shuffling through a handful of documents. He didn't enter completely and casually stated, "I'm going over to Yuri's to finish up his report on this."

"The dead girl?"

"Yeah, her. I'll take what we have as well as a picture to confirm her identification with Matchmaker just in case. Just want to make absolutely sure."

"Well... okay... I guess it can't hurt."

"Be back in a bit."

II

It was 10:50 in the evening and Clint was sitting on his sofa watching a DVD of Law and Order, when his mobile rang. He glanced quickly at its face and grimaced in disgust. It was Billups' number and he instinctively knew that it must be something big. Shit, he thought as he grabbed the remote control and pressed the mute button.

"Yeah, what's up?" His answer was unemotional, still was in shock.

"It's unbelievable, Clint. Fucking huge!" Billups exclaimed with a tone that was filled with exasperation and futility.

"What are you talking about?" Clint insisted

"Shit, man! You haven't been watching television, have you?"

"No... I mean I was out with Yuri working on this case, and then came home to watch Law and Order. What the hell's going on?"

"Turn on to Fox News or, hell, even CNN, for Christ's sake. Fox has some interesting news, as if my boss hasn't already chewed my ass out already on this story."

"Oh, crap, I'm turning it on now. You going to tell me what the hell happened?"

"We need to meet soon, but let's not talk by phone. The diner?"

"Yeah, sure. I guess that works. When?""Give me thirty. I'm sure by then you'll understand the urgency."

"Alright, I'm flipping channels now. See you soon."

Clint was taken by the pressing call and the urgency in Billups' voice. The diner was actually a hole in the wall joint that they found when the director came over one evening. Later on they went out looking for a bar and found 'Tila's', which served some of the best Mexican food they had ever had. Ever since, Tila's became a staple for a beer and a place to unwind. Lucky for Clint it was less than a ten minute walk away, which gave him some time to decipher Billups' cryptic panic.

Then he knew. It all started to unfold right in front of him on his oversized flat-screen TV. A giant headline under Breaking News hinted at the scope of Billups' panic, while a stream of text ran on the bottom. What the fuck? he thought as he quickly raised the volume. Instinctively Clint moved to the edge of his sofa and focused intently on the reporter, who was in mid-sentence. He couldn't help but notice the large Taliban arms scandal written above the reporter, and the running verbiage that mentioned 'White House' and 'selling to terrorists'.

The reporter stood in front of an illuminated Red Square and was talking to the anchor who had just asked her if the scandal was reminiscent of the Iran-Contra scandal. Clint listened intently to the reporter, who held her microphone with one hand and pressed her earpiece with the other.

"Yes, Mike," she replied, "The similarities are alarmingly comparable. You may remember that the Reagan administration was then supplying arms to the Iranians through Israel, while a portion of those proceeds went to support the Nicaraguan Contras. Of course, this current scandal has no hostages at the centre of the deal, but the funnelling of money for weapons via a secondary party, in this case Russia, to support tribal Afghan rebels is eerily similar."

Oh fuck! This can't be! No! Clint thought in horror. The realisation of it all suddenly became clear. Clint immediately turned off the television and jumped off the sofa, and he threw the remote on the coffee table. He raced out of the room and slipped into his jacket in a single fluid movement, as if he were a superhero changing instantly in their costume.

A few minutes later Clint flung open the door to the little diner and saw that his boss had yet to make it. At this hour, only a pair of Russian men and an older man was there. He glanced at his watch and it was just a past 11:10. Another fifty minutes and the grease pit would be closed.

A waiter approached and Clint ordered his usual – a can of coke, no glass. Billups strode over to the table and glided into the empty plastic bench as the gaunt waiter left. His face was a storybook with a tale that was written all over it. Clint had worked long enough with the old veteran to read his many furrows and wrinkles. This face was a wreck, or at least had seen the carnage of one.

"Okay, what the hell's going on?"

"You saw the news?" Billups replied in hushed anger.

"This is us, isn't it? Tell me what you know."

Billups looked around to see if anyone was listening, but the two guys laughing were three booths away and too drunk to notice the American pair.

"Fox News received a tape and a DVD with incriminating secretive information of a deal between us and the Russians. Who sent it we can only guess, but it was clearly an inside job."

"One of us?" Clint interrupted.

"No. It looks to be someone who was involved in this project on the other end. Frankly, it just doesn't make sense."

Clint looked up and nodded his head, just as the waiter approached with the drinks. Billups turned around and the two said nothing as the drinks were placed before them.

"Would you like something to eat?"

Clint raised his hand and replied, "No, that's all."

The waiter slowly turned away, looking bedraggled from a long shift. As he walked off behind the counter, Clint turned back to his boss and shook his head, thinking of who could possibly have sent this information to a news network. Why? he thought.

Billups took a mighty drink from his beer, and while he gulped Clint asked, "What else?"

The director exhaled. "The project appears to centre around arms being secretly bought and then siphoned off to Afghan rebels. The rebels would potentially fight al-Qaeda forces in the northern region where the US hopes to contain the guerrilla warfare in that region."

"Does this have anything to do with our mission on Krokav? I mean, shit, he's working with the Egyptians and the Syrians, for Christ's sake!"

"Maybe. Probably. At least that's what Rhodes was chewing my ass about."

"Director Rhodes is in Langley. What does he know?"

"He doesn't get to be the head of global covert projects for nothing. I hate to say it, but the bastard was a genius back in the day."

"So what? He should be asking around in Washington and Langley then. We've been whitewashed. Left out in the dark chasing shadows, while someone high up has been undermining everything we are doing."

Billups could only agree with a quiet nod of his head, and by taking another full gulp from his beer.

After he had finished, Billups replied calmly, "You know this goes way up?"

The manner which Billups stressed 'way' suggested he thought the same as Clint. If their government was dealing with the Russians on some plan to arm the very forces they were at war with, then surely someone very high up the food chain was involved. High enough that the breaking scandal would ensure other heads would roll.

"Why the Taliban?" Clint asked.

"Well, you see, Clint, that is what will make Fox News and all the other media millionaires. Sensationalise everything and scare the public. That's what they do, you know?"

Clint was less convinced, although he had always been particularly unimpressed with Fox and their appeal to the average uneducated viewer.

"So what?"

"So now, all those couch potatoes that we work our ass off to protect will be running around like a swarm of ants after their hill gets razed. Just like after nine-eleven when everyone was afraid to go in an office building or their local mall. Unfounded fear fed by the media."

Billups emphatically drank the last of his beer, slammed the empty glass down on the table and gave a look of disgust as he continued, "Now they will see we had some deal with the Taliban and they will be running around like Chicken Little for the next months. The media will convince them that the sky really is falling."

"It is bad if we were selling to them, you know?" Clint retorted.

The director lurched towards Clint and in a venomous hush replied angrily, "Damn straight it is, but I can already guess what the plan is about and it ain't worth all this sensationalism. Would have been just fine to keep this all under the radar and let everyone just trust us on how to best protect them."

Clint actually understood the director. If any normal citizen was sitting there then for sure Billups would have been seen as a heretic and a complete idiot, but not Clint. He had worked far too long in the intelligence community and with Ron to know that everything is purely black and white, good and bad. In fact, the world was grey.

He suddenly thought about Alexandra, who was the epitome of grey. She was good. He knew it deep down. Even though there was plenty of black in her moral fibre and judgment, there was also plenty of white. Most would never understand and easily just compartmentalise her as one or the other. Clint hated that about the people back home. He found that they largely leaned to one opinion or the other, one way of thinking or the other with little care to the grey that truly defined people. Being in the agency, and so long in Europe, broadened his view of the world and its people.

"Do you know yet who we were arming?"

"You know how many people back home all collectively thought that Saddam Hussein was the worst thing on the planet because 'he killed his own people'?"

Billups accentuated the last part of his question by using his fingers as quotation marks. Clint wasn't sure where this was going, yet knew that Billups often diverged in order to come back to the original argument. He knew that eventually his boss would answer his question.

"Yeah, sure, I remember. Hell, I was one of those people."

"Hell yeah you were, because you were all wet behind the ears and hadn't figured out the world yet! You didn't actually know that that region of earth called Iraq was a centuries-long battlefield for the Kurds, Shiites and Arab Sunnis. Hell, man! Iraqis been slaughtering each other long before Saddam came along. He actually kept it all together." Billups looked down and shook his head.

"Now I ain't saying he was a good guy, but all Americans knew was that he killed his own people. Why? Because that was what the media said! Like they haven't a fucking clue what it was like in Iraq! As if everyone was all holding hands and singing kumbaya or something."

"And let me guess. The Taliban is the same?" Clint had finally got the where Billups was going.

"Hell yeah! That's a whole other can of worms. But the media just lumps all those tribes and groups in that region as one united group. Mention the word Taliban, and you've just compartmentalised the whole of Afghanistan and Pakistan. We know there are thousands of fickle Talibans that would do anything for money. I'm sure if we were supplying some of them with arms then it was for a greater good."

"Maybe, but it doesn't matter right now. Like you said, who is going to split that fine hair?"

"No-one. Fucking media is the curse of good intelligence and defence."

"You know, going back to Saddam, you may think I liked that low-life scumbag, which isn't true. No-one, absolutely no-one I ever met knew that imperialistic England stole a part of Iraq and set up what is now the country of Kuwait. England gets in there, deals away a part of Iraq, supports a puppet regime and sticks it to Iraq. Ever since then Iraq had been fighting behind the scenes to reclaim their lost borders, but to no avail. Then Saddam saves them from Iran back in the day when Iraq was at war with Iran, asks for Kuwait to help pay some of the debt they occurred to protect Kuwait, and they in turn give him the middle finger."

Clint looked at his boss totally dumbfounded. "Hell, I didn't know that. It still didn't give him a right to invade though."

"Hell no it doesn't, but it explains it. And that story was never told. Now every Tom, Dick and Harry labels Iraq as something it ain't. No-one studies history, yet you and I – we live it."

Billups leaned back and exhaled in a resigned sigh. "All I'm saying is that not everything seems to be what it is, especially when the media is covering it. They need to cover it how to best sell it. We know differently, guys like you and me."

"Yeah. Yeah we do," Clint sighed.

Billups was clearly both bitter and nostalgic, and needed Clint as an outlet for his frustration. Being an indirect part of an unravelling scandal that could tarnish his reputation assured him of his melancholy.

"You know. I started this career back in 1968, and back then I was sure we would have another World War with those crazy Russians. They scared the hell out of me, and we didn't have CNN or Fox News back then to fan the fire every single minute on national television." Billups smiled as he reflected, and he paused before continuing.

"And now, look at the bastards. Here I am in their capital talking to you while we're practically their bed buddies. God knows I would have never believed it twenty years ago."

"Things really change, huh?" Clint asked in reflection.

"Hell yeah they do! But one thing has never changed. Our government is always supporting someone our fellow citizens would be outraged if they knew about it. Contra rebels or Saddam yesterday, Taliban today. It will never change."

"What happens next?"

"I have a conference call from the folks in Langley in forty-five minutes. I get briefed from them while passing on everything we know to the director."

"Damn! Up at one in the morning with the bureaucrats," Clint said apologetically while shaking his head.

"And then I brief you guys at nine sharp. So let's get out of here, because I need to get going."

"Yeah... well... I don't know what to say." Clint was truly at a loss for words.

"Just watch the TV like everyone else is doing across the Atlantic and get all your information by the networks. I'm sure this will be the top story for days."

Billups began to slide out of his bench as he reached in his back pocket for his wallet. Then he concluded, "We haven't even got to the political fallout yet."

Clint could only shake his head in agreement. "I'm not so sure if I really want to know."

"You will, son. We all will."

III

The room was just as it always was, except this time the atmosphere was electric. The news of the breaking scandal had been seen by nearly everyone in the room, either on television or the internet. Each person knew that everything could change the moment Director Billups spoke.

The chatter had never been quite like this, as each person discussed the implications of the breaking story. They were in the centre of the storm - in Moscow, and secretly working to prevent the sale of arms to fringe terrorists. The irony that their government was going against their efforts was a source of both shock and resentment.

Then the door opened to reveal the director as they had never quite seen him before. Clearly tired, stressed, and wearing the weight of a mission compromised, the director looked disheveled and out of sorts. Instead of striding confidently to the front of the room, he walked with a casual saunter.

Clint knew why, because he too was feeling the effects of a late night. The emotional explosion of professional and personal setbacks had left Clint without much sleep. He was working on his own project, desperately using every source and every bit of his pull to find out everything about the secretive life of his lost lover.

Director Billups leaned forward and clutched at his podium tightly. His face wore the news of everything his team already knew, as well as from what they didn't. It was a combination of the two that everyone saw.

"Alright. I'm sure everyone was expecting this, so here we are. Gaby," he nodded. The room was silenced completely as everyone seemed to hold their collective breath.

"What we know now is that a tape was sent a couple days ago from Moscow to the headquarters of Fox News in New York, as well as CNN in Atlanta. Apparently CNN was sensitive enough to the material to contact the White House before running it, but Fox simply went straight to air."

"Do we know who sent the tape?" Florian asked.

"No, but we have a theory. Let me get through everything, and then I'll open it up for questions."

"Sorry sir."

Actually, Florian's quick outburst was the one question everyone wanted an answer to. Now the director would have to keep the team riveted a bit longer.

"All right then. The tape apparently depicts two individuals here in Moscow; a Defence Minister by the name of Vladimir Gorban and the creator of the tape, a banker from Sberbank who has suddenly disappeared, probably having gone underground when all this broke. This banker, a Mikhail Markov, appears to have filmed and recorded a meeting between them negotiating the payment of arms into an account set up by the US government named Condor. Condor payments were deposited by a group within the US and overseen by this man, Simon Wolf."

The screen flashed a photograph of the same man they had photographed with Krokav weeks before. The photo of Simon was one of those taken by Logan many days previously, and everyone began to murmur. The full scale of what Billups confessed began to be fully realised. Everyone knew the scandal was legitimate, and that their government was truly involved in a way that deflated them all.

"We now know what all of you in this room suspects. That is that Krokav, our target here, was the guy supplying the arms."

The agency and their mission had been created as some sort of watchdog to an illegal operation which they never broke. The whole time they were trailing Krokav, someone else was further along to what was really happening.

"All right! Quiet down! I know you all are just as shocked as I was, but settle down so I can continue.

What we don't know is the extent to which these two people behind me were involved, but they were certainly involved somehow."

Clint could only bite his lower lip and fold his arms tightly when the picture of Victoria Popslavskaya went up.

"We suspect that Victoria was actually Sasha, an escort whose website's photo you see here, but who was somehow associated to a mafia group or even to the bank itself. She was seen with Krokav on one of our stakeouts. Perhaps she had seen too much or was involved in something that posed a danger to Krokav. Miroslav Abramov is much more interesting. He was the bank president of Sberbank, the very branch where the Condor account was set up. His name comes up on the tape from his understudy – none other than our guy Mikhail Markov. We suspect he may have made the tape as some sort of protection or blackmail for his own safety. We're not sure why or how that tape was sent to the American media and police, and our agents are diligently looking for Markov as we speak. Now, your questions."

"Sir," Florian asked, "Where is Gorban now?"

"Yes, of course. As of one hour ago, our famous television star from the Kremlin is in police custody. Later this afternoon, our contact Yuri Richov will be providing us a statement of what he says. The minister will be a tricky one since he's in the Duma, but Markov should more likely provide us with something when law enforcement eventually catches up with him."

Clint stepped out of the corner and asked with the steadfast calm, "And the girl? Any new developments on her?"

"None."

With the one-word answer, Billups summed up Sasha's importance to the case. To Clint she was so much more, and he was aware that her assassination had to have been part of something far greater than anyone here in this room knew. Or could imagine.

Gaby then raised her hand and spoke when Billups nodded his head. "And Krokav? Do we know where he is?"

"Yes. He was followed late last night to a new hotel where he still is. We assume he knows what has happened and will likely try to move out of Moscow ASAP. I am hiring a directive what to do with him any minute from my superiors, so he remains our number-one priority."

"Sir?" Frank had sat so patiently, but now he had to ask the one question perhaps everyone else was too reticent to ask. "What about the agency? How does this impact us?"

"Let me worry about that, Frank. Believe me when I say I will let you all know when I know, yeah?" The silence in the room was the convincing proof of their trust, but did little to stop the rampant churning of their insides.

"So, team," he barked, "Let's get cracking! Boys! Our friends are on surveillance now, but I want a full report on him immediately!"

As everyone started to talk wildly and scamper out of the room, Billups mumbled, "Even if the whole world is watching the US."

Billups always referred to the team of Darrell, Logan Florian and Marco as 'boys', and the four already knew their expectation before the director had ordered them to another stakeout. They were in the middle of a four day relief by their Russian counterparts who shared surveillance of Krokav. Everybody knew that once the director said that Krokav had moved, they would be immediately camped outside his hotel.

While everyone left the office and scurried about outside in a sea of bustling activity, Clint stayed inside and dialled from his mobile. He waited a few seconds as the phone dialled, before finally speaking softly.

"Hey, it's me. You got it?" he asked.

A few seconds of silence meant the other party was talking. A lot.

"Including a new passport, I assume?" Again he listened. "And that includes all registrations, changed documents and everything, yes?"

Clint fumbled to pull his pen out of his jacket and to write on a piece of free paper that was left stranded on the conference room table. While he scribbled, his eyes flicked back and forth, although he always kept a watchful look out for his colleagues.

"Okay then. Listen – keep an eye out on the number and let me know if you get anything else. Right now the last call was yesterday, right?"

An answer was given before Clint continued, "Alright then, just let me know if anything changes." He folded the piece of paper and listened to the last of his conversation before ending it simply, "We talk later."

Clint left the small room and headed straight for Billups' office, where he saw the director speaking to Darrell and Florian. His boss was outlining their plan and had just said that his next phone call would be to the chief of police regarding extra men to more fully encompass the hotel. Krokav was going down and his arrest would only be hours away, he told them. At least that was the plan he was told by his own boss, who was to call him eminently to confirm.

"That's it!" he exclaimed with a clap of his hands. "Get going!" he demanded, before he turned to Clint, who was leaning casually in the doorframe.

"And?"

Clint snapped back to his feet and calmly stated, "Listen, I'm going out for a little while. Going down to meet Yuri at the station to check out those phone taps we have on Krokav, as well as chasing a new lead."

"A new lead?"

"Well… maybe it's something. Maybe a dead end. I'll let you know for sure."

"Damn straight you will. Now, get out of here and on to it. Can't talk to me and do that at the same time, now can you?"

Clint could only smile knowingly. Indeed he couldn't.

Chapter 22

I

It was now evening and three cars and two vans sat parked outside of the chain fence. Another four police cars were placed further away, while behind the vans hunched a dozen concealed Russian SWAT officers, who were fully ready to rush the facility. Inside the dowdy building was Krokav.

The Americans knew what was happening. He was probably only hours away from leaving Russia and their watchful eyes. Soon he would slip away into the recesses of some obscure location, far from any field agents. He might resurface again months later, but never would he be as transparent as he now was.

Billups had got approval to bring him in this morning. Thirty-six hours previously Washington and Interpol had authorised the arrest on grounds of selling weapons illegally to al-Qaeda, as well as to Columbia's FARC rebels. Those deals were the only two of dozen suspected deals which could be proven. Krokav had become infamous to governments for his deals irrespective of ideology, as he was even known to supply arms to both side of conflicts, especially amongst the Africans.

Now Clint and his team awaited the signal in the cool morning sunlight. Everyone was antsy and the nervous energy that permeated from inside each vehicle was overwhelming. Every man privately hoped for an organised takedown, but was resigned to the fact that gun fire and bloodshed would likely ensue. How many that would die today was the mystery which weighed on everyone's mind.

Clint glanced at his watch, now ticking just past ten o'clock. Billups said he would confirm the takedown at ten and now he could do nothing but wait. No activity was evident, and the place was eerily silent.

"Jesus, it looks dead in there. It's almost as if they are waiting inside for us," Clint said to Darrell, who stared straight ahead.

Their van spearheaded the group of police vehicles that sat parked near the entrance, and their view of the dilapidated compound was complete. It amazed Clint that a multi-millionaire would actually operate in such rundown conditions. He expected so much more from Krokav.

Just then his earpiece crackled and he touched his inner ear instinctively. It was Billups, who he was expecting.

"Abort operation immediately. Pull out and return to base. It's a wrap."

Billups' voice was filled with authority and distress. Clint knew his boss too well to miss the disappointment that he heard.

He leaned into his microphone and repeated, "We are here directly in front of the warehouse. Are you sure we are to abort?"

Clint's question seemed stupid on the surface, as only a couple of hours before the whole team was briefed about every detail of the takedown and the urgency to act on this particular evening. Now the director was calling off the mission, and Clint knew Krokav was off the hook.

"Abort now, God damn it!"

Billups' voice reflected his frustration. Immediately, Clint knew.

Washington, he thought as he clenched the microphone hard and grit his teeth with equal force. Fucking bureaucrats! "Yes Sir," he replied, disgustedly and disappointedly.

Clint knew it was over as he looked over at Darrell, who motioned with his hands in confusion. The others in the back leaned forward and Florian muttered, "What the fuck?" Clint slightly shook his head in response and flipped to the frequency where the others could hear him.

"We are to abort immediately!" he said with impassioned disdain. "Repeat. Abort now and pull back to base."

"Sir?" was the immediate response from Boris, the head of the Russian SWAT. The doubt in his voice mirrored Clint's, but all Clint could do was reply, "That's a confirmed abort."

Silence and quiet replaced the tension, and privately most in the cars felt some relief to the imminent chaos that would have followed only minutes later. Instead of shouting and shooting, the Moscow wind gently whistled through the crack of the car's open window. The silence was eerie and everyone seemed pensive and brooding.

Clint shook his head as he started the van and placed the lever in drive. He couldn't wait to find out how they were being manipulated by the pencil pushers eight time-zones away.

II

An hour later, Clint burst through the doors of the unit. He was a volcano ready to erupt. The longer he drove back, the more frustrated he became. The mission had been compromised, and Victoria's indirect killer had gone free. The case had become so much more personal since her death. Throwing himself into the mission was all he had done since Frank had broken the news.

He was ready to shout at the top of his lungs and perhaps to break the first thing that that came his way;

however, all that changed instantly when he saw what was completely unexpected. The gang of men who followed him into the office all stopped too, and their looks of confusion complimented their boss's sheer dumbfounded desperation.

What Clint saw immediately subdued him, and at that very second he knew everything was over. His colleagues were all packing, and everything was in the process of finality. Billups stood like a lost child in the room's centre – his face and body a complete picture of defeat and inevitability.

"What the hell is this, Ron?" Clint demanded.

"It's all over, boys. Everything. The plug has been pulled with immediate effect. I just got the call right after the assholes told me to cancel Krokav's takedown. Apparently there's a bigger picture."

"Fuck the bigger picture!" Clint shouted. Everyone suddenly stopped to stare.

The two leaders stood opposing each other, and clearly Clint wasn't ready to back down. No-one ever yelled at the director, and a new tension filled the room. Instead of the eruption that everyone braced for, the director merely shrugged his limp shoulders and motioned with his head for Clint to follow.

"Come on. Follow me," he said calmly.

A moment later the two were entering Billups' office and Clint slammed the door shut – his frustration still evident.

"What's going on, Ron?"

Clint was a bag of raw emotions, dazed and confused. He boiled inside, but also was on the verge of tears. Deep down he knew what was happening, and it scared him. Everything was so perfect only days ago. Suddenly everything that was comfortable and his own had been taken away. Now he just desperately needed Billups to say why.

"Director Stewart called me just before ten o'clock to say that the project is over and to forget Krokav. Our unit is finished with immediate effect and we are to hand over everything we have to a special investigator who has already been appointed. They want all files packed and sent back to Langley immediately. A group will arrive tomorrow and help us clean up, while ensuring the integrity of our work."

Clint was stunned, and Billups' own daze was obvious. Who was more dejected was a matter of debate as Billups continued, "We're finished, son. Big brother has pulled the plug."

"But bringing in Krokav would have refuted that we were dealing wrongly with the Taliban," Clint pleaded.

"Maybe that was the problem," Billups quipped.

"I don't understand," Clint said, now walking towards his deflated boss. "With all his shit that has just come out, we could have disproved most of it with his arrest."

"Or maybe he would have proven it. Ever thought of that?"

In fact, Clint hadn't. Actually he hadn't thought of anything, because his mind was still numb. Right now Clint was too full of confusion to think about diabolical conspiracies. He shook his head slowly as he muttered, "No. Not really."

"Well, you need to. You need to get your head around the fact that we are nothing more than shitty little pawns that get yanked around by guys back home who are playing their own damn game of chess. I've been too long in this business, and it gets harder and harder with every year. I used to be so full of pure ideology and couldn't see beyond those red, white and blue stripes." Billups slowly walked to his chair and collapsed in it like the defeated warrior he was.

"It was a different time when I was young. Our enemies were clear, their politics evil. Communism was the only dark force on the planet. Hell! Africa, most of Asia and the Middle East were backwaters in the fifties. Now it's so much more complex, and our politicians are more misguided. You think I respect those idiots we've got in the White House?"

Clint knew better. Billups thought Bush was a bumbling fool, and it pained him to have to see Cheney's and Rumsfeld's arrogance reach new highs with each passing month. Maybe the director saw a bit of himself in them, but he also felt they had waged an empty war with shitty intelligence and with no real tangible exit strategy.

Billups continued, as he opened his desk drawer and pulled out a candy bar that he often resorted to when he was stressed, "This scandal and us – we are all linked. I'm sure there are those in Washington who were dealing with the Taliban. The media is dead right on this one. They have all the evidence, and we're here in Moscow fighting the noble fight while the whole time getting jerked around."

"How high does this go?"

"Do you really have to ask?" Billups replied sarcastically. "Think about it for a second. Just think about it."

Clint did, and it didn't take long to figure out. They were a project created by the Joint Chief of Staff, who deferred the unit to the Defence Department. Both of these had oversight from the oval office, and especially Cheny. It didn't take much deduction to assume that the Vice-President could have been involved.

"So why let Krokav go?" Clint asked again. "You think he was working for a governmental buyer, don't you?"

"Of course he was. When you take out the political posturing we've been doing on this guy for years, it all makes sense. Our administration has been all high and mighty, but as soon as we can benefit from this parasite then we jump in bed with him." Clint shook his head in agreement, because he knew Billups was right.

"Remember my Saddam example. The US was wary of him until they saw an opportunity to use him against Iran. We gave, not sold, a whole arsenal of weapons to him. Iraq was the third-highest country in terms of our foreign spending at one time. Then when we are done with him we go in and take him out."

"Guess they figure Krokav can be taken out another time, huh?"

"The administration has egg on their face. The media is all over this story, and it is here to stay. Krokav could only hurt them more. No American citizen has ever heard of this guy, and if we bring him in and he starts talking then suddenly he becomes a household name. This guy could bring down the presidency."

"Hence why we got pulled," Clint answered with a resigned sigh.

"Exactly," Billups replied.

"It really is that simple, isn't it?" Clint asked rhetorically.

"Misguided stupidity. The definition of our administration's foreign policy, and we're at the eye of the storm. Makes you really want to find a new line of work, doesn't it?"

The director's words cut at the heart of everything at that moment. Clint probably didn't feel as disenfranchised as Billups, but he did feel disillusioned. The director bit from his Mars bar and spoke while chewing. "I was hoping to retire here, you know? Just punch my clock for another two years, catch a bad guy or two, and just get away from it all."

"You still can, Ron."

"They'll crucify me. I can see the handwriting on the wall."

"You can't be a fall guy," Clint retorted immediately.

"I've been around the block too long, but I ain't going down without a good old fashioned fist-fight."

Billups smiled wryly. Clint knew his boss was tougher than a Texas rattlesnake and just as mean. Any hardened bureaucrat would have their hands full with the well-connected and grizzled veteran.

"Listen, Ron," Clint said after a long pause, "I need to do something. I need to get away for a couple of days and fix something personally."

Ron's face snapped like an elastic band, from disdain to surprise. "You? Time off?"

After an uncomfortable pause where both men said nothing, Billups replied, "Shit... why not? Nothing happening now except getting babysat by top-secret movers. They're here late tomorrow and then for a couple more days to unplug, disassemble and pack everything." Billups paused and took the last bite from his candy bar before finally continuing, "Be back Friday. Give you enough time?"

"Yeah... yeah," Clint answered as he looked down at the floor. "I guess we all leave pretty soon, huh?"

"Director Stewart said sometime next week. I'm not sure what that means for you, but you'll be okay. I'll make sure of it."

Billups confirmed that indeed it was all over, and only one thing remained to do before he would have to leave the country. He knew it was a long shot; however, he felt nearly certain he could find the needed closure before stepping foot on the airplane that would take him away from all that had just happened.

"Thanks," he muttered as he turned to leave the office. He turned the handle, then looked back at the director and paused momentarily. He looked at his old friend, mentor and boss nostalgically, and smiled knowingly. The two men didn't need to speak – their unspoken gaze spoke for them.

Clint merely nodded his head and gave a two-finger salute to Billups as he walked out of his office and back into the commotion of his busy peers. He took his phone, and with a single push he dialled the second number of his speed dial.

"Yeah, it's me. I need it now. I'll be over in twenty minutes."

Chapter 23

I

Clint drove onwards, but his eyes had barely blinked for several minutes, his body was a prisoner to the thoughts that consumed him completely. He thought of it all and everything that had happened. Now he drove away from Moscow to nowhere.

His face was tortured still from all that had been turned upside-down so quickly. How could this happen? he thought. Being a spy meant being immune to personal involvement. Or so he thought. The past days had snuck up upon him like one of his own stealthy suspects and stabbed him fatally without ever knowing why or how. He still felt the pain of losing Alexandra who he had wished so much for. It wasn't supposed to have ended like this.

The road so far away from Moscow was bumpy and full of potholes. It had stopped being smooth four hours ago and only seemed to be getting worse. Nonetheless, the jar of the car being rocked as if hit by a battering ram was not enough to jolt Clint out of his sorry mood. He was locked into another worldly dimension where his mind raced and his body felt numb because of it.

Eventually his eyelids gradually drooped, but it wasn't because he was tired. There was far too much adrenaline to be tired. Instead he closed them for a full two seconds to escape his trance. When he opened them again, nothing had changed. The long road was nearly empty. Only a truck was ahead in the far away distance, and two small cars were nearing from the other direction.

The navigation device indicated only sixty-seven more kilometres to go. Clint had left Moscow at four o'clock, when the huge city was still nestled sleeping in its blanket of darkness. After the four hundred kilometre drive to Novgorod he had made his first stop, and then continued driving for another six hours until he reached Chelny. He was exhausted from driving. He had never driven so far in one day, but, then again, why would he ever have ever driven twelve hundred kilometres and fourteen hours?

Clint saw Alexandra again in his mind, and imagined her sitting in his empty passenger seat. He remembered their last date, when it occurred to him that he had truly fallen in love with this stranger who had come from nowhere. He had so much more still to learn and experience with her. The pangs of new love had been a distant feeling for him, not felt since years earlier when he met Aleeka.

That dream was now over. The fantasy of a blue cloudless sky with infinite sunshine had been replaced with the drab grey that Moscow is so famous for. Big dreams often crash heroically, and the anaesthetised realisation of that was all he felt.

Knowing that he would never be able to be with Alexandra was what literally drove him so far from Moscow. It was the escape of everything that had happened, and the final act of closure that he desperately needed. Only one thing now remained – only one final bridge to cross before he could ever move on again. That was now only sixty kilometres away.

II

It was nearly seven o'clock as he turned off the road and onto a packed dirt path that left him wondering. The GPS indicated eight hundred metres to the final destination; however, he still felt unsure. The forest seemed so thick and the road seemed too unused to be correct, but there was no other alternative.

Can this be? he wondered as he peered intensely into his surroundings. The day was slowly slipping away as dusk was setting in. The tall trees further darkened the road; nonetheless, he pressed ahead. Clint drove slowly and his car rocked and swayed on the uneven surface. It was a road he thought fit only for tractors and farm machinery, not his BMW.

Eventually he was there at its end, and the tree-lined path gave way to a clearing of some small homes and a sign that assured him that he had finally found his destination. A shimmering lake was only a hundred metres further away and was fronted by a wooden lodge and other small cabins. The motif was that of a rustic camp, and it was easily the most attractive thing he had seen since he left Moscow.

He parked and stepped outside into the stillness of the Ural's tranquil environs. Moscow seemed such a world away. The air here seemed lighter, crisper, and he inhaled deeply. Sucking in so much rich oxygen left him immediately invigorated, and the chilly temperature caused his skin to pimple and shiver.

Clint reached in the back seat and grabbed his jacket and, as he did, he noticed a couple walking together hand in hand towards the lake's edge. He smiled at the romantic nature of the sight, and it occurred to him that he had never gone camping or visited nature quite like this. The closest thing to nature Clint ever experienced was playing golf, which he felt was a way to connect to nature. In fact, it was a clumsy alternative that now reminded him how much of an urban dweller he truly was. The appeal of what he was now surrounded by was undeniable, yet felt so alien nonetheless.

He grabbed his soft leather messenger bag and headed to the central lodge. He felt the unbelievable anticipation of conquest, which was now at his fingertips and only metres away. The sudden feeling of realisation caused him to pause momentarily. Clint reached inside his bag and took the familiar handle from his Beretta and looked at it longingly for a second, thinking just how long it had been since the last time he used it outside of the firing range. He slipped it into the holster, which he wore at the back of his pants, and proceeded forward – prepared, yet pensive.

He climbed up the few steps to the lodge that groaned under his weight before pulling open the front door, which squeaked loudly. Clint entered the comfortable interior, a warm reprieve from the outside chill. A gigantic fireplace burned in the opposite corner and large paintings depicting rustic and mountainous scenes hung throughout the spacious cabin. A clustering of soft brown velour chairs filled an area aimed at relaxation, while a small bar attended to two overweight men only metres away.

Clint noticed the smiling receptionist looking at him. Even out here in the middle of nowhere the women still were beautiful. Her blonde hair and features were similar to Alexandra's, and she possessed the same slender smile that seemed genetic to all Russian women.

"Privet," she said, looking Clint up and down. She tilted her head and looked at him coyly.

He had seen this before and knew the tell-tale signs of a flirt when he saw one. Clint was so obviously a foreigner, and somehow it seemed Russian women were magically drawn to attractive non-Russian men like flying insects to lights. She thrust her shoulders back and cocked her head ever so slightly in an instinctive manner to maximise her body and all its perfect curves, even if it was covered by a plain pale green uniform. If he was here for pleasure then he would have likely indulged her subtle flirting with playful banter, and perhaps even asked her out if his suspicions were confirmed. A girl like this would likely be yet another sexual conquest at any other time. He had long since stopped counting the number of forward Russian women who ultimately became a fun and casual sexual distraction. Symbiosis, he assumed, went both ways.

Clint was the consummate flirt and had been for so long, yet he was in no mood and disinterested in anything other than the task at hand. Instead of an indulgent playful cat and mouse he approached her directly and without a smile. Frankly, he had no reason to smile.

"Privet," he replied sternly. He reached into his bag, pulled out a folder and opened it before the smiling receptionist."

"Do you have a reservation, Mr...?" she asked in Russian. Her melodic voice danced along playfully in an accent that was definitely not from Moscow.

"No. No I don't," he replied back firmly. Clint spoke decent conversational Russian so conversing in these situations wasn't a problem; however, his accent was pure American, and the woman across from him immediately recognised it.

She grinned widely and flicked again at her hair. "Ah, you are American, yes?" she asked in her best English. Her voice, so smooth in Russian, had been replaced by a syrupy thick accent that lost its charm. Her curiosity was piqued by the rarity of any foreigner visiting this place, let alone an American.

Clint knew better than to answer, as this visit was strictly under the radar and low-key. Instead he pulled a photo, and revealed a badge that he now laid in front of her. Clint glanced at her badge and noticed her name before he continued in Russian, "Is this person one of your guests... Eva?" He tapped at the photo with his index finger and looked down at her. He saw her eyes drift first to the photo, and then to his badge.

She had surely never seen such a badge before. He carried an international police badge that had been assigned by the Russian government, who had co-sponsored the project. It gave him limited police powers although he was only authorised to use them in the presence of a Russian police officer. Clint assumed that Eva hadn't quite figured out the hair-splitting of just how limited his powers actually were. Eva's smile slowly disappeared and her eyes spoke, even though she remained momentarily silent.

"Where can I find this person?" he asked with assurance.

"In cabin number three," she replied in Russian. Clint snapped away the photo and badge and thanked her hastily, his mind already flashing ahead.

"Do you need the name, sir?" she asked cautiously. Clint paused only for a second as he searched for an answer. A name? he thought to himself. How ironic.

"No. That won't be necessary," he replied.

Clint saw her nervousness as she fidgeted with a pen. He stopped and smiled before speaking. "Don't worry. There is no problem." He spoke to quell her anxiety as much as he did to reduce any evidence that he was there. He wanted to be invisible. She smiled softly, although it seemed forced and conscious.

"Thank you, Eva."

He strode away and back out the door, which seemed to creak even louder than before. The steps groaned too, and he stopped on the last stair to scan the panoramic view of lake and cabins in the fading light. A wooden post next to a nearby bulletin board indicated the cabin numbers with two opposing arrows. His mind raced again, and he felt exhilarated.

Each cabin was like its neighbour and was built solely from wood. He paused and his hand found its way to the back of his pants, where the handle of his gun felt warm and tactile. He adjusted his coat and blew into his hand in a feeble attempt to warm it. The striking chill of the air was a sharp contrast to the warmth of what was beyond the wooden walls he was now only metres from.

The smoke that billowed from the small cabin's fireplace stretched into infinity, and eventually disappeared when the sky's colour changed from light blue to the deep indigo that touched the barely-visible stars. Clint was caught in a distraction of the heavens. The stars barely twinkled, and it suddenly occurred to him that he hadn't seen a starry night since he had been in Russia.

He gazed once again at the maroon-coloured door that seemed to become darker by the second. The cabin's interior was illuminated by soft light, which gave him hope to confront the person he had driven so long to see. Closure was so near, yet remained tantalisingly so far away. His arms felt heavy and his body seemed temporarily paralysed. The Siberian wilderness had its grip on the outsider who was a stranger in its midst.

Clint inhaled one last time and closed his eyes momentarily to prepare himself for the final confrontation. The mystery of the puzzle that had taken so long to piece together lacked a singular jagged piece; without it there would be no finality, no closure and no way to ever move forward.

He opened his eyes once again and walked slowly to the steps. His nervous scan assured him that he was alone and invisible to anyone who might be out. He stood directly at the foot of the door and pushed the tiny doorbell. It rang with an old time sounding clang that reminded him of a preschooler's bicycle.

He heard nothing inside, and took a step sideways to avoid standing directly in the door's middle. A second later the scene was instantly illuminated when the front light flashed on. A raised yet familiar voice from the other side of the door could now be heard. "Coming, coming!"

He could hear the door's lock turn and the slide of the safety latch as the reply continued, "But I didn't order..."

The words stopped in the instant that the two saw one another. At that moment, the world and all its reality stood perfectly still. Their eyes were locked in a frozen stare, and the air suddenly felt so heavy and toxic. The ominous figure looming in front of her was hardly who she had expected. Although the high collar of his jacket partially concealed his profile, there was enough light to reveal who actually stood before her. Clint could see her mouth open; however, no words escaped.

He too felt the sudden pang of the moment. Alexandra was there in front of him, alive and real. Seeing her again quelled his pain and breathed life back into his emptiness. He had wondered about this moment for so long and his hunch and detective work had paid off, although what his eyes saw seemed so unbelievable. She was a living ghost that should be dead.

Or at least that was what the official record declared; however, she now stood in front of him in complete shock. His repressed feelings once again were ignited, and he didn't know what to do or feel. Every emotion ran through him like the high-powered voltage given to a death row inmate. Neither knew what to say or do. Alexandra peered half-exposed from the door that shielded her, while Clint was the illuminated entity that she had resigned to never see again. Each were ghosts that had been strangely reunited in the middle of the Russian Siberia, so far from the glitz, glare and concrete that had once defined their reality.

Clint spoke first, although his words seemed to be in slow motion. "I had a hunch." Alexandra laughed in a way that was both ironic and nervous.

It all started from the birthmark that wasn't on the dead woman. Clint knew then that Victoria must have been Alexandra's twin, which sent him on a frantic ride to prove it. Yuri had helped him. Mobile phone calls can be traced and, although Alexandra had only made two calls since the killing, it was enough to convince him of her whereabouts.

"How..."

"I'll answer that later, but first things first." He stepped forward into the inviting warmth of the cosy cabin's interior. She closed the door, engulfed within a white terry-clothed bath robe and without any makeup. Nonetheless, she somehow exuded the radiance of an angel. Maybe it was the white, or perhaps it was his own subjectivity that idolised his lover. Either way he stepped boldly to her, and she hugged him passionately. He caught her gingerly, and at that very instant they were locked together in a kiss that paralysed her. Their mouths interlocked in a familiar passion that had been nearly forgotten.

"I've missed you," he whispered, staring into the eyes of the truth he knew so well.

It wasn't his words but rather the sound of his familiar voice that caused her to swoon. Energy raced through her, flooding her like some sort of ocean wave and leaving Alexandra consumed. It was if his lips had been coated with some sort of poison that instantly drugged her and now left her weakened to the point of complete paralysis. All of her fear from the past several days suddenly vanished, as if by magic.

"How.....how did you know?" she struggled to ask.

In reality, it hadn't been that difficult to find her. At least not for a spy with access to tools and influential friends.

"You told me," he confessed. Her face told him she didn't remember.

"After Casanova's a couple weeks ago. Remember?"

In fact, she didn't.

"You told me that Gayva would be where you would return one day if you could."

Alexandra was stunned. "You actually remembered that?" she asked in total awe.

"I did. But..." He paused and looked awkward, struggling to release his confession. After a couple more seconds of silence and a prod from Alexandra's eyes, he admitted to what assured him of her place here so far away from Moscow. "I traced your calls from your mobile," he acknowledged sheepishly.

"You did what?"

Oddly this came as a greater shock than did his remembering their pillow talk and her childhood fantasies. "How did you...?"

"I ran a trace," he interrupted. "Big Brother is always watching."

Alexandra could only smile and shake her head in defeat. "How did you run a trace?" She saw her man as the artificially created illusion that Clint had so carefully constructed. It was no different than what she had done with him; however the difference now was that only one of them truly knew the other. She saw him as a simple bureaucrat and a tender man that she wanted to be with – at least to explore herself being with, and perhaps commit to in a way she had never before. If she only knew that the truth would now shatter any hope of those desires.

For Alexandra, the other side meant casting away every element of her soiled past to be amongst the pure – the people who lived a life of children, gatherings with couples and even in-laws. Indulgence in the ordinary was something which she now longed to experience. Clint could have been the man to introduce her to that. Or so she thought.

She wanted to tell him everything at that moment. She wanted him to protect her from those she feared wanted her dead, and she wanted him to make love to her as well. She wanted so much, and she felt torn.

Clint closed the door slowly behind him and locked it. He took her hand gently inside his and walked her over to the large brown and cream sofa. His eyes never left her.

"There's so much I need to tell you."

She already knew his words were an understatement. Indeed she wanted answers, and none more than why he was here. However, there was even more she wanted to tell him.

"Clint," she began, "I'm in trouble and I don't really know why."

"I know."

His reply struck her like a body blow. A simple two-word answer felt like a ton of stones crashing down on her, leaving her to inhale deeply and then slowly breathe out.

"Okay... and how?"

"Alexandra... I'm not exactly who you think I am."

She snapped her head back and stiffened like a wooden board. Her skin prickled and her mind raced.

"What do you mean by that?" she retorted sharply. "Do you know that I'm on the run?"

"I can explain everything. I want you to know what all has happened. For your own protection." Clint saw the opening he needed and seized the moment by blurting, "I know everything, Alex. The escort thing, Minister Gorban, everything."

Alexandra spun in stunned shock and faced her lover with widened eyes. She felt a surge of adrenalin shoot through her. Not the kind that comes from fear, but rather the exhilaration and shortness of breath that happens when caught in a terrible lie. Suddenly the fresh air seemed so heavy and humid. She felt the weight of his knowledge like the force of a car crash that sent her into the dashboard, leaving her breathless from the impact. The thoughts, feelings and words to say flew through her faster than her mind could digest, and the only reply that she could muster was, "How?"

It had come down to a single one-syllable word. How did he know? How could he know? Her distressed eyes searched his in frantic desperation.

"I could say the same thing about me, Alex," he replied calmly as his gaze fell back down at the bed. "I'm not just approving visas and such, and I don't exactly work for the Embassy."

His confession sent Alexandra to raise and eventually settle in a sitting position that now saw her looking down at Clint in bewilderment. She wanted to shout at his deception, but knew better. Her shame prevented causing a scandal when she knew that the life she had portrayed had been largely a lie.

"Okay," she muttered.

"I do work for the US government, but for the Department of Defence in a special project sponsored by the Homeland Security Act. A small group of us work in secret to thwart terrorist activity."

Alexandra sat back and pursed her lips as she thought momentarily before replying in apparent relief, "That's not so bad. You could have told me that."

"No, no. I couldn't, Alex," he retorted in immediate denial. "I'm going to trust you now that you will never repeat this to anyone." The fierce look from his eyes told of the seriousness of his confession, and Alexandra knew that she owed him this.

"Of course not."

"Actually, I'm more a spy than a bureaucrat. I'm here in Russia because we know that there is a rogue arms dealer who was selling to terrorists that threaten US security. I can't be known as anything more than a simple paper-pusher in the eyes of everyone here."

Suddenly, it all started to make sense. He must have been spying on her, but why? The only answer she found that flashed before her instantly was that spies were always spying on everybody, even those around them.

"So you were spying on me, huh?"

She hung her head down in both shame and disappointment. She felt the mix of personal guilt for what she did, but also equal disappointment that he was somehow not honest and wholly trustworthy to her deception.

"Actually no, Alexandra."

He rarely called her by her full name, and his direct answer was stated with such emphatic denial that she somehow believed him. His eyes and face were a picture of seriousness and complete honesty. She wished to kiss him, however she knew that it was impossible.

"Vladimir... one of your clients..."

"Wait!" she blurted. "I ended all that when I began to realise that you and I were..."

She couldn't find the words to complete her thoughts, and her interruption was a vain attempt to justify having been with one man while also sleeping with another. Now, for the first time, she spoke of her feelings that she had for Clint, even if she couldn't finish. Clint knew, though.

"You don't have to justify anything, Alex. I was just saying that you were discovered indirectly about two weeks ago, but I didn't know it was you at the time."

Alexandra felt even more confused, because somehow he had already said that he knew she was an escort. Having a lover while with Clint, coupled with her escort sex, left her clinching the sides of the couch and feeling shame like never before. Alexandra had never answered to a man in her past and, oddly, she didn't need to answer to Clint. However, she couldn't help but feel deeply dirty.

"You were photographed on a stakeout with a subject, who we later knew had underworld ties and is a major arms dealer. At the time we thought you may be a girlfriend or even... well..."

She rolled her eyes and knew what he refused to say. "A hooker," she snapped back with shameful vengeance.

"Not a hooker, but maybe a date or something," he whispered defensively. In fact, he had thought she was a prostitute; however, he would never tell her this. There was no need to agonise her unnecessarily. "Eventually we matched you to Moscow Elite, and began to look into you further."

A tear trickled out of Alexandra's swollen eyes and her mouth, quivered although she tried to force it shut. She looked away shamefully and softly muttered, "We, huh? So everyone in your department knows I'm an escort."

Clint rubbed away her tear and the one that was just beginning to escape the corner of her eye. "Shh. You're only a subject to them. It's not personal."

"Well, it is for me! Did they know I was fucking you?" she retorted angrily.

With calm reassurance Clint replied, "No. No-one knows about us. Well... except for one person, but he's the one that has helped me with you. He can be trusted."

Alexandra tossed her head the other way, looked out towards the window and into nowhere. The uneasiness of the moment left her feeling so many emotions, and all of them were raw.

Clint continued. "We later established a connection to you and the minister, who you were also seen with, which is how you became a subject to our investigation. It was then that you were positively identified. These things sometime take time."

"I saw a paper with a photo of a woman killed who was supposed to be me!" she blurted while sniffing deeply. "She looked exactly like me!"

"You saw this?" Clint asked in bewildered shock.

"The reporter linked this Victoria woman to some sort of chain where Mikhail and others had been killed. That's when I knew that they had killed the wrong woman – that the real target should have been me." Alexandra sniffed again before continuing. "They're going to come back, you know? It's only a matter of time! If you found out...."

"He's not going to find out, Alex," Clint snapped.

"Unless he is dead, I am never safe," she stressed agonisingly.

"You are dead," Clint countered.

Clint's rebuttal was quick and so certain. Alexandra jerked her head back and stroked back her hair in disbelief. Of course she was alive, and sitting there facing her lover. It was bad enough that she was running scared; but dead?

"So you're saying we both are ghosts right now?" she quipped sarcastically.

Clint replied calmly, "This guy who killed the woman thinks you are dead, so to him you are. If he does, then whoever else he associates with thinks the same. But Alex – you're not that important to these people. It's over now."

"So why then? Who did he kill if it wasn't me? For Christ's sake! I saw that woman and it was like looking in a mirror. He could find out that he made a mistake, and then he would…"

"Alex! Stop right there! Listen to me."

Clint clasped her with both hands, one holding tightly on each of her shaking arms. He felt her fear as it raced through her, and he looked directly into her panicked eyes.

"There's so much you need to know, and then you will realise that you are safe."

"What?" she sighed in utter disbelief. "What could possibly make me think that none of this ever happened?"

"It did happen, but the woman killed was your twin sister, Alex. Her name was Victoria. I'm assuming you never knew your twin, did you?"

Alexandra's face told of the sheer shock of his words, striking her like a heavyweight's right hook. She felt the impact hit her square in the body, leaving her breathless and dazed.

"I…I…" She struggled to speak and she could barely open her mouth. "I didn't know I had a sister." Alexandra's gaze had fallen as her head hung low, and Clint was left to explain.

"Your mother had you and Victoria, but your sister was adopted as a baby to a family that moved to

Moscow in 1983. She went to school and lived a normal life, before eventually marrying nine years ago. You stayed at the orphanage much longer, so it's possible you were never told or could know."

Alexandra didn't know what to feel or think. Instantly she felt the shock that she had a sister – an actual blood sibling that she never knew of, and her shock was compounded because it was her lover who now revealed this. She felt a violation of sorts. His information proved that he had access to every part of her life that she had kept so secretive. He calmly recanted her life as if it was a merely another case from some sort of bureaucratic file.

"What don't you know?" she snapped angrily as she threw herself away from him and against the back of the couch. "My life is some fucking case for all you Americans to know? I have... I had a sister? Why didn't you tell me?"

Her anger was justified, albeit unfounded. It wasn't personal and no-one would know, but right now Alexandra would never believe it.

"It's not just a case, Alex," Clint replied sympathetically, "I only just discovered your sister."

It didn't occur to him what he would have done if he had discovered earlier Alexandra was a twin. He may have fished around wondering why she denied her, but then it came to mind that Alexandra had always said she was an only child. He reached out to touch her arm, but she slapped his hand away with authority.

"You are not just a case to me!" he said firmly and with a raised pitch that underscored his seriousness.

Alexandra could only look away and out to the emptiness before her. "I never knew," she muttered as she began to cry. "I never knew I had a sister right under my nose. I would have loved having a sister."

Her voice tailed away and she looked back at her tormenter, whose empathy she now felt. "And I will only ever remember her lying dead on the concrete."

Alexandra let her tears stream like a waterfall; she cried for all that had happened and could have happened. She felt the sheer weight of her past, and blamed herself in some twisted way. She could have never known about Victoria, but it didn't stop her from blaming herself.

"I'm sorry," Clint said softly. "I think she knew you somehow, though."

"How do you mean?" Alexandra replied curiously, through a sniff.

"Her son was named Alexander. That's nearly the same as your name, so perhaps she felt you in some sort of subconscious way."

Alexandra smiled, sniffed some more and brushed away the tear that trickled down her flushed cheek.

"You're safe now," he whispered with absolute reassurance as his hand found its way to her exposed leg.

"How can you be so sure?"

"Because Victoria became you in an instant."

Alexandra's blank stare spoke of her absolute confusion.

"Victoria, mother and wife, lived a double life working as an administrator at a local mental health centre while simultaneously serving as an escort for Moscow Elite Escorts. It was when servicing a client with known underworld connections that she inadvertently became involved in a deadly triangle involving her husband, who worked in a weapons facility. Her client eventually found out, tried extorting her, and had her killed when she refused or when he got what he needed."

"What?" she asked with sheer indignation. None of this made any sense, and Alexandra truly doubted that such a fantastical story would ever survive scrutiny.

"Right now the police are looking in to your sister's husband, Stefan Popslavski. By all accounts he's a good guy, hard-working, never did anything to piss anyone off who seems unlikely to have ordered her hit, but it all makes sense. For you, at least."

"How? By blaming an innocent person?"

"Yes, Alexandra! Yes! By putting your life on someone who can't say it's not true! That's how you are going to live a long and hopefully quiet life! The only other person who knows it isn't true is your friend Elena, and she is willing to testify that Sasha was in fact Victoria. I've talked to her already. Remember, I traced your call to her. She tells me you are like her daughter, and because of that we changed all the files she has on you to indicate you are Victoria. Don't worry. In a few months I will arrange for my friend to tell Stefan the full story –and we'll make him understand why he can't repeat it."

Clint's raised voice spoke of an inconvenient truth whose duplicity was beyond the visible. It was the kind of manufactured lie that governments or secret agents create for their own personal gain. Now Alexandra was a part of the conspiracy. He could so easily say it; however, she would have to live it. It seemed so unfair... but shamefully necessary.

"You can't take back her death, but you can take back your life, Alex."

Clint was right, and she recognised it. She nodded approvingly and knew that he wasn't wrong. However words were so easy to say, and she felt suddenly alone and completely vulnerable. She knew that the prism of life would now become harder than ever before, and that reclaiming anything 'normal' would take time.

"How did she become involved?"

"Simple bad luck... for her."

She squinted disbelieving and didn't quite believe it could be that simple.

"Her last call was to her husband as she left a gym called Body and Soul..."

Before he could speak Alexandra blurted, "That's my gym!"

"I know. My partner and I followed every lead and investigated the membership at this gym where I found you both belonged. I'm assuming the killer followed Victoria instead of you. You know you are damn lucky, don't you? It's amazing you never ran into her. She died near where you work and live," he added.

"My God," Alexandra mumbled in stunned surprise. She couldn't believe how life could have played its hand. She could have seen her twin sister any time, and wondered privately what it would have been like.

Alexandra looked upwards with a blank stare. "I never saw her until that day."

His hand tightened its grip on hers, and he paused as he looked down. Clint searched for a beginning, knowing only the end and everything in between. He looked at her staring back intently. He saw her hope, her fears and the closure she desperately needed. He wasn't sure if he saw love, but at that moment his heart truly skipped and he gasped ever so slightly.

He felt the raw energy of the deep-seated fire that always shone when she was near. It was a sexual energy that stoked deeper, more pure emotions that left him feeling exhilarated, yet wanting to curl within her warm and tender embrace. She made him feel like what no other woman had ever been able to do – sexual, but simultaneously tender and loving.

The silence between them and the look in her eyes told him she was feeling the same. Somehow all that needed to be said slid quickly to the background, revealing only their desires to be dealt with. He leaned forward slowly, almost cautiously. She never moved, except for her eyelids, closing as he drew ever nearer.

A second later their lips touched and the electricity of that moment sent both into a raw kiss that seemed to last forever. Alexandra gasped. His unexpected passion had ignited all the emotions she had for him at that very moment. Her feelings were both primeval and nurtured, and she felt their full fury as he pulled away. He seemed to know exactly what she needed to replace the fear that had gripped her over the past days. She cupped his face with both hands and whispered, "Make love to me."

III

Clint awoke to the morning light. It illuminated the sparsely-furnished bedroom to reveal a translucent haze that filled it completely. He turned to see a mess of blonde peeking out from the thickness of the plaid comforter. Alexandra slept softly yet soundly.

He thought of how beautiful she was during these times. He knew that this morning would be his last like this. He savoured how she breathed and the waviness of her hair. He was careful not to touch her and wake her, because sleep was the only freedom that she now knew.

He laid and watched her like some sort of sentry guarding a prisoner. Except Alexandra was a prisoner; not to his watchful gaze, but of a past which she one day would have to resolve. It was a return to innocence for her, yet the gravity of love was still far from being realised. Her journey had indeed taken her here to Perm and far from her life in Moscow. What she had just done was much more than a physical voyage, but rather an odyssey of the mind. She had fled Moscow for fear of her life; however, she had discovered what she must become if she were ever to return.

Clint propped himself up on one elbow and glanced at his watch. It was already 8:38, which was late for him. Making love, talking, and the raw emotion of the night had taken its place over sleep.

Slowly and carefully, he rolled out of the bed so as to not awaken the girl who still breathed rhythmically in her sleep. Once out of the warm cocoon, Clint felt the chill of the new morning. The floor was cold and he tip-toed his way to the bathroom awkwardly, as if to avoid imaginary glass shards that had been strewn across the chilly surface.

Upon entering the bathroom, he stood on a small furry rug that was directly in front of the sink and he noticed himself in the mirror. He looked tired and thought himself unattractive with his messed hair and puffed eyes. He noted Alexandra's personal effects as well as the tinfoil packet of pills that caused him to close his eyes and grimace. Seeing her birth control pills pained him, as it was the stinging reminder that they were one of the critical necessities of her life.

There was a time not long ago that Clint imagined Alexandra meeting his parents, and he even saw her as a mother to his child. He had always admitted to the unfairness of the Madonna and whore complex, yet deeply knew that he viewed women with such a mentality. Alexandra was so perfect in bed; he loved her raw sexuality and how easily she seemed to handle his body. Yet still he found himself beginning to idolise her into something that she was not. The virtuosity and purity that he projected on to her was merely the fantasy of a man setting unrealistic expectations. He blinked his eyes rapidly to remove the thought of strange men with her, and moved towards the shower quickly. He let the water run over him completely and he closed his eyes in delight.

For a moment he floated back to the restaurant where he first saw Alexandra, and to the first time he saw her nakedness before him. He remembered her first cunning quip, and what she whispered into his ear just the night before. He saw his lover in extremes, and the images that flashed inside him were truly symbolic of the duplicity of their relationship. In fact, he too was guilty of posing as something he was not, and his deception only now pained him.

He was an agent of a country which forbade him such disclosure, and there was no handbook as to how to settle the paradox. How could he work in such secrecy and honestly be able to share himself with a woman? It was the cruel contradiction that would always prove the downfall of having a genuine relationship. Alexandra had been the second woman to remind him of that.

Clint lathered himself in the vanilla-scented soap. He wore the smell of desire just like Alexandra, and he breathed in the aroma as deeply as he could. As he let the water rinse him completely, he thought of what he needed to tell her when she woke up, and just how fleeting his time was.

He felt that she had kept so much of herself secret from him and, while that was part of her appeal in a bizarre kind of way, it was not what he wanted in a woman long-term. As a romance it was exciting –as a lover, her mystery was enticing. But what he wanted in a wife and the possible mother of his children was someone more straightforward, more loving, more predictable. Clint had always felt that Alexandra would never completely give herself emotionally to anyone, and that left him wanting her more – as the conquest was never complete - but it also left him slightly empty and unfulfilled. He wanted someone warmer, someone who he knew loved him more completely and with less self-control.

He felt that Alexandra would always ultimately put herself first - above him, above their possible children, above everything - and that he could never entirely trust her. The quality made him pursue her harder and want her more, but the thought of what it could lead to long-term left him cold and repelled. She had continued to fuck clients through their intimacy and romance, often on the same day that she had told Clint she loved him or he'd said the same to her. So what would stop her continuing to do so when they were married and the excitement and intensity had died down? What would their children think if they found out - or, worse still, what if his family found out?

Alexandra was vulnerable; not in a soft way, but rather in a spiky, defensive way. Clint wanted to be with someone he really felt he could take care of. Not just financially, but emotionally too. He also wanted someone who would take care of him. With Alexandra she had only seen the best side of him and that obviously hadn't been enough as she'd continued to see clients – so what about when she got bored of him or saw the less impressive sides? No, ultimately Clint wanted someone more stable, someone softer.

Although he tiptoed his way back into the bedroom, his attempt to not be heard was in vain. Alexandra rolled over and muttered, "Early shower?"

"Oh, sorry. Did I wake you?"

"Uh... yeah."

"It's really not so late. About nine, actually."

"It's all right. Hope you finished before the cold..."

"Too late. I feel like I just swam in the North Sea," he interrupted, now inching closer to Alexandra. The bed was exactly what he needed – dry, warm, and alive with Alexandra.

Both were propped on their elbows, and they faced each other in smiling silence. Each privately wondered what would happen in the next hours, although Clint knew more than she. He knew what was inside his bag, and he knew that an answer to why he was there right now had to be given. His silence must be heard.

"I heard the elks last night," he said softly. "Or I think it was them that I heard."

Alexandra smiled knowingly.

"They probably missed you, Alex. Probably calling you out to join them in the forest."

A delicate grin was enough to tell Clint what he thought. "I can see why you came here. It's so....so..."

"Peaceful," she replied.

"Yeah, peaceful," he confirmed with a slight nod. "Sure ain't Moscow, that's for sure."

"No. It isn't Moscow at all," she answered back assuredly.

Alexandra sighed and then crashed back into her pillow. "I don't know what the hell was happening, Clint. There's stuff that I never..." She hesitated slightly before continuing, "Never told you about me."

Alexandra leapt from the bed and walked away, completely naked. The filtered sun illuminated her milky skin and her blonde hair, which seemed to glisten with radiance. She entered the bathroom as she wiped her eyes with the palm of her hand. "I'm taking a shower." Clint heard her from behind the thin walls, and knew what he had to do.

Ten minutes later she reappeared, her nipples firm from the fresh air of the bedroom. Alexandra stopped as she saw her lover fully-dressed and sitting in the small chair by the window. She reached to the adjacent dresser and pulled out a T-shirt.

"I see you are all ready. Going somewhere?" she asked pensively.

Clint rose and approached her with something in his hand. Her arms were crossed in subconscious defensiveness, and she looked at him nervously.

"What's that?" she asked with a nod towards his hand.

"Perhaps part of your future. It's all yours if you want it." He handed her an envelope that she took tentatively, before eventually opening it in stilled silence. As she peered over the contents, Clint explained.

"Your mother's name is Mariya," he said assuredly, as if he personally knew her mother. "She lives alone not too far from here in downtown Perm, along the river. She's never married and has no children. No family, in fact. Except for you, Alex."

The words and information on the papers before her eyes confirmed the truth. To think that her mother was now something more than imaginary was paralysing.

"I think she might like to get to know you. Everything you need is there."

She didn't know what to say, let alone feel. Then it occurred to her.

"And my father?"

She knew in an instant from the expression of his face what the answer was.

"Your father died several years ago; nevertheless, the names of his two sons are in there as well. I hope you reach out to them, and, if you do, I hope they accept you."

She looked at him with rounded eyes that swelled with both astonishment and fear. "Can you join me?"

Clint clinched his mouth shut, and his discomfort was obvious. His eyes dropped, and a saddened glaze covered his face. "I can't," he muttered.

After a temporary pause he continued as his eyes met hers, "I could have loved you. I mean, really loved you."

She wanted to fly into his arms and hold him, except she knew otherwise. She knew what was happening. It was the only thing that could happen.

"It's not about your past. Not really."

Her mind raced, and somehow she didn't entirely believe him.

"It's everything, really. Me, the mission, what I am and what I do. We could never be together in a normal sense."

Somehow, she didn't care about normalcy. She wanted him and the simple chance to be with him, even when the obstacles were so great.

"I fly back to Washington in two days. Everything has been shut down. They're pulling me back, Alex."

Alexandra felt a sea of emotion as he spoke – relief, surprise, and sadness. He had managed to deliver it all to her, and her head felt light from the last fourteen hours. He had reappeared out of nowhere like some sort of mystic voyager, and would disappear back into it. She wanted him to somehow take her back to whatever world he lived in, and her face told him so.

"I want you to be happy, Alex. Find yourself again and start over from where you left off here in Perm."

Clint then stood and went over to his briefcase, resting by the side of her dresser. He took it, tossed it on the bed, and opened it up. He calmly handed her a large, bulging, folder.

"Everything you need for a new life is here in this folder."

She wondered if finding herself could be so easy. She had thought about it ever since the moment she boarded the train that left Moscow. Alexandra pondered a whole new beginning for a day and a half while the train zigzagged its way to Perm. She had barely slept during those long restless hours as her mind thought of how life would be different.

"What do you mean by a new life?" she asked as she opened the folder.

"You can start totally over, Alex. I mean totally over. New name and everything. You'll be off the grid completely. Everything has been taken care of."

"What grid?"

"You know, government, anyone who may one day run background checks on you."

"You said I was safe," she retorted sharply, while crossing her arms.

"From Igor and his contacts, yes. Most likely."

"Most likely! That's the best you can say?"

Alexandra's fury was a result of the fear that she could one day face the man who had wanted her dead. She looked away and exhaled loudly as she began to bite her nails.

Clint touched her softly on her elbow and countered, "Listen, for all practical purposes you are a hit that is finished. These guys move on and have no reason to believe that you are alive. Still, if you were to live in Moscow then having a new identity is your absolute insurance."

"And you can just give me that so easily?" she replied with a snap of her finger. "You aren't even Russian, and somehow you can create this."

"I've got my connections, Alex," he replied defensively. "The paperwork is all there, as is the business card with the only man you are to contact. He works with us on placing moles underground and secret witness protection cases. You can keep your first name; however, your new family name is there."

Her eyes fell on the application, where she saw the name Alexandra Gromova. Her birth date had changed to September 7th and her address was now listed in Perm. There was an identity card, registration authorisation, and both the travel passport and personal passport with fresh stamps. In fact, there was much more, and it all seemed so overwhelming and unreal.

"How can you do this?" she asked in disbelief as she raised her passport to him.

"I'm a guy with connections. Don't forget Yuri's number. He's your new guardian angel. Consider him your friendly parole officer."

He stepped towards her and kissed her gently on the top of her head. Her hair smelled like flowers, and he breathed her scent for what he knew would be the final time. He wanted a part of her to be inside him forever.

"The bank card that's in the envelope," he whispered quietly, "It has a few thousand dollars on it. Consider it start-up money. Compliments from the Duma. Be sure to have Yuri close out your current bank accounts. That's the only loose end."

Clint looked Alexandra squarely in her eyes, and said nothing. His smile hid his torment. She always made him smile, even now when he was leaving her.

"What could have been," he sighed. A firm tightening of his hands on her slender shoulders signalled the end. "Go and be happy. It all starts here." The look in his face told her that he spoke the truth. "I'm sure your mother will find you as wonderful as I do."

"We'll see," she replied. Her reply was assured and hopeful. Admitting she would see the mother she never knew gave him peace of mind that she just might find personal happiness.

Clint turned and opened the door cautiously, as if he wanted to stay. Deep inside he knew that their life paths were now at the point of divergence. They had met briefly in the grand scheme of things; however, they were now about to dramatically drift apart. His life would take him back to America where she would likely find herself in the shadows of the Ural Mountains – at least for a while.

Alexandra followed him out the door and stood in the opening as she watched him leave, his head hung low. The morning sun was gleaming over the lake, and the freshness of the air caused her to shiver. Suddenly she saw him stop and look into the distance, staring momentarily. Across the lake, a few hundred metres away, they could see a small gathering of wild elk which stood at the forest's edge. The large male with huge antlers seemed to notice them as he stood motionless. Both stared at one another.

Clint looked back towards the cabin and saw Alexandra looking at the faraway pack of animals with a look of contentment and a soft smile.

"He's here for you," he shouted. "He knows you're back. Just as it was when you were a little girl!"

Alexandra smiled brightly before replying, "I am back."

He stood frozen and wanted a final look at her – to burn a permanent silhouette of Alexandra into his mind. He examined her every feature from a short distance, and he couldn't help but smile. He always grinned when he saw her. She was as magical as ever, and he knew he was going to miss her with every fibre in his aching body. At least he could leave knowing she was alive.

"I love you," she mouthed, waving gently and then blowing him a discreet kiss.

And then it hit him. Like a proverbial falling piano from a great height, her three words struck him as hard as a two by four with all its force. All of a sudden, Aleeka came back while he stared at Alexandra. It occurred to him that this was exactly the last thing that she said to him before she slipped away into a final slumber. He could barely hear her utter those same words back in 2002 because cancer had stolen her once-magical voice. Now he could only read those same words from Alexandra's lips.

"Mea Culpa," he mouthed back as he waved at Alexandra.

He turned away, feeling like he was once again entering an age of loneliness. Losing the second women he had ever loved left him deflated and remorseful. He had been powerless in Aleeka's case, but at least felt some satisfaction realising that he had helped Alexandra. It could have cost him his career, and even meeting her like this was professionally stupid.

Maybe he had given her a head-start in a new life partly because of Aleeka. Either way, he walked away fully conscious it was now over and this was the best closure he could ever expect. Clint was aware that part of the reason that he had found Alexandra so attractive was that she reminded him of Aleeka – the girl he had never really stopped loving.

Losing Alexandra meant that in some way he was losing Aleeka once again. He wasn't sure which hurt him more, but he suspected Aleeka's loss was more devastating. Nonetheless there was something there too that could have led them to enjoy something deeper, something permanent. Clint could have seen him and Aleeka growing old together and, while he had tried to imagine it with Alexandra, it hadn't rung true. Aleeka would remain his only true love.

Aleeka had been similar in some ways to Alexandra, but vitally different in others. She was independent and feisty but ultimately she needed Clint more than Alexandra did or ever would. Clint felt that Alexandra needed him but more to fill a void, a lonely and lost emptiness in herself, and he felt that she would not be able to fill that with another person. Aleeka meanwhile had needed him, but he felt that this was caused entirely by her love for him and that, if she had not met him, she would have been complete without him.

Alexandra watched him stroll away into the distance. Within seconds he was out of sight. Eventually even the sound of his car tracking over the dirt and potholes disappeared, leaving her once again in stilled silence. She looked back to where the pack of elk had been, but they too had left as if they had only been a mirage.

Alexandra felt strangely calm about the break-up as she understood Clint's reasons for leaving and, despite feeling sad, she accepted that the circumstances had changed. He had not known that she was a call-girl previously, and now he did. Whereas he could have treated her with disrespect his manner showed nothing of the kind, and he had gone far out of his way to help her.

She knew that Clint still had a certain amount of love and fascination for her in his heart, and this left her feeling warm. When her first love Andrei had left her, he had done it so suddenly and coldly that it left her disorientated and confused. Clint, meanwhile, was the same person he had been. He was leaving, but he was leaving as the same person. Alexandra reflected that perhaps they might be able to be together again, but only after some time had passed to heal the wounds that her deception must have caused Clint. For now she understood that he needed space, and she knew that fighting that would just make him more resistant to ever giving things a second chance.

Alexandra nevertheless felt stronger than she ever had before. Finally having the means to contact her mother made an enormous difference. She knew that it shouldn't matter so much, and yet it did. It meant that the void she always felt could be healed. Alexandra hoped that she could, through knowing her mother, get over her mother's initial abandonment of her –an abandonment which had led her to believe that she was always alone and that relationships simply caused pain and were unreliable. These beliefs had shaped her life and left her independent to the point of extreme loneliness. She could not remember crying in front of anyone. Only she had ever seen her tears reflected in her mirror or window-pane.

She hoped that they could be close, and that ultimately that she would be able to cry in front of her mother and trust her enough to tell her the truth about her life and work as a call-girl. More importantly, she hoped to speak of her innermost thoughts and feelings – to not have to feel that she needed to emotionally protect herself. Alexandra needed to tell her mother this and, if her mother accepted her and understood, she would feel that she could accept herself more fully as a result.

The fact that Clint accepted her and had not shown her any repulsion on account of what she did reassured her. Alexandra respected herself in some respects and yet a hidden, almost subconscious, part of her – which she normally repressed - questioned her choices, and disapproved. She felt torn and upset by the fact that she had not been able to explain her sudden departure to Clint. His appearance and understanding ultimately healed her. She also felt relieved that someone, other than her clients, at last knew her secrets.

At the same time it left her with a sense of invaded privacy and claustrophobia, and she felt a strong urge to run away and never see Clint again. Her pride refused to allow her to apologise for any deception, and she felt disgusted at the thought of having to explain herself to anyone. It was obviously over now, and to really explain why she'd made the choices she had would involve too much emotional honesty –something she was not comfortable with, and a part of herself she was not willing to expose.

Alexandra stepped back into the cabin and closed the door gently, feeling its warmth as an embrace of sorts. She took the folder and sat on the same chair that Clint had been on only moments before, and opened it once again. The sunlight illuminated the papers and she examined each piece of paper thoroughly. Ultimately it was just a single piece of paper that she held nervously in her hand.

She reached for the green telephone that sat alone on the adjacent table and raised the receiver to her right ear. Slowly and methodically, Alexandra turned each of the rotary dial numbers. She dialled the final number of the local call deliberately and waited for the electronic pulses to finish as she collected her breath. The pause between the final dialled number and the first ring seemed to last for eternity, and Alexandra's mind was a blur of thoughts while her body was tense in anticipation.

Alexandra had been in Perm only weeks before looking for the ultimate answer, and now she sat only seconds away from discovering the final leg of her long journey. Alexandra was finally about to experience a new chapter in her life's book. This new life's path began when the soothing and tender voice on the other line replied, "Privet."

Chapter 24

I

In the depths of Moscow's midnight, Igor slowly drove his BMW to the familiar space in front of Slovij's. The restaurant was closed; however, several men were inside waiting for the hit-man to come. One of those was Viktor himself.

He parked and quickly made his way through the pouring April rain to the wooden front door. Once under the protective relief of the overhead canopy he rapped twice on the closed door, which opened immediately. Predictably, Ruslan and Pavel were present, flanking either side just as always.

Igor entered and before he could take one step, Oleg jumped up out of his chair and shouted, "Privet, comrade!"

Igor approached his sponsor and quietly greeted Oleg back, but his eyes were focused on the other man who sat waiting at the table. It was Viktor, and he had come to see his prized assassin and business assistant in person. Igor calmly walked over to the old man, who was even more frail and feeble than he was back in September, six months ago.

"Viktor," Igor said with the kind of certainty and respect that was only afforded to his mentor and father figure.

"I called this meeting to congratulate you in person. Excuse me if I am too weak to get up."

Viktor was declining in health rapidly, but at age eighty-three it could be expected. A hard life that had seen him through the worst of the Great Patriotic War and then of crushing communism had taken its toll. He was physically frail; nonetheless, he was just as sharp now as he was when he was a twenty-year-old prisoner of the Nazis. The same ingenuity and resourcefulness that had served him so well in 1943 was still there with him today. He was a survivor, and Igor always saw his strength.

"It's no problem, sir. Please sit and let me toast you to your success."

Viktor chuckled softly, his laugh more a croaky whimper than a hearty laugh. Time, alcohol and tobacco had left their marks, nevertheless, it didn't stop the old mob boss from pouring everyone a glass of vodka.

"My son tells me of your success, but I don't need his word to know it. It's on television every hour."

All the men laughed out loud and simultaneously raised their glasses together in a toast. Each small glass clanked together before the three downed their swig in a single gulp.

Viktor coughed slightly before continuing, "Ten, even five years ago I would have had Krokav and Vladimir killed. Or at least one of them. Now, however, I am learning the ways of the new world. I've learned that I can use my best hit-man for more than his gun to bring down the Americans." Viktor again laughed a slight chuckle.

"I never thought I'd see the day when our family was behind such greatness. I grew up hating the Americans, and now I will have lived to see my defining moment. And I owe much of that to you."

The old man poured each of the empty glasses slowly, and leaned forward from his squeaky chair.

"I want to give you this Igor," he said as he pulled out a thick envelope from his jacket. He slid the beige envelope to his protégé and smiled knowingly. "All the Condor money is now mine, and I think it's only fair you get a bonus."

Igor was rarely surprised, but this wad of cash was truly a shock. He didn't have the heart to tell Viktor and his family that he had decided to get out of the business, and the look into his proud sponsor's eyes assured him of their approval when he would eventually tell them. The cash they gave him would compliment what he had saved over the years. Igor had already picked out a small cottage in a picturesque village on the Black Sea, and was thinking of moving there next month so he could enjoy the summer. He wanted to avoid the last of the harsh Moscow winters that he had grown to hate.

"Thank you, dear friend," he said humbly.

"No. Thank you. What we managed to do was to bring down Gorban, Krokav and the Americans with one crafty plan. Total and complete embarrassment and the end of Gorban's political career - plus, criminal charges please us more than if you had killed him."

The men all chuckled at their ultimate revenge before Oleg continued, "And only two people had to be whacked. I assume you disposed of our banker friend properly?"

Igor swallowed a sip from his glass before acknowledging, "Mr Markov is about twenty metres deep in the Moskva River, tied down by cement blocks. He served his purpose quite well, don't you think."

"Good, then. Everything ties back to Vladimir, and we get all of Krokav's customers while he runs from everyone. I don't even think our dear President could have come up with such a plan."

The three men laughed out loud, and Oleg slapped the table, as he always did when he became rambunctious. Their laughter drowned out as Viktor poured the last drops from the bottle of vodka.

Eight time zones away, it was early morning in Virginia. Clint was sitting in the emptiness and chaos of his new apartment. While Viktor, Oleg and Igor downed their vodka, Clint sipped from his glass of orange juice and watched the television. His television was the first thing that had been connected, as everything else was still packed away in one of the dozens of cartons that filled his apartment. His things arrived from Moscow only yesterday, and his new apartment was in need of re-arranging.

For now, the amount of work ahead made him procrastinate and feel overwhelmed. Moving was always hell, but this time was worse. The sudden end to the project and the quick return to the States made him feel as if he had been kicked in the gut and he felt bitter, confused and doubtful.

The only thing he didn't doubt was his closure with Alexandra. He and Yuri had found her, and Clint had expunged any trace of Alexandra from the software. He had erased all personal governmental records, identity registrations, and her address history. He and Yuri used the same methods that the Russians had use for their own witness-protection programme, except this one was done on the fly and without anyone else being aware of their secretive plan. Clint he sat fully aware that her life would be safe forever.

The commercial break was over and the television news report blared again. He leaned back into his sofa and listened to the dialogue more.

"And we welcome you back to CNN's non-stop coverage of the Taliban arms scandal. Reporting now from the steps of Capital Hill is our own Sandra Rogers, who has the latest developments in the bizarre events that continues to grip the beleaguered administration.

Sandra – what can you tell us about the developing scandal, and what should we expect from the hearings that will be starting this morning?"

"Well, Tom, that's the million dollar question everyone around here is asking. The whole country and especially the D.C. area is full of anticipation of this ever developing scandal that begins to look more and more like the White House was knowingly involved.

Here's what we know so far. Just earlier today the Secretary of Defence, Donald Rumsfeld, issued a statement that denied any involvement in the 'arms for loyalty' deal that the scandal centres around. Also denying any part of the scandal is the Chairman of the Joint Chiefs of Staff, Michael Mullen. Both will be here behind me in an emergency Senate hearing that will grill these two, plus five other senior Department of Defence officials, over what they know or don't.

What's clear is that evidence uncovered shows that in a period of up to six months there were up to 50,000 AK-47 assault rifles plus grenade launchers and other ammunition sold by a Russian war lord to the US who, in turn, gave these arms to Taliban tribal leaders throughout the Tora Bora region of Afghanistan. The deal allegedly helps US coalition forces against entrenched al-Qaeda Taliban fighters by turning small roaming forces against their own on the tab of US tax dollars. These forces reportedly are pseudo-mercenary armies that have been bought or contracted by the Defence Department, and could help break the deadlock in the unstable region near Pakistan that many argue is key to the total defeat of al-Qaeda in that part of Afghanistan.

What is not clear is the exact involvement of the Kremlin and whether they arranged or knew the dealer who supplied these weapons. His name is Krokav Pilkin, and is known as the 'Merchant of Death' for his penchant of supplying governments and dictators with arms. Currently Krokav is reportedly underground, and was in Moscow when the scandal broke out. Reports also directly link payments from secretive US bank accounts to him.

All this, plus much more, will be the focus of today's hearings, which indirectly may shed light on what exactly the President or Vice-President knew, as well as Donald Rumsfeld. Many here are saying that Vice-President Dick Cheney and Rumsfeld would have likely known, or even initiated such a plan. Tom."

"Sandra, what do we know for sure regarding the validity of the evidence?"

"Yes, Tom, that's what caused this scandal to explode in the first place, and mostly what has initiated these extraordinary hearings. Apparently the Senate has a tape, or a copy of a tape, that provides video-recorded discussions of a bank account called 'Condor' that openly discusses the US depositing money for arms by a Russian Duma Minister to a banker where the account was set up. Condor supposedly was a temporary account to Mr Pilkin, who then supplied the Taliban leaders with weapons; however, what justified the scrutiny was the mentioning of a State Department official by name, who allegedly was the facilitator and go-between in the deal.

That is the primary source of evidence, but we also have new evidence provided by the State Department which was gathered during an internal investigation that went directly to the Department of Justice, as well as to the National Security Council. The Senators today are especially interested in this information, which seems to be unfolding by the hour. Tom."

"Sandra, the political fallout from this is almost becoming a bigger story than the deal itself. What else can you report on that will elaborate the political going-ons behind the scene right now?"

"Well, Tom, as we all know the popularity of President's Bush's War on Terror has been losing momentum and public support by the month. The dip in polls over the last months have given minority Democrats confidence to really criticise the President about how badly the war is turning out. Consistently, though, Republicans have always focused on the message of 'trust our judgment, trust our intelligence and trust our President'. Now however, even the staunchest Republicans are beginning to distance themselves from this scandal.

Just last evening Senator Majority Leader Bill Frist spoke of possible censorship of the President. The allegations are linked to the oval office and, of course, many Republicans have already gone further, calling for impeachment. Nonetheless, one would have to assume that Democrats are licking their chops, as they already have been eyeing the 2008 Presidential elections and the current unpopularity of President Bush. This scandal would give them an argument for change, as they say that another Republican term would not serve the country's best interest. Tom."

"Thank you for the report, Sandra, and we'll get back in touch with you for another live report in one hour.

Sitting next to me is Reginald Bowles, a political lawyer and my guest for the next several minutes who will shed some light at what possible..."

Clint had seen enough. He was tired of the scandal which he was unwittingly involved in. For so many the shame of what was happening in the oval office was certain, while others couldn't believe that their own government would deal with their enemy. Ron was right, and his words rang in Clint's ears. Nothing was ever black and white.

He wondered if Ron was okay now. Just yesterday he had gotten a call from his former supervisor. It had been the longest twelve days since he last saw his friend and boss. He thought he would never see him again, and this was even more likely when Ron called to tell him he was back home in New Mexico, settled in the small ranch that he had always planned to retire to. Billups had been cleared of any wrongdoings, but had been given a gentle push out of the agency. He said he would get full retirement benefits, even though he was still twenty months short. The giddiness was back in his voice; the stress had been erased.

Clint was in life's no-man's land. He had been reassigned to Langley, while almost every other person from the unit was somewhere else in the world. Billups had promised him he would be okay, and he was. Clint wasn't sure if it had been Ron who had pushed through the new promotion he had received, but he was now three GS pay scales higher in salary. Being a Deputy Director earned him a comfy salary, even if he was only overseeing a small department that dealt with illegal trafficking from Eastern Europe. It was a relatively new department, but one that was growing and could use his experience, especially his experience from his time in Moscow.

Working on this new assignment would be his daily torment. Each and every day he knew he would be reminded of Alexandra. He would see her face, her country and the images of Perm in his mind, and he wondered what would happen to her. She had Yuri's business card as her sole contact and maybe, just maybe, Yuri would give her Clint's details if she ever needed him.

He had forgiven her completely for her deceit. Maybe it was because he had forgiven himself for his. Providing her with assistance for her new life had eased his anguish and indirectly freed him from her. He could leave her in a better place and safe from the people that had nearly killed her.

If only he could have done that with Aleeka, he pondered - and then it struck him that he couldn't have done anything. His closure from Alexandra had now also given him closure from Aleeka. For years he had questioned how he could have had her cancer noticed earlier, but this was now replaced by his calm reassurance that he could not have done anything differently. Both Alexandra and Aleeka were in better places, and both left him with the same thought. Those three tiny words that he would never forget – three words that surely would leave him simultaneously comforted and haunted.

The End